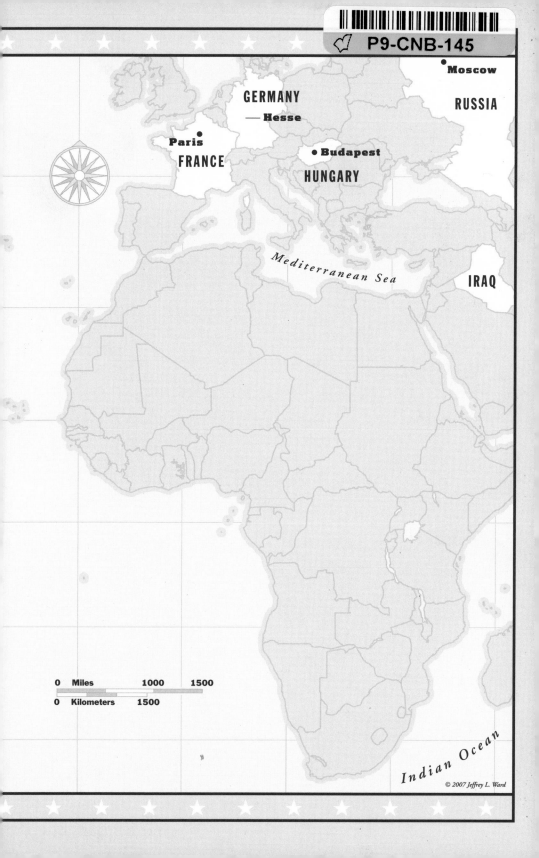

P9-CNB-145

Moscow

GERMANY
— Hesse
RUSSIA

Paris
FRANCE
Budapest
HUNGARY

IRAQ

Mediterranean Sea

0   Miles   1000   1500
0   Kilometers   1500

Indian Ocean

© 2007 Jeffrey L. Ward

THE
SHOOTERS

ALSO BY W. E. B. GRIFFIN

THE
SHOOTERS

W.E.B. GRIFFIN

G. P. PUTNAM'S SONS

NEW YORK

G. P. PUTNAM'S SONS
Publishers Since 1838
Published by the Penguin Group
Penguin Group (USA) Inc., 375 Hudson Street, New York, New York 10014, USA • Penguin Group
(Canada), 90 Eglinton Avenue East, Suite 700, Toronto, Ontario M4P 2Y3, Canada (a division of Pearson
Penguin Canada Inc.) • Penguin Books Ltd, 80 Strand, London WC2R 0RL, England • Penguin Ireland,
25 St Stephen's Green, Dublin 2, Ireland (a division of Penguin Books Ltd) • Penguin Group (Australia),
250 Camberwell Road, Camberwell, Victoria 3124, Australia (a division of Pearson Australia Group Pty Ltd) •
Penguin Books India Pvt Ltd, 11 Community Centre, Panchsheel Park, New Delhi–110 017, India •
Penguin Group (NZ), 67 Apollo Drive, Rosedale, North Shore 0632, New Zealand (a division of
Pearson New Zealand Ltd) • Penguin Books (South Africa) (Pty) Ltd, 24 Sturdee Avenue,
Rosebank, Johannesburg 2196, South Africa

Penguin Books Ltd, Registered Offices: 80 Strand, London WC2R 0RL, England

Library of Congress Cataloging-in-Publication Data

Griffin, W. E. B.
The shooters / W. E. B. Griffin.
p.   cm.
ISBN-13: 978-0-399-15440-9
1. United States. Army. Delta Force—Fiction.   2. Undercover operations—Fiction.
3. Drug dealers—Uruguay—Fiction.   I. Title.
PS3557.R489137S47   2008   2007038587
813'.54—dc22

Printed in the United States of America
1   3   5   7   9   10   8   6   4   2

This is a work of fiction. Names, characters, places, and incidents either are the product of the author's imagination
or are used fictitiously, and any resemblance to actual persons, living or dead, businesses, companies, events, or locales
is entirely coincidental.

While the author has made every effort to provide accurate telephone numbers and Internet addresses at the time of
publication, neither the publisher nor the author assumes any responsibility for errors, or for changes that occur after
publication. Further, the publisher does not have any control over and does not assume any responsibility for author
or third-party websites or their content.

26 July 1777

The necessity of procuring good intelligence is apparent and need not be further urged.

George Washington
General and Commander in Chief
The Continental Army

JOHNNY REITZEL
An Army Special Operations officer
who could have terminated the head terrorist of the seized cruise ship
Achille Lauro but could not get permission to do so.

RALPH PETERS
An Army intelligence officer
who has written the best analysis of our war against terrorists
and of our enemy that I have ever seen.

★

AND FOR THE NEW BREED

MARC L
A senior intelligence officer who, despite his youth,
reminds me of Bill Colby more and more each day.

FRANK L
A legendary Defense Intelligence Agency officer
who retired and now follows in Billy Waugh's footsteps.

OUR NATION OWES ALL OF THESE PATRIOTS
A DEBT BEYOND REPAYMENT.

I

When Byron J. Timmons, Jr., saw what was causing the airport-bound traffic to be stopped and backed up for at least a kilometer, he muttered an obscenity that was absolutely not appropriate for an assistant legal attaché of the embassy of the United States of America.

The twenty-nine-year-old—who was six feet one and weighed two hundred five pounds—had a reservation on the Aerolíneas Argentinas five-thirty flight to Buenos Aires and it looked to him to be entirely likely that these bastards were going to make him miss it.

Timmons looked at the driver of his embassy vehicle, a lightly armored Chevrolet TrailBlazer.

Franco Julio César—a quiet thirty-nine-year-old Paraguayan national who was employed as a chauffeur by the U.S. embassy—was silently shaking his head in frustration. He, too, knew what was going on.

These bastards were officers of the Paraguayan Highway Police and they were running a roadblock. There was a Highway Police car and a Peugeot van on the shoulder. The van had a sliding side door—now open—so that it could serve as sort of a mobile booking station. Inside was a small desk behind which sat a booking sergeant. He would decide whether the miscreant caught by the roadblock would be simply given a summons or hauled away in handcuffs.

There were three police forces in Paraguay. In addition to the Highway Police, which was run by the Minister of Public Works & Communication, the Minister of the Interior had a Capital Police Force, which patrolled Asunción, and a National Police Force, which patrolled the rest of the country.

The opinion Timmons held of all three was as pejoratively vulgar as the obscenity he uttered when he saw the Highway Police roadblock. His opinion was based on his experiences with the various police forces since arriving in Paraguay, and his criterion for judgment was that he thought of himself as a cop.

He actually had been a police officer, briefly, but the real reason he thought of himself as a cop was that that was what the Timmons family did—be cops.

His paternal grandfather, Francis, used to say that he was one of the only two really honest cops on the job in Chicago. He refused to identify the other one.

Francis and Mary-Margaret Timmons had five children, three boys and two girls. Two of the boys—Aloysius and Byron—went on the force. Francis Junior became a priest. Dorothy became Sister Alexandria. Elizabeth married a cop, Patrick Donnehy. Father Francis, who was assigned to Saint Rose of Lima's, spent most of his time as a police chaplain.

Aloysius and Joanne Timmons had four children, all boys. Three went on the force and one went in the Army. Byron and Helen Timmons had five children, three girls and two boys. Two of the girls married cops, and Matthew went on the force.

Byron Junior skipped the third grade at Saint Rose's, primarily because he was much larger than the other kids but also because the sisters understood that he already knew what they were going to teach him in the third grade—he never seemed to have his nose out of a book.

The sisters also got him a scholarship to Cristo Rey Jesuit High School. His Uncle Francis and his mother were delighted. His grandfather and father were not. They quite irreverently agreed that The Goddamn Jesuits wanted him for the priesthood.

At age sixteen, Junior, as he was known in the family, graduated from Cristo Rey with honors and without having felt the call to Holy Orders. He immediately became a Police Cadet, although you were supposed to be eighteen. Before the summer was over, the Society of Jesus reentered the picture.

Loyola University (Chicago) was prepared to offer Junior, based on his academic record at Cristo Rey, a full scholarship. This time his father and grandfather disagreed. His father offered another quite irreverent opinion: that you had to admire those tenacious bastards; they never give up when they're trying to grab some smart kid for their priesthood.

His grandfather disagreed, and suggested that Junior had two options.

One was to spend the next nearly four years in a gray cadet uniform riding in the backseat of a patrol car, or filing crap in a precinct basement someplace— he couldn't even get into the academy until he was twenty years and six months old—or he could spend that time getting a college education on the Jesuits' dime.

For the next three years, Junior studied during the school year and returned to the police cadet program in the summers. On his graduation, *cum laude*, he immediately entered the police academy. Three months later, he was graduated from there and—with most of the family watching—became a sworn officer of the Chicago Police Department.

He had been on the job doing what rookies do for six months when Grandfather Francis reentered the picture.

"Go federal," Grandpa advised. "The pay is better. Maybe the U.S. Marshals or even the Secret Service."

To which Byron—no longer universally known as "Junior" after he made good on a promise to knock his sister Ellen's husband, Charley Mullroney, on his ass the next time he called him that—replied that he'd already looked into it, was thinking of the Federal Bureau of Investigation, and going down that road, was really thinking of getting a law degree.

He told his grandfather he'd talked to people at Loyola, and they not only were going to let him in the law school but had arranged for him a job as a rent-a-cop on campus. Christ knew he couldn't go to college if he had to change shifts on the job every three months.

Byron graduated, again with honors, and passed the bar examination on his first try. By then he had just turned twenty-eight and had seen enough of the FBI to decide that wasn't for him. The Border Patrol looked interesting, but then he met a guy from the Drug Enforcement Administration whom his brother-in-law Charley Mullroney had been working with in Narcotics.

Stanley Wyskowski said Byron was just the kind of guy the DEA was looking for. He'd been a cop, and he had a law degree, and he spoke passable Spanish.

Actually, he spoke better than passable Spanish. He had the grammar down pat because he'd had Latin his last two years at Saint Rose's and his first two at Cristo Rey, and then he'd had two years of Spanish at Cristo Rey—somebody had tipped him that if you had Latin, Spanish was the easiest language—and four more years of it at Loyola. And he had polished his colloquial Spanish with a young lady named María González, with whom he'd had an on-and-off carnal relationship for several years when he was at Loyola.

Wyskowski said if Byron wanted, he'd ask his boss.

Byron J. Timmons, Jr., entered the Federal Service two weeks later, as a GS-7. On his graduation from the Federal Law Enforcement Training Center at Glynco, Georgia, he received both his credentials as a Special Agent of the Drug Enforcement Administration and a promotion to GS-9, because of his law degree.

He was initially assigned to Washington, D.C.—the DEA is part of the Department of Homeland Security—where, he understood, they wanted to have a look at him. Two months later, they offered him his choice of the Legal Section (which carried an almost automatic promotion to GS-11 after two years), or The Field.

He had seen what was going on in the Legal Department—pushing papers held absolutely no appeal—so he chose The Field.

That wasn't the answer they wanted.

They reminded him of the automatic promotion that came with the Legal Section, and told him that the only vacancies in The Field were in El Paso, Los Angeles, Miami, Mexico City, and Asunción, Paraguay. Timmons didn't like the sound of El Paso, Mexico City, or Los Angeles, and had only the vaguest idea of where in hell Asunción, Paraguay, even was.

So, when he said "Miami," he was not very surprised that they sent him to Asunción, Paraguay. They were really pissed that he had turned down the Legal Section—twice.

No regrets, though. He wanted to be a cop, not a lawyer preparing cases for prosecution by the Justice Department.

Specifically, he wanted to be a drug cop.

In Byron's mind, there wasn't much difference between a guy who did Murder One—roughly defined as with premeditation, or during the course of a Class One Felony, like armed robbery—and some guy who got a kid started on hard drugs. In both cases, a life was over.

If there was a difference, in Byron's mind it was that the drug bastards were the worse of the two. A murder victim, or some convenience store clerk, died right there. Tough, but it was over quick. It usually took a long time for a drug addict to die, and he almost always hooked a lot of other people before he did. If that wasn't multiple murder, what was?

Not to mention the pain a drug addict caused his family.

Another difference was that dealing in prohibited substances—even for the clowns standing on a street corner peddling nickel bags of crack—paid a lot better than sticking up a bank did.

And that was the problem—money. It was bad in the States, where entirely too many cops went bad because they really couldn't see the harm in looking the other way for fifteen minutes in exchange for a year's pay, and it was even worse here.

Byron knew too much about the job to think that when he came to Paraguay he personally was going to be able to shut off the flow of drugs, or even to slow it down very much. But he thought that he could probably cost the people moving the stuff a lot of money and maybe even send a few of them to the slam.

He'd had some success—nothing that was going to see him named DEA

Agent of the Year, or anything like that—but enough to know that he was earning his paycheck and making the bad guys hurt a little. Making them hurt a little was better than not making them hurt at all.

And that was why he was pissed now that it looked like the goddamn Highway Police were going to make him miss his plane.

He was going to Buenos Aires to see an Argentine cop he'd met. Truth being stranger than fiction, an *Irish* Argentine cop by the name of Liam Duffy. Duffy's family had gone to Argentina at about the same time as Grandfather Francis's parents had gone to the States.

Duffy was a comandante (major) in the Gendarmería Nacional Argentina. They wore brown uniforms, not blue, and looked more like soldiers than cops. Most of the time they went around carrying 9mm submachine guns. But cops they were. And from what Timmons had seen, far more honest cops than the Policía Federal.

That was part of the good thing he had going with Liam Duffy. The other part was that Duffy didn't like drug people any more than he did.

Even before he had met Duffy, Timmons had pretty well figured out for himself how the drugs were moved, and why. There had been briefings in Washington, of course, before they sent him to Asunción, but that had been pretty much second- or third-hand information. And he had been briefed when he got to the embassy in Asunción, although he'd come away from those briefings with the idea that Rule One in the Suppression of the Drug Trade was *We're guests in Paraguay, so don't piss off the locals.*

It hadn't taken Timmons long to understand what was going on. Paraguay was bordered by Brazil, Bolivia, and Argentina. The drugs came from Bolivia, where the cultivation of the coca plant was as common as the cultivation of corn in Kansas. It was refined into cocaine in Bolivia. Some of the refined product went to Brazil, where some was consumed and some exported. Most of it went to—actually through—Paraguay to Argentina.

Although there was a substantial, and growing, market for cocaine in Argentina—this explained Liam Duffy's interest—most of the cocaine simply changed hands in Argentina. The coke then was exported by its new owners through the port of Buenos Aires, near downtown, and the international airport, Ezeiza, some twenty kilometers to the southwest, the bulk of it going to the United States, but a good deal to Europe, and some even to Australia.

There were some imaginative ways of moving the cocaine, a crystalline powder, across borders. These ranged from packing it in caskets—or body cavities—of the deceased being returned home for burial to putting an ounce or more in a latex condom, which was then tied, swallowed by a human smuggler—or "mule"—and either regurgitated or defecated once across the border. (Unless, of course, one or more of the condoms were to rupture en route—which they often did—causing the mule severe toxicity . . . then death.)

Most of the drug, however, was commonly packed in plastic bags, one kilogram—two point two pounds—of cocaine to a package.

These sometimes were not concealed or disguised at all, if the shippers were confident the customs officials at the border had been adequately bribed. Or the kilo bags were hidden in myriad ways—in the tires of cars or trucks, for example, or packed in a crate with something legitimate—operative word *myriad.*

The only way to interdict a "worthwhile" shipment was to know when it was to be made and/or the method of shipment. For example, that one hundred kilos of cocaine were to be concealed in the spare tires of a Scandia eighteen-wheeler of the Jorge Manso e Hijos truck line carrying bagged soybeans, which would cross the border at a certain crossing on a certain date.

This information could be obtained most commonly in one of two ways. It could be bought. The trouble here was that the U.S. government was reluctant to come up with enough money for this purpose and did so only rarely. The Paraguayan government came up with no money for such a purpose.

Sometimes, however, there was money as the result of a successful interdiction—any money over a reasonable expectation of a truck driver's expenses was considered to be as much contraband as any cocaine found—and this was used.

The most common source of information, however, was to take someone who had been apprehended moving drugs and turn him into a snitch. The wheels of justice in Paraguay set a world standard for slow grinding. Getting arraigned might take upward of a year. The wait for a trial was usually a period longer than that. But when the sentence finally came down, it was pretty stiff. Paraguay wanted the world to know it was doing its part in the war on the trafficking of illegal drugs.

The people who owned the cocaine—who arranged its transport through Paraguay into Argentina and who profited the most from the business—as a rule never rode in the trucks or in the light aircraft that moved it over the border. Thus, they didn't get arrested. The most they ever lost was the shipment itself and maybe the transport vehicle. So basically not much, considering that the cocaine—worth a fortune in Miami or Buenos Aires or London or Brisbane—was a cheap commodity until it actually got across the Argentine border.

What really burned the bad guys—far better than grabbing a hundred kilos of cocaine every week—was grabbing the cash after the Argentine dealers paid for it in Argentina. Even better: grabbing the cocaine *and* the money. That really stung the bastards.

Timmons and Duffy were working on this. Step One was to find out how and when a shipment would be made. Snitches gave Timmons this information. Step Two was to pass it to Duffy.

The Gendarmería Nacional had authority all over Argentina. They could show up at a Policía Federal roadblock and make sure the Federals did their job. Or they could set up their own roadblocks to grab the cocaine and/or turn the couriers into snitches.

With a little bit of luck, Timmons and Duffy believed, they could track the cocaine until it changed hands, then grab both the merchandise and the money the dealers in Argentina were using to pay for it.

The problem Timmons had with this was getting the information from the snitches to Duffy without anyone hearing about it. It wasn't much of a secret that the bad guys had taps on both Timmons's and Duffy's telephones.

The only way for Timmons to get the information to Duffy without its being compromised, and in time for Duffy to be able to use it, was to personally take it to him.

Which, again, explained why Timmons was heartsick when he saw the Highway Police roadblock on the road to the airport.

The information he had gathered with so much effort would be useless unless he could get it to Duffy in Buenos Aires tonight. If he missed his flight, the next wasn't until tomorrow morning. Before that plane left, the Scandia eighteen-wheeler of the Jorge Manso e Hijos truck line, Argentine license plate number DSD 6774, which had two hundred one-kilo bags of cocaine concealed in bags of soybeans on the second pallet from the top, center row, rear, would be lined up to get on the ferry that would carry it across the Río Paraguay— the border—to Formosa.

And all Timmons's work over the last seventeen days would be down the toilet.

What was particularly grating to Timmons was that he knew the moment a Highway Policeman saw the diplomatic plates on his embassy Chevrolet Trail-Blazer, the vehicle would be waved through the roadblock. The Highway Police had no authority to stop a car with CD plates, and no authority of any kind over an accredited diplomat. The problem was to actually get up to the Highway Policemen.

That had taken a long time, almost twenty precious minutes, but the line of vehicles moved so that finally the TrailBlazer had worked its way to where the Peugeot van sat with its door open.

The embassy vehicle with CD plates, however, didn't get waved through.

Instead, two Highway Policemen approached.

"Shit," Timmons said.

César remained silent behind the wheel.

Timmons angrily took both his diplomatic passport and his diplomatic carnet—a driver's license-size plastic sealed card issued by the Paraguayan Foreign Ministry identifying him as an accredited diplomat—and hurriedly held them out the window.

"Diplomat, diplomat," he said impatiently.

"Please step out of the car, Señor," one of the Highway Policemen said.

"Didn't you hear what I said?" Timmons demanded. Waving his diplomatic credentials, he added, "Don't you know what these are?"

"Step out of the car, please, Señor."

One of the Highway Policemen now pointed the muzzle of his submachine gun at Timmons.

Timmons told himself not to lose his temper. He got out of the TrailBlazer.

"Please take me to your officer," he said politely.

The muzzle of the submachine gun now directed him to the open door of the panel van.

He went to it. He ducked his head to get inside, and as he entered the van he suddenly had the sensation of what felt like a bee sting in his buttocks.

Then everything went black.

One of the Highway Policemen pushed his body all the way into the van and the door closed. The other Highway Policeman ordered Timmons's driver out from behind the wheel, handcuffed him, then forced him into the backseat.

Then he got behind the wheel and drove off toward the airport.

The Peugeot panel van followed.

[TWO]
Nuestra Pequeña Casa
Mayerling Country Club
Pilar, Buenos Aires Province, Argentina
1645 31 August 2005

"Sergeant Kensington," Lieutenant Colonel C. G. Castillo said, "if you say 'un-fucking-believable' one more time, I'm going to have the sergeant major wash your mouth out with soap."

Sergeant Robert Kensington—a smallish, trim twenty-one-year-old—

turned from a huge flat-screen television screen mounted on the wall of the sitting room and looked uneasily at Lieutenant Colonel Castillo, who was thirty-six, blue-eyed, had a nice thick head of hair, and stood a shade over six feet tall and one hundred ninety pounds.

Sergeant Major John K. Davidson, who was thirty-two and a little larger than Lieutenant Colonel Castillo, looked at him, smiled, and said, "With all possible respect, Colonel, sir, the sergeant is right. It *is* un-fucking-believable."

"He's got you there, Ace," a nondescript man in his late fifties wearing a blue denim shirt and brown corduroy trousers said, chuckling. " 'Un-fucking-believable' fits like a glove."

His name was Edgar Delchamps, and though technically subordinate to the lieutenant colonel, he was not particularly awed by Castillo. Men who have spent more than thirty years in the clandestine service of the Central Intelligence Agency tend not to be awed by thirty-six-year-old recently promoted light birds.

"Lester's around here someplace," Castillo said. "I don't want Kensington corrupting him any more than he already has."

Delchamps, Davidson, Colonel Alfredo Munz, and Sándor Tor chuckled.

Munz, a blond-headed stocky man in his forties, until recently had been the head of SIDE, which combines the functions of the Argentine versions of the FBI and the CIA. He was of German heritage and fluent in that language and several others.

Tor, a Hungarian, was director of security for the newspaper *Budapester Tages Zeitung*. Before that, he had been an Inspector of Police in Budapest, and in his youth had done a hitch in the French Foreign Legion.

"I cannot hear what that woman is saying over all this brilliant repartee," Eric Billy Kocian announced indignantly, in faintly accented English. The managing director and editor-in-chief of the *Budapester Tages Zeitung* was a tall man with a full head of silver hair who looked to be in his sixties. He was in fact eighty-two years of age.

Delchamps made a megaphone with his hands and called loudly, clearly implying that Kocian was deaf or senile, or both: "Billy, it looks like they've got a little storm in New Orleans."

Everybody laughed.

Kocian threw his hands up in disgust and said something obscene and unflattering in Hungarian.

But then the chuckles subsided and they all returned their attention to the television.

In deference to Kocian, Munz, and Tor, they were watching Deutsche Welle, the German version, more or less, of Fox News. It was covering Hurricane

Katrina in the Gulf Coast of the United States and had just reported, with some stunning accompanying video, that eighty percent of New Orleans was flooded, some parts of the port city under twenty feet of water, its entire population forced to flee.

Castillo stared at the images of one of America's major cities in complete chaos, and at the collection onscreen of talking heads representing local, state, and federal government officials—all unequivocally with their thumbs up their collective asses while blaming one another for failure after failure—and heard himself mutter, "Un-fucking-believable. . . ."

Not much in Nuestra Pequeña Casa was what it appeared to be. Starting with the fact that Our Little House was in fact a very large house, bordering on a mansion. It was in the upscale Mayerling Country Club in the Buenos Aires suburb of Pilar.

It had been rented, furnished except for lightbulbs and linen, just over three weeks before to a Señor Paul Sieno and his wife, Susanna. The owner believed them to be a nice and affluent young couple from Mendoza. They had signed a year's lease for four thousand U.S. dollars a month, with the first and last month due on signing, plus another two months' up front for a security deposit.

The Sienos had paid the sixteen thousand in cash.

Cash payments of that size are not at all uncommon in Argentina, where the government taxes every transaction paid by check and where almost no one trusts the banks.

Both el Señor y la Señora Sieno were in fact agents of the Central Intelligence Agency, and what they had really been after was a "safe house," which is usually defined within the intelligence community as a place nobody else knows about where one may hide things and people.

Nuestra Pequeña Casa—the owner had named it—was ideal for this purpose.

The Mayerling Country Club, which is several kilometers off the Panamericana Highway, about fifty kilometers north of the center of Buenos Aires, held about one hundred houses very similar to Nuestra Pequeña Casa. Each sat upon about a hectare (or about two and a half acres). It also held a Jack Nicklaus golf course, five polo fields, stables, tennis courts, and a clubhouse with a dining room that featured a thirty-foot-high ceiling and half a dozen Czechoslovakian crystal chandeliers suspended over a highly polished marble floor.

The entire country club was surrounded by a nine-foot-tall fence, topped with razor wire, and equipped with motion-sensing devices. When triggered, an alarm went off in the Edificio de Seguridad and floodlights came on where the intrusion had been detected. Then members of the Mayerling Security

Force, armed with everything from semiautomatic pistols and shotguns to fully automatic Uzis, rushed to the scene on foot, by auto, and in golf carts.

None of this had anything to do with intelligence, espionage, or even the trade in illegal drugs, but rather with kidnapping. The kidnapping of well-to-do men, their wives, offspring, parents—sometimes even their horses and dogs—was Argentina's second-largest cottage industry, so the wags said, larger than all others except the teaching of the English language.

Just about all of the houses within the Mayerling Country Club were individually fenced on three sides, most often by fences concealed in closely packed pine trees. They, too, had motion-sensing devices.

Motion-sensing devices also prevented anyone from approaching the unfenced front of the houses without being detected.

Nuestra Pequeña Casa was for Mayerling not an unusually large house. It had six bedrooms, all with bath; three other toilets with bidets; a library, a sitting room, a dining room, a kitchen, servants' quarters (for the housing of four), a swimming pool, and, in the backyard near the pool, a *quincho.*

A quincho, Paul Sieno explained, was much like an American pool house, except that it was equipped with a *parrilla*—a wood-fired grill—and was primarily intended as a place to eat, more or less outdoors. It was an extremely sturdy structure, built solidly of masonry, and had a rugged roof of mottled red Spanish tiles. The front of the quincho had a deep verandah, which also was covered by the tile roof, and a wall of sliding glass doors that overlooked the pool and backyard and which served as the entrance from the verandah into the main room of the building.

The group had moved from the big house out to the quincho.

Paul Sieno was kneeled down before the parrilla, which was built into one wall of the *cocina,* or kitchen. He worked with great effort—and as yet not much success—to get the wood that he had carefully arranged under the heavy black iron grill to catch fire.

Susanna Sieno stood behind him, leaning against the polished marble countertop to the left of the parrilla, handing her husband sheets of newspaper for use as tinder.

On the countertop, beside the stainless steel sink, was an impressively large wooden platter piled high with an even more impressively large stack of a dozen *lomos,* each filet mignon hand cut from tenderloins of beef to a thickness of two inches. Nearby were the makings for side dishes of seasoned potatoes and tossed salad.

In the adjoining main room of the quincho there was a brand-new flat-screen television mounted on a wall that was identical to the one in Nuestra Pequeña Casa.

The DirecTV dish antenna on the quincho's red tile roof was identical to the one mounted on the big house. The television set in the quincho, however, was hooked to a repeater connected to the DirecTV antenna on the big house. This allowed for the antenna on the quincho roof to be aimed at an IntelSat satellite in permanent orbit some 27,000 miles above the earth's surface—and thus to be part of a system that provided the safe house with instant encrypted voice, visual, and data communication. It communicated with similar proprietary devices at the Office of Homeland Security in the Nebraska Avenue Complex in Washington, D.C., and ones in what had at one time been the Post Stockade at Fort Bragg, North Carolina, and was now the headquarters of Delta Force and even more clandestine special operations forces.

Most of the group was sitting in teak deck chairs that they had pulled inside from the verandah.

The TV was now tuned to the English-language CNN, not because its nonstop coverage of the disaster that was Hurricane Katrina was any better than that of Deutsche Welle—it arguably was worse—but because DW was repeating ad nauseam the same footage and interviews. The on-air "talent"—both on location and in the various news bureaus—had long ago stopped offering any real reporting and had instead resorted to the basic equivalent of a live camera simply airing the obvious. And, while it was only a matter of time before CNN's so-called in-depth coverage would begin to loop, at least for now the group was seeing and hearing something somewhat different.

This same dynamic happened during the Desert Wars, Lieutenant C. G. Castillo thought with more than a little disgust. *Sticking a camera crew out in the middle of a hot zone—with a clueless commentator, someone with no real understanding of what's going on around them—is worse than there being no, quote, reporting, unquote, at all.*

Watching RPG rounds and tracers in a firefight—or people looting a flooded food store—without an educated source on screen to put what you're seeing in context of the big picture only serves to drive the hysteria.

It damn sure doesn't help someone sitting in the comfort of their living room better understand what the hell is really going on.

Castillo turned from the TV and glanced around the quincho.

Of the people watching CNN, three could—and in fact often did—pass as Argentines. They were the Sienos (who now had the parrilla wood burning) and a twenty-three-year-old from San Antonio, Texas, named Ricardo Solez, who had come to Argentina as an agent of the Drug Enforcement Administration. All had mastered the *Porteño* accent of a Buenos Aires native.

Anthony J. "Tony" Santini, a special agent of the U.S. Secret Service, a stocky and somewhat swarthy forty-two-year-old, could pass for a Porteño until he had to say something, whereupon his accent usually gave him away.

None of the others watching the TV in the quincho even tried to pass themselves off as Argentines.

Special Agent David W. Yung of the FBI, a thirty-two-year-old of Chinese ancestry—who spoke Spanish and three other languages, none of them Oriental—felt that his race made trying to fob himself off as an Argentine almost a silly exercise.

The language skills of various others were rudimentary.

As Colonel Jacob D. "Jake" Torine, United States Air Force, put it, "It's as if the moment I get out of the States, a neon sign starts flashing over my head— *American! Throw rocks!*"

Inspector John J. Doherty of the FBI understood what Torine meant. Lieutenant Colonel Castillo had once remarked, "Torine and Doherty look like somebody called Central Casting and said, 'Send us an airline pilot and an Irish cop.' " Neither had taken offense.

One viewer of what Katrina was doing to New Orleans and the Gulf Coast was in a category of his own.

Corporal Lester Bradley, United States Marine Corps, was not quite twenty. He appeared to be about seventeen. He stood five feet five inches tall and weighed a little under one hundred forty pounds. Looking at him now—attired in a knit polo shirt, khaki trousers, and red and gold striped Nike sport shoes— very few people would think of associating him with the military at all, much less with the elite special operations.

The truth here was that Bradley, fresh from Parris Island boot camp, had earned his corporal's stripes as a "designated marksman" with the Marines on the march to Baghdad. On his return to the United States, he had been assigned to the USMC guard detachment at the American embassy in Buenos Aires, where he mostly functioned as a clerk typist until the day he had been detailed—as the man the gunny felt he could most easily spare—to drive a GMC Yukon XL to Uruguay.

Three days after that, Bradley found himself part of a hastily organized special operations mission during which he saved the life of then-Major C. G. Castillo by using a borrowed sniper's rifle to take out two of the bad guys with head shots.

Bradley thus had learned too much about a very secret operation—and the reasons for said operation—for him to be returned to the care of the gunny, who could be counted on to demand a full account of where his young corporal had been and what he had done. So Bradley next had been aboard the aircraft on which Castillo and the body of Sergeant First Class Seymour Kranz—who had been killed during the operation—returned to the United States.

Not knowing what to do with Bradley back in the States, Castillo had "put him on ice" at Camp Mackall, North Carolina, the Special Forces training base, until he could find a solution. Camp Mackall's sergeant major, Jack Davidson, had taken one look at the boyish Marine, concluded that his assignment to Mackall was a practical joke being played on Davidson by a Marine master gunnery sergeant acquaintance, and put him to work pushing the keys on a computer.

The first that Davidson learned of who Bradley really was—and that he had saved the life of Castillo, with whom Davidson had been around the block many times, most recently in Afghanistan—came when Lieutenant General Bruce J. McNab showed up at Mackall to arrange for Bradley to attend Sergeant Kranz's funeral at Arlington National Cemetery.

Davidson had also been around the block several times with General McNab, and several times with McNab and Castillo together. He had not been at all bashful to tell the general (a) that Castillo's idea that Bradley could be hidden at Mackall made about as much sense as suggesting a giraffe could be hidden on the White House lawn, and (b) that if Charley was doing something interesting, it only made sense that Sergeant Major Davidson be assigned to do it with him, as the general well knew how prone Charley, absent the wise counsel of Sergeant Major Davidson, was to do things that made large waves, and got everybody in trouble, and that this was not very likely to be changed just because they'd just made Charley a light bird.

Shortly after the final rites of Sergeant Kranz at Arlington National Cemetery, Sergeant Major Davidson and Corporal Bradley were en route to Buenos Aires.

And shortly after going to Nuestra Pequeña Casa, while serving as the driver of a Renault Trafic van, Corporal Bradley found himself participating in an unpleasant firefight in the basement garage of the Pilar Sheraton Hotel and Convention Center, during which he took down one of the bad guys with a Model 1911A1 Colt semiautomatic pistol and contributed to the demise of another with the same .45-caliber weapon.

Following that, it was Castillo's judgment that Corporal Bradley really deserved to be formally assigned to the Office of Organizational Analysis.

He called the director of National Intelligence, who called the secretary of defense, who called the secretary of the Navy, who directed the commandant of the Marine Corps—"Just do it, don't ask questions"—to issue the appropriate orders:

TOP SECRET—PRESIDENTIAL

THE WHITE HOUSE, WASHINGTON, D.C.

DUPLICATION FORBIDDEN

COPY 2 OF 3 (SECRETARY COHEN)

JULY 25, 2005.

PRESIDENTIAL FINDING.

IT HAS BEEN FOUND THAT THE ASSASSINATION OF J. WINSLOW
MASTERSON, DEPUTY CHIEF OF MISSION OF THE UNITED STATES
EMBASSY IN BUENOS AIRES, ARGENTINA; THE ABDUCTION OF
MR. MASTERSON'S WIFE, MRS. ELIZABETH LORIMER MASTERSON;
THE ASSASSINATION OF SERGEANT ROGER MARKHAM, USMC; AND
THE ATTEMPTED ASSASSINATION OF SECRET SERVICE SPECIAL
AGENT ELIZABETH T. SCHNEIDER INDICATE BEYOND ANY
REASONABLE DOUBT THE EXISTENCE OF A CONTINUING PLOT OR
PLOTS BY TERRORISTS, OR TERRORIST ORGANIZATIONS, TO
CAUSE SERIOUS DAMAGE TO THE INTERESTS OF THE UNITED
STATES, ITS DIPLOMATIC OFFICERS, AND ITS CITIZENS, AND
THAT THIS SITUATION CANNOT BE TOLERATED.

IT IS FURTHER FOUND THAT THE EFFORTS AND ACTIONS TAKEN
AND TO BE TAKEN BY THE SEVERAL BRANCHES OF THE UNITED
STATES GOVERNMENT TO DETECT AND APPREHEND THOSE
INDIVIDUALS WHO COMMITTED THE TERRORIST ACTS PREVIOUSLY
DESCRIBED, AND TO PREVENT SIMILAR SUCH ACTS IN THE
FUTURE ARE BEING AND WILL BE HAMPERED AND RENDERED LESS
EFFECTIVE BY STRICT ADHERENCE TO APPLICABLE LAWS
AND REGULATIONS.

IT IS THEREFORE FOUND THAT CLANDESTINE AND COVERT
ACTION UNDER THE SOLE SUPERVISION OF THE PRESIDENT
IS NECESSARY.

IT IS DIRECTED AND ORDERED THAT THERE IMMEDIATELY BE ESTABLISHED A CLANDESTINE AND COVERT ORGANIZATION WITH THE MISSION OF DETERMINING THE IDENTITY OF THE TERRORISTS INVOLVED IN THE ASSASSINATIONS, ABDUCTION, AND ATTEMPTED ASSASSINATION PREVIOUSLY DESCRIBED AND TO RENDER THEM HARMLESS. AND TO PERFORM SUCH OTHER COVERT AND CLANDESTINE ACTIVITIES AS THE PRESIDENT MAY ELECT TO ASSIGN.

FOR PURPOSES OF CONCEALMENT, THE AFOREMENTIONED CLANDESTINE AND COVERT ORGANIZATION WILL BE KNOWN AS THE OFFICE OF ORGANIZATIONAL ANALYSIS, WITHIN THE DEPARTMENT OF HOMELAND SECURITY. FUNDING WILL INITIALLY BE FROM DISCRETIONARY FUNDS OF THE OFFICE OF THE PRESIDENT. THE MANNING OF THE ORGANIZATION WILL BE DECIDED BY THE PRESIDENT ACTING ON THE ADVICE OF THE CHIEF, OFFICE OF ORGANIZATIONAL ANALYSIS.

MAJOR CARLOS G. CASTILLO, SPECIAL FORCES, U.S. ARMY, IS HEREWITH APPOINTED CHIEF, OFFICE OF ORGANIZATIONAL ANALYSIS, WITH IMMEDIATE EFFECT.

SIGNED:

PRESIDENT OF THE UNITED STATES OF AMERICA

WITNESS:

Natalie G. Cohen

SECRETARY OF STATE

TOP SECRET—PRESIDENTIAL

The identification of the bodies in the Sheraton garage—and of two others shortly thereafter in the Conrad Resort & Casino in Punta del Este, Uruguay—pretty well "determined the identity of the terrorists."

And, obviously, they had been "rendered harmless" as called for by the Finding.

This accomplishment, however, did not mean that the Office of Organizational Analysis now could be shut down, or that the Finding could be filed in the Presidential Documents Not To Be Declassified For Fifty Years, or that the OOA personnel could be returned whence they had come.

Just about the opposite was true.

The investigation had been going on in Nuestra Pequeña Casa for nearly three weeks. To say that no end was in sight was a gross understatement.

The turning over of the rocks had revealed an astonishing number of ugly worms of interest to the director of National Intelligence, the Department of Justice, the Internal Revenue Service, the Department of State, and other governmental agencies.

"What we have here isn't an investigation," Inspector Doherty, who was on the staff of the director of the FBI and who had given the subject a good deal of thought, said very seriously the night before at dinner, "it's an investigation to determine what has to be investigated."

Doherty had reluctantly—another gross understatement—become part of the investigation only after the President had personally ordered the FBI director to loan the best man he had to OOA, not the senior FBI man who could be most easily spared.

Edgar Delchamps, of the CIA, had replied, "You got it, Sherlock."

Delchamps, too, had come to the OOA reluctantly. So reluctantly that when transferred from his posting as the CIA station chief in Paris, he had reported to Castillo only after he had stopped by CIA headquarters in Langley, Virginia, to put in for retirement.

When Castillo found out about that, it had taken a personal call from the director of National Intelligence, Ambassador Charles W. Montvale, to the director of the Central Intelligence Agency to get Delchamps to put off his retirement "for the time being." Montvale told the DCI that the President had personally ordered that the OOA—meaning Delchamps—be given absolute access to any intelligence the agency had gathered on any subject.

Doherty and Delchamps had not at first gotten along. Both were middle-aged and set in their ways. Doherty's way—which had seen him rise high in the FBI hierarchy—was to scrupulously follow the book, never bending, much less breaking, the law. Delchamps had spent most of his career operating clandestinely, often using a fictitious name. There was no book for what he did, of course, because the clandestine service does not—*cannot*—operate that way. So far as Delchamps was concerned, the end really justified the means.

Yet surprisingly they had become close—even friends—in recent weeks, largely because, Castillo had decided, they were older than everybody but Eric Kocian. They regarded everyone else—including Castillo—as inexperienced youngsters and were agreed that the President had erred in giving Castillo the authority he had given him. (Castillo thought they were probably right.)

What Doherty the night before had called the "investigation to determine what has to be investigated" now was just about over.

Castillo and Colonel Torine had flown the OOA's private jet—a Gulfstream III registered to the Lorimer Charitable & Benevolent Fund—down to Argentina to quietly ferry Delchamps, Doherty, and some of the others—not to mention the results of the investigation, which now filled one small filing cabinet and a dozen computer external hard drives—back to Washington.

Eric Kocian and his two dogs would go with them, too. His notes about the Iraqi Oil for Food scandal had provided keys to much of the information now on the hard drives.

So far as Castillo, Delchamps, and Doherty were concerned, Kocian was going to Washington to serve as a sort of living reference library as their investigation moved into the data banks of the FBI, the CIA, and other elements of the intelligence community.

So far as Kocian was concerned, however, he was going to Washington because there was a direct Delta Airlines flight from Washington Dulles International Airport to Budapest. It would allow him to take his dogs. There was no such flight from Buenos Aires.

Kocian owned two Bouvier des Flandres dogs, a male named Max and a bitch named Mädchen. At one hundred–plus pounds, Max was time-and-a-half the size of a large boxer. Mädchen was just a little smaller. There always had been a Max in Kocian's life since right after World War II, all of them named Max. Mädchen was a recent addition, a gift from the Lorimer Charitable & Benevolent Fund, not necessarily as a pet for Kocian, but as a companion for Max.

Max's alertness in Budapest had warned Castillo in time for him to be able to use a suppressed Ruger MKII .22-caliber semiautomatic pistol to render harmless two men who had broken into his hotel room bent on his assassination.

As Castillo later had put it—perhaps indelicately—to Edgar Delchamps, "I don't know how things are done in the spook world, but in the Army when someone saves your ass, the least you can do for him is get him laid."

It had been love at first sight between Max and Mädchen. But the playful frolicking of two canines weighing more than two hundred pounds between them had caused some serious damage to the furnishings of Nuestra Pequeña Casa. Although they slept on the floor in Kocian's bedroom, they mostly had been banished to the backyard and to the quincho, where they had sort of adopted Corporal Lester Bradley, sensing that not only did he like to kick a soccer ball for them, but while manning the secure satellite communication device had the time to do so.

Everyone was so used to seeing Max, Mädchen, and Lester together that hardly anyone noticed when Lester went to Ricardo Solez, touched his shoulder, and pointed to the secure radio. Solez nodded his understanding that if the radio went off, he was to answer the call.

Solez thought that Lester and Max and Mädchen were leaving the quincho so that the dogs could meet the call of nature and Lester would then kick the soccer ball for them to retrieve. Both dogs could get a soccer ball in their mouths with no more effort than lesser breeds had with a tennis ball.

The first person to sense that that had not been Corporal Bradley's intention was Edgar Delchamps, who happened to glance out of the quincho into the backyard.

"Hey, Ace!" he called to Lieutenant Colonel Castillo. "As much as I would like to think the kid's playing cops and robbers, I don't think so."

Castillo looked at him in confusion, then followed Delchamps's nod toward the backyard.

Corporal Bradley, holding a Model 1911A1 .45 ACP pistol in both hands, was marching across the grass by the swimming pool. Ahead of Bradley was a young man in a suit and tie who held his hands locked in the small of his neck. Max walked on one side of them, showing his teeth, and Mädchen on the other showing hers.

"What the hell?" Castillo exclaimed.

Sándor Tor, with almost amazing grace for his bulk, got out of his chair and walked toward the door, brushing aside his suit jacket enough to uncover a black SIG-Sauer 9mm P228 semiautomatic pistol in a skeleton holster on his belt.

Castillo moved quickly to the drapes gathered at one side of the plateglass window and snatched a 9mm Micro Uzi submachine gun from behind them.

He opened the door as they approached the verandah of the quincho.

"What's up, Lester?" he asked.

Corporal Bradley did not reply directly.

"On the porch," he ordered the man. "Drop to your knees, and then get on your stomach on the tiles."

"Permission to speak, sir?" the young man in the suit asked.

"I told you to get on your stomach," Bradley ordered as sternly as he could. He did not have much of what is known as a "command voice."

"I'd do what he says, pal," Edgar Delchamps suggested, conversationally. "Lester's been known to use that .45, and Max likes to bite people."

The young man dropped to his knees, then went flat to the tile of the shaded verandah. Max leaned over him, showing his teeth. Mädchen sat on her haunches across from him.

"I apprehended the intruder behind the pine trees, sir," Bradley announced, "as he was making his way toward the house."

"He was inside the fence?" Castillo asked. "What happened to the motion detectors?"

"He was inside the fence, sir," Bradley said. "Perhaps there is a malfunction of the motion-detecting system."

Tony Santini, carrying a Mini Uzi, and Ricardo Solez, holding a CAR-4, came out of the quincho.

"Jesus Christ, Pegleg!" Solez exclaimed. "What the fuck are you doing here?"

"Right now I'm laying on my goddamn stomach," the young man said.

"You know this guy, Ricardo?" Castillo asked.

"Yes, sir," Solez said.

Castillo waited a moment, then asked, "Well?"

"He's an assistant military attaché at the embassy in Asunción."

"Permission to speak, sir?" the man on the tile said.

"See what he's got in his pockets, Sándor," Castillo ordered.

Sándor Tor bent over the man on the tile, took a wallet from his hip pocket, and tossed it to Castillo. Then he rolled the man onto his back and went into the pockets of his jacket. He came up with an American diplomatic passport and tossed that to Castillo.

Castillo examined it.

"Sit, Max," he ordered.

Max looked at him, head cocked.

"He's probably not a bad guy," Castillo added.

After a moment, as if he had considered, then accepted, what Castillo had said, Max sat back on his haunches.

"Permission to speak, sir?" the man on the tile said.

"Why not?" Castillo said.

"Sir, I request to see Lieutenant Colonel Costello."

"Nobody here by that name," Castillo said. "Why don't we talk about what the hell you're doing here?"

"Sir, I came to see Colonel Costello."

"And if this Colonel Costello was here, what were you going to say to him?" Castillo asked.

"I was going to ask him for his help."

"Help about what?" Castillo asked, but before the man had a chance to open his mouth, Castillo asked another question. "You sneaked in here to ask somebody for help?"

"Sir, I didn't know what name you were using for the safe house. And even if I did, I didn't think you would pass me through the gate to this place. So I had to come in surreptitiously."

"Son," Edgar Delchamps asked, "how'd you get past the motion sensors on the fence? *Fences,* plural?"

"Dry ice, sir. I froze the mercury switches."

"Where'd you get the dry ice?"

"I bought it from a kid who delivers ice cream on a motorbike from the Freddo's ice cream store in the shopping mall."

"And where'd you learn to use dry ice on mercury switches?"

"Fort Huachuca, sir."

He pronounced that correctly, Castillo thought. *"Wah-choo-kuh."*

"What were you doing at Huachuca?" Delchamps challenged.

"Going through the Intelligence School."

"You're an Army intelligence officer?"

"Yes, sir. First Lieutenant Edmund Lorimer, sir."

"*Lorimer?*" Castillo said. "Your name is *Lorimer?*"

"Yes, sir. Same as that UN guy who got himself whacked in Uruguay."

"Your witness, Colonel," Delchamps said, gesturing grandly.

"You're Colonel Costello?" Lorimer asked.

"For the time being, I'll ask the questions," Castillo snapped, and was immediately sorry. "You may get up, Lieutenant Lorimer."

"Thank you, sir."

"You can put the .45 away, Bradley," Castillo said. He added, "But good job, Lester."

"Thank you, sir. The credit is due Max. He either detected unusual movement in the pines or perhaps smelled him."

"Take them inside the quincho, tell them 'good dog!', and give them each a bone."

"Yes, sir. Sir, when Max has too many bones—and he's already had several today—he suffers flatulence."

"Use your good judgment, Lester."

"Yes, sir. Thank you, sir."

Castillo had been watching Lorimer out of the corner of his eye, idly wondering why he was getting to his feet slowly and carefully. He saw that Lorimer was smiling at Bradley, probably at the word "flatulence."

Lorimer's eyes met Castillo's for a moment, and when Lorimer was half-sitting on the table there, Castillo saw what had caused him to get to his feet so slowly and carefully.

And why Ricardo had called him "Pegleg."

Lorimer's right trouser leg had been pulled up. Rising from his stockinged ankle was a dully shining metal tube.

Titanium, Castillo thought. *They now make those things out of titanium. How do I know that?*

"What happened to your leg?" Castillo asked gently.

"RPG," Lorimer said.

"Where?"

"Afghanistan. We got bushwhacked on the way to Mazar. On Highway A76."

Castillo knew well the Mazar airfield—and, for that matter, Highway A76, the road to it from Kabul. The next to last time he had been there, he had "borrowed" a Black Hawk helicopter to make an extraction of the crew of another Black Hawk that had been shot down. Far senior officers had reluctantly concluded that the weather was so bad that making such an attempt would have been suicidal.

The last time he'd been at Mazar was to board a USAF C-5 Galaxy for the States, which carried him home with a vaguely phrased letter of reprimand for "knowingly and flagrantly violating flight safety rules."

The letter of reprimand was the compromise reached between several very senior officers who wished to recommend him for the Distinguished Service Cross—or perhaps even The Medal—and other very senior officers who wished to bring the crazy Special Forces sonofabitch before a General Court-Martial for willful disobedience of orders.

"How far up does that thing go?" Castillo asked.

"To the knee. Actually, the knee's part of it. All titanium."

"What were you doing in Afghanistan?"

"I thought I was winning their hearts and minds until this happened."

"You were Special Forces?"

Lorimer nodded. "Was. Now I'm Intelligence. DIA."

"How did that happen?"

"Well, for a while I thought I could do a Freddy Franks, but that didn't work."

General Frederick M. Franks Jr., then an Army major, lost a leg to wounds suffered in the Cambodian Incursion during the Vietnam War. He managed to stay in the Army by proving he could pass any physical test required of any officer. He became both the first one-legged general since the Civil War and, as a four-star general, the commander of ground forces in the First Desert War. Franks served as an inspiration to all—particularly to amputees.

"Why not?"

"It hurt too much."

"Okay. Who told you about this place?" Castillo asked.

"I asked around, sir."

"I asked *who*, Lieutenant."

Castillo looked at Ricardo Solez, who proclaimed his innocence by shaking his head and wagging both hands palms outward.

Lorimer said, "A lot people, sir. I just put it together."

"Among them Solez?"

"He was one of them, but he wouldn't tell me anything. But he's how I found out where you were."

Castillo glanced at Solez, who motioned to maintain his innocence, then looked back at Lorimer.

"He told you where we were?" Castillo said.

Lorimer shook his head. "I followed him and that kid with the .45 out here from the embassy."

Solez and Bradley, who had been posted to the embassy before they had been drafted by Castillo, had been assigned to make daily—sometimes twice-daily—errand runs from Nuestra Pequeña Casa to the embassy specifically and to Buenos Aires generally. The theory was they were familiar faces and would attract the least attention.

Castillo looked at Solez, whose face now showed pain.

Castillo was tempted to let it go, but changed his mind. Getting followed was inexcusable.

"No rearview mirrors on the Trafic, right, Ricardo?" Castillo asked.

"Jesus Christ, Carlos, I'm sorry."

His embarrassment—shame—was clear in his voice.

"He's pretty good, Colonel," Lorimer said. "He led me up and down every back street between here and Palermo."

"But you're better, right?"

"Yes, sir. I guess I am."

"Okay. So you're here. Why?"

"A friend of mine, a DEA agent, got kidnapped about a week ago. I need some help to get him back. I figured you were the guy who could help, maybe the only one," Lorimer said.

"Why would you think that?"

"Because you got the bad guys who kidnapped Jack the Stack's wife and whacked him."

"What if I told you I have no idea what you're talking about?"

"Sir, I would expect you to say just that," Lorimer said. "But, sir, with respect, you better get used to the idea that the cat's out of the bag. I even heard of what went down and I'm pretty low down on the pay scale. And in Paraguay."

Castillo looked at Delchamps.

"Write this down, Ace," Delchamps said. "There's no such thing as a secret."

"Oh, shit!" Castillo said, and shook his head. Then he turned to Lorimer.

"Lieutenant Lorimer, I am Lieutenant Colonel C. G. *Castillo*, Special Forces, U.S. Army."

"Yes, sir."

"I inform you herewith that I am here operating on the authority of a Presidential Finding. . . ."

"Yes, sir."

"Close your mouth until I'm finished, Lieutenant. You are advised herewith that each and every aspect of this operation is classified Top Secret Presidential. From this moment on, you will not discuss with anyone what you think you may have learned, or what you think you may have surmised, about anything connected with this operation. That includes the names of personnel, and the location of personnel or facilities, and what I or anyone connected with this operation may or may not have done. Any breach of these instructions will result in your trial by General Court-Martial—at which, trust me, you will be found guilty—and being placed in solitary confinement at probably Leavenworth until the details of this operation are no longer of interest to anyone. You run off at the mouth, and you'll wish the RPG had got all of you. Got it?"

"Yes, sir."

He's got it. His face is white. And I feel like a shit.

"You heard what he said, Ace, about the cat being out of the bag?" Delchamps asked, but it sounded to Castillo like a statement.

"Edgar, butt out," Castillo said.

"I was thinking about collateral damage," Delchamps said. "Who's he been talking to? Which of them has been running at the mouth? What are you going to do about shutting them up?"

There I go again, underestimating Delchamps!

"Let's go to the house," Castillo said, gesturing. "You, Ed, and Tony and—somebody go inside and get Sieno."

"Which one, Colonel?" Davidson asked.

"Both of them," Castillo ordered. "And, Jack, sit on Lieutenant Lorimer here. If he even looks like he's thinking of taking off, shoot him in his good leg."

There were two suites of rooms on the second floor of Nuestra Pequeña Casa, each containing a large bedroom, a walk-in-closet, and a bathroom. The Sienos occupied the larger of the two. Castillo had taken the slightly smaller one for himself.

Castillo's bedroom had one chair—at a dressing table—and a chaise lounge. Susanna Sieno—a trim, pale-freckled-skin redhead who did not look like what came to mind when "an officer of the clandestine service of the CIA" was said—took the dressing table chair. Delchamps and Paul Sieno sat side by side on the chaise lounge. Solez wordlessly asked permission to sit on the edge of the bed. When Castillo nodded, and he had, Tony Santini sat beside Solez.

Castillo leaned against the wall by the door, and after a moment said, "The word that comes to mind is 'compromised' . . . goddammit!"

"It happens, Ace," Delchamps said.

"Okay, we shut down. We were going to the States anyway in a couple of days. Now we go now."

There were nods of agreement.

"I'd love to know how this happened," Castillo said.

"I'd say Uruguay," Susanna Sieno said.

Castillo looked at her, then made a *come on* gesture.

"The OK Corral shoot-out took place there," she explained. "And you jerked Dave Yung and Julio Artigas out of the embassy, which was sure to cause gossip in the embassy, and then they found Howard Kennedy's body in the Conrad in Punta del Este. . . ."

"What's that got to with this Lieutenant Lorimer in Paraguay?" Castillo interrupted.

"The spooks and the cops in Asunción find a lot of reasons to, quote, confer, close quote, with the spooks and the cops in Montevideo," she said. "Like the dentists who go to Hawaii for two weeks, all tax-deductible, to confer for two hours on how to drill a molar with caries."

Delchamps chuckled.

"I'm not sure I understand," Castillo said.

"I think Susanna is onto it, Ace," Delchamps said. "I'll put it in soldier terms for you. You know what R&R is, right?"

Castillo nodded. "Rest and Recuperation."

"Sometimes known as I & I, for Intercourse and Intoxication," Delchamps went on. "And we know how every second lieutenant is required to memorize, 'If indiscretions you must have, have them a hundred miles from the flagpole.' "

Castillo smiled. "Okay."

"I don't know anything about this, of course," Susanna Sieno said, "but my husband, who as far as I know never lies to me, says that healthy young men not lucky enough to be accompanied by their wives on an assignment to someplace like Asunción have unsatisfied physical desires. . . ."

"When you were in short pants, Ace, and I was in Moscow," Delchamps said, "I used to confer with my professional associates in Vienna every couple of months. It wasn't smart to accept the female companionship offered to horny young spooks by the KGB in Moscow. Getting the picture, or do I have to be more graphic and make you blush?"

"I'm getting the picture," Castillo said.

"So try this scenario on for size," Susanna Sieno said. "Agent X, of the firm, or the DIA, or the DEA, or the FBI, checks in with his peers at the embassy in Montevideo. This satisfies the requirements of his temporary-duty orders. He spends an hour in the embassy, and then it's off to the sandy beaches and the bikini-clad maidens of Punta del Este. So Agent X asks, 'Well, what's new, Willy?'

"And Willy says, 'Nothing much here, but you heard about Jack the Stack Masterson getting whacked in front of his wife in Buenos Aires?'

"And Agent X says, 'Yeah, what was that all about?'

"And Willy says, 'God only knows, but what's interesting is that a Washington hotshot—I don't know this, but I heard that he's an Army officer sent by the President—has taken over the investigation.'

"So Agent X goes back to Asunción and tells this interesting story to the boys. And then Agent Y goes on R&R to Montevideo.

" 'Willy, tell me about Jack the Stack's murder and the hotshot.'

"To which Willy replies, 'I don't know much, but it's getting interesting. First, Dave Yung, one the FBI guys, gets jerked out of here and onto a plane for Washington. No explanation. And then, two days ago, right after Yung mysteriously disappeared, they find an American, who worked for the UN, and six guys all dressed like Ninjas, all dead at an estancia named—would you believe it?—*Shangri-La*. Nobody has a clue what that was all about.'

"So Agent Y, his physical desires satisfied, goes back to Asunción and tells his pal, Agent Z, what he heard in Montevideo. Agent Z then takes his R&R in Montevideo, where he asks Willy—or Tom, Dick, and Harry—'Tell me more about the six dead Ninjas and the UN guy.'

" 'Curiouser and curiouser,' he's told. 'Turns out the dead American was a drug dealer *and* Jack the Stack's brother-in-law. There's a very interesting rumor that a special operations team, probably run by the hotshot—he's an Army officer by the name of Costello; we found that out—whacked the Ninjas and maybe also the drug guy—his name was Lorimer—and then they jerked another FBI guy, Artigas, out of here. No explanation.' "

Susanna paused.

"End of scenario," she said after a moment.

"Good scenario," Castillo said.

"These are all bright, clever guys, Charley," she said. "Trained investigators."

"With diarrhea of the mouth," Castillo said.

"Nobody told them all this was Top Secret Presidential," Sieno said. "Call it shop talk."

"No excuse," Castillo said.

"It wasn't as if they were running off at the mouth in a bar," Delchamps said. "These guys were swapping gossip with people they knew had the same security clearances they did. Arguably, their sharing of such information could hold a kernel that would prove to be a missing piece of a puzzle they were working, one they otherwise would not have had. . . ."

"That's not an excuse, Ed, and you know it," Castillo said.

"I didn't say it was right, Ace. I said I think it explains what happened. I think Susanna's right on the money. And it explains the young man with the titanium leg coming here. His pal got snatched and now he's desperate. . . ."

"I didn't hear about that," Susanna said.

"What he said was his pal, a DEA agent, was snatched a week ago," Delchamps explained. "And, though he didn't say this, I'll bet nobody in Paraguay is doing anything at all to get him back that might annoy the host government in any way. So he came looking for John Wayne here."

"So the question then becomes 'What do we do about it?' "

"About getting the DEA guy back?" Delchamps asked.

"The DEA guy is not my problem," Castillo said.

"No, he's not," Delchamps said. "Write that down."

Castillo flashed him a cold look.

"Meaning what?"

"Meaning for a moment there, Ace, I thought you were starting to think you really are John Wayne, flitting around the world righting wrongs," Delchamps said.

"My primary concern is making sure this operation isn't compromised any more than it already is," Castillo said.

"How are you going to do that?"

"Well, first we're going to get out of here. There's no reason we can't move it to the Nebraska Avenue Complex. Or is there?"

Delchamps shook his head.

"The Sienos, Tony, and Alex Darby will be here. Plus Bob Howell in Montevideo," Delchamps said. "They can handle anything that comes up with regard to this . . ." He gestured in the direction of the quincho.

Castillo nodded. Darby was the CIA station chief in Buenos Aires and Howell his counterpart in Montevideo.

"But what are you going to do about the guy downstairs?" Tony Santini asked. "You can't trust him to keep his mouth shut."

"Particularly since Charley's not going to rescue his pal from the bad guys," Susanna said.

"He goes with us," Castillo said. "Unless somebody's got a better idea?"

"Tony, who do you know in the embassy in Asunción?" Delchamps asked.

"I've been up there, of course," Santini said. "But I don't have any pals there, if that's what you're asking."

"You're not alone," Susanna said.

Castillo and Delchamps looked at her. When she didn't respond, Delchamps asked, "Who's the station chief?"

"His name is White," Paul Sieno said. "Robert J. White."

Delchamps looked thoughtful a moment, then shook his head.

Susanna said: "He can't understand why someone like himself, who has kissed all the appropriate buttocks in Langley for years, gets assigned to Asunción when troublemakers like Paul and Alex and me got to go to Buenos Aires."

"What about the military attaché?" Castillo asked.

"He and the station chief are great pals," Santini said. "I don't think talking to them would work, Charley."

"And I don't want to go to the ambassador there, or involve Silvio any more than I already have," Castillo said, almost thoughtfully. "If this thing blows up in our faces, the less he knows the better."

Juan Manuel Silvio was the United States Ambassador to Argentina. He had put his career at risk to help Castillo to carry out the Presidential Finding.

"So?" Delchamps asked.

"So, I guess I have to go to the other ambassador."

The other ambassador was the Honorable Charles W. Montvale, the former deputy secretary of State, former secretary of the Treasury, and former ambassador to the European Union. And now the director of National Intelligence.

Castillo shook his head and said, "I now know how Lee felt at Appomattox Court House when he said, 'I would rather face a thousand deaths, but now I must go and treat with General Grant.' "

"Is he really that bad, Charley?" Susanna asked.

"Right now, Susie, I feel like a small white mouse about to be put into the cobra's cage," Castillo said.

He pushed himself away from the wall, walked to the bed, and gestured to Solez to give up his seat.

"You want some privacy, Ace?" Delchamps said.

"No. I want everybody to hear this," Castillo said, sat down on the bed, and punched the SPEAKER PHONE button on what looked like an ordinary telephone.

"Corporal Bradley speaking, sir," Lester's voice came over the speaker.

"Is the Local Secure LED lit, Lester?"

"Yes, sir."

"Get Major Miller on here, secure."

"Aye, aye, sir."

Ten seconds later, a male voice came very clearly over the speaker.

"And how are things down in Buenos Aires on this miserable, blistering, humid afternoon in our beloved nation's capital?"

"Verify secure," Bradley's voice piped.

"Ah, the pride of the Marine Corps! The little green light is glowing brightly, Lester."

"Colonel, the line is secure. I believe Major Miller is the party answering."

"Thank you, Bradley," Castillo said. "Hey, Dick!"

"*A sus órdenes, mi coronel*," Miller said.

"Get Agnes on an extension, and then patch me through secure to the White House."

"I don't like the tone of your voice," Miller said, seriously. "Hold one, Charley."

Twenty seconds later, a female voice announced, "White House."

"You on, Agnes?" Castillo asked.

"Uh-huh," Mrs. Agnes Forbison, the deputy chief for administration of the Office of Organizational Analysis, said.

"You and Dick stay on the line," Castillo said. "Don't record or take notes, but pay attention."

"Why do I think I know what you're going to say next?" Agnes Forbison asked.

"White House," the female operator repeated.

"You're prescient, Agnes," Castillo said, and then, "Operator, this is Colonel Castillo. Will you get me Ambassador Montvale on a secure line, please?"

"Hold one, Colonel. It may take a moment. He's in the mountains with the boss."

Oh, shit!

Ten seconds later, a male voice came on.

"Ambassador Montvale's line."

"Colonel Castillo for Ambassador Montvale," the White House operator said. "The line is secure."

"The ambassador is with the President. I'm not sure he can be disturbed."

"Is that Mr. Ellsworth?" Castillo asked.

Truman C. Ellsworth had risen high in government service as Ambassador Montvale's trusted deputy. He was not an admirer of Lieutenant Colonel Castillo, whom he viewed as a threat to Montvale.

"Good afternoon, Colonel," Ellsworth said in his somewhat nasal voice.

"I have to speak to the ambassador. Your call, Mr. Ellsworth, as to if he can be interrupted when he's with the President."

There was no reply, but in five seconds another male voice, one somewhat impatient, came over the speakers.

"Yes?"

Ellsworth, you sonofabitch!

"This is Castillo, Mr. President. Sorry to bother you, sir. I was trying to get the ambassador."

"My line rang," the President said, and then corrected himself. "*Flashed.* How are you, Charley?"

"Very well, thank you, sir."

"You're in Argentina, right?"

"Yes, sir."

"What kind of television do you get down there?"

"We've been watching Fox and Deutsche Welle, Mr. President."

"So you know what's going on in New Orleans and along the Gulf Coast?"

"Yes, sir."

"We're watching. Hard to believe, isn't it?"

Un-fucking-believable, sir.

"Yes, Mr. President, it is."

"I want to see you as soon as you get back up here, Charley. When is that going to be?"

"Probably late tomorrow, sir."

"Okay. I'll see you then. Unless I'm down there overseeing this disaster. You find me, either way."

"Yes, sir."

"Charles," Castillo heard the President say, "it's Charley for you."

Ambassador Montvale came on the line a moment later.

"Good to hear from you, Colonel," he said. "What can I do for you?"

"Buy Mr. Ellsworth a new pair of glasses."

"Excuse me?"

"I can think of no reason but fuzzy eyesight for his pushing the President's button when he knew I wanted to talk to you, can you?"

"I'm sure that it was inadvertent."

"Oh, me too," Castillo said, sarcastically. "I can't imagine him doing it on purpose, hoping it would cause the President to be annoyed with me. It just *has to be* his glasses."

"What can I do for you, Charley?" Montvale asked, his annoyance clear in his voice.

"There's a risk of compromise down here that I want to stop before it goes any further."

"At this late date?"

"Yes, sir."

"What needs to be done?"

"Two things. First, please call the station chief in Paraguay and tell him that Alex Darby is coming to see him and will speak with your authority."

"My authority about what?"

"To tell his people to stop guessing between them what happened in Uruguay and here, and stop talking about it, period."

"Should I call the ambassador there?"

"Let's leave him out of it, if we can."

"Your call. But forewarned is forearmed, as you know."

"And then call Fort Meade and have the DIA immediately transfer First Lieutenant Edmund Lorimer, an assistant military attaché at the embassy in Asunción, to OOA."

"What's that about?"

"He was clever enough to learn my name and find the safe house. I don't want to leave him here."

"A troublemaker, in other words?"

"Mr. Ambassador, he's done nothing but what I would have done in his shoes."

"Why don't I find that comforting, do you suppose?"

Castillo ignored the response.

"We're shutting down here," Castillo went on, "just to be safe. We're just about finished here anyway. We ought to be in Washington sometime late tomorrow. I'm going to bring Lorimer with us."

"Come see me when you get here."

"Yes, sir. Of course."

"I'll get right on this."

"Thank you, sir."

Castillo waited until the White House operator, detecting that the telephone in Camp David had been hung up, asked, "Are you through, Colonel?"

"Break it down, please, thank you," Castillo said, and then, after a moment, "You heard that, Agnes? Dick?"

"Why do I think Mr. Ellsworth doesn't like you?" Agnes asked.

"With a little bit of luck, I can stop this before it gets any worse," Castillo said. "But I wanted you to have a heads-up if it goes wrong. I'll give you a call when we're a couple hours out of Baltimore. We're going to need three Yukons."

"They'll be there," Agnes said.

"Where do we live now, Dick?"

"I was about to call you about that," Miller said. "You know West Boulevard Drive in Alexandria?"

"Maybe. I think so."

"Agnes knows a real estate guy, and he put her onto a place at 7200 West Boulevard Drive. An old couple lived there, she died, and then a month later, three months ago, he did. Their kids didn't want it, and they want the money quick. They went through it and took out the valuable stuff, but what's left is nice."

"And the house?"

"You'll like everything about it but the price, boss," Agnes said.

"Which is how much? And why will I like it?"

"Right now you are renting it, furnished, for ten thousand a month, with an option to buy at $2,950,000 with the furniture, and I don't really know how much without."

"Done deal?"

"You told Dick to get you out of the Monica Lewinsky Motel right now, and yesterday would be better. Yeah, it's a done deal. I gave them a check two hours ago," Agnes said.

"On my account, I hope? I don't want the Lorimer Benevolent & Charitable Trust involved in this."

"You're paying for it," Agnes said. "But on that subject, we just got confirmation of that substantial deposit to the trust we've been expecting."

"Well, presuming we can keep that a secret, that's good news. Can I go to this place straight from the airport? And can I stash Lieutenant Lorimer there until I figure out what to do with him?"

"You can go there from the airport," Agnes said. "But there's no sheets or towels, food, etcetera. And yes, you can take somebody there. Six bedrooms, six baths. And it's off the road; nobody can look into the windows from the street. I told them to get a radio in there tomorrow, but it will probably be a couple of days before you have a secure White House telephone."

"Dick, can you get our stuff out of the Mayflower and over there before I get there? And stop by Sam's Club or someplace and buy sheets, etcetera, and food? Charge that to the Trust."

"Yes, sir, Colonel, sir. Dare I to presume that was an invitation to share your new quarters?"

"Yeah, but no guests of the opposite sex above the first floor," Castillo said. "We are going to be paragons of virtue in our new home."

Agnes laughed.

"That I'll have to see," she said.

Castillo had a new thought: "Who's going to take care of this place?"

"That's another problem I'm working on," Agnes said. "You're going to need a housekeeper and a yardman. At least. Dick said maybe we could put an ad in the *Army Times* and see if we could find a retired sergeant and his wife. Maybe they'd have security clearances."

"What would I do without you, Agnes?"

"I shudder to consider the possibility," she said.

"Unless you've got something else, we'll see you tomorrow," Castillo said.

"Can't think of anything that won't wait," she said.

When it became evident that Miller wasn't going to say anything, Castillo ordered, "Break it down, Lester."

"Aye, aye, sir."

Castillo hung up the phone.

"Okay," he said, "in the immortal words of General George S. Patton, let's saddle up and get this show on the road."

"I don't think Patton said that, Ace," Edgar Delchamps said.

"If he didn't, he should have," Castillo said.

"What about the steaks?" Susanna Sieno said.

"Fire should be ready about now," Paul Sieno added.

Castillo considered that a moment, then said, "Good idea, Susanna. 'An Army marches on its stomach.' I don't know if Patton said that or not. And I don't care—I'm hungry. Let's eat."

II

They had gone wheels-up at Jorge Newbery Airport in Buenos Aires a few minutes after six that morning. They'd flown diagonally across South America to Quito, Ecuador, where they had taken on fuel and had lunch. From Quito, they'd flown north, passing over Panama into the Gulf of Mexico, skirted around the western tip of Cuba, and then flown almost straight north to the Panhandle of Florida.

The flight plan they filed gave Hurlburt Field, near Destin, Florida, as their destination. Hurlburt was headquarters of the Air Force Special Operations Command. Far fewer questions, Jake Torine had suggested, would be asked there than anywhere else, and even if questions were asked, Hurlburt had instant communication with the Special Operations Command at MacDill Air Force Base in Tampa, Florida, where they could be quickly—and, as important, quietly—answered.

It now looked as if that logical plan wasn't going to work.

"Aircraft calling Hurlburt Approach Control, this is Eglin Approach."

"Uh-oh," Castillo said, and then triggering his mike, replied, "Eglin Approach Control, Gulfstream Three Seven Nine."

"Gulfstream Three Seven Nine, be advised that Hurlburt Field is closed to all traffic. Acknowledge."

Jake Torine made an impatient gesture for Castillo to take control of the airplane.

"Eglin, Three Seven Nine, this aircraft is in the service of the United States government. Colonel Jacob Torine, USAF, is pilot in command. We wish to land at Hurlburt."

"Sir, Katrina knocked Hurlburt out."

Castillo and Torine exchanged *What the hell?* glances.

"Okay," Torine replied. "Turning on transponder at this time. We are approximately a hundred miles south of your station. Let me know when you have us."

Fifteen seconds later, Eglin Approach Control reported, "Three Seven Nine, I have you at flight level 30, 450 knots, approximately nine five miles south."

"Okay, Eglin Approach. Give me approach and landing, please."

"Three Seven Nine, be advised that Eglin is closed to all but emergency traffic."

"Son, did you hear what I said about this aircraft being in government service?"

"Yes, sir. Do you wish to declare an emergency at this time?"

Castillo triggered his microphone.

"Eglin," he said, "is Cairns Army Airfield open?"

"Three Seven Nine, I believe Cairns is open, but be advised it is closed to civilian traffic."

"Thank you, Eglin," Castillo said. "Three Seven Nine is not, repeat not, declaring an emergency at this time."

He turned to Torine.

"Jake, if you'll take it and steer about thirty-five degrees, I'll see if I can find the approach charts to Cairns."

"I gather, first officer, that you have been to this place before?"

"Once or twice, pilot in command, sir," Castillo said, as he began rummaging through his Jeppesen case.

THIRTEEN YEARS EARLIER

[-I-]
Base Operations
Cairns Army Airfield
The Army Aviation Center
Fort Rucker, Alabama
1145 2 February 1992

Lieutenant Colonel F. Mason Edmonds, Aviation—a starting-to-get-a-little-chubby thirty-nine-year-old who sported a bushy mustache—stood behind one of the double plateglass doors of Base Operations, looking out at the airfield.

On the wall behind him was an oil portrait of Major General Bogardus S.

Cairns, for whom the airfield was named. General Cairns, a West Pointer and at the time the commanding general of Fort Rucker, had crashed to his death in an H-13 Sioux helicopter on 9 December 1958. There was an unpleasant story that the crash had been due to General Cairns's failure to turn on his aircraft's pitot heat.

True or not, Colonel Edmonds did not like the story. It tended to detract from the positive image of Army Aviation, and Colonel Edmonds considered himself to be probably the most important guardian of that image. He was the information officer of the Army Aviation Center and Fort Rucker, Alabama.

A year before, the fact that Colonel Edmonds had been granted a bachelor of fine arts degree in journalism by Temple University had come to light when personnel officers in the Pentagon were reviewing his records to see what could be done with him now that some sort of unpronounceable inner-ear malady had caused him to fail his annual flight physical examination and he could no longer be assigned to flight duty.

Finding a round peg for the round hole had pleased both the personnel officers and Colonel Edmonds. He had been afraid, now that he was grounded, that he would be assigned to some maintenance billet, or some supply billet, or wind up in some other nothing assignment, like dependent housing officer.

Being the information officer for the Army Aviation Center and Fort Rucker was a horse of an entirely different hue. He had always believed he had a flair for journalism and the written word, and had often wondered if he had made the right decision in staying in the Army after his compulsory-after-ROTC five-year initial tour. He could have gotten out and tried his hand as a journalist. Or perhaps even as a novelist.

His experience since he'd become the IO had confirmed his opinion of his ability as a journalist. Surprising most his staff—made up of half civilian, half military—instead of just sitting behind his desk supervising things and reviewing press releases to make sure they reflected well on Army Aviation, he had gotten right down to his new profession and gotten his hands dirty.

That was to say, he took it upon himself to write some of the stories that would be published in *The Army Flier*, the base newspaper, or sent out as press releases. Only the important stories, of course, not the run-of-the-mill pieces.

He was on such a yarn today, one that he intended to run on page one of *The Army Flier*, and one he was reasonably sure would be printed in newspapers across the land. In his judgment, it had just the right mixture of human interest, military history, and a little good old-fashioned emotion. And, of course, it could not help but burnish the image of Army Aviation and indeed the Army itself.

A sergeant walked up to him.

"Sir?"

Edmonds turned to look at him and nodded.

"Colonel, that Mohawk you've been looking for just turned on final."

"And it will park on the tarmac here?"

"Yes, sir. It's a Blue Flight aircraft, Colonel. They always park here."

"Thank you, Sergeant."

"Yes, sir."

Blue Flight was the name assigned to a special function of the Aviation School's flight training program. If, for example, it was determined for some reason that a nonflying field-grade officer—sometimes a major, most often a lieutenant colonel—needed to learn how to fly, he was sent to Rucker and assigned to Blue Flight.

He—or she, as the case might be—was then subjected to what amounted to a cram course in flying.

This was not to suggest that the course of instruction was less thorough in any way than the regular flight training programs of the Aviation School. If anything, Blue Flight instruction—the best instructors were assigned temporarily to Blue Flight as needed—might just be a little better than that offered by the school.

As Colonel Edmonds thought of it, there were several factors driving the philosophy of Blue Flight instruction. High among them was the realization that it was in the Army's interest to send a senior officer student back as a fully qualified pilot to whatever assignment had necessitated that he or she become a pilot as quickly as possible.

Further, if the Army felt an officer in midcareer needed to be a pilot, it made little sense to send them to Rucker only to have them fail the course of instruction. With this in mind, Blue Flight students were *tutored*, rather than simply taught. It was in the Army's interest that they earn their wings.

While most Blue Flight students were majors or lieutenant colonels, there were exceptions at both ends of the rank hierarchy. Most of these officers were colonels, but there was—far less commonly—the occasional captain or even lieutenant.

In the case of the junior officers, they were most often aides-de-camp to general officers who were already qualified rotary-wing aviators. They were assigned to Blue Flight for transition into fixed-wing aircraft. It made sense to have an aide-de-camp who could fly his general in both a helicopter and in the C-12 Huron, a twin turboprop, used to fly senior officers around.

"Huron" was the Army's name for the Beechcraft Super King Air. It annoyed Colonel Edmonds that Army Aviators almost invariably called the aircraft the King Air rather than the Huron, but he couldn't do much about it except ensure that the term "King Air" never appeared in news stories emanating from his office.

Such a junior officer—this one a lieutenant, a general officer's aide-de-camp sent to Blue Flight for transition training into the C-12 Huron—was to be the subject of the story Colonel Edmonds planned to write today.

Colonel Edmonds was more than a little annoyed that he had had to dig up the story himself. He should have been told, not have had to hear a rumor and then run down the rumor.

He had happened to mention this to the post commander, when he suggested to the general that if he were to release a photograph of the general standing together with the lieutenant before a building named for the lieutenant's father, it would more than likely be printed widely and reflect well upon Army Aviation and the Army itself.

Two months before, Colonel Edmonds had thought he was onto another story, one just as good, perhaps, as the one he was onto today. That one, however, hadn't worked out.

What had happened was that Colonel Edmonds had seen a familiar name on the bronze dedicatory plaque of the building. He had inquired of Brigadier General Harold F. Wilson, deputy commander of the Army Aviation Center and Fort Rucker, if there was any connection between himself and Second Lieutenant H. F. Wilson, whose name was on the dedicatory plaque.

It had been too much to hope for, and asking General Wilson had been a mistake.

"Colonel, I have been asked that question many times before," the general had said. "I will tell you what I have told everyone else who's asked it: Don't ask it again, and whenever you hear that rumor someplace else, repeat this conversation of ours."

Obviously, General Wilson, himself a highly decorated Army Aviator, was anxious not to bask in the reflected glory of another hero who happened to have a similar name.

With that encounter with General Wilson in mind—and knowing the odds were that General Wilson would not be enthusiastic about what he had in mind—Colonel Edmonds had taken his idea directly to Major General Charles M. Augustus, Jr., the commanding general of the Army Aviation Center and Fort Rucker.

General Augustus, not very enthusiastically, agreed that it was a good idea, and told Edmonds to set it up. But he didn't respond to Edmonds's complaint that he had not been advised, as he should have been, that the lieutenant was a member of Blue Flight.

Edmonds further suspected that the Blue Flight people were either unaware of what the lieutenant was doing or didn't care.

When he called Blue Flight to ask that the lieutenant be directed to report to him at his office, in Class A uniform at 1300, they said that might be a little difficult, as the lieutenant was involved in a cross-country training flight in the Mohawk under simulated instrument conditions, and that he might be back at Cairns a little before noon, and then again he might not. No telling.

Like the C-12 Huron, the Grumman Mohawk also was a twin-turboprop aircraft, but not a light transport designed to move senior officers in comfort from one place to another. It was, instead, designed as an electronic surveillance aircraft, normally assigned to military intelligence units. The only people it carried were its two pilots.

The military intelligence connection gave it a certain élan with Army Aviators, as did the fact that it was the fastest airplane in the inventory. The pilots assigned to fly it were most often the more experienced ones.

So, Edmonds concluded, there was something extraordinary in a lieutenant being trained by Blue Flight to fly the Mohawk.

The only thing Colonel Edmonds could think of to explain the situation was that they might be using the Mohawk as an instrument flight training aircraft. Yet when he really thought some more about that, it didn't make sense.

He looked up at the sky and saw a triple-tailed Mohawk approaching, and he followed it through touchdown until he lost sight of it. And then suddenly there it was, taxiing up to the tarmac in front of Base Ops.

He remembered only then that it was said of the Mohawk that it could land on a dime. This was accomplished by reversing the propellers' pitch at the instant of touchdown—or a split second before.

Ground handlers laid ladders against the Mohawk's bulbous cockpit. The two men in the aircraft unbuckled their harnesses and climbed down and then started walking toward Base Operations.

One of them was an older man, and the other—logically, the lieutenant whom Edmonds was looking for—was much younger.

As they came closer, Colonel Edmonds had doubts that this was the officer he was looking for. He was a tall, fair-skinned, blue-eyed young man who didn't look as if his name was Carlos Guillermo Castillo. One would expect someone with a name like that to have a darker skin and more than likely dark eyes.

Edmonds now saw the older man was Chief Warrant Officer-4 Pete Kowalski, who was not only a master Army Aviator but vice president of the Instrument Examiner Board. Edmonds was surprised that Kowalski was teaching a lowly lieutenant.

Both saluted Colonel Edmonds as they got close to where he stood by the Base Ops door.

"Lieutenant Castillo?" Colonel Edmonds asked.

Castillo stopped and said, "Yes, sir."

Maybe this isn't the right Castillo. It's not that unusual a name.

"*Carlos Guillermo* Castillo?" Edmonds challenged.

"Yes, sir."

"Lieutenant, I'm Colonel Edmonds, the information officer. Between now and 1300, we have to get you into a Class A uniform and out to the Castillo Classroom Building on the post."

"Sir?"

"Where you will be photographed with the commanding general standing by the building named after your father," Edmonds explained.

"Sir, with respect, what's this all about?"

"I'm reasonably confident that the photograph will shortly appear in several hundred newspapers across the country."

"Colonel, I'm Special Forces," Castillo said. "We try to keep our pictures *out* of the newspapers."

Edmonds thought, *What does he mean, he's "Special Forces"?*

He's a pilot; he's Aviation.

He may be assigned to support Special Forces, but he's Aviation.

"Be that as it may, Lieutenant," Edmonds said, "you will be photographed with the commanding general at the Castillo Building at 1300."

"Yes, sir."

"Do you have a car here?"

"Yes, sir."

"Well, in that case, I will follow you to your BOQ. But in case we become separated, which BOQ is it?"

"Sir, I'm in the Daleville Inn."

The Daleville Inn was a motel in a village crammed with gasoline stations, fast-food emporiums, hock shops, trailer parks, and used-car lots. It lay between Cairns Army Airfield and Fort Rucker.

"You're not in a BOQ? Why not?"

"Sir, I thought I would have a quieter place to study if I were in the Daleville Inn than I would in a BOQ. When I went through chopper school here, the BOQs were a little noisy."

"But isn't that a little expensive?"

"Yes, sir, it is."

Edmonds shook his head in amazement, then said, "Well, let's get going."

"Mr. Kowalski, what do I do?" Lieutenant Castillo asked. "I'm between two masters."

"Lieutenant," CWO Kowalski said, smiling, "you being a West Pointer, I'm surprised nobody told you that you always obey the last order you got from a senior officer. You go get your picture taken with the general."

"Thank you," Castillo said.

"Call me when you've had your picture taken, and we'll go flying again," Kowalski said. "I'll take care of the paperwork here."

"And did I pass the check ride?"

"Well, I'm reasonably sure that after another couple of hours—if you don't do something really stupid—I will feel confident in certifying you as competent to fly the Mohawk on instruments."

Colonel Edmonds was a pilot. He knew what the translation of that was.

Castillo had passed—without question—his check ride. Otherwise Instructor Pilot Kowalski would not have said what he did. What the two of them were going to do later was take the Mohawk for a ride. Play with it. Maybe fly down to Panama City, Florida, and fly over the beach "practicing visual observation." Or maybe do some aerobatics.

"Would you like to come in, sir, while I shower and change?" Lieutenant Castillo asked when they had reached the Daleville Inn.

"Thank you," Edmonds said.

He's a West Pointer. He will have an immaculate Class A uniform hanging in his closet. And he will probably shave again when he showers. But there is no sense taking a chance.

Lieutenant Castillo did not have a motel room. He had a three-room suite: a living room with a bar, a bedroom, and a smaller second bedroom that had been turned into an office by shoving the bed in there against a wall and moving in a desk.

I don't know what this is costing him, but whatever it is, it's a hell of a lot more than his per diem allowance.

If he somehow managed to get permission to live off post and is getting per diem.

And why don't I believe him when he said he moved in here to have a quiet place to study? Probably because there are half a dozen assorted half-empty liquor bottles on the bar. And a beer case on the floor behind it.

He's spending all this money to have a place to entertain members of the opposite sex. They've been cracking down on that sort of thing in the BOQs.

Well, why not? He's young and the hormones are raging.

When Castillo went into the bedroom to shower and change, Colonel Edmonds looked around the living room. On a shelf under the coffee table he saw a newspaper and pulled it out.

It was a German newspaper.

What the hell is that doing here?

Maybe he's studying German. I read somewhere that Special Forces officers are supposed to have, or acquire, a second language.

That would explain the German newspaper, but it doesn't explain what he said about his branch being Special Forces, not Aviation. What in the hell was that all about?

When Lieutenant Castillo appeared ten minutes later, freshly shaven and in a Class A uniform, Colonel Edmonds was glad that he had accompanied him to his room.

While technically there was nothing wrong with the uniform—it was crisply pressed and well fitting—it left a good deal to be desired.

The only insignia on it were the lieutenant's silver bars on the epaulets, the U.S. and Aviation insignias on the lapels, and the aviator's wings on the breast. There were no ribbons indicating awards for valor or campaigns. And there was no unit insignia sewn to the shoulder.

"Two questions, Lieutenant," Colonel Edmonds said. "First, didn't you tell me you were Special Forces and not Aviation? I ask because you are wearing Aviation branch insignia."

"Yes, sir."

"Excuse me?"

"Yes, sir, I'm Special Forces."

"But wearing Aviation insignia?"

"Sir, with all respect, if I'm wearing Aviation insignia, no one will connect me with Special Forces."

Colonel Edmonds considered that, then said, "Question Two: Where is the rest of your insignia? I was informed you are assigned to the Special Warfare Center at Fort Bragg. Aren't you supposed to be wearing the Third Army shoulder insignia?"

"Sir, at Bragg I wear the Special Forces shoulder insignia, and the Special Warfare Center insignia on my blaze."

"On your what?"

"The embroidered patch worn on the green beret, sir. We're under DCSOPS, not Third Army, sir."

"Lieutenant, I don't know what you're up to here, but I don't have time to play games. Do you have a tunic to which is affixed all the insignia and decorations to which you are entitled?"

"Yes, sir."

"Then go put it on."

"Sir, permission to speak?"

"Granted," Colonel Edmonds snapped.

"Sir, as I tried to tell the colonel before, we're supposed to maintain a low profile. That is what I'm trying to do, sir."

"Go put on your tunic and every last item of uniform to which you are entitled, Lieutenant."

"Yes, sir."

In five minutes, Lieutenant Castillo returned.

He now was wearing both aviator's and parachutist's wings, and a Combat Infantryman's badge was pinned above both. He had three rows of ribbons on his breast, among which Colonel Edmonds recognized the Distinguished Flying Cross, the Bronze Star medal with V device, signifying it had been awarded for valor in combat, and the Purple Heart medal with one oak-leaf cluster. The silver aiguillette of an aide-de-camp hung from his epaulet, and on his lapels were the one-starred shields reflecting that he was an aide-de-camp to a brigadier general. He had a green beret on his head, and his trousers were bloused around highly polished parachutist's jump boots.

Colonel Edmonds had a sudden, unpleasant thought, which he quickly suppressed:

Jesus Christ, is he entitled to all that stuff?

Of course he is. He's a West Pointer. He wouldn't wear anything to which he was not entitled.

"Much better, Lieutenant," Colonel Edmonds said. "And now we'd better get going. We don't want to keep the general waiting, do we?"

The story appeared on the front page of *The Army Flier* two days later, which was a Friday. It included a photograph of Lieutenant Castillo and the Fort Rucker commander standing as if reading what was cast into a bronze plaque mounted on the wall beside the main door to the WOJG Jorge A. Castillo Classroom Building of the Army Aviation School.

LIVING TRADITION

By LTC F. Mason Edmonds
Information Officer
Fort Rucker, Al., and the Army Aviation Center

Major General Charles M. Augustus, Jr. (right), Commanding General of Fort Rucker and the Army Aviation Center and 1LT Carlos G. Castillo examine the dedication plaque of the WOJG Jorge A. Castillo Classroom Building at the Army Aviation School.

WOJG Castillo, 1LT Castillo's father, was posthumously awarded the Medal of Honor, the nation's highest award for gallantry, in the Vietnam War. He was killed when his HU-1D helicopter was struck by enemy fire and exploded on 5 April 1971 during Operation Lam Sol 719. He was on his fifty-second rescue mission of downed fellow Army Aviators in a thirty-six-hour period when he was killed, and was flying despite his having suffered both painful burns and shrapnel wounds. The HU-1D in which he died was the fourth helicopter he flew during this period, the others having been rendered un-airworthy by enemy fire.

His sadly prophetic last words were to his co-pilot, 2LT H. F. Wilson, as he ordered him out of the helicopter in which twenty minutes later he made the supreme sacrifice: "Get out, Lieutenant. There's no point in both of us getting killed."

Those heroic words are cast into the plaque MG Augustus, Jr., and 1LT Castillo are examining.

Following in his father's footsteps, 1LT Castillo became an Army Aviator after his graduation from the United States Military Academy at West Point.

The opening hours of the Desert War saw him flying deep inside enemy lines as co-pilot of an AH-64B Apache attack helicopter charged with destroying Iraqi anti-aircraft radar facilities.

The Apache was struck by enemy fire, seriously wounding the pilot and destroying the helicopter's windshield and navigation equipment.

Despite his own wounds, 1LT Castillo took command of the badly damaged helicopter and flew it more than 100 miles to safety. He was awarded the Distinguished Flying Cross for this action.

Now a flying aide-de-camp to a general officer, 1LT Castillo returned to the Aviation School for transition training to qualify him as a pilot of the C-12 Huron.

LT Castillo is the grandson of Mr. and Mrs. J. F. Castillo of San Antonio, Texas.

(U.S. Army Photograph by CPL Roger Marshutz)

[·II·]
Room 202
The Daleville Inn
Daleville, Alabama
1625 5 February 1992

The door to Room 202 was opened by a six-foot-two, two-hundred-twenty-pound, very black young man in a gray tattered West Point sweatshirt. He was holding a bottle of Coors beer and looking visibly surprised to see two crisply uniformed officers—one of them a brigadier general—standing outside the door.

"May I help the general, sir?" he asked after a moment's hesitation.

"Dick, we're looking for Lieutenant Castillo," the other officer, a captain wearing aide-de-camp's insignia, said.

He could have been the general's son. Both were tall, slim, and erect. The general's hair was starting to gray, but that was really the only significant physical difference between them.

"He's in the shower," the huge young black man said.

"You know each other?" the general asked.

"Yes, sir. We were at the Point together," the captain said.

"I'd really like to see Lieutenant Castillo," the general said to the huge young black man.

"Yes, sir," he replied, and opening the door all the way, added, "Would the general like to come in, sir? I'm sure he won't be long."

"Thank you," the general said, and entered the motel suite.

"General Wilson," the captain said, "this is Lieutenant H. Richard Miller, Jr."

"How do you do, Lieutenant?" General Wilson said. "You're Dick Miller's son?"

"Yes, sir."

"Tom, General Miller and I toured scenic Panama together a couple of years ago," Wilson said, then asked Miller, "How is your dad?"

"Happy, sir. He just got his second star."

"I saw that. Please pass on my regards."

"Yes, sir. I'll do that."

"You're assigned here, are you?"

"Yes, sir. I just started Apache school."

"Meaning you were one of the top three in your basic flight course. Congratulations. Your father must be proud of you."

"Actually, sir, as the general probably already knows, my father is not at all sure Army Aviation is here to stay."

"Yes, I know," Wilson said, smiling. "He's mentioned that once or twice."

Miller held up his bottle of beer. "Sir, would it be appropriate for me to offer the general a beer? Or something stronger?"

He immediately saw on the captain's face that it was not appropriate.

After a moment's hesitation, however, the general said, "I would really like a drink, if that's possible."

Miller then saw genuine surprise on the captain's face.

"Very possible, sir," Miller said. He gestured at a wet bar. "Would the general prefer bourbon or scotch or gin . . ."

"Scotch would do nicely," Wilson said. "Neat."

"Yes, sir."

"You can have one, too, Tom," Wilson added. "And I would feel better if you did."

"Yes, sir. Thank you, sir. The same, Dick, please."

Lieutenant C. G. Castillo, wearing only a towel, came into the living room as General Wilson was about to take a sip of his scotch. Wilson looked at him for a long moment, then took a healthy swallow.

"Sir," Miller said, "this is Lieutenant C. G. Castillo."

"I'm Harry Wilson," the general said.

"Yes, sir," Castillo said. It was obvious the name meant nothing to him. "Is there something I can do for the general, sir?"

"I'm here to straighten something out, Lieutenant," General Wilson said.

"Sir?"

"I was your father's copilot," General Wilson said.

"Jesus Christ!" Castillo blurted.

"Until I saw the story in *The Army Flier* right after lunch," General Wilson said, "I didn't even know you existed. It took us this long to find you. The housing office had never heard of you, and Blue Flight had shut down for the weekend."

Castillo looked at him but didn't speak.

"What your father said," General Wilson said, "just before he took off . . . that day . . . was, 'Get the fuck out, Harry. The way you're shaking, you're going to get both of us killed.' "

Castillo still didn't reply.

"Not what it says on that plaque," General Wilson added softly. "So I got out, and he lifted off."

He paused, then went on: "I've been waiting—what is it, twenty-two years, twenty-three?—to tell somebody besides my wife what Jorge . . . your father . . . really said that day."

"Sonofabitch!" Miller said softly.

"I think, under the circumstances," Castillo finally said, obviously making an effort to control his voice, "that a small libation *is* in order."

He walked to the bar, splashed scotch into a glass, and took a healthy swallow.

"Sir," Castillo then said, "I presume Lieutenant Miller has introduced himself?"

General Wilson nodded.

"And you remember Captain Prentiss, don't you, Charley?" Miller asked.

"Yeah, sure. Nice to see you again, sir."

"With the general's permission, I will withdraw," Miller said.

"No, you won't," Castillo said sharply.

"You sure, Charley?" Miller asked.

"Goddamn sure," Castillo said.

" 'Charley'?" General Wilson said. "I thought I read your name was Carlos."

"Yes, sir, it is. But people call me Charley."

"Your . . . dad . . . made me call him *Hor-hay*," Wilson said. "Not George. He said he was a wetback and proud of it, and wanted to be called Hor-hay."

"Sir, I think he was pulling your chain," Castillo said. "From what I've learned of my father, he was proud of being a Texican. Not a wetback."

"A Texican?"

Castillo nodded. "Yes, sir. A Texan with long-ago Mexican roots. A wetback is somebody who came across the border yesterday."

"No offense intended, Lieutenant."

"None taken, sir," Castillo said. "Sir, how long did you fly with my father?"

Wilson looked around the room, then took a seat on the couch and sipped at his drink.

"About three months," Wilson said. "We arrived in-country the same day. I was fresh out of West Point, and here he was an old-timer; he'd done a six-months tour in Germany before they shipped him to Vietnam. They put us together, with him in the right seat because he had more time. He took me under his wing—he was a really good pilot—and taught me the things the Aviation School didn't teach. We shared a hootch." He paused a moment in thought, then finished, "Became close friends, although he warned me that that wasn't smart."

"An old-timer?" Castillo said. "He was nineteen when he was killed. Christ, I'm twenty-two."

"I was twenty-two, too," Wilson said softly.

"A friend of mine told me there were a lot of teenaged Huey pilots in Vietnam," Castillo said.

"There were," Wilson said, then added, "I can't understand why he never mentioned you. As I said, I had no idea you existed. Until today."

"He didn't know about me," Castillo said. "He was killed before I was born. I don't think he even knew my mother was pregnant."

"I realize this may sound selfish, Lieutenant—I realize doing so would probably open old wounds—but I'd like to go see your mother."

"May I ask why you would want to do that, sir?" Castillo asked.

"Well, first I'd like to apologize for not looking her up when I came home. And I'd like her to know that I know I'm alive because of your father. If he hadn't told me to . . . 'get the fuck out, Harry' . . . both of us would have died when that chopper blew up."

"My mother died ten years ago, sir," Castillo said.

"I'm sorry," Wilson said. "I should have picked that up from the story in *The Army Flier*. It mentioned only your grandparents."

"Yes, sir. They raised me. I know they'd like to talk to you, sir. Would you be willing to do that?"

"Of course I would. I'd be honored."

"Well, let me set that up," Castillo said. "Then I'll put my pants on."

He walked to the telephone on the wet bar and punched in a number from memory.

There followed a brief exchange in Spanish, then Castillo held out the telephone to General Wilson.

"Sir, my grandfather—Juan Fernando Castillo, generally referred to as Don Fernando—would like to speak with you."

Wilson got quickly off the couch and walked to the wet bar.

"He speaks English, right?" he asked softly.

"It might be better if you spoke slowly, sir," Castillo said, and handed him the phone.

"Oh, Jesus, Charley," Miller said. "You have a dangerous sense of humor."

"I remember," Captain Prentiss said.

"Good afternoon, Mr. Castillo," General Wilson said, carefully pronouncing each syllable. "My name is Harold Wilson, and I had the privilege of serving with your son Hor-hay."

There was a reply, which caused General Wilson to shake his head and flash Lieutenant Castillo a dirty look.

Castillo smiled and poured more scotch into his glass.

After a minute or so, Wilson handed Castillo the telephone and there followed another conversation in Spanish. Finally, Castillo put the handset back in the base.

"Like father, like son, right, Castillo?" General Wilson said, smiling. "You like pulling people's chains? Your grandfather speaks English like a Harvard lawyer."

"I guess I shouldn't have done that, sir," Castillo said. "I have an awful problem resisting temptation."

"That, sir," Miller said, "is what is known as a monumental understatement."

"Your grandfather and grandmother are coming here tomorrow, I guess he told you," Wilson said. "I'm presuming he'll call you back with the details when he's made his reservations."

"He has a plane, sir. He said they'll leave right after breakfast. That should put them in here about noon. What I've got to do now is arrange permission for them to land at Cairns and get them some place to stay. I think I can probably get them in here."

"They will stay in the VIP quarters," General Wilson said. "And I'll arrange for permission for his plane to land at Cairns. Or Tom will. Right, Tom?"

"Yes, sir," Prentiss said, then looked at Castillo as he took a notebook from his shirt pocket. "What kind of a plane is it?"

"A Learjet."

"Got the tail number?" Prentiss asked.

Castillo gave it to him.

"Your grandfather has a Learjet?" General Wilson asked.

"Yes, sir. And until a year ago, when my grandmother made him stop, he used to fly it himself. My cousin Fernando will be flying it tomorrow."

"Your father painted a very colorful picture of his life as a wetback," Wilson said. "The benefits of a serape and sandals; how to make tortillas and refry beans. He said he played the trumpet in a mariachi band. And until just now I believed every word."

"Sir, according to my grandfather, what my father did before he joined the Army—he was booted out of Texas A&M and was one step ahead of his draft board—was fly Sikorskys, the civilian version of the H-19, ferrying people and supplies to oil rigs in the Gulf of Mexico."

"Can I get you another one of those, sir?" Miller asked, nodding at the general's empty glass.

"Yes, please," General Wilson said. "This time, put a little water and some ice in it, please."

"Yes, sir," Miller said.

"General, may I ask a favor?" Castillo asked.

"Absolutely."

"Sir, I stood still for that picture because I was ordered to. My general is not a great believer in publicity. I don't know how he'll react when he sees that story—but I do know that he will. My grandfather is much the same way, sir; he doesn't like his name in the newspapers. Is there some way you can turn the IO off?"

Wilson nodded. "Okay, he's off. I understand how you feel." He paused and then smiled. "I guess you really can't cast in bronze 'Get the fuck out, Harry,' can you?"

"That might raise some eyebrows, sir," Castillo said.

"Anything else I can do for you?"

"No, sir. That's about it. Thank you."

"Who is your general, Charley? You don't mind if I call you Charley, do you?"

"Not at all, sir. General McNab, sir. He's deputy commander of the Special Warfare Center at Bragg."

"He was three years ahead of me at the Point," Wilson said. "Interesting man."

"Yes, sir, he is that."

"May I use your telephone?"

"Yes, sir, of course," Castillo said.

As he walked to the wet bar, General Wilson said, "When there is more than one call to make, you should make the one to the most important person first. You may wish to write that down."

General Wilson appeared clearly pleased with his humor, causing Castillo to wonder, *Is he a little plastered? On two drinks?*

"Yes, sir," Castillo and Miller, both sounding confused, said almost in unison.

The explanation came almost immediately.

"Sweetheart," General Wilson said into the phone, "Tom found him. We're with him right now in the Daleville Inn.

"He doesn't look like his father, darling, but he has Hor-hay's sense of humor."

"So that means two things, baby. First, there will be two more for supper tonight. And Hor-hay's parents are coming in tomorrow.

"Yes, really. Young Castillo called them just now. Can you do a really nice lunch for them? And dinner, too?

"No, I thought they'd be more comfortable in the VIP house.

"We'll be there shortly.

"Is Randy there?"

General Wilson looked at Miller and asked, "What's your class?"

"Ninety, sir," Miller said.

General Wilson said into the receiver, "Tell Randy he'll have another class-mate there tonight. Lieutenant H. Richard Miller, Jr.

"Yeah. His son.

"That's about it, sweetheart. We'll be over there shortly."

He put the receiver in its base and pointed to the telephone.

"Your turn, Tom," he ordered. "First, call protocol and reserve one of the VIP houses for a Mr. and Mrs. Castillo for tomorrow night and the next night. If there's someone already in there, have them moved, and then call Cairns and clear Mr. Castillo's airplane to land there tomorrow."

"Yes, sir," Captain Prentiss said.

"While he's doing that," General Wilson said, "may I help myself to another little taste?"

"Yes, sir, of course," Miller said.

Castillo thought: *He's getting plastered. Does he have a problem with the sauce?*

"Tonight," General Wilson said, "my daughter's broiling steaks for her fiancé, Randy—Randolph—Richardson, and some other of his—your—classmates. I presume you know him?"

"Yes, sir, I know Lieutenant Richardson," Miller said.

"Righteous Randolph," Castillo said, and shook his head.

"I somehow suspect that my announcement that you're about to get together with some of your classmates is not being met with the smiles of pleasure I anticipated."

"Sir, with all respect," Castillo said carefully, "I don't think our having supper with Lieutenant Richardson is a very good idea. Could we pass, with thanks, sir?"

"I've already told my wife you're coming."

"Yes, sir, I understand," Castillo said. "Nevertheless, sir, I think it would be best if we did that some other time."

General Wilson stared at Castillo for a long moment. There was no longer a question in Castillo's mind that the general was feeling the drinks.

"Okay," Wilson said, "what happened between you?"

Neither Castillo nor Miller replied.

"That question is in the nature of an order, gentlemen," General Wilson said, and now there was a cold tone in his voice.

"A book fell off a shelf, sir," Miller said. "Striking Cadet First Sergeant Richardson on the face. He alleged that his broken nose had actually been caused by Cadet Private Castillo having punched him. An inquiry was held. I was called as a witness and confirmed Cadet Private Castillo's version. Richardson then brought us before a Court of Honor."

"For violating the honor code? 'A cadet will not lie, cheat, or steal, nor tolerate those who do'?"

"Yes, sir."

"And?"

"We were acquitted, sir."

"As a purely hypothetical question," Wilson said, "why would a cadet private take a punch at a cadet first sergeant?"

Neither replied.

"Your turn, Castillo," General Wilson said.

"Sir, in the hypothetical situation the general describes, I could imagine that a cadet private might lose his temper upon learning that a cadet first sergeant had gone to his tactical officer and reported his suspicions that a cadet lieutenant had arranged for a car to pick him up at the Hotel Thayer with the intention of going to New York for the weekend."

"Had the cadet lieutenant done so?"

"Yes, sir."

"Who was he? A friend?"

"Me, sir. When my tac officer called me on it, I admitted it, and he had no choice but to bust me, sir."

"For just sneaking into the city on a weekend? I did that routinely."

"I was on academic restriction at the time, sir," Castillo said.

"Oh, God, you are your father's son," General Wilson said.

"Sir?"

"We had a captain who had the unpleasant habit of grabbing the nearest soldier and having him clean his bird. I'm not talking about shining it up for an IG inspection. I'm talking about getting rid of the vomit and blood and excreta with which they were too often fouled. Your father told the captain that the next time he grabbed our crew chief to do his dirty work, he was going to shove him headfirst into a honey bucket. You know what a honey bucket is, presumably?"

"Yes, sir."

"The captain did, and your father did, and the captain had him brought up on charges of assault upon a senior officer. The company commander—a wise, senior major—just about told your father that if he would take an Article 15, he could expect no worse punishment than being restricted to the company area for two weeks. That was meaningless, actually, as we were in the boonies, and there was nowhere to go.

"Your father demanded trial by court-martial. And he exercised his right to defense counsel of his choice. Me. He could not be dissuaded from that, either. He told me when they put his accuser on the stand, I was to get into great detail about his shoving the captain's head in the honey bucket.

"I was convinced your father was going to go to the Long Bihn stockade. But—your dad was one of those natural leaders who are able to get people to do whatever they are asked to do, even if it sounds insane—I did what he asked."

He stopped when Miller handed him his fresh drink.

"I'm not at all sure I need this," General Wilson said. "But thank you."

And then he laughed.

"Well, as I said," he went on, smiling, "I did my best to carry out my client's instructions. I asked the captain over and over about the details of the assault upon him. Finally, the president of the court had enough. 'Wind it up, Lieutenant, you've been over and over this. One more question.' So I said, 'Yes, sir.' And I tried to think of a good final question. I came up with a doozy. Not on purpose. It just came out of my mouth. 'Captain,' I said, 'please tell the court what you found in the honey bucket when you allege Mr. Castillo shoved your head in it.' "

"Jesus Christ!" Miller said, and laughed delightedly.

"That caused some coughing on the part of the members of the court," General Wilson went on. "Then the captain replied, very angrily, 'Shit is what I found in the honey bucket. I damned near drowned in it.'

"Well, the court broke up, literally became hysterical. The president banged his gavel and fled the room. The other members followed him. The trial was held in a Quonset hut, and we could hear them laughing in the other end of the building for a long time.

"Finally, they came back in. I announced that the defense rested. The lieutenant prosecuting gave his closing argument, which was of course devastating, and I gave mine, which was ludicrous. Then the court retired. They were out thirty minutes, and then they came back and found your father not guilty of all charges and specifications."

"That's a great story," Castillo said, smiling.

"Unfortunately, he didn't have much time to savor his victory. Two weeks later, he was dead."

General Wilson took a sip of his scotch, then went on: "I had a purpose in telling that story. For one thing, it has been my experience that there is more justice in the Army than people are usually willing to recognize. We are supposed to be judged by our peers. In the Army, we really are. Soldiers who understand soldiering judge their fellow soldiers. They almost always return verdicts that are just, even if they sort of stray from legal niceties. I would suggest that court of honor which found you two not guilty and the court which found Charley's father not guilty based their decision on the circumstances rather than on the cold facts.

"I suspect your fellow cadets liked Cadet Lieutenant Castillo and thought Randy had gotten what he deserved from him. And I suspect that the officers on the court liked your father, admired his sticking up for our crew chief, and that the captain got what he deserved, too, and that it would serve neither justice nor good order and discipline to make things any worse than they were.

"Furthermore, that's all water long under the dam. Vietnam and West Point are both long ago. Tonight, when you see Randy, I'm sure that what passed between you will seem—as indeed it is—no longer important. You might even be glad you had a chance to get together with him. He really can't be all bad. Beth is absolutely crazy about him."

Castillo and Miller did not respond.

"Beth is of course off-limits. But there will be other young women there tonight and—presuming they are neither engaged nor married—the hunting may interest you. And I promised my wife you would be there. My quarters—Number Two—are on Red Cloud Road. Can you find that?"

"Yes, sir," Miller said. "I know where it is."

"Well, having talked too much, drunk too much, and pontificated too much, Tom and I will now leave. We will see you in about thirty minutes, right?"

"Yes, sir," Miller and Castillo said in chorus.

"Thank you for your hospitality, gentlemen," General Wilson said.

"Our pleasure, sir," Miller and Castillo said, almost in chorus.

General Wilson was almost at the door when he stopped and turned.

"Two things," he said.

"Yes, sir?" they said.

"One, the dress is informal"—he pointed at Miller's sweatshirt—"but, two, not that informal."

"Yes, sir," Miller said.

Wilson looked at Castillo.

"Did I pick up that you're Class of '90 too, Charley? You and Miller and your good friend Randy are all classmates?"

"Yes, sir," Castillo said.

"Then how in *hell* did you manage to get to the Desert War flying an Apache?"

"That's a long story, sir."

"It can't be that long."

"Sir, I had just reported to Fort Knox to begin the basic officer course when I was told I had been selected to fill an 'unexpected' slot in Rotary Wing Primary Class 90-7. I suspect it was because of my father. When I got here, they found out I had two-hundred-odd hours of Huey time, so they gave me my wings, transferred me to RW Advanced Class 90-8, and the next thing I knew, there I was flying over the Iraqi desert with Mr. Kowalski at oh dark hundred in an Apache with people shooting at us. The distinction I really have, sir, was in having been the least qualified Apache pilot in the Army."

"Warrant Officer Kowalski? The Blue Flight Instructor Pilot?"

"Yes, sir. There we were, probably the best Apache pilot in the Army and the worst one."

"I will want to hear that story more in detail, Charley. But you're wrong. The distinction you have is the Distinguished Flying Cross you earned flying a shot-up Apache a hundred miles or so across the Iraqi sand at oh dark hundred." He paused. "Thirty minutes, gentlemen. Thank you again for your hospitality."

Captain Prentiss opened the door for General Wilson, they went through it, and Prentiss pulled it shut behind him.

After a moment, Miller moved aside the venetian blind of the front window to make sure General Wilson was really gone. He turned to Castillo and said, "I think that's what they call a memorable experience."

"Yeah. I suspect the general had more to drink than he usually does."

"I got the feeling from Prentiss that he doesn't drink at all. This upset him. And why not? 'Get the fuck out, Harry. You're shaking so much you'll get us both killed.' As opposed to the heroic bullshit on the whatever you call it on that building."

Castillo nodded. "When I got that Apache back across the berm, and they started pulling Kowalski out of the Apache—he wasn't hurt as bad as it looked, but all I could see was blood where his face was supposed to be, and there was blood all over the cockpit—I started to shake so bad they had to hold me up. Then I started throwing up stuff I had eaten two years before." Castillo paused, then went on, "I understand that. I think he thinks he did the wrong thing by getting out. He didn't."

"You never told me about that before," Miller said softly.

"You don't want to think about it; you put it out of your mind. Jesus, Dick, think about what they went through. They'd been picking up bloody bodies for hours. What's amazing is they were still doing it. Better men than thee and me, Richard. All it took was one shot-up helicopter and Kowalski and I were out of it."

Miller looked at him for a long moment without responding. Then he forced a laugh to change the subject and said, "And your father shoved some chickenshit captain down a honey bucket. He must have been quite a guy."

"And got away with it," Castillo added, grinning.

"You're not going to tell your folks about that?"

"Not Abuela. Grandpa, sure. If I don't, Fernando will, and I definitely have to share that story with Fernando."

Miller nodded, then said, "We are to be reunited with Righteous Randolph. I've bumped into him a half dozen times here. I'm invisible to him. As far as he's concerned, I am a disgrace to the Long Gray Line."

"Just you? I'd hoped never to see the miserable sonofabitch again. I think he was born a prick."

"I just had a very unpleasant thought," Miller said.

"I didn't know you had any other kind."

"Charley, you're not thinking of nailing Wilson's daughter, are you?"

"Where did that come from?"

"Answer the question."

"For one thing, she's a general's daughter. I learned, painfully, the dangers of nailing a general's daughter with Jennifer."

"That didn't slow you down with the next one, Casanova. What was her name? Delores?"

"Daphne," Castillo furnished. "Hey, General Wilson is not only a nice guy, but he was my father's buddy. I'm not going to try to nail his daughter. What kind of a prick do you think I am?"

"I know damned well what kind: The kind who will forget all those noble sentiments the instant you start thinking with your dick. And/or that it might be fun to nail Righteous Randolph's girlfriend, just for old times' sake. Don't do it, Charley."

"Put your evil imagination at rest."

"In case I didn't say this before: Don't do it, Charley. I'm serious."

[-III-]
2002 Red Cloud Road
Fort Rucker, Alabama
1735 5 February 1992

The quarters assigned to the deputy commanding general of the Army Aviation Center and Fort Rucker, Alabama, were larger, but not by much, than the quarters assigned to officers of lesser rank.

Castillo thought the dependent housing area of Fort Rucker—more than a thousand one-story frame buildings, ninety percent of them duplexes, spread over several hundred acres of pine-covered, gently rolling land—looked like an *Absolutely no money down! Move right in!* housing development outside, say, Houston or Philadelphia.

His boss, Brigadier General Bruce J. McNab, lived in a spacious, two-story brick colonial house on an elm-shaded street at Fort Bragg. The reason for the difference was that the senior officer housing at Bragg had been built before World War II, while all the housing at Rucker had gone up immediately before and during the Vietnam War.

The driveway to General Wilson's quarters was lined with automobiles, half of them ordinary Fords and Chevrolets, the other half sports cars. Miller said that was how you told which lieutenants were married and which were not. It was impossible to support both a wife and a Porsche on a lieutenant's pay, even a lieutenant on flight pay. Miller himself drove a Ford; Castillo, a Chevrolet coupe.

There was a handmade sign on the front door of Quarters Two. It had an arrow and the words "Around in Back" in bold type.

Around in back of the house was the patio. This consisted of a concrete pad enclosed by an eight-foot slat fence painted an odd shade of blue. On the patio were two gas-fired barbecue stoves, two picnic tables, two round tables with folded umbrellas, four large ice-filled containers, and about twenty young men and women.

All the young men—including Miller and Castillo—were dressed very much alike: sports jackets, slacks, open-collared shirts, and well-shined shoes. It was not hard to imagine them in uniform.

The young women were similarly dressed in their own same style: skirts and either sweaters or blouses.

Castillo's eye fell on one of the latter, a blonde standing by one of the smoking stoves. Even across the patio, Castillo could see her brassiere through the sheer blouse. He had always found this fascinating, and was so taken with this one that he didn't notice a couple walking across the patio until Miller whispered, "Heads-up, here comes Righteous Randolph."

The female with Righteous Randolph, also a blonde, was every bit as good-looking as the one cooking steaks. She wore a skirt topped with a tight sweater.

"And good evening to you, Righteous," Miller said.

"You're Miller and Castillo, right?" the blonde asked.

"Guilty," Miller said.

"I couldn't believe Randy when he said you would have the gall to show up here," the blonde said.

"Charles, my boy," Miller said. "I suspect that our invitation to mingle with these charming people has been withdrawn."

"Odd, I'm getting the same feeling," Castillo said. "I suspect we withdraw. With Righteous's permission, of course."

"You're right, sweetheart," the blonde said. "They think it's funny, and they're oh, so clever."

"And hers, too, of course," Castillo said.

"You two are really disgusting," Lieutenant Randolph Richardson said.

Castillo was already behind the wheel of his Chevrolet and Miller was having his usual trouble fastening the seat belt around his bulk when Captain Prentiss came running down the drive.

"Where the hell are you going?" Prentiss demanded.

"We tried to tell the general—you were there—that our coming here was probably going to be a mistake," Castillo said. "A stunning blonde, who I strongly suspect is the general's daughter, just confirmed that prognosis."

"My feelings are crushed beyond measure," Miller said. "Righteous Randolph just told us we are really disgusting. I'm about to break into tears, and I didn't want to do that for fear of bringing discredit upon the Long Gray Line."

"Gentlemen," Prentiss said. "General Wilson's compliments. The general requests that you attend him at your earliest convenience."

"What the blonde said was she couldn't believe we'd have the gall to show up here," Castillo said.

"Gentlemen," Prentiss repeated. "General Wilson's compliments. The general requests that you attend him at your earliest convenience."

"That sounds pretty goddamn official, Tom," Miller said.

"As goddamn official as I know how to make it, Lieutenant," Prentiss said. He pulled open the passenger-side door.

A trim blonde who was visibly the mother of the one on the patio was waiting at the open door of Quarters Two.

"You're Miller and Castillo, right? Dick and Charley?"

"Yes, ma'am," they said.

"I'm Bethany Wilson," she said with a smile. "Where were you going?" Prentiss answered for them.

"Beth apparently believes they are responsible for the general's condition," he said. "And greeted them with something less than enthusiasm."

"If anyone is responsible for the general's condition, you are, Tom," Mrs. Wilson said. "What did Beth say?"

"The one responsible for the general's condition is the general," General Wilson said, coming to the door from inside the house.

"Good evening, sir," Miller and Castillo said.

"The general's condition, in case you're wondering," he said, "is that he cannot—never has been able to—handle any more than one drink in a ninety-minute period. As you may have noticed, I had four drinks in about forty-five minutes at your apartment. And then I came home. And fell out of the car, before at least a dozen of my daughter's guests. Then, to prove to the world that all I had done was stumble a little, I got onto my wife's bicycle and went merrily down the drive—until I collided with the car of another arriving guest. At that point, Tom finally caught up with me and got me into the house."

He looked between Miller and Castillo and said, "You may smile. It certainly wasn't your fault, but I would consider it a personal favor, Lieutenant Miller, if you did not tell your father about this amusing little episode."

"I beg the general's pardon, but I didn't hear a thing that was said," Miller said.

"Quickly changing the subject," Mrs. Wilson said, "what can I get you to drink? Or would you rather just go out to the patio and join the other young people?"

"There's one more thing, dear," General Wilson said. "Dick and Charley don't get along well with Randy."

"Oh, I'm sorry to hear that," she said. "Do I get to hear why?"

"No," General Wilson said. "You were saying something about offering them drinks? Then I suggest we show them the scrapbook—there's a number of pictures of your dad, Charley, and yours too, Dick—and then, throwing poor Tom yet again into the breach, Tom can cook us some steaks to eat in here."

"Sir," Prentiss said, "I'm sorry that I didn't—"

"Didn't what?" Wilson interrupted, and looked at Castillo. "Charley, you're an aide. Would you dare to tell your general to go easy on the sauce?"

"No, sir, I would not," Castillo replied.

"There you go, Tom. Nobody's fault but mine. Subject closed."

[·IV·]
2002 Red Cloud Road
Fort Rucker, Alabama
0755 6 February 1992

Captain Tom Prentiss walked to the kitchen door of Quarters Two and lightly tapped one of the panes with his ring. Brigadier General Harry Wilson, who was sitting at the kitchen table in his bathrobe, gestured for him to come in. He entered.

"Did you have to knock so loudly?" General Wilson inquired.

Prentiss exchanged smiles with Mrs. Bethany Wilson, who stood at the stove.

"Good morning, ma'am."

"*Good morning*, Tom," she replied, her tone teeming with an exaggerated cheeriness.

General Wilson glared at her over his coffee mug. Miss Beth Wilson, who was sitting across the table from her father, rolled her eyes.

"The general is not his chipper self this morning?" Prentiss said to him. "We are not going to have our morning trot up and down Red Cloud?"

"For one thing, it's Saturday. For another, in my condition, I could not trot down the drive to Red Cloud, much less up and down Red Cloud itself."

"Well, Harry," Mrs. Wilson said, turning from the stove, "you know what they say about the wages of sin." She looked at Prentiss. "Your timing is perfect. You want fried or scrambled?"

"I was hoping you'd make the offer," Prentiss said. "Scrambled, please."

"You know where the coffee is," she said.

"Bring the pot, please, Tom," General Wilson said. "Unless you have an oxygen flask in your pocket."

"I can have one here in five minutes, sir," Prentiss said.

He took the decanter from the coffee machine and carried it to the table.

"And how are you this morning, Miss Beth?" Prentiss said.

Beth Wilson flashed him an icy look, but didn't reply.

"Does oxygen really work, Tom?" Mrs. Wilson asked.

"Yes, ma'am, it does."

"You heard that? Or you know from personal experience?"

"I respectfully claim my privilege against self-incrimination under the fifth amendment to the constitution," Prentiss said.

"Seriously, Tom," General Wilson said, "how much trouble would it be to get your hands on an oxygen flask before we go to meet the Castillos?"

"You want it right now, sir?"

"You heard what she said about the wages of sin," General Wilson said. "I'm about to die."

"Let me make a call," Prentiss said, and started to get up.

"Eat your breakfast first," Mrs. Wilson said. "Let him suffer a little."

"Oh, God!" General Wilson said. "Is there no pity in the world for a suffering man?"

His wife and his aide-de-camp chuckled.

His daughter said, "You all make me sick!"

"I beg your pardon?" General Wilson said.

"You're all acting as if it's all very funny."

"There are elements of humor mingled with the gloom," General Wilson said.

"Randy said he did it on purpose," Beth said.

"Randy did what on purpose?" her mother asked.

"*Castillo* did it on purpose. *Castillo* got Daddy drunk on purpose, hoping he would make an ass of himself."

General Wilson said, "Well, Daddy did in fact make sort of an ass of himself, but Charley Castillo wasn't responsible. Daddy was."

"Actually, I thought you careening down the drive on my bike was hilarious," his wife said.

General Wilson raised his eyebrows at that, then said, "It's not the sort of behavior general officers should display before a group of young officers, and I'm well aware of that. But the sky is not falling, and I am being punished, as your mother points out, for my sins."

"Randy says he was always doing that, trying to humiliate his betters," Beth said.

"You knew him at the Point, Tom," General Wilson said. "Was he?"

"Well, he was one of the prime suspects, the other being Dick Miller, in 'The Case of Who Put Miracle Glue on the Regimental Commander's Saber.' "

"Really?" Mrs. Wilson asked, as she laid a plate of scrambled eggs before him.

Prentiss nodded. "He couldn't get it out of the scabbard on the Friday retreat parade. Talk about humiliation!"

"And then he lied about it!" Beth said. "Randy told me all about that."

"What they did was claim their right against self-incrimination, Beth," Prentiss said. "That's not the same thing as lying."

"Randy said he lied," she insisted.

"I was there. Randy wasn't," Prentiss said. "I was the tactical officer supervising the Court of Honor. The court knew they did it, but they couldn't prove it. Nobody actually saw them."

"So they let him—them—go?" Beth said.

"They had no choice. Nobody saw them do it."

"Was that the real reason?" she challenged. "It wasn't because his father won that medal?"

"You get that from Randy, too?" General Wilson asked softly.

"Randy said that the only reason they weren't thrown out of West Point was because Castillo's father had that medal . . . that the only reason he was in West Point to begin with was because his father had that medal."

"Sons of Medal of Honor recipients are granted *entrance* to West Point," General Wilson said. "*Staying* in the Corps of Cadets is not covered."

"And he said that no one had the courage to expel the son of a black general," Beth went on, "no matter what he'd done."

"And what does Randy have to say about Lieutenant Castillo's Distinguished Flying Cross?" General Wilson asked, softly.

"He said it's impossible to believe that someone could graduate in ninety and be through flight school and flying an Apache in the Desert War when Castillo says he was unless a lot of strings were pulled."

"I am in no condition to debate this with you now, Beth," General Wilson said. "But just as soon as the Castillos leave, you, Randy, and I are going to have to talk. While the Castillos are here, I don't think it would be a good idea if you were around them."

"You're throwing me out?" Beth said somewhat indignantly.

"I'm suggesting that you spend the day, and tonight, with a friend. Patricia, maybe?"

"I've got a date with Randy tonight. Where am I supposed to get dressed?"

"Doesn't Patricia have a bedroom? Take what clothing you need with you. I don't want you around here when the Castillos are here."

"Yes, *sir*," she snapped, and jumped up from the table.

"Tom, would you take her to the Gremmiers'?"

"Yes, sir," Prentiss said, then added a little hesitantly, "General, I was sort of hoping I could get Beth to help me at the VIP house; make sure everything's right. And I know Mrs. Wilson is . . ."

"Get her to help you at the VIP house, then take her to the Gremmiers'," Mrs. Wilson ordered.

"I'm perfectly capable of driving myself," Beth said.

"We're probably going to need both cars," General Wilson said. "End of discussion."

[·V·]
Magnolia Cottage
Fort Rucker, Alabama
0845 6 February 1992

Camp Rucker had been built on a vast area of sandy, worn-out-from-cotton-farming land in southern Alabama in the opening months of World War II. It was intended for use first as a division training area, and then for the confinement of prisoners of war. An army of workmen had erected thousands of two-story frame barracks, concrete-block mess halls, theaters, chapels, headquarters, warehouses, officers' clubs, and all the other facilities needed to accomplish this purpose, including a half-dozen small frame buildings intended to house general officers and colonels.

After the war and the repatriation of the POWs, the camp was closed, only to be reopened briefly for the Korean War, where it again served as a division training base. Then it was closed for good.

Several years after the Korean War, with Camp Rucker placed on the list of bases to be wiped from the books, the decision was made to greatly expand Army Aviation. United States Senator John Sparkman (Democrat, Alabama)—to whom a large number of fellow senators owed many favors—suggested that Camp Rucker would be a fine place to have an Army Aviation Center. His fellow senators voted in agreement with their esteemed colleague.

Thus, the facility was then reopened and declared a fort, a permanent base. Another army of workmen swarmed over it, building airfields and classrooms and whatever else was needed for a flying army. They also tore down most of the old frame buildings—most, not all.

Chapels and theaters remained, and the warehouses, and the officer's clubs, and the post headquarters building, and four of the cottages originally built in the early 1940s to last only five to ten years for the housing of general officers and senior colonels. Two of these four—including Building T-1104, which had been renamed "Magnolia Cottage"—were near the main gate, outside of which was Daleville.

They were fixed up as nicely as possible, air-conditioned, furnished with the most elegant furniture to be found in Army warehouses, provided with a kitchen, and became VIP quarters in which distinguished visitors to the post were housed.

When Captain Tom Prentiss pushed open the door of Magnolia House and waved Beth Wilson into the living room, they found the place was immaculate. There were even fresh flowers in a vase in the center of the dining table.

"Looks fine to me," Beth Wilson said.

Prentiss didn't reply directly. Instead, he said, "I've got to make a telephone call. Have a seat."

"That sounds like an order," she snapped.

"Not at all. If you'd rather, stand."

He used the telephone in the small kitchen and, not really curious, she nevertheless managed to hear Prentiss's side of the conversation:

"Tom Prentiss. I'm glad I caught you at home. I need a big favor.

"Could you come to Magnolia House right now? It shouldn't take more than a few minutes.

"No, don't worry about that. He's not here.

"I stand in your debt, sir."

Beth Wilson wondered what that was all about, but was not going to ask.

When Prentiss hung up the phone, she said, "Will you tell me what you want me to do, so I can do it and get out of here?"

"There doesn't seem to be anything that needs doing," Prentiss said. "But we're going to have to wait until somebody comes here."

She locked eyes with him.

He went on: "You upset your dad with that recitation of what your boyfriend had to think about just about everything. I suppose you know that?"

"Is that really any of your business?"

"Let me explain where I'm coming from," Prentiss said coldly. "I admire your father more than I do anyone else I've ever met. If you were to look in a dictionary, there would be a picture of your dad in the definition of officer and gentleman."

"Maybe you should have thought of that when you let Castillo get him drunk and make a fool of himself."

"You're right. I should have," Prentiss said. "But your question, Beth, was 'Is it any of my business' that you upset your father by quoting your boyfriend to him and making him damned uncomfortable. And the answer is, 'Yeah, it is my business.' It's my duty to do something to straighten you out."

"Straighten *me* out?"

"Yeah, and your boyfriend, too. He's next on my list."

"I can't believe this conversation," Beth said. "And I don't think my parents are going to like it a bit when I tell them about it."

"I'll have to take my chances about that," Prentiss said.

"I'm leaving," she said. "I don't have to put up with this."

"I can't stop you, of course, but if you leave, you'll walk. And it's a long way from here to Colonel Gremmier's quarters."

He walked out of the living room and went through the dining room into the kitchen.

Beth started for the door, then stopped.

That arrogant bastard is right about one thing. I can't walk from here to the Gremmiers'.

So what do I do?

She was still staring at the door three minutes later when it opened and a middle-aged man wearing a woolen shirt, a zipper jacket, and blue jeans came through it.

He looked at her and said, "I'm looking for Tom Prentiss."

"I'm in the kitchen, Pete," Prentiss called. "Be right there."

When he came into the living room, Prentiss said, "Jesus, that was quick."

"Well, you said you needed a favor," the man said.

"Do you know Miss Wilson?" Prentiss asked.

"I know who she is."

"Beth, this is Mr. Kowalski. He was my instructor pilot when I went through Blue Flight. He was with Lieutenant Castillo in the desert."

Beth nodded coldly at Kowalski.

Kowalski looked at Prentiss.

"How'd you hear about that?" Kowalski said.

"From him," Prentiss said. "What he told the general was something like 'There we were, the best Apache pilot in the Army and the worst one, flying an Apache over the Iraqi desert at oh dark hundred with people shooting at us.' "

Kowalski chuckled.

"Well," he said, "that's a pretty good description. Except, as he shortly proved, he was a much better Apache pilot than he or I thought he was."

"Would you please tell Miss Wilson about that?"

Kowalski glanced at her, then looked back at Prentiss and said, "What's this all about, Tom? Did somebody tell the general what Charley's really doing here?"

"I don't know what he's really doing here," Prentiss said, "but I'll take my chances about learning that, too. Start with the desert, please, Pete."

"It would help if I knew what this is all about, Tom."

"Okay. A source in whom Miss Wilson places a good deal of faith has implied that the only reason Castillo was in an Apache in the desert was because his father had the Medal of Honor."

"Absolutely true," Kowalski said. He shook his head. "Jesus Christ, I'd pretty much forgotten that!"

Beth flashed Prentiss a triumphant glance.

Then Kowalski went on: "What happened was a week, maybe ten days before we went over the berm, the old man, Colonel Stevens? He was then a light colonel"—Prentiss nodded—"Stevens called me in and said I wasn't going to believe what he was going to tell me."

"Which was?" Prentiss said.

"That I was about to have a new copilot. That said new copilot had a little over three hundred hours' total time, forty of which were in the Apache, and had been in the Army since last June, when he'd graduated from West Point. And the explanation for this insanity was that this kid's father had won the Medal of Honor, and they thought it would make a nice story for the newspapers that the son of a Medal of Honor guy had been involved in the first action . . . etcetera. Get the point?"

"Now, Tom, isn't that very much what Randy said?" Beth asked in an artificially sweet tone.

"I'm not finished," Kowalski said. "Tom said I was to tell you what happened."

"Oh, please do," Beth said.

"Well, I shortly afterward met Second Lieutenant Charley Castillo," Kowalski continued. "And he was your typical bushy-tailed West Point second john. He was going to win the war all by himself. But I also picked up that he was so dumb that he had no idea what they were doing to him.

"And I sort of liked him, right off. He was like a puppy, wagging his tail and trying to please. So because of that, and because I was deeply interested in preserving my own skin, I spent a lot of time in the next week or whatever it was, giving him a cram course in the Kowalski Method of Apache Flying. He wasn't a bad pilot; he just didn't have the Apache time, the experience.

"And then we went over the berm and—what did Castillo say?—'There we were flying over the Iraqi desert at oh dark hundred with people shooting at us.'

"What we were doing was taking out Iraqi air defense radar. If the radar didn't work, they not only couldn't shoot at the Air Force but they wouldn't even know where it was.

"I was flying, and Charley was shooting. He was good at that, and like he said, he wasn't the world's best Apache pilot.

"And then some raghead got lucky. I don't think they were shooting at us; what I think happened was they were shooting in the air and we ran into it. Anyway, I think it was probably an explosive-headed 30mm that hit us. It came through my windshield, and all of a sudden I was blind. . . .

"And I figured, 'Oh, fuck' "—he glanced at Beth Wilson—"sorry. I figured, 'We're going in. The kid'll be so shook up he'll freeze and never even think of grabbing the controls'—did I mention, we lost intercom?—'and we're going to fly into the sandpile about as fast as an Apache will fly.'

"And then, all of a sudden, I sense that he *is* flying the sonofabitch, that what he's trying to do is gain a little altitude so that he can set it down someplace where the ragheads aren't.

"And then I sense—like I said, I can't see a goddamned thing—that he's flying the bird. That he's trying to go home."

"When he really should have been trying to land?" Beth asked.

"Yeah, when he really should have been trying to land," Kowalski said. "When most pilots would have tried to land."

"Then why didn't he?" Beth asked.

"Because when he had to wipe my blood from his helmet visor, he figured—damned rightly—that if he set it down, even if there no were ragheads waiting to shoot us—which there were—it would be a long time before anybody found us, and I would die.

"From the way the bird was shaking, from the noise it was making, I thought that we were going to die anyway; the bird was either going to come apart or blow up."

"So he should have landed, then?" Beth asked.

"Either I'm not making myself clear, young lady, or you don't want to hear what I'm saying," Kowalski said, not pleasantly. "If Charley had set it down, he would have lived, and maybe I wouldn't have. He knew that all those long miles back to across the berm. And he had enough time in rotary-wing aircraft to think what I was thinking—*Any second now, this sonofabitch is going to come apart, and we'll both die.* Knowing that, he kept flying. In case there is any question in your mind, I am the founding member of the Charley Castillo Fan Club."

"That's a very interesting story," Beth said.

"Well, you asked for it," Kowalski said. "I don't know where you got your story, but you got it wrong."

"What happened then, Pete?" Prentiss asked.

"Well, when I got out of the hospital—I wasn't hurt as bad as it looked; there's a lot of blood in the head, and I lost a lot, and that's what blinded me— I went looking for him. But he was already gone. I asked around and found out that when the public relations guys learned that Colonel Stevens had put Charley in for the impact award of the DFC—which he damned sure deserved, that and the Purple Heart, because he'd taken some shrapnel in his hands— they'd arranged to have him flown to Riyadh, so that General Schwarzkopf could personally pin the awards on him. A picture of that would really have gotten in all the newspapers.

"But at Riyadh, one of the brass—I heard it was General Naylor, who was Schwartzkopf's operations officer; he just got put in for a third star, they're giving him V Corps, I saw that in *The Army Times*—"

"I know who he is," Prentiss said.

Kowalski nodded. "Anyway, someone took a close look at this second lieutenant fresh from West Point flying an Apache and decided something wasn't kosher. What I heard first was that Charley had been reassigned to fly Hueys for some civil affairs outfit to get him out of the line of fire, so to speak—"

"I don't understand 'what you heard first,' " Beth interrupted.

"—then I heard," Kowalski went on, ignoring her while looking at Prentiss, "what Charley was really doing was flying Scotty McNab around the desert in a Huey. The story I got was that was the only place Naylor thought he could stash him safe from the public relations guys, who couldn't wait to either put Charley back in an Apache or send him on a speechmaking tour."

"You said something before, Pete, about what Castillo is 'really doing here'?" Prentiss asked.

"You really don't know?"

Prentiss shook his head.

"And the general doesn't know either? Or maybe heard something? Why the questions?"

"I don't know what you're talking about," Prentiss said. "I heard he was getting Blue Flight transition into the King Air."

"Then I think we should leave it there," Kowalski said. "If you don't mind."

"If I tell you, and Miss Wilson agrees, that anything you tell us won't go any farther than this room . . ."

"I really would like an explanation of that," Beth said.

"Okay, with the understanding that I'll deny everything if anybody asks me," Kowalski said.

"Understood," Prentiss said.

"Agreed," Beth said.

"Well, the original idea, as I understand it, was to stash Charley where he should have been all along—flying in the left seat of a Huey in an aviation company. Christ, he'd just gotten out of flight school, and he didn't even go through the Huey training; they just gave him a check ride. In a company, he could build up some hours. But Naylor figured if he sent him to a regular company, the same people who'd put him in an Apache would put him back in one. So he sent him to McNab, who had this civil affairs outfit as a cover for what he was really doing in the desert."

"Which was?" Beth asked.

"Special Forces, honey," Kowalski said. "The guys with the Green Beanies."

"Oh," she said.

"But it didn't work out that way. McNab heard about the kid who'd flown the shot-up Apache back across the berm, went for a look, liked what he saw, and put him to work flying him around. I understand they got involved in a lot of interesting stuff. And then McNab found out that Charley speaks German and Russian. I mean really speaks it, like a native. And that was really useful to McNab.

"So the war's over. McNab gets his star . . . there were a lot people who didn't think that would ever happen—"

"How is it that he speaks German and Russian like a native?" Beth interrupted.

"His mother was German; he was raised there. I don't know where he got the Russian. And some other languages, too. Anyway, McNab is now a general. He's entitled to an aide, so he takes Charley to Bragg with him as his aide . . ."

Kowalski stopped and smiled and shook his head.

"Why are you smiling?" Beth asked.

"Charley thought he was really hot stuff. And why not? He wasn't out of West Point a year, and here he was an aviator with the DFC, two Purple Hearts, a Bronze Star, and the Combat Infantry Badge. And now a general's aide."

"I didn't know about the CIB and the Bronze Star," Prentiss said. "Where'd he get those?"

"I saw the Bronze Star citation," Kowalski said. "It says he 'distinguished himself while engaged in intensive combat action of a clandestine and covert nature.' I guess he got the CIB and the second Purple Heart from the same place."

"That's all it said?" Prentiss asked.

"God only knows what McNab did over there, all of it covert and clandestine. He came out of that war—and you know how long it lasted; it took me longer to walk out of Cambodia—with a Distinguished Service Medal, a Purple Heart, a star for his CIB, and the star that most people never thought he'd get.

"Anyway, when Charley got to Bragg, McNab quickly took the wind out of his sails."

"I'd like to know how he managed to do that," Beth said sweetly.

Kowalski gave her a look that was half curiosity and half frown, then went on, "When I heard Charley was at Bragg, I went to see him the first time. He wasn't in McNab's office; he was out in the boonies, at Camp Mackall, taking Green Beanie qualification training. Eating snakes and all that crap, you know? And *before* that, McNab had sent him to jump school. That'll take the wind out of anybody's sails."

"I thought he was General McNab's aide," Beth said.

"Oh, he was, but first he had to go to Benning and Mackall. Then, as an aide, McNab really ran his ass ragged. What he was doing, of course, was training him. But Charley didn't know that. He decided that God really didn't like him after all, that the fickle finger of fate had got him, that he was working for one mean sonofabitch.

"He told me that when his tour as an aide was up, it was sayonara, Special Forces, back to Aviation for him. McNab was of course one, two jumps ahead of him. I was up there to see Charley maybe two, three months ago on a, quote, Blue Flight cross-country exercise, end quote. McNab sent for me, told me the conversation was private, and asked me what I thought of the 160th."

"The Special Forces Aviation Regiment?" Beth asked.

Kowalski nodded.

"Special Operations Aviation Regiment. SOAR. I told him what I thought—which is that it's pretty good, and I would much rather be at Campbell flying with the Night Stalkers than teaching field-grade officers to fly here.

"He said he thought it would be just the place for Charley to go when his aide tour was up. I told him I didn't think that with as little time as Charley had—either total hours or in the Army—they'd take him. He said what he was thinking of doing was sending Charley over here for Blue Flight transition into the King Air—which he already knew how to fly—and what could be done while he was here to train him in something else, something that would appeal to the 160th?

"He said he knew two people who were going to have a quiet word in the ear of whoever selected people for the 160th saying that they'd flown with him in combat, and thought he could make it in the 160th. Then he pointed to me and him.

"And he said, 'If I hear you told him, or even if he finds out about this, I will shoot you in both knees with a .22 hollow-point.' " Kowalski laughed. "McNab really likes Charley. They're two of a kind."

"So what are you doing for him here?" Prentiss asked.

"If it's got wings or rotary blades, by the time I send him back to Bragg, he will be checked out in it as pilot-in-command," Kowalski said. "I've even checked him out in stuff the Aviation Board has for testing that the Army hasn't even bought yet."

"How do you get away with that?" Prentiss asked.

"I'm the vice president of the Instrument Examiner Board and the training scheduler for Blue Flight," Kowalski said. "Very few people ask me why I'm doing something. And a lot of people owe me favors. Like I figure I owe Charley several big ones."

Prentiss nodded

"Thanks, Pete," he said.

"This is the favor you wanted? Telling you about Charley?"

"Yeah. And now I need one more. You going home from here?"

"Yeah," Kowalski said.

"How about dropping Miss Wilson at Colonel Gremmier's quarters? I have the feeling she'd rather be with anyone but me right now."

Kowalski looked at the girl, then back at Prentiss.

"You going to explain that?" Kowalski said.

"You don't want to know, Pete."

"Yeah, sure. Gremmier's house is right on my way."

[-VI-]
2002 Red Cloud Road
Fort Rucker, Alabama
1955 6 February 1992

"These are really wonderful photos," Juan Fernando Castillo said. He glanced up from the thick photo album on the coffee table in the Wilsons' living room and met Brigadier General Harold F. Wilson's eyes.

"They mean a lot to me, Don Fernando," the general said.

The last snapshot that Don Fernando was looking at was a five-by-seven color photograph of Second Lieutenant Harold F. Wilson and WOJG Jorge A. Castillo standing by the nose of an HU-1D helicopter of the 322nd Attack Helicopter Company. Both were smiling broadly.

Don Fernando—no one had ever dared call him Don Juan, for the obvious reason—was a tall, heavyset man with a full head of dark hair. He wore a well-tailored nearly black double-breasted pin-striped suit. He looked very much like one of his grandsons, Fernando Manuel Lopez, who sat on one side of him on the Wilsons' couch, and not at all like his other grandson, Carlos Guillermo Castillo, who sat on the other side of him.

"Let me tell you what I've decided to do with those photos, Don Fernando," Wilson said. "And a good decision is a good decision, even if it is made much longer after it should have been."

"Excuse me?" Don Fernando said.

"I have decided that many of them should be hanging, suitably framed, in the Jorge Castillo Classroom Building. The first thing Monday morning, I will take them to our state-of-the-art photo lab."

"I think that's a very good idea, General," Don Fernando said.

"You're not going to stop that, are you? Calling me 'General'?"

"You have to understand, *Harry*," Don Fernando said, "that I never got any higher than major, and never very close to general officers."

"When Jorge and I were in 'Nam, we thought majors were God," Wilson said.

"So did we majors in Korea," Don Fernando said.

They laughed.

"I never thought majors were God, did you, Gringo?" Fernando Lopez asked Charley in a mock innocent tone.

"Fernando!" Doña Alicia Castillo said.

The wife of Don Fernando—and grandmother of Fernando Lopez and Charley Castillo—was a slight woman, her black hair heavily streaked with gray and pulled tight around her head. She wore a single strand of large pearls around her neck. Her only other jewelry consisted of two gold, miniature branch insignias—Armor and Aviation, honoring Fernando and Charley, respectively—pinned to the bosom of her simple black dress and her wedding and engagement rings.

She was an elegant, dignified, and formidable lady.

Don Fernando smiled. "My darling, Fernando's been calling him that from the moment Carlos got off the plane. What makes you think he'll stop now?"

"Actually, Fernando," Charley said, "now that I think about it, no, I never thought majors were God-like. *Other* comparisons, however, have occurred to me from time to time."

Doña Alicia shook her head.

"May I finish, gentlemen?" Wilson asked. "As I was saying, I will order that they be copied with great care, enlarged, and three copies made of each. You should have your complete set in San Antonio by Friday."

"Oh, my God, you don't have to do that," Don Fernando said.

"Oh, yes, I do," Wilson said. "I'm only sorry that I didn't . . ."

"What happened, happened," Don Fernando said. "You tried."

"And our number is unlisted," Doña Alicia said. "You couldn't be expected to find someone who isn't in the book."

"My wife and I were deeply touched by your letter," Don Fernando said.

"Yes, we were, Harry," Doña Alicia said. "It was heartfelt. And then the maid threw it out before I could reply. *Things* happened that kept us from getting together before this. I'm just so glad it finally happened."

"General," Castillo said, "may I ask a question?"

"Of course, Charley."

"Sir, aren't you a little concerned that somebody might recognize the second lieutenant standing next to my father?"

"Yes, I am. But I don't see what I can do about that, do you?"

"I don't understand," Doña Alicia said.

"For what it's worth, General, I hope a lot of people do," Castillo said.

The general didn't reply.

"Thank you, Charley," Mrs. Bethany Wilson said. "And so do I."

"I have hanging in my office," Don Fernando said, "Jorge's medal and a photograph, a terrible one taken when he graduated from flight school. I will replace the photograph with this one."

"That's a great idea," Charley said.

Doña Alicia asked, "What about—would this be possible?—getting a photo of the plaque on that building to put beside it? Or perhaps having a replica made for the same purpose?"

"Abuela," Charley said. "Trust me. That's a lousy idea."

"Why is it a lousy idea?"

"The gringo's right, Abuela," Fernando said. "Just the photo. The photo's a great idea."

"Don't call Carlos that," Doña Alicia said, but then she let the matter drop.

[-VII-]
Room 202
The Daleville Inn
Daleville, Alabama
1920 8 February 1992

Dripping water, Charley Castillo was wearing a thick terry-cloth bathrobe—and not a damn thing else—when he went to answer his door. The somewhat sour-toned chime had been bonging steadily—amid the downpour drumming on the roof—since before he had stepped out from the shower.

There's no telling how long it's been bonging like that.

Either the motel is on fire or some sonofabitch has stuck a toothpick in the button.

Or, more likely, it's Pete Kowalski with the wonderful news that he's got his hands on an Apache and we can get in a couple of hours airborne tonight.

And my ass is dragging.

It was instead Miss Beth Wilson.

It was one of the rare occasions where he found himself momentarily speechless.

But then his mouth went on autopilot.

"I can't believe that you have the gall to show up here," he said, paraphrasing her greeting to him when he and Miller had first arrived at Quarters Two.

"You are a sonofabitch, aren't you?" Beth said.

"Actually, I'm a bastard," he said. "There's a difference. My mother was a lady."

"Are you going to ask me in? It's raining out here, in case you didn't notice."

"Since I seriously doubt you came here with designs on my body, may I ask why you want to come in?"

"I'm here to apologize," she said, "and to ask a big favor."

"You're kidding, right?"

"No, I am not kidding."

"You realize what will happen if you pass through this portal and Righteous Randolph hears about it?"

"I'm asking you as nicely as I know how. Please. I'm getting soaked."

"Won't you come in, Miss Wilson?" Castillo asked, and opened the door fully.

She entered the living room, took off her head scarf and then her raincoat. She was wearing a skirt and, under a sweater vest, a nearly transparent blouse.

Where are you now, Dick Miller, Self-Appointed Keeper of Castillo's Morals, you sonofabitch, when I really need you?

"Do you think this will take long, Miss Wilson?"

"It'll take a little time."

"In that case—you may have noticed that you've interrupted my toilette— please excuse me for a moment while I slip into something more comfortable."

When Castillo came out of the bedroom three minutes later—wearing slacks and a sweater and shower thongs—Beth Wilson was sitting on the couch holding a copy of the *Tages Zeitung*.

"What's this?" she said.

"They call that a newspaper."

"It's German."

"I noticed."

"What do you do, use this to keep your German up?"

"Keep my German up where?" Castillo asked innocently, and then took pity on her. "My mother's family was in the newspaper business. They send it to me. And yeah, I read it to practice my German."

She gave him a faint smile.

"Now that I am appropriately dressed," Castillo said, "and in a position to proclaim my innocence of even harboring any indecent thoughts of any kind whatsoever should Randolph come bursting through the door, his eyes blazing with righteousness, you mentioned something about an apology?"

"Randy's on a cross-country, round-robin RON," she said. "He won't come bursting through the door."

A round robin was a flight that began and ended, after one or more intermediate stops, at the same place. Cross-country meant what it sounded like. RON stood for "Remain Over Night."

"Oh, you speak aviation?" he said.

"My father is an aviator, you might recall."

"Now that you mention it . . ."

She shook her head.

He went on: "Lieutenant Miller is also on that recruiting flight. Remember him? You met him, briefly—"

"Recruiting flight?"

"You mean you don't know?"

"Know what?"

"What they do when these splendid young fledgling birdmen are about to finish their course of instruction and graduate—"

"Randy graduates next Friday," she offered. "We'll be married on Sunday at three in Chapel One."

"Thank you for sharing that with me," Castillo said. "As I was saying, when they are about to finish, they schedule one of those cross-country, round-robin

RON training flights you mention, with stops at Forts Benning, Stewart, and—depending on the weather—either Knox or Bragg.

"Eight or ten—for that matter, two—Apaches coming in for a landing is a sight that will impress young officers. Some of these fledgling birdmen will even be bright enough to extrapolate from that that driving one such machine, and getting flight pay to do so, would seem to be a far smarter way to serve one's country than mucking about in the mud, etcetera, as they are doing. They then apply for flight training. This is called recruiting. Hence the term 'recruiting flights.' "

"I almost believe that."

"Miss Wilson, there is no limit to what terrible things certain people will do to further Army Aviation."

She looked at him for a moment before smiling again.

"Well, anyway," she said, "you don't have to worry about Randy bursting through your door. He called me from Fort Stewart about an hour ago."

"And suggested you come over here and say 'hi' if you were bored?"

"God, you just don't stop, do you?"

"Are we back to the apology, or have I said something that's changed your mind?"

"You're making it hard, but I haven't changed my mind."

"Are you familiar with Ed McMahon, the entertainer, Miss Wilson?"

"Can you call me 'Beth'?"

"Obviously, I can. The questions would seem to be *Will I?* and/or *Why should I?*"

"Because it would make things easier for me. And, yes, I know who McMahon is. Why?"

"Because, *Beth*—"

"Thank you."

"You're welcome, *Beth*. Mr. McMahon said that drink is God's payment for hard work. And as I've worked hard all day—"

"Doing what?"

"I spent three hours in an Apache and two-thirty in a Mohawk. Thank you for your interest. As I was saying, I worked hard all day, and in the shower I was planning to accept my just pay the moment I was dry. But then you started bonging at my door. So, what I am going to do now, while you rehearse your apology, is make myself a drink."

"All right."

He went to the wet bar, took out a silver set of martini-making necessities from the freezer compartment of the refrigerator, and very seriously set about constructing himself a martini in the manner practiced by and passed on to him by Brigadier General Bruce J. McNab.

This involved, among other things, rinsing out both the martini mixer and the martini glass with vermouth before adding a precisely measured *hefty* amount of Gilbey's gin to the ice in the mixer. He then stirred the mixture precisely one hundred times before pouring it into two large, long-stemmed martini glasses and adding two pickled onions on a toothpick to each.

He took one of the martinis, very carefully placed it in the freezer, and gently closed the freezer door. Then, carefully carrying the other martini, he walked to the couch and sat down as far away from Beth Wilson as the couch would permit.

He brought the glass to his lips, looked at her over the rim, and said, "You may begin the apology."

Then he took his first sip.

"Where's mine?" she said.

"You're kidding, right?"

"You are not going to offer me a drink? After that long Ed McMahon speech?"

" 'What work did you do today?' is one question that pops to mind," Castillo said.

"I told you, I'm getting married on Sunday. I spent all day—with half a dozen giggling women—getting ready."

"I can see where that would be tiring," Castillo said. "The next question is a little delicate. Your father—"

"My father has a problem with alcohol," she said. "Something about his metabolism. My mother and I don't."

"And you want a martini?"

"If it wouldn't be too much trouble. I happened to notice you made two."

"There is a reason for that. You know what they say about martinis."

"I'll bet you're about to tell me."

"Martinis are like a woman's breasts," Castillo said, solemnly. "One is not enough, and three is too many."

"My God! That's disgusting! I can't believe you said that to me!"

She could not, however hard she tried, completely restrain the smile that came to her face.

"I made two because I planned to drink two," Castillo said. "The idea of making one for you never entered my mind."

"Well, now that it has, are you going to give me one?"

"I'm not sure that would be wise."

"Why not?"

"Well, if a couple of belts puts your father on a bicycle, there's no telling what one martini would do to you," Castillo said. And then his mouth went on autopilot: "You might, for example, tear off your clothes and throw yourself into my arms."

She looked at him incredulously for a moment, then got off the couch and walked to the refrigerator, commenting en route, "Don't hold your breath! My God! You're an absolute lunatic."

She took the second martini out of the freezer and carried it back to the couch. She extended it to him.

"Let's start over, okay?"

He shrugged. "Why not?"

They tapped glasses. Both took a sip.

"I came here, Castillo—"

"I call you Beth and you call me *Castillo*? Is that the way to commence an apology?"

"I came here, *Charley* . . ."

"Better," he said.

". . . to apologize for my behavior at my house on Saturday . . ."

"And well you should. You nearly reduced poor Dick Miller to tears. He's very sensitive."

She shook her head, took another sip of the martini, and went doggedly on: ". . . and to ask a favor."

"Well, that certainly explains why you felt you needed a drink. Asking a favor—much less apologizing—to the likes of me has to be very difficult for someone like you."

"What is that supposed to mean?"

"You are a general's daughter. You are not the first general's daughter I . . . have encountered."

"Randy told me about her," Beth said.

"Well, I'm sure that was fascinating. Did he manage to suggest that my behavior was ungentlemanly?"

"As a matter of fact, yes."

"Well, my conscience is clear. From Day One I made it absolutely clear to Daphne that I had no intention of marching up the aisle of the cadet chapel with her the day after I graduated."

"Daphne? Randy said her name was Jennifer."

"Same story. Jennifer was before Daphne, but I made it perfectly clear to her, too, that if she was looking for a husband, she was looking in the wrong place."

"Oh, you're not only a sonofabitch, but you're proud of being a son-ofabitch!"

"No. As I said before, I am a bastard, not a sonofabitch."

"I know why you and Randy don't get along."

"I don't think so, but what does it matter? I accept your apology. Now, what's the favor you want?"

"I can't believe you drank that already," she said.

"Here is the proof," he said, holding the martini glass upside down. "And now I am going to have to make myself another, having let chivalry get in the way of my common sense."

"What the hell does that mean?"

"I gave you my second martini," he said.

He got up and walked to the wet bar.

"You may ask me the favor," he said, as he went to the freezer for another frozen glass.

There were two glasses in the freezer. He looked at them a long moment, and then took both out.

That would seem to prove that I am indeed the sonofabitch that she thinks—and Dick knows—I am.

But not to worry. Virtue will triumph.

If I so much as lightly touch her shoulder, she will throw the martini in my face and then kick me with practiced skill in the scrotum.

He set about making a second duo of dry martini cocktails according to the famous recipe of Brigadier General Bruce J. McNab.

Beth came across the room to where he stood.

He looked at her and then away.

"You might as well go sit back down," he said, stirring the gin-and-ice mixture. "You have had your ration of martinis."

"My family likes, really likes, your family," Beth said. "That was all they talked about at breakfast."

"And my family likes your family. Since both families are extraordinarily nice people, why does that surprise you?"

"My mother and father are going to San Antonio. Did you know that?"

"Abuela told me."

"Abuela?"

"My grandmother. Doña Alicia."

"Why do they call her that?"

"*They* don't call her Abuela. Fernando and I do. It means 'grandmother' in Spanish. *They* call *our* abuela 'Doña Alicia' as a mark of respect."

"I'm going to marry Randy," she said.

"I seem to recall having heard that somewhere."

"That will make Randy part of my family."

"Yeah, I guess it will."

"What I would like to do is patch things up between you and Randy."

"There's not much chance of that, Beth," he said seriously, and their eyes met again.

He averted his quickly, and very carefully poured the two glasses full.

"Starting with you being part of our wedding," she said.

"Not a chance."

"There's going to be an arch of swords outside the chapel. I'm sure Randy—you're classmates—would love to have you be one of the . . . whatever they're called."

"Beth, for Christ's sake, no. I can't stand the sonofabitch."

"I thought you didn't use that term. You preferred 'bastard.' "

"I didn't say I preferred it. I said that *I* wasn't a sonofabitch because *my* mother was the antithesis of a bitch."

He met her eyes again, averted them, picked up his martini glass, and took a healthy swallow.

"But you don't mind being called a bastard?"

"I am a bastard," he said, meeting her eyes. "There's not much I can do about it."

"A bastard being defined as someone who is hardheaded? Arrogant? Infuriating? And revels in it?"

"A bastard is a child born out of wedlock," Castillo said.

"I don't understand," she said. "Your parents weren't married?"

He shook his head.

He said: "The estimates vary that between fifty thousand and one hundred fifty thousand children were born outside the bonds of holy matrimony to German girls and their American boyfriends—some of whom were general officers. I am one of those so born. I'm a lot luckier than any of the others I've run into, but I'm one of them."

"Because of your father, you mean?"

"No. Because of my mother. My father was only in at the beginning, so to speak. Because of my mother. My mother was something special."

"Why are you telling me this?" she asked.

"I don't know. Possibly in the hope that it will send you fleeing before this situation gets any more out of hand than it is."

"I want to hear this," she said. "Does my father know?"

"Your father is a very intelligent man. He's probably put it all together by now. Or your mother has. Or Abuela told them."

He took another sip of his martini.

As Beth watched, she said, "That's your second you're gulping down, you know."

"I can count. And as soon as you leave, I will have the third."

"I'm not leaving until you tell me. What happened?"

"When my father finished flight school, they sent him to Germany, rather than straight to Vietnam. They tried to do that, send kids straight from flight school over there. The idea was that they would build some hours, be better pilots when they got into combat. And while he was in Germany he met a German girl, and here I am."

"The sonofabitch!" Beth exploded.

"No. Now you're talking about his *madre*—my Abuela—and she is indeed another who is the antithesis of bitch."

"He . . . made your mother pregnant and then just left? I don't care if you like it or not, that makes him a sonofabitch in my book. Oh, Charley, I'm so sorry."

"Hold the pity," he said. "For one thing, we don't *know* that he behaved dishonorably. For one thing, he didn't know she was pregnant. He did promise her he would write, and then never did. It is entirely possible that had he written, and had she been able to reply that she was in the family way, he would have done something about it. I like to think that's the case. Genes are strong, and he was my grandparents' son. But he didn't write, he didn't know, and we'll never know whether or not he would have gone back to Germany when he came home from Vietnam"—he drained his martini glass—"because he didn't come back from Vietnam."

"Your poor mother," Beth said. "How awful for her."

"And it's not as if my mother had to go scrub floors or stand under Lili Marlene's streetlamp to feed her bastard son," Castillo said, just a little thickly. "She was the eighteen-year-old princess in the castle, who'd made a little mistake that no one dared talk about.

"Her father, my grandfather, was a tough old Hessian. He was a lieutenant colonel at Stalingrad. He was one of the, quote, lucky ones, unquote—the really seriously wounded who were evacuated just before it fell. He was also an aristocrat. The family name is von und zu Gossinger. Not just 'von' and not just 'zu.' Both. That sort of thing is important in the Almanac de Gotha."

"You sound as if you didn't like him," she said.

"Actually, I liked him very much. He was kind to me. What I think now is that he wasn't all that unhappy that an American, a Mexican-American with a name like Jorge Castillo, had not come back to further pollute the von und zu Gossinger bloodline."

He met her eyes again, quickly averted them again, and reached for the other full martini glass. She snatched it away before his hand touched it.

"You've had enough," she said.

"That decision is mine, don't you think?" Castillo asked, not very pleasantly. She glowered at him. Then she put the glass to her mouth and drained it.

"Not anymore, it's not," she said.

"You're out of your mind. You'll pass out."

"Finish the story," she said.

"How the hell am I going to get you home?"

"Finish the story," she repeated.

"That's it."

"How did you wind up in San Antonio?"

"Oh."

"Yeah, *oh*."

He shrugged. "Well, my grandfather and my uncle Willi went off a bridge on the autobahn, and that left my mother and me alone in the castle."

"Why didn't your mother try to get in contact with your father?"

"When he didn't write or come back as he promised, I guess she decided he didn't want to. And I suspect that my grandfather managed to suggest two or three thousand times that it was probably better that he hadn't. I just don't know."

"How did you get to San Antonio?"

"Oh, yeah. Well, you've heard that good luck comes in threes?"

"Of course."

"A year or so after my grandfather and uncle Willi went off the bridge, my mother was diagnosed with a terminal case of pancreatic cancer."

"Oh, God!"

"At that point, my mother apparently decided that wetback Mexican relatives in Texas would be better than no family at all for the soon-to-be orphan son. So she went to the Army, which had been running patrols along the East/West German border fence on our land. She knew a couple of officers, one of them a major named Allan Naylor."

"General Naylor?" she asked.

When Castillo nodded, she added, "He's a friend of my father's."

"I am not surprised," Castillo said. "Anyway, Naylor was shortly able to tell her the reason that my father had not come back as promised was because he was interred in the National Cemetery in San Antonio." He paused, then— his voice breaking—added: "So at least she had that. It wasn't much, but she had that."

Beth saw tears forming. Her own watered.

He turned his face from hers and coughed to get his voice under control.

He then asked, "If I take a beer from the cooler, are you going to snatch it away from me and gulp it down?"

"No," she said softly, almost in a whisper.

He took a bottle of Schlitz from the refrigerator and twisted off the cap. As he went to take a swig, raising it to his mouth, he lost enough of his balance so that he had to quickly back up against the counter.

Without missing a beat, he went on, "So . . . so one day Major Allan Naylor shows up in San Antonio, nobly determined to protect as well as he can the considerable assets the German kid is about to inherit from the natural avarice of the wetback family into which the German bastard is about to be dumped."

"Oh, Charley!"

"My grandfather was in New York on business, so Naylor had to deliver the news to Doña Alicia that WOJG Jorge Castillo had left a love child behind in Germany."

"What happened?"

"She called my grandfather in New York, told him, and his reaction to the news was that she was to do nothing until he could get back to Texas. He didn't want to be cruel, but, on the other hand, he didn't want to open the family safe to some German woman just because she claimed her bastard was his son's."

"Oh, Charley!"

"You keep saying that," Castillo said. He took another swig and went on: "Couldn't blame him. I'd have done the same thing. Asked for proof."

"So how long did that take? Proving who you were?"

"Not long. Thirty minutes after she hung up on Grandpa, the Lear went wheels-up out of San Antonio with Abuela and Naylor on it. They caught the five-fifteen Pan American flight out of New York to Frankfurt that afternoon. Abuela was at the Haus im Wald at eleven o'clock the next morning."

"Haus in Wald? What's that?"

"Means house in the woods. It's not really a castle. Really ugly building."

"Oh. And she went there?"

"And I didn't want to let her in," Castillo said, now speaking very carefully. "My mother was pretty heavily into the sauce. What she had was very painful. I was twelve, had never seen this woman before, and I was Karl Wilhelm von und zu Gossinger. I was not about to display my drunken mother to some Mexican from America.

"So Abuela grabbed my arm and marched me into the house, and into mother's bedroom, and my mother, somewhat belligerently, said, 'Who the hell are you, and what are you doing in my bedroom?' Abuela said she didn't speak German, so my mother switched to English and asked exactly the same question. And Abuela said"—Castillo's voice broke, and he started to sob—"and Abuela said, 'I'm Jorge's mother, my dear, and I'm here to take care of you and the boy.'"

He turned his back to Beth and she saw him shaking with sobs.

And she saw him raise the bottle of Schlitz.

And she ran to him to take it away from him.

And he didn't want to give it up.

They wrestled for it, then he fell backward onto the floor, pulling the bottle and Beth on top of him as he went down.

Neither remembered much of what happened after that, or the exact sequence in which it happened.

Just that it had.

The next thing they both knew was Beth asking, "Charley, are you awake?"

"I'm afraid so. I was hoping it was a dream."

"It's half past ten," she said.

"Time marches on."

"My God!" she said. "What happened?"

"You don't remember?"

"You sonofabitch!" she said, and swung at him.

He caught her wrist, and she fell on him.

"I told you not to call me that," he said.

And then it happened again.

[-VIII-]
The Daleville Inn
Daleville, Alabama
2005 9 February 1992

The rain was coming down in buckets, and First Lieutenant C. G. Castillo, who had gotten drenched going from the Apache to Base Ops and then drenched again going from Base Ops to his car, got drenched a third time going from where he had parked his car to the motel building.

The Daleville Inn was full of parents and wives who had come to see their offspring and mates get their wings pinned on them, and one of these had inconsiderately parked in the slot reserved for Room 202.

As he walked past the car and started up the stairs to the second floor, the car in his slot flashed its lights at him and then blew its horn.

He was tempted to go to the car and deliver a lecture on motel parking lot courtesy, but decided that was likely to get out of hand and satisfied himself with giving the driver the finger as he continued up the stairs.

He was standing at his door, patting the many pockets of his soaking-wet flight suit in search of his key, when he heard someone bonging their way up the steel stairs. Then he sensed someone standing behind him.

"I was just about to give up," Beth Wilson said. "I've been sitting out there since six."

"I was afraid of this," he said.

"Afraid that I'd be here?"

"Or that you wouldn't," he said.

"We have to talk, Charley."

"Oh, yeah."

"Just talk. Nothing else."

"Would you believe I expected you to say something like that?"

He found the key. He opened the door, waved her through it, followed her in, closed the door, and only then turned the lights on.

"You could have turned them on before you pushed me in here," Beth said. "I almost fell over your wastebasket."

"But no one saw the general's daughter and the affianced of Righteous Randolph in Castillo's room, did they? As they would have had I turned the lights on first."

"You're soaking wet," Beth said. "Where have you been?"

"Where would you guess I've been, dressed as I am in my GI rompers?"

"You haven't been flying?"

"Oh, yes, I have."

"Randy called and said they were weathered in. That there was weather all over this area and nobody could fly."

"Except courageous seagulls and Pete Kowalski. He holds that coveted green special instrument card which permits him to decide for himself whether it's safe to take off. He told me that it would be educational, and it was."

"Where were you?"

"The last leg was Fulton County to here. Can you amuse yourself while I take a shower? We're going flying again in the morning, and I'd rather not have pneumonia when I do that."

"Go ahead," she said.

Beth was sitting on the couch with her legs curled up under her skirt when he came into the living room, She was wearing another transparent blouse through which he could see her brassiere.

I know she didn't do that on purpose.

"I am now going to have a drink," Castillo announced. "Not, I hasten to add, a martini. We have learned our lesson about martinis, haven't we?"

"I really wish you wouldn't."

"I've told you about Ed McMahon. And, oh boy, did I earn it today."

"Do whatever you want."

"I don't think you really mean that," he said.

"I meant about taking a drink."

"Oh."

"And you knew it," she said. "Goddamn you, Charley. You never quit."

He made himself a stiff scotch on the rocks and carried it to the couch.

"You will notice I didn't offer you one," he said, raising the glass.

"I noticed. Thank you."

"So what have you decided to do about Righteous?"

"I wish you wouldn't call him that."

"So what have you decided to do about He Who Is Nameless?"

"What do you mean, what am I going to do about him?"

"If I may dare to offer some advice, when you tell him you've thought things over and the wedding is off, don't mention what caused you to do some serious reconsidering."

"The wedding's not off," she said, surprised.

"You're still going to marry him?"

"Of course. What did you think I was going to do, elope with you to Panama City or someplace?"

"Aware of the risk of having you throw something at me, I have to tell you that is not one of your options."

"I never thought it was."

"I'm glad we can agree on at least that," Castillo said. "So you're going ahead with the wedding?"

"Why is that so hard for you to understand?"

"Think about it, Beth."

"What happened last night was a mistake."

"Yes, it was. It made me reconsider the merits of the Roman Catholic Church."

"Now, what is that supposed to mean?"

"If you're a Catholic—and all the Castillos but this one are devout Roman Catholics—when you have sinned, all you have to do is go to confession. *Forgive me, Father, for I have sinned.* Convince the priest that you're sorry, and he grants you absolution, and all is forgiven. Clean slate. Forget it."

"Well, at least you're sorry about yesterday."

"On a strictly philosophical, moral level, yeah. But Satan has his claws in me, and on another level, I'm not sorry, and I don't think I'll ever forget it."

"Does that mean you're sorry or not?"

"I don't like the prospect of having always to remember that I plied my father's buddy's about-to-be-married daughter with martinis and had my wicked way with her."

"My God!"

"Not that I seem to recall there was much resistance involved."

"You *bastard*!"

"You're learning," Castillo said, and sipped his scotch.

"It happened. What we have to do is decide what we're going to do about it."

"Is one of my options doing it again? The cow, so to speak, being already out of the barn."

"I won't even respond to that. What I came to ask you is what I came to ask you last night. Will you take a part in the wedding?"

"Jesus Christ! I'm a bastard, not a hypocrite!"

"My mother, this morning, said she was going to ask you. My father said it probably wasn't that good an idea. She told him to ask you. At supper he said he couldn't, because you were stuck someplace because of the weather. But he'll ask you tomorrow."

"He won't find me tomorrow, trust me."

She didn't reply.

He said, "I just can't believe you're going to marry Righteous. Just can't understand it."

"I love him. Can you understand that?"

"No."

"It's as simple as that, Charley. We have a lot in common. I understand him. He understands me."

"I don't think he would understand what happened last night."

"He's never going to know what happened last night . . . is he?"

"As tempting as it is for me to consider having it whispered down the Long Gray Line that Castillo nailed Righteous Randolph's fiancée five days before they got hitched, I couldn't do that to you or your parents. Our sordid little secret will remain our sordid little secret."

"Thank you."

"You're welcome."

Beth got off the couch and said, "I'll say good night."

"Good night."

She walked to the door. He went with her.

She looked up at him.

"Thank you again," she said. "Good luck."

"You're welcome again," he said.

She took the lock off the door.

"Beth," he said, very seriously. "There's something I've got to tell you."

"What's that?"

"Don't get your hopes up too high about the wedding night, the honeymoon."

"Excuse me?"

"I've seen Righteous in the shower. I've seen bigger you-know-whats on a Pekingese."

He held up his right hand with the thumb and index finger barely apart to give her some idea of scale.

She swung her purse at him.

He caught her wrist.

She spit in his face . . . then fell into his arms.

She didn't go home until it was almost midnight.

By then it had stopped raining.

THIRTEEN YEARS LATER

[TWO]
Cairns Army Airfield
Fort Rucker, Alabama
1820 1 September 2005

The glistening white Gulfstream III taxied up to the visitors' tarmac in front of the Base Operations building. Waving wands, ground handlers directed it into a parking space between two Army King Air turboprops.

Colonel Jake Torine looked out the cockpit window.

"Our reception committee apparently includes a buck general, Charley," he said. "You want me to do the talking?"

The reception committee walking toward them included four military policemen and half a dozen other men in uniform. Three of them were armed and wearing brassards on their sleeves, making Castillo think they were probably the AOD, the FOD, and the OD, which translated to mean the Air Officer of the Day, the Field Grade Officer of the Day, and the Officer of the Day.

One of the others was a general officer, and another man was more than likely his aide. Castillo hoped that a public information officer was not among them, but that was a very real possibility.

Cairns had not wanted them to land, and they had had to declare an emergency.

"Please, Jake," Castillo said. "And take Doherty with you. Maybe they'll be impressed with the FBI."

He followed Torine into the passenger compartment.

"Jack," he said to Inspector Doherty, "would you come flash your badge at these people? They didn't want us to land."

Doherty nodded and stood up.

Castillo opened the stair door. Max came charging up the aisle, headed for the door with Mädchen behind him. They pushed Torine out of the way and jumped to the ground. Max ran to one of the King Airs and raised his leg at the nose gear. Mädchen met the call of nature under the wing.

Torine went down the stairs and saluted the general.

"Torine, sir," he said. "Colonel, USAF, attached to the Department of Homeland Security. This is Inspector Doherty of the FBI. Would you like to see our identification?"

"I think that would be a good idea, Colonel," the general said.

Torine handed his identity card to the general. Doherty took out his credentials and held them open.

The general examined both carefully.

"Welcome to Fort Rucker," he said. "I'm Brigadier General Crenshaw, the deputy post commander."

"I'm sorry about causing the fuss, sir," Torine said. "But we had planned to land at Hurlburt—"

"They took a pretty bad hit from Katrina," General Crenshaw said.

"—and we were getting pretty low on fuel."

"Where'd you come from?"

"I'm sorry, sir, but that's classified," Torine said.

"The reason I asked had to do with customs and immigration, Colonel."

"We'll do that when we get to Washington, sir. Presuming we can get fuel from you."

"That's a civilian airplane," General Crenshaw said.

"Sir, if you will contact General McNab at Special Operations Command, I'm sure he'll authorize you to fuel us."

"You work for Scotty McNab, do you?"

"With him, sir."

"Okay, Colonel. You have an honest face, and the FBI seems to be vouching for you. We'll fuel you. Anything else we can do for you?"

"Two things, sir. Forget we were ever here, and . . . uh . . . the dogs aren't the only ones who need a pit stop."

"They did have the urge, didn't they?" General Crenshaw said. "Not a problem. We can even feed you."

"Very kind of you, sir. We'll pass on the food, but some coffee would be really appreciated."

"Is there a problem with me having a look at your airplane?"

"None at all, sir," Torine said, and waved the general toward the door stairs.

Castillo stepped away from the door as Crenshaw mounted the steps.

"Hello," Crenshaw said to him as he stepped inside. "Who are you?"

"I'm the copilot, sir."

"Air Force?"

"Secret Service."

Crenshaw studied him a moment, then nodded. Then he raised his voice to those in the cabin:

"Although I understand you're not here, gentlemen, welcome to Cairns Army Airfield and the Army Aviation Center. If you'd care to use our facilities while you're here, we'll throw in coffee and doughnuts."

Then he turned to Castillo again.

"Where'd you learn how to fly? If you don't mind my asking?"

"In Texas, sir."

Crenshaw looked at him again, then nodded, and went down the stairs.

Did he remember my face from somewhere?

He didn't ask my name.

My replies to his questions weren't the truth, the whole truth, and nothing but the truth, but I really did learn to fly in Texas, rather than here, which is what I think he was asking. And I have bona fide credentials of a Secret Service supervisory agent in my pocket.

So why am I uncomfortable?

Because while I'm wildly out of step with others in the Long Gray Line, I'm still in it. And a cadet does not lie, or cheat, or tolerate those who do.

How the hell did a nice young West Pointer like me wind up doing what I'm doing?

Thirty-five minutes later, Cairns departure control cleared Gulfstream Three Seven Nine for immediate takeoff.

[ONE]
Signature Flight Support, Inc.
Baltimore—Washington International Airport
Baltimore, Maryland
2205 1 September 2005

A black Chevrolet sedan with a United States Customs and Border Protection Service decal on the door and four identical dark blue GMC Yukon XL Denalis were waiting for the Gulfstream III when it taxied up to the Signature tarmac.

Two uniformed customs officers got out of the Chevrolet sedan and walked across the tarmac toward the aircraft. Major H. Richard Miller, Jr., in civilian clothing, slid gingerly out of the front seat of the first Yukon in the line, turned and retrieved a crutch, stuck it under his arm, and moved with surprising agility after them.

As soon as the stair door opened into place, one of the customs officers, a gray-haired man in his fifties, bounded quickly up it, then stopped, exclaimed, "Jesus Christ!" and then backed up so quickly that he knocked the second customs officer, by then right behind him, off the stairs and then fell backward onto him.

Max appeared in the door, growling deeply and showing an impressive array of teeth. Mädchen moved beside him and added her voice and teeth to the display.

Castillo appeared in the door.

"Gentlemen," he said, solemnly, "you have just personally witnessed the Office of Organizational Analysis Aircraft Anti-Intrusion Team in action."

The gray-haired customs officer gained his feet, glared for a moment at the stair door, and then, shaking his head, smiled.

"Very impressive, Colonel," he said, finally.

"They're okay, Max," Castillo said, in Hungarian. "You may now go piss."

Max looked at him, stopped growling, went down the stairs, and headed for the nose gear. Mädchen went modestly to the other side of the fuselage.

"You all right?" Castillo said.

"What the hell kind of dogs are they?" the gray-haired customs officer asked.

"Bouvier des Flandres," Castillo said.

The customs officer shook his head. "What do they weigh?" he asked.

"Max has been known to hit one-thirty-five, Mädchen maybe one-ten."

"You understand, Colonel, sir," Miller said, "that you may now expect these gentlemen to *really* search your person and luggage?"

"What I'm hoping you'll say, Colonel," the customs officer said, "is that you're going to show me evidence that you passed through customs someplace else."

"No," Castillo said. "We were going to do that at Hurlburt Field, but the hurricane got Hurlburt. We refueled at Fort Rucker, but we have to do the customs and immigration here."

"Everybody aboard American?"

"No," Castillo replied, and waved them onto the Gulfstream. "No more surprises, I promise."

"Welcome to the United States," the large customs officer said when he had stepped into the cabin. "Or welcome home, whichever the case may be. There would be a band, but I have been led to believe that everybody would prefer to enter the United States as quietly as possible. What we're going to do is collect the American passports and run them through the computers in the main terminal. Then—presuming the computer doesn't tell us there are outstanding warrants on anybody—they will be returned to you and you can be on your way."

He looked around the cabin and continued: "I just learned that some of you are not American citizens, which means that we'll have to check your visas. I think we can run them through the computers without any trouble, but I think we'd better have a look at them before we try to do that. Understood?"

When there were nods, he pulled a heavy plastic bag from his pocket and finished his speech: "And if any of you are carrying forbidden substances, not only mood-altering chemicals of one kind or another but raw fruits and vegetables, any meat product not in an unopened can—that sort of thing—now is the time to deposit them in this bag."

"As my patriotic duty," Castillo said, "I have to mention that the cigarettes that Irishman has been smoking don't smell like Marlboros."

He pointed. The customs officer looked.

"And I've seen his picture hanging in the post office, too," the customs officer said, and walked to the man with his hand extended. "How are you, Jack? And what the hell are you doing with this crew?"

"Hoping nobody sees me," Inspector Doherty said. "And what are you doing in a uniform?"

"The director of National Intelligence suggested it would be appropriate."

"Say hello to Edgar Delchamps," Doherty said. "I'll vouch for him. Use your judgment about the others. Ed, this is Chief Inspector Bob Mitchell."

The men shook hands.

"You're with the bureau?" Mitchell asked.

"Ed's the exception to the rule about people who get paid from Langley," Doherty said. "When he shakes your hand, Bob, you get all five fingers back."

"Actually, I'm with the Fish and Wildlife Service," Delchamps said.

Mitchell chuckled.

The other customs officer handed Mitchell several passports.

"Take a look at these, Inspector," he said. "When was the last time you saw a handwritten, non-expiring, multivisit visa signed by an ambassador?"

"It's been a while," Mitchell said. He looked at the passports and added, "An Argentine, a German, and two Hungarians. All issued the same day in Buenos Aires. Interesting. I'd love to know what's going on here."

"But you were told not to ask, right?" Doherty said. "Sorry, Bob."

"We also serve who look but do not see or ask questions," Mitchell said. "Well, I think I had better run these through the computer myself. I'm sure all kinds of warning bells and whistles are going to go off."

"Thank you, Mr. Mitchell," Castillo said.

"I always try to be nice to people I feel sorry for, Colonel," Mitchell said. "Excuse me?"

"I bear a message from our boss, Colonel. The ambassador said, quote, Ask Colonel Castillo to please call me the minute he gets off the airplane, unquote."

"Oh. I see what you mean."

"That's the first time I can remember the ambassador saying 'please.' "

"That's probably because he's not my boss," Castillo replied. "He just thinks he is."

"That's probably even worse, isn't it?"

"Yes, it is," Castillo agreed.

Mitchell smiled and nodded.

"Okay, this'll take ten or fifteen minutes. You can start unloading whatever you have to unload."

"Thank you," Castillo said.

"Consider it your hearty meal for the condemned man," Mitchell said, shook his hand, and went to the stair door.

Castillo turned to Miller.

"So where do I find a secure phone?"

"There's one in your Yukon."

"I said a *secure* phone."

"And I said, Colonel, sir, 'In your Yukon,' " Miller said, and made a grand gesture toward the stair door.

Miller motioned for Castillo to precede him into the backseat of one of the dark blue Yukons. Then, not without difficulty, he stowed his crutch, got in beside him, and closed the door.

There was a telephone handset mounted on the rear of the driver's seat in the Yukon. Except for an extraordinarily thick cord, it looked like a perfectly normal handset.

"That's secure?" Castillo asked.

"Secure and brand-new," Miller replied. "A present from your pal Aloysius."

"Really?"

"He called up three or four days ago, asked of your general health and welfare, then asked if there was anything he could do for us. I told him I couldn't think of a thing. He said he had a new toy he thought you might like to play with, one in its developmental phase."

Miller pointed at the telephone.

"So yesterday, I was not surprised when the Secret Service guy said there were some people from AFC seeking access to your throne room in the complex. I was surprised when they came up to see that one of them was Aloysius in the flesh."

Aloysius Francis Casey (Ph.D., Electrical Engineering, MIT) was a small, pale-faced man who customarily dressed in baggy black suits. He also was the founder, chairman of the board, and principal stockholder of the AFC Corporation. AFC had a vast laboratory and three manufacturing facilities that provided a substantial portion of worldwide encrypted communications to industry in the form of leased technology.

During the Vietnam War, then-Sergeant Casey had served with distinction as the commo man on several Special Forces A-Teams. He had decided, immediately after the First Desert War, that it was payback time. Preceded by a telephone call from the senior U.S. senator from Nevada, he had arrived at Fort Bragg in one of AFC's smaller jets and explained to then–Major General Bruce J. McNab that, save for the confidence that being a Green Beanie had given him, he would almost certainly have become either a Boston cop—or maybe a postman—after his Vietnam service.

Not that Casey found either occupation wanting.

Instead, he said, his Green Beanie service had given him the confidence to attempt the impossible. In his case, he explained, that meant getting into MIT without a high school diploma on the strength of his self-taught comprehension of both radio wave propagation and cryptographic algorithms.

"A professor," Casey had said, "took a chance on a scrawny little Irishman with the balls to ask for something like getting into MIT and arranged for me to audit classes. By the end of my freshman year, I got my high school diploma. By the end of my second year, I had my BS. The next year, I got my master's and started AFC. By the time I got my doctorate two years later, AFC was up and running. The professor who gave me my chance—Heinz Walle—is now AFC's vice president of research and development. I now have more money than I can spend, so it's payback time."

General McNab had asked him exactly what he had in mind. Dr. Casey replied that he knew the Army's equipment was two, three years obsolete before the first piece of it was delivered.

"What I'm going to do is see that Special Forces has state-of-the-art stuff."

General McNab said that was a great idea, but as Sergeant/Dr. Casey must know, procurement of signal equipment was handled by Signal Corps procurement officials, over whom Special Forces had absolutely no control.

"I'm not about to get involved trying to *sell* anything to those paper-pushing bastards," Dr. Casey had said. "What I'm going to do is *give* you the stuff and charge it off to R&D."

General McNab was never one to pass up an opportunity, and asked, "It sounds like a great idea. How would you suggest we get started?"

Dr. Casey had then jerked his thumb at General McNab's aide-de-camp, Second Lieutenant C. G. Castillo, who had met Dr. Casey's Lear at Pope AFB.

Because General McNab had better things to do with his time than entertain some [expletive deleted] civilian with friends in the [expletive deleted] U.S. Senate any further than buying the [expletive deleted] lunch, Lieutenant Castillo had taken Dr. Casey on a helicopter tour of Fort Bragg and Fayetteville, North Carolina, until lunchtime.

By the time they landed on the Officers' Club lawn, Dr. Casey had learned the young officer had earned both the pilot's wings and Combat Infantry Badge sewn to his BDU jacket and decided he was one tough and smart little son-ofabitch.

"What about me taking the boy wonder here back to Vegas with me after lunch? He can see what we have and what you need, and we can wing it from there."

"Charley," General McNab had ordered Lieutenant Castillo, "go pack a bag. And try to stay out of trouble in Las Vegas."

"Aloysius had this put in?" Castillo asked, picking up the handset.

"You're not listening, Colonel, sir," Dick Miller said. "Aloysius put it in with his own freckled fingers."

"White House," the handset announced.

"Jesus!" Castillo said.

"I'm afraid he's not on the circuit," the White House operator said. "Anyone else you'd like to speak to?"

"This line is secure?" Castillo asked, doubtfully.

"This line is secure."

"I'll be damned!"

"If you keep up the profanity, you probably will be, Colonel."

"How do you know I'm a Colonel?" Castillo said.

"Because this link is listed as Colonel Castillo's Mobile One," the operator said, "and because the voice identification circuit just identified you as Colonel Castillo himself."

"I will be damned."

"It's amazing, isn't it?" the operator said. "And aside from Major Miller, you're the first call we've handled. Even my boss is amazed. Can I put you through to someone, Colonel? Or are you just seeing how it works?"

"Ambassador Montvale on a secure line, please."

"Montvale."

"Good evening, sir. Castillo."

"Didn't take you long to find a secure line, did it, Charley? You've been on the ground only twelve minutes."

"Well, I'm using the one in my Yukon."

"Then this is not a secure line?"

"The White House assures me it's secure, sir."

"In your truck?"

"Yes, sir. Don't you have a secure line in your vehicle?"

There was a pause, which caused Castillo to smirk at the mental image he had of the face that Montvale was now making.

"We'll talk about that when I see you," Montvale said. "How long is it going to take you to get to your Alexandria house?"

"Well, I think we can leave here in fifteen minutes or so. And then however long it takes to get to the house. I've never been there."

"Who's with you, Charley?" Montvale asked, and then before Castillo could answer, went on: "Bring everybody with you who might know something about the possible compromise."

"I gather that you mean, sir, to the house in Alexandria?"

"Are there any problems with that?"

"None, sir, except—"

"You and I are meeting with the President at eight o'clock tomorrow morning," Montvale interrupted. "I don't want to meet him unprepared. Any problems with that?"

"Inspector Doherty was just on the phone to his wife, telling her he'd be right home."

"Well, I especially want to see him. Have him call her back and tell her he's being delayed. I want everybody at your house."

"Excuse me, Mr. Ambassador, but isn't there an agreement between us that you don't give me orders?"

"For the moment, there is," Montvale said, icily. "Let me rephrase. I'll be grateful, Colonel, for the opportunity to meet with you and everybody with knowledge of the possible compromise at your earliest convenience. Say in approximately one hour in Alexandria?"

"I'll do my best to have everyone there as soon as possible, Mr. Ambassador."

There was a click on the line as Montvale hung up without saying anything else.

Castillo put the handset in its cradle.

"I didn't see Doherty using his cellular," Miller said.

"Either did I," Castillo said.

"You just like to pull the tiger's tail, right?"

"If I don't, Dick, I'd find myself asking permission to take a leak."

"Yeah," Miller said thoughtfully after a moment. Then he asked, "What has to go to the complex?"

"Not that much. One filing cabinet just about full of paper. And then a dozen external hard drives. What do I do about the weapons?"

"I'd take them to the house," Miller said.

"Okay," Castillo said.

"You heard all this, Stan?" Miller asked the Secret Service driver.

"Uh-huh. I'll take care of it."

"Somebody'll have to sit on the filing cabinet and the hard drives," Castillo said. "Unless we can get everything into the vault tonight."

"I think I'll have somebody sit on the vault, Colonel, after we get everything inside."

"Thank you," Castillo said.

[TWO]
7200 West Boulevard Drive
Alexandria, Virginia
2325 1 September 2005

The first impression Castillo had of the new property was that it was a typical Alexandria redbrick two-story home. The exception being, perhaps, the size of its lot; the front lawn was at least one hundred yards from West Boulevard Drive.

But his first impression changed as the Yukon rolled up the driveway.

Castillo saw that the rise in the lawn concealed both a circular drive in front of the house and a large area in front of the basement garage on the right. There was another Yukon XL parked there, and a Buick sedan, but there was still room enough for the three Yukons in the convoy to park easily.

The Yukon's probably Montvale's. He's too exalted to drive a lowly Buick, particularly since a Yukon with a Secret Service driver from the White House pool is the status symbol in Washington.

And if it is his, he's waiting for me in the living room, in the largest chair, finally having succeeded in summoning me to the throne room.

As the first Yukon reached the house, the triple garage doors opened one by one. The Secret Service driver of Castillo's Yukon drove inside the garage and the other two followed suit. The doors began to close.

The garage ran all the way under the house. There was room for three more Yukons. And some other vehicles. The walls were lined with shelves, and on them were old cans of paint, coils of water hose, and other things that people stored in garages.

Well, Miller told me that the kids of the people who owned this place had removed the valuable stuff.

Paint cans and water hoses don't count as valuable stuff.

There were two familiar faces standing at the foot of an extraordinarily wide basement-to-house stairway. One of them, a large, red-haired Irishman, was Secret Service Supervisory Special Agent Thomas McGuire, who had joined the Office of Organizational Analysis at its beginning. The other was Mrs. Agnes Forbison, a gray-haired, getting-just-a-little-chubby lady in her late forties who had been one of then–Secretary of Homeland Security Matt Hall's executive assistants and who also had joined OOA at its beginning. Her title now was OOA's deputy chief for administration.

Well, the Buick is probably Agnes's and the Yukon Tom's.

So where is the ambassador?

Castillo got out of the Yukon and walked to them.

He and McGuire shook hands. Agnes kissed his cheek.

"Montvale?" Castillo asked.

"I expect he'll be here shortly," Agnes said, and then, "Jesus, Mary, and Joseph!"

Max and Mädchen had been freed from one of the other Yukons and made right for them.

"This is Max and his lady friend, Mädchen," Castillo explained.

Agnes squatted and rubbed Max's ears.

"Pretty puppy," she said.

Mädchen shouldered Max out of the way.

"And you, too, sweetheart!" Agnes added, now rubbing Mädchen's ears.

Tom McGuire eyed both animals warily.

"Montvale's meeting us here," Castillo said.

"You didn't think he would be waiting for you, did you, Chief?" Agnes said, looking up at him, and then added, "We bought everything we could think of. Except, of course, dog food."

"If you bought a rib roast, that'd do," Castillo said.

Agnes stood up.

"You want a look around before the ambassador gets here?" she asked.

"Please," Castillo said. "How many beds do we have?"

"How many do you need?"

"That many," Castillo said, pointing to the others, who were now standing around the Yukons. "Less Doherty, who'll probably go home."

Agnes used her index finger to count Colonel Jake Torine, USAF; First Lieutenant Edmund Lorimer, USA; Corporal Lester Bradley, USMC; Sergeant Major John K. Davidson, USA; Colonel Alfredo Munz; Edgar Delchamps; Special Agent David W. Yung of the FBI; Sándor Tor; and Eric Kocian.

"Not counting Inspector Doherty," she computed aloud, "that's nine, plus you and Dick. That's a total of eleven. No problem. There's six bedrooms all with double beds. One of you will actually be alone."

"That would be me, madam," Eric Kocian announced, advancing on her. "The sacrifices I am willing to make to contribute to this enterprise do not include sharing a bedroom."

"Mrs. Forbison, Eric Kocian," Castillo said.

"I am charmed, madam," Kocian said, taking the hand Agnes extended and raising it to his lips.

From the look on her face—the pleased look—I think it's been some time since she has had her hand kissed.

"I hope you will not take offense, madam," Kocian went on, "if I say I have urgent need of a restroom, preferably one inside?"

"We'll put you in my room, Billy," Castillo said. "I'll bunk with Miller."

"Splendid!" Kocian said.

"Has this place got a fenced backyard?" Castillo asked.

"Uh-huh," Agnes said.

"If you'll show me that, I'll put Max and Mädchen out, and Tom can show the old gentleman to his quarters—"

"Old gentleman!" Kocian snorted.

"—and then we can get everybody settled in before we have to face the dragon."

Agnes's tour of the house ended in a small study. Bookcases lined three of its walls. A stuffed mallard and two stuffed fish—a trout and a king mackerel— were mounted on the remaining wall. There were a few books scattered on the shelves, mostly ten-year-old and older novels. Windows opened to the left and rear. Through it, Castillo saw that floodlights around a decent-sized swimming pool had been turned on. Max was happily paddling about in the pool while Mädchen stood on the side and barked at him.

The study was furnished with a small desk, a well-worn blue leather judge's chair, and a soiled, well-worn chaise lounge, none of which had obviously struck the heirs as worth taking.

There was a telephone on the desk, but Castillo didn't pay much attention to it until it buzzed and a red light began to flash on its base. Then he saw the thick cord that identified it as a secure telephone.

Agnes picked it up.

"C. G. Castillo's line," she said, then, "Yes, the colonel is available for Ambassador Montvale," and handed him the phone.

"Castillo."

"Charles Montvale, Colonel. We will be at your door in approximately five minutes."

"I'm looking forward to it, sir," Castillo replied, and then, when a click told him that Montvale had hung up, added, "about as much as I would visiting an Afghan dentist with a foot-powered drill."

Agnes looked at him.

"I gather you're speaking from experience?"

"Painful experience," Castillo said. "With both."

"How do you want to handle this?"

"I will receive the ambassador in here, where he will find me carefully studying my computer, which I will close when he enters. Have everybody but Kocian, Tor, Bradley, and, of course, Lieutenant Lorimer in the living room. We'll have to bring chairs from the kitchen or someplace else for them, I guess."

The living room had a beamed ceiling, a brick fireplace, and hardwood floors. There were two small and rather battered carpets that the children of the former owner also had apparently decided were not of value to them. Marks on the floor showed where the valuable carpets had lain, and marks on the wall showed where picture frames had hung.

There were four red leather armchairs and a matching couch that also had apparently missed the cut, although they looked fine to Castillo. Another stuffed trout was mounted above the fireplace, and there was some kind of animal hoof—maybe an elk's, Castillo guessed—converted into an ashtray that sat on a heavy and battered coffee table scarred with whiskey glass rings and cigarette burns.

Castillo had decided he probably would have liked the former owners. He was already feeling comfortable in their house.

"Ambassador Montvale, Colonel," Agnes announced from the study door five minutes later.

Castillo closed the lid of his laptop and stood up.

"Please come in, Mr. Ambassador," he said.

Montvale wordlessly shook his hand.

"I haven't had a chance to make this place homey," Castillo said. "The chaise lounge all right? Or would you rather sit in that?"

He pointed to the judge's chair.

"This'll be fine, thank you," Montvale said, and sat at the foot of the chaise lounge.

It was a very low chaise lounge. Montvale's knees were now higher than his buttocks.

"Getting right to it, Charley," Montvale said. "How bad is the compromise situation?"

"I think it's under control."

"I'd be happier if you said you're confident it's under control."

"*Think* is the best I can do for now. Sorry."

"Tell me what's happened, and then I'll tell you why it's so dangerous."

"We were all watching Hurricane Katrina on the television when Corporal Bradley marched in with a guy at gunpoint, a guy Max had caught coming through the fence—"

"Max?" Montvale interrupted. "Who the hell is Max?"

Castillo walked to the window and pointed.

Less than gracefully, Montvale got to his feet, joined him at the window, and looked out.

Max had tired of his swim, climbed out of the pool, and in the moment Montvale looked out, was shaking himself dry.

"You could have said, 'Our watchdog,' Charley," Montvale said disapprovingly. Then curiosity overwhelmed him. "God, he's enormous! What is he?"

"*They* are Bouvier des Flandres. There's a pretty credible story that Hitler lost one of his testicles to one of them when he was Corporal Schickelgruber in Flanders. It is a fact that when he went back to Flanders as Der Führer he ordered the breed eliminated."

"Fascinating," Montvale said as he walked to the judge's leather chair and sat down. "It is also a fact that when Hitler was a corporal he was Corporal Hitler. That Schickelgruber business was something the OSS came up with during World War Two. It's known as ridiculing your enemy."

"Really?" Castillo said, then thought: *You sonofabitch, you grabbed my chair! Well, I'll be goddamned if I'm going to sit on that chaise lounge and look up at you.*

Castillo leaned on the wall beside the window and folded his arms over his chest.

"Trust me," Montvale said. "It's a fact. Now, getting back to what happened after that outsized dog caught the guy . . ."

"He turned out to be an assistant military attaché in our embassy in Asunción, Paraguay. First Lieutenant Edmund Lorimer. Formerly of Special Forces, now of Intelligence. One of his pals, a DEA agent—"

"Name?"

"I can get it from Lorimer, if it's important to you."

"Lorimer? Any connection with our Lorimers?"

"Just a coincidence."

"Where is this chap?"

"Upstairs."

"Go on."

"Well, Lorimer is clever. He put together all the gossip, and when the drug guys kidnapped his DEA agent pal, he decided that Colonel Costello—getting my name wrong was about the only mistake he made—was just the man who could play James Bond and get back his pal. And he came looking for me. And found me."

"Charley, how would you go about getting this DEA agent back?"

"I don't know how—or if—that could be done. And I haven't given it any thought because it's none of my business."

"You have no idea how pleased I am that you realize that," Montvale said. "It is none of your business, and I strongly recommend you don't forget that."

Castillo didn't reply, but his face clearly showed that Montvale's comment interested him.

Montvale nodded in reply, indicating that he was about to explain himself.

"Senator Homer Johns came to see me several days ago," Montvale said. "The junior senator from New Hampshire? Of the Senate Intelligence Committee?"

Castillo nodded to show that he knew of Johns.

"He told me that the day before he had spoken with his brother-in-law . . ." Montvale paused for dramatic effect, then went on. ". . . who is the President's envoy plenipotentiary and extraordinary to the Republic of Uruguay, Ambassador Michael A. McGrory."

He paused again.

"I think I now have your full attention, Charley, don't I?"

Castillo chuckled and nodded.

"This is not a laughing matter," Montvale said, waited for that to register, and then went on: "There are those who think McGrory owes his present job to the senator. His career in the State Department had been, kindly, mediocre before he was named ambassador to Uruguay.

"The senator said he was calling to send his sister best wishes on her birthday. In the course of their conversation, however, the ambassador just happened to mention—possibly to make the point that there he was on the front line of international diplomacy, proving he indeed was worthy of the influence the senator had exercised on his behalf—the trouble he was having with the Uruguayan Foreign Ministry.

"Specifically, he said that shortly after a drug dealer, one Dr. Jean-Paul Lorimer, an American employed by the UN, had been assassinated on his estancia, the deputy foreign minister had made an unofficial call on him, during which he as much as accused the ambassador of concealing from him that the assassins were American Special Forces troops."

"Ouch!" Castillo said.

"Indeed," Montvale replied. "According to Senator Johns, the ambassador proudly related how he had dealt with the situation. McGrory apparently threw the deputy foreign minister out of his office. But then Johns—the senator said his curiosity was piqued—had a chat with the Uruguayan ambassador here in D.C., who assured him Lorimer's murder had been thoroughly investigated by the Uruguayan authorities, who were convinced that it was drug related, as was the death of another American, one Howard Kennedy, who was found beaten to death in the Conrad Hotel in Punta del Este. The ambassador told the senator, off the record, that there was reason to believe Kennedy was associated with your good friend Aleksandr Pevsner, who he had heard is in that part of the world, and that Pevsner was probably behind everything."

"And what do you think Senator Johns believes?" Castillo asked.

"I don't know what he believes. I think he suspects that something took place down there that his brilliant brother-in-law doesn't know, something that the government of Uruguay would just as soon sweep under the rug. *And* I suspect that the senator would love to find out that the President sent Special Forces down there."

"He didn't. He sent me."

"That's splitting a hair, Charley, and you know it. The question, then, is is your operation going to be blown?"

"I don't think so—"

"There's that word 'think' again," Montvale interrupted.

"I don't *think* there will be any trouble starting in Uruguay," Castillo said. "The head of the Interior Police Division of the Uruguayan Policía Nacional, Chief Inspector José Ordóñez—I thought I told you this."

"Tell me again," Montvale said.

"Ordóñez was at the Conrad when we got there. He actually took us to see the bodies—"

"Bodies? Plural?"

"Plural. The other one was Lieutenant Colonel Viktor Zhdankov of the FSB's Service for the Protection of the Constitutional System and the Fight against Terrorism. Delchamps told Ordóñez who it was, and Ordóñez made the point that Delchamps was wrong, that Zhdankov was a Czech businessman. Quietly, Ordóñez said it would provide problems for him, and the Uruguayan government, if he had to start investigating the murders of a senior Russian intelligence officer and a man known to have close ties to Aleksandr Pevsner."

Now it was Castillo's turn to let what he had said sink in.

After a moment, Montvale nodded thoughtfully.

Castillo went on: "Ordóñez then said his investigation of the bodies at Lorimer's estancia had made him believe that it was another drug deal gone wrong, that he doubted that any arrests would be made, and that for all practical purposes the case was closed. He added that he thought it would be a good idea for us to leave Uruguay right then and stay away until all the, quote, bad memories, unquote, had a chance to fade."

"And you think he knows the truth?"

"The first time I told you about this—and now I remember when I did—I told you that he's a very smart cop and has a very good idea of exactly what happened. That's why I—here comes that word again, sorry—*think* that we're safe as far as Uruguay is concerned."

"And in Argentina? You left bodies lying around there, too."

"Munz says he *thinks* the Argentine government would like the whole business—Masterson's murder in particular, but what happened in the Sheraton garage, too—forgotten. Munz—and I remember telling you this, too—says he *thinks* the Argentine government is perfectly happy to chalk up the Sheraton shooting to drug dealers; their alternative being investigating what Lieutenant Colonel Yevgeny Komogorov of the FSB was doing with a Uzi in his hand when he got blown away in the garage. They couldn't keep that out of the newspapers."

Montvale considered that, grunted, and asked. "Where is Munz?"

"In the living room with the others."

"Delchamps, too?"

"You said 'everybody,' Ambassador."

"Let's go talk to them," Montvale said, and then, as if remembering Castillo didn't like being ordered around, added: "I'd like confirmation of what you told me, Charley. No offense."

"None taken."

"Or would you rather ask them to come in here?"

Castillo pushed himself away from the wall and gestured toward the door.

The battered coffee table in the living room now held a bottle of Famous Grouse, a bottle of Jack Daniel's, and a cheap plastic water pitcher, telling Castillo the odds were that he now was entertaining everybody with his liquor stock from his vacated suite in the Mayflower Hotel.

"Keep your seats, gentlemen," Montvale ordered somewhat grandly and entirely unnecessarily, as nobody in the room showed the slightest indication of wanting to stand up for any reason.

They all looked at him, however, as he scanned the room and finally selected the fireplace as his podium. He was tall enough so that he could rest his elbow on the mantel. He was seeking to establish an informal, friendly ambience. He failed. Everyone knew what his relationship with Castillo was.

"The situation is this, gentlemen," Montvale began. "Senator Johns has an inkling of what went on in Uruguay and Argentina. Colonel Castillo tells me that he doesn't think the operation has been compromised. I'm concerned about a possible serious embarrassment to the President, and therefore I'd like to be sure that it's not going to blow up in our faces."

No one responded.

"Mr. Delchamps? Would you care to comment?"

Delchamps took a healthy swallow of his drink.

"I vote with Charley," he said simply. "Thirty minutes after the kid marched Lorimer into the living room, Charley ordered the shutdown, and we were out of Argentina within hours. Charley ordered what I thought were exactly the right actions to shut the mouths of anyone else who might be theorizing. But shit happens. This may get compromised. I just don't think it will."

Delchamps looked at the others in the room, who nodded their agreement.

Montvale chuckled.

"Did I say something funny?" Delchamps challenged.

"Oh, no. Not at all," Montvale said quickly. "What I was thinking was it's really a rather amusing situation. What we have in this room are very skilled, highly experienced intelligence officers, enjoying the confidence of the President, who were nonetheless forced to shut down their operation—what did you say, you were 'out of Argentina within hours'?—because of one unimportant little lieutenant who had no idea what he was sticking his nose into. You'll have to admit, that is rather amusing."

No one else seemed to find it amusing.

Delchamps took another swallow of his drink, looked thoughtful—if not annoyed—for a moment, then shrugged his shoulders.

"Let me tell you about that unimportant little lieutenant, Mr. Montvale," he said, an edge to his tone.

"Please do," Montvale said sarcastically.

"Jack Doherty and I had a long talk with him on the trip from B.A.," Delchamps said. "It's not that he was running at the mouth . . . even willing to talk. What it was, Mr. Montvale, is that Jack and I, between us, have more experience pulling things from reluctant people than you are old."

Montvale's face showed no response to that.

"We started out to learn who he'd been running his mouth to," Delchamps went on, "and what he'd said. The first impression we got was that he had been listening, not running his mouth, and that was the impression we had when we finished. Right, Jack?"

"That's it," Doherty agreed. "He's one hell of a young man, Mr. Ambassador."

"Who talks too much," Montvale said, "and has come close to compromising your operation."

"Listen to what I'm saying, for Christ's sake!" Delchamps said.

"Just who do you think you're talking to?" Montvale demanded.

"Your name, I understand, is Montvale. Do you know who *you're* talking to?"

"I'll wager you're about to tell me," Montvale said, icily. "Something more, I mean, than that you're a midlevel officer of the CIA."

"I wondered how long it would take you to get around to that," Delchamps said. "Christ, you're all alike."

"Who's all alike?" Montvale challenged.

"What the good guys in the clandestine service call the 'Washington assholes,' " Delchamps said, matter-of-factly.

"I will not be talked to like that," Montvale flared. " 'Washington asshole' or not, I'm the director of National Intelligence."

Delchamps smiled. "You won't be DNI long if this Presidential Finding blows up in your face. The President will feed you to Senator Johns. The term for that is 'sacrificial lamb.' You, Montvale, not Charley. Charley is not fat enough to be fed as a sacrificial lamb to the Senate committee on intelligence. They like large, well-known sacrificial lambs for the headlines and sound bites with their names."

They locked eyes for a moment, then Delchamps went on, calmly, "As I was saying, it is my professional assessment, and that of Inspector Doherty, that

Lieutenant Lorimer did not, at any time, share with anyone anything that he suspected might be classified.

"What he did, as I said before, Mr. Montvale, was listen. And, with a skill belying his youth and experience, put together a rather complete picture of what Colonel Castillo has done in compliance with the Presidential Finding.

"And then he made a mistake, which, considering his youth and inexperience, is perfectly understandable. He's naïve, in other words. He believed that there had to be someone in the system somewhere who would really care about his pal Timmons and do the right thing."

"The right thing?" Montvale repeated, drily.

"Do something but wring their hands."

"Such as?"

Delchamps ignored the question.

Instead, he said, "Let me paint the picture for you, Mr. Montvale. The Paraguayan authorities notified our ambassador that an embassy vehicle had been found parked against the fence surrounding Silvio Pettirossi International Airport, directly across the field from the terminal building.

"In the backseat of the SUV, on the floor, was the body of one Franco Julio César, thirty-nine years old, a Paraguayan national, employed as a chauffeur by the U.S. embassy. El Señor César was dead of asphyxiation, caused by a metallic garrote having been placed around his neck by party or parties unknown—"

"This guy had been garroted?" Castillo interrupted. "A *metal* garrote?"

"Yeah, Ace, that's what the Paraguayan cops reported," Delchamps said.

"Is that of some significance?" Montvale asked.

Delchamps ignored him again.

"A check of embassy records revealed that Señor César had been dispatched to drive Special Agent Byron J. Timmons, Jr., of the DEA to the airport. Nothing was known of Agent Timmons at that time.

"Late the next morning, however, a motorcycle messenger delivered an envelope to the embassy, which contained a color photograph of Special Agent Timmons. It showed him sitting in a chair, holding a copy of that day's *Ultima Hora*, one of the local newspapers. There were four men, their faces concealed by balaclava masks, standing with Special Agent Timmons. One of them held the tag end of a metallic garrote which was around Timmons's neck—one yank on that, and he'd wind up like el Señor César."

"Sonofabitch!" Castillo muttered.

"There was no message of any kind," Delchamps went on. "At this point, the senior DEA agent in charge summoned Lieutenant Lorimer to his office.

When Lorimer got there he found the consul general, who Lorimer suspected was in fact the CIA station chief, and the legal attaché.

"They asked Lieutenant Lorimer, who was known to be Timmons's friend and who occupied an apartment immediately next to Timmons's, if he had any idea who might have kidnapped Special Agent Timmons.

"To which Lorimer replied, 'Gypsies? You know—blasphemy omitted—well who kidnapped him,' or words to that effect, and then asked, 'So what are we going to do about getting him back?'

"To which the CIA station chief replied, 'The matter is, of course, being handled by the Paraguayan Capital Police Force, which has promised to notify us promptly of any developments, and there is every reason to believe that Timmons will be ultimately freed.' Or words to that effect.

"To which Lieutenant Lorimer replied, 'As a—blasphemy deleted—junkie you mean, providing we don't do our—blasphemy deleted—job.' At which point, after being admonished to get his emotions under control and ordered not to discuss the kidnapping with anyone, Lorimer was dismissed. And so he went looking for Colonel Costello, in the belief that this Costello was not your typical candy-ass."

"Ed, what's that about 'as a junkie'?" Castillo asked.

"Well, Ace, according to Lorimer—and Doherty agrees with me that Lorimer probably isn't making this up—the way things work down there—there have been four other kidnappings Lorimer says he knows about—what the bad guys do is snatch a DEA guy—or an FBI guy or a DIA guy—then let the embassy know he's alive. If shortly thereafter some heavy movement of cocaine goes off all right, they turn him loose. Payment for everybody looking the other way."

"But what's with the 'junkie'?" Castillo pursued.

"I'm getting to that. To show their contempt for gringos generally, and to keep their prisoner captive and quiet, by the time they turn him loose, his arm is riddled with needle tracks. He's lucky to have a vein that's not collapsed. They've turned him into a coke—sometimes a crack—junkie."

Castillo shook his head in amazement.

"And if their movement of drugs is interdicted?" he asked softly.

"According to Lorimer, there have been four kidnappings of DEA agents in Paraguay since he's been there—five, counting Timmons. Three have been turned loose, full of drugs. One was found dead of an overdose, shortly after about five hundred kilos—more than half a ton—of refined coke was grabbed in Argentina on a fruit boat floating down the Paraguay River."

"Not garroted?" Castillo asked.

Delchamps shook his head.

"Full of cocaine," he said.

"What happens to the ones who are turned loose?"

"They are quietly given the best medical attention available for drug addiction," Delchamps said, " 'in anticipation of their return to full duty.' " He paused. "Want to guess how often that works?"

"Probably not very often," Ambassador Montvale said.

"And that doesn't bother you?" Castillo snapped.

"Of course it bothers me."

"But we have to look at the big picture, right?" Delchamps said, sarcastically. "DEA agents know their duties are going to place them in danger?"

Montvale nodded.

He said, "How likely do you think it is that this DEA agent—"

"His name is Timmons," Delchamps said.

"Very well," Montvale replied. "How likely do you think it is that *Special Agent Timmons*—and every other DEA agent, DIA agent—Lieutenant Lorimer, for example—and CIA officer in the embassy in Asunción volunteered for the assignment?"

Delchamps looked at him for a moment, then said, "And that means Lorimer is an unimportant little lieutenant, and Timmons is an unimportant little DEA agent, right?"

"That was an unfortunate choice of words," Montvale said, "but isn't 'important' a relative term? Which would you say is more important, Mr. Delchamps: preserving the confidentiality of the Presidential Finding, the compromise of which would embarrass the President and just about destroy the fruits of the investigation you and Inspector Doherty and the others are about to complete, or sending an unimportant little lieutenant to a weather station in the Aleutian Islands for a year or two to make sure he keeps his mouth shut?"

Delchamps didn't reply.

Montvale went on: "Or which would be less wise: to send Colonel Castillo and his merry band to Paraguay to take on a drug cartel, which could carry with it, obviously, the very real risk of compromising the Finding, and, in addition, render the OOA impotent, or letting the people for whom Special Agent Timmons works in Paraguay deal with the matter?"

"No one is suggesting that Charley's guys go rescue Timmons," Delchamps said. "We all know that wouldn't work."

"I'm glad you realize that," Montvale said.

"Lorimer is not going to be sent to the Aleutian Islands," Castillo said, "or anything like that."

Both Montvale and Delchamps looked at him, surprised that he had gone off on a tangent.

"What are you going to do with him, Ace?" Delchamps asked after a moment.

"The first thing that comes to mind is to send him to Bragg. Let him be an instructor or something."

"That'll work?" Delchamps asked.

"I think so."

"I don't think that's a satisfactory solution," Montvale said. "How can you guarantee he won't do something irrational at Fort Bragg?"

"I can't. But since the decision about how to deal with him is mine to make, that's where he's going. He may in fact be an unimportant little lieutenant in your big picture, but in mine he's a dedicated soldier who did exactly what I would have done in the circumstances."

"You told me something like that before," Montvale said. "You remember my response?"

Castillo nodded. "Something to the effect that his having done what I would have done made you uncomfortable. The implication was that I'm also a loose cannon."

"There is that matter of the Black Hawk helicopter you 'borrowed' in Afghanistan," Montvale said. "That might make some people think that way."

"Yeah, I'd agree with that," Delchamps said. "But on the other hand, the bottom line is the President doesn't think he is."

Montvale glared at him.

Delchamps went on: "I hate to be a party pooper, Mr. Montvale, but unless you want to kick the can around some more, it's now about one in the morning, and an old man like me needs his rest."

"Yes, and I would agree that we're through here," Montvale said. "Eight o'clock in the apartment, Colonel Castillo. Based on what you and these gentlemen have told me, I don't think we need concern the President that the Southern Cone operations may have been compromised, do you?"

"I don't *think* it has, or will be, Mr. Ambassador," Castillo said.

"Good evening, gentlemen," Montvale said. "Thank you for your time."

He nodded at all of them and walked out of the room.

[THREE]
The Breakfast Room
The Presidential Apartments
The White House
1600 Pennsylvania Avenue, NW
Washington, D.C.
0755 2 September 2005

The only person in the breakfast room when the Secret Service agent opened the door for Ambassador Montvale and Lieutenant Colonel Castillo was Secretary of State Natalie Cohen, a small, slight, pale-skinned woman who wore her black hair in a pageboy cut.

She was standing by the window, holding a cup of coffee, as she watched the Presidential helicopter flutter down to the lawn. When she saw Montvale and Castillo, she smiled, set her coffee cup on a small table, and walked to them.

"I was hoping I'd have a moment alone with you, Charles," she said, "so that I could ask you where our wandering boy was."

"Natalie," Montvale said, as the secretary of State walked to Castillo and kissed his cheek.

"Welcome home, Wandering Boy," she said. "When did you get back?"

"Last night, Madam Secretary," Castillo said.

"We have a little problem, Charley," she said.

"Yes, ma'am?"

"Katrina has put fifteen feet of water over Ambassador Lorimer's home in New Orleans," she said. "He and his wife are at the Masterson plantation—which is apparently just outside the area of mass destruction along the Mississippi Gulf Coast—and he called me to ask if I could give him the precise address of his late son's plantation—estancia—in Uruguay, at which he intends to live until he can move back into his house in New Orleans."

"Jesus!" Castillo said.

"When I told him I didn't have the address, he said that Mr. Masterson had told him that you know where it is, and asked how he could get in touch with you."

"At the risk of repeating myself, Madame Secretary," Castillo said, "Jesus!"

"May I reasonably infer from your reaction that there's a problem with this?"

"Yes, ma'am, there's a problem with that," Castillo said. "Why can't he just stay with the Mastersons?"

"That question occurred to me, too, but of course, I couldn't ask it. What's the nature of the problem?"

"What about the apartment in Paris?" Castillo said. "He inherited that, too."

"I suggested to the ambassador that he would probably be more comfortable in an apartment in Paris than on a ranch—an estancia—in Uruguay. His response to that suggested he's about as much a Francophobe as you are, Charley. He wants to go to the estancia and there's not much we can do to stop him. Except, of course, you talking him out of going down there. I asked you what the problem is?"

Castillo looked at Montvale, then raised his hands in a gesture of helplessness.

"Things happened down there, Natalie," Montvale said, "which suggested the possibility the Presidential Finding might be at risk of compromise. Castillo thinks, operative word *thinks*, that his shutting down his operation there has removed the threat. But Lorimer going down there would pose problems."

"Why, Charley?" the secretary asked simply. "More important, what things happened down there?"

"A too-clever young DIA officer assigned to our embassy in Asunción has pretty well figured out what's taken place down there," Montvale answered for him.

"Oh, God!"

"Castillo has brought this young officer back with him, and intends to send him to Fort Bragg in what I think is the rather wishful belief that there he will keep what he has learned to himself."

"I've also taken steps to shut mouths in Montevideo, Buenos Aires, and Asunción," Castillo said. "And I think the threat of compromise is pretty well reduced."

"Again the operative word is *thinks*," Montvale said. "Although I don't believe we should worry the President with the situation at this time."

"But Ambassador Lorimer going down there might change that?" she replied, and then, before anyone could answer, she asked, "Why, Charley?"

"There is a very clever Uruguayan cop, Chief Inspector José Ordóñez, who has figured out just about everything that happened down there," Castillo said. "I talked with him in Punta del Este, right after they found the bodies of Howard Kennedy and Lieutenant Colonel Viktor Zhdankov of the FSB beaten to death in the Conrade—a plush hotel and casino. He said he believed Kennedy was a drug dealer, and Zhdankov the Czech businessman that his passport said he was. And that the bodies at Shangri-La, Lorimer's estancia, including Lorimer's, were also the result of a drug deal gone wrong, and that he doubted if anyone would ever be arrested. And then he suggested that I leave Uruguay as quickly as possible and not return until, quote, the bad memories had time to fade, unquote. Which, of course, I did."

"And Ambassador Lorimer going down there would possibly pull the scab off this?" she asked.

Castillo nodded.

"There's more, Natalie," Montvale said. "Senator Johns came to see me, and implied that he thinks his brother-in-law the ambassador was kept in the dark about a Special Forces team operating in Uruguay."

"God!" she said. "How bad is that?"

"At the moment, under control. But if Lorimer goes down there . . ."

"If Lorimer goes down where?" the President of the United States asked as he walked into the breakfast room heading for the coffee service.

"Good morning, Mr. President," the secretary of State, the director of National Intelligence, and Lieutenant Colonel Castillo said almost in unison.

"Good morning," the President said as he poured himself a cup of coffee. Then he turned. "I'm especially glad to see you, Charley. You have this wonderful ability to show up at the exact moment I need you. When did you get back?"

"Last night, Mr. President."

" 'If Lorimer goes down there' what?" the President asked.

Natalie Cohen said, "Ambassador Lorimer's home in New Orleans is under the water, Mr.—"

"His and several hundred thousand other people's," the President interrupted. "My God, what a disaster!"

"—and he called me and asked for directions to his son's ranch in Uruguay in which, or at which, he intends to live until he can get back in his home."

"And that poses problems?"

"It may, sir," Montvale said.

"How bad problems?" the President asked.

"Not catastrophic, Mr. President," Montvale said, "but potentially dangerous."

"I can't imagine why the hell . . . yeah, now that I think about it, I *can* imagine why he'd want to go down there. Far from the mess in New Orleans, and it's cheap—right, Charley? —to live down there."

"Yes, sir, it is."

"If it's not going to cause catastrophic problems for us, I don't think it's any of our business what he does," the President said. "We have other problems to deal with. Aside from Katrina, I mean."

"Sir?" Natalie Cohen asked.

The President sipped his coffee, then said, "Two days ago, the mayor of Chicago called me. Now, I know you two are above sordid politics, but I'll bet Charley can guess how important Cook County is to me. Right, Charley?"

"I think I have an idea, Mr. President," Castillo said.

"And knowing that, you'll all understand why I responded in the affirmative when the mayor asked me to do him a personal favor."

"Yes, sir," the three said, chuckling almost in unison.

"And when I heard what favor he was asking, I was glad that I had replied in the affirmative, because it pissed me off, too. If I'd known about this, I would have taken action myself."

"Known about what, Mr. President?" Montvale said.

"You're the director of National Intelligence, Charles," the President said, "so I am presuming you (a) know what's going on in Paraguay and (b) have a good reason for not telling me about it."

"I'm afraid I don't know what you're talking about, Mr. President," Montvale said.

"You have any idea what I'm talking about, Natalie?"

"I'm afraid not, Mr. President."

"Well, then, let me tell you," the President said. "What the drug cartel down there has been doing is kidnapping our agents and then either turning them into junkies or giving them fatal overdoses of what we euphemistically call 'controlled substances.' Are you learning this for the first time, Charles?"

"No, sir. Of course, I'm aware of the situation—"

"Natalie?"

"I've heard of the abductions, Mr. President, but not about the . . . uh . . . business of making the agents drug addicts."

"Charley, are you learning this for the first time now?"

"No, sir."

"Why doesn't that surprise me?" the President said. "Sometime when we have time, Charles, we can have a long philosophical discussion of what the DNI should, or should not, pass on to the commander-in-chief, but right now all we have time for is dealing with the problem.

"I have come by my intelligence regarding this situation from His Honor the Mayor. It seems that his father, who was, you recall, His Honor the Mayor for a *very* long time, had a lifelong pal, one Francis "Big Frank" Timmons, who the current mayor told me his father said was one of the only two really honest cops in Chicago.

"The mayor told me that Big Frank Timmons called him and asked him for a favor. The mayor, who was bounced on Big Frank's knees as an infant and calls him 'Uncle Frank,' said 'Name it,' or something like that.

"Big Frank told the mayor that his son Byron—who is a captain on the Chicago Police Force—just had a visit from an official of the Drug Enforcement Administration, who told him that his son, Special Agent Byron J. Timmons, Jr., of the DEA, was missing from his assignment at the U.S. embassy in . . . whatever the hell the capital city is . . . in Paraguay . . ."

"Asunción," Castillo furnished without thinking.

The President's face showed that he was not very grateful for the information.

". . . and that the possibility he had been kidnapped had to be faced, although they had no proof of that."

Castillo exhaled audibly.

"What's with the deep breathing, Charley?" the President asked.

"Pardon me, Mr. President."

"What does it mean, Colonel?" the President demanded coldly.

"Sir, I don't know if the DEA man in Chicago knew this, but the embassy in Asunción knew the day after Timmons disappeared that he had been kidnapped. They sent a photograph of him, surrounded by men in balaclava masks, and with a garrote around his neck."

"How long have you known about this?" the President asked.

"That Timmons had been kidnapped, about"—he paused and did the arithmetic—"thirty-six hours, Mr. President. I learned about the photograph being sent to the embassy about midnight last night, sir."

"And you, Charles?" the President asked.

"I learned of this incident for the first time last night, Mr. President, when Colonel Castillo did."

"And you, Natalie?"

"I'm hearing about this man . . . Special Agent Timmons . . . for the first time now, Mr. President. I'm sure the embassy made a report. I can simply presume it never made it to my desk."

"I guess not," the President said. "Well, it seems that Special Agent Timmons wrote his grandfather—who bounced the mayor on his knee, you will recall—about what was happening down there. He said there have been four such kidnappings. His makes five. So neither he nor Captain Timmons was very much impressed with what the DEA representative had told them. The word they used to describe it, forgive me, Madam Secretary, was 'bullshit.' At that point, Big Frank Timmons called the mayor."

"Mr. President," Montvale said, "just as soon as you're finished with us, I'll get on the telephone to our ambassador in Paraguay."

"No, you won't, Charles," the President said.

"Sir?"

"What I told the mayor was that I have an in-house expert for dealing with matters like this, and just as soon as I could lay my hands on him, I was going to tell him that his first priority was to get Special Agent Timmons back from these bastards."

"Sir, you don't mean Charley?" the secretary of State asked.

"Natalie, who else could I possibly mean?" the President said. But it clearly was more a statement than a question.

"Mr. President," she said, "I don't think that's a very good idea."

"Your objection noted," the President said.

"Mr. President, with all possible respect," Castillo said, "I don't know anything about dealing with something like this."

"How much did you know about finding a stolen airliner, Colonel? Or a missing UN official?"

"Sir, with respect, I know nothing about the drug trade. . . ."

"I thought the way this works is the superior officer gives an order and the subordinate officer says, 'yes, sir,' and then does his goddamnedest to carry it out. Am I wrong?"

"Yes, sir," Castillo said.

"I'm wrong?"

"No, sir. I meant to say—"

"I know what you meant to say, Charley," the President said, and smiled. "And to assist you in carrying out your orders, the DNI and Secretary Cohen will provide you with whatever you think may be useful. As will the secretary of Defense and the attorney general. I will inform them of this just as soon as I can get to Andrews, where both are waiting for me. We're going to have a look at what Katrina has done." He paused. "Any questions?"

There was a chorus of "No, sir."

The President had another thought: "I'm going to call the mayor from Air Force One and tell him that I am sending you up there to talk to him and Big Frank and Captain Timmons and anyone else who needs reassurance that I'm doing everything in my power to right this wrong."

"Yes, sir," Castillo said.

"Wear your uniform," the President said. "I think they'll find that reassuring. My wife says you look like a recruiting poster in your uniform."

He gave his hand to Castillo, then walked out of the breakfast room with only a nod of his head to Montvale and Cohen.

"My God!" Natalie Cohen said when the door had closed after him.

Montvale shook his head, then walked to the window. Cohen followed him after a moment, and then Castillo did.

No one said a word until after the President had walked quickly across the lawn to the Sikorsky VH-3D and gotten aboard, and the helicopter had gone airborne.

"Colonel," Montvale said, breaking the silence, "by the time you return from Chicago, the experts on the drug trade will be waiting for you in your office. And I suggest you make the flight in my Gulfstream. You have just flown yours eight thousand miles. It—and you—must be tired."

"Thank you."

"Unnecessary," Montvale said. "While it might be a wonderful solution to this problem, if you were to crash and burn flying your own airplane, I fear the President would suspect I had something to do with it."

"I can't believe you said that, Charles," Natalie Cohen said, appearing genuinely shocked. She touched Castillo's arm. "Maybe you can reason with Ambassador Lorimer. I really don't think he should be going to Uruguay, especially now."

Castillo nodded.

IV

[ONE]
The White House
1600 Pennsylvania Avenue, NW
Washington, D.C.
0845 2 September 2005

"Madame Secretary, Mr. Director," the uniformed Secret Service man at the door to the north side drive apologized, "it'll be just a moment for your vehicles."

They had come down from the presidential apartment before the Secret Service agent on duty there passed word to the uniformed Secret Service agent in charge of the motor pool "downstairs" that they were coming.

"Not a problem," Natalie Cohen said. "Thank you."

Castillo had learned the cars would be brought to the door following protocol. The secretary of State was senior to the director of National Intelligence. Her armored Cadillac limousine would arrive before Montvale's black Yukon XL Denali.

And since I am at the bottom of the protocol totem pole, mine will arrive last.

If at all.

The secretary of State put her hand on Castillo's arm and led him outside, out of hearing of the Secret Service uniformed officer and, of course, DNI Montvale, who hurried to catch up.

"Charley," she said, "I'm going to do my best to talk him out of this. But I'm not sure I'll be able to."

Castillo nodded.

"Do I have to ask you to try hard not to make waves?"

"No, ma'am."

"Let me know what I can do to help."

"Yes, ma'am. Thank you."

Her limousine rolled up. A burly man—obviously an agent of the Bureau of Diplomatic Security, which protects the secretary of State—got quickly out of the front seat and glanced around carefully as he opened the rear for Cohen. He saw Castillo and eyed him suspiciously.

Castillo winked at him, which obviously displeased him.

Oh, for Christ's sake! What are the odds that somebody wanting to do her harm is going to walk out of the White House with her and the director of National Intelligence?

Montvale's Denali rolled up. Castillo saw his coming up the drive.

"I'll call the Eighty-ninth," Montvale said, "and tell them that you'll be using my Gulfstream."

The 89th Airlift Wing at Andrews Air Force Base provided the White House with its fleet of airplanes, including the two VC-25A Boeings that had the call sign of Air Force One when flying the President.

"I thought you were kidding," Castillo said.

"Not at all."

"Thanks just the same. I think it would be smarter if I used my own."

"My God, aren't you tired?"

"Exhausted. But not a problem. I'll just set the autopilot and the alarm on my wristwatch. Then I can sleep all the way to Chicago."

It took a moment for Montvale to realize his chain was being pulled. When that showed on his face, Castillo said, "I'd rather not have people asking, 'Who's the guy in the presidential G-IV?' But thanks anyway."

"My God, Castillo!" Montvale said, and got in the rear seat of his vehicle.

His Yukon rolled off, Castillo's rolled up, and Castillo got in the backseat.

"Where to, sir?" the driver asked.

"Why don't you move this thing so it's not blocking the door while I find out?" Castillo said, and reached for the telephone.

"White House."

"If you can guess who this is, can you ring my office?"

"Oh, you heard about the voice recognition, did you, Colonel?"

"God, ain't we clever?"

There was a chuckle, then Agnes's voice.

"Colonel Castillo's line."

"Good morning," Castillo said.

"How'd it go with the President?"

"Disastrously. Guess who's supposed to get that DEA agent back from the bad guys?"

"Oh, no!"

"Oh, yes. Is Tom there?"

"He's at your house. Or at the Alexandria Police Department on the way to your house. He wanted to keep them from getting curious about all the sudden activity at the house."

"Can you get him on the horn and ask him to meet me at the house?"

"Done."

"Thank you. I'll bring you up to speed later, Agnes."

"That would probably be a very good idea, boss."

The connection was broken.

"Home, James," Castillo regally ordered the driver, who smiled and shook his head as he put the Yukon into motion.

"We have a Secret Service radio in here, Colonel," he said. "I can probably get McGuire for you, if you want."

"Thank you, but no. McGuire's likely to cause me trouble, but he's too smart to argue with Agnes."

"Are you through, Colonel?" the White House operator asked.

"Can you get my house, please?"

A moment later, a male voice announced, "Colonel Castillo's line."

There was something about the less than vibrant timbre of the voice that gave Castillo pause. And then he understood.

Jesus, it didn't take them long to put Lester to work, did it?

"Colonel Castillo, Lester."

"Yes, sir, I know. There's a voice recognition system on this. Just as soon as you said, 'Colonel Castillo,' your name popped up."

"What do you think it would have done if I had said, 'Clint Eastwood'?"

"Sir, as efficient as this system seems to be, I think it would have reported, 'Colonel Castillo.' "

"Yeah, it probably would have. Is Major Miller around there?"

"Yes, sir. One moment, sir. I'll get him for you, sir."

A few seconds later, Miller came on the connection.

"Yes, sir, Colonel, sir?"

"Dick, two things. First, keep everybody there."

"Too late. Mrs. Doherty drove off with him right after you left."

"Damn."

"He lives near here. I have a number. Want me to get him back?"

"No. If I need him, we can call. Anybody else gone?"

"No, but the troops are getting a little restless."

"Well, keep everybody there. I'm on my way."

"Done. And?"

"And?"

"You said two things."

"Oh, yeah. See if Lorimer has a uniform. If he does, put him in it. And I'm presuming you brought mine from the hotel?"

"Freshly run one last time through their very expensive dry-cleaning operation. If I were to infer that the trumpets have sounded and that you and Peg-leg are about to rush to the sound of musketry, would I be close?"

"A lot worse than that. I'll explain when I get there."

As the Yukon turned onto West Boulevard Drive, a red light-emitting diode (LED) on the telephone began to flash. Castillo looked at it, wondered what it was, and had just decided it meant he'd better pick up the phone when the driver said, "I think you'd better pick up, Colonel. That's the White House calling."

Oh, boy, another friendly offer of help from Montvale!

"Castillo."

"I just talked to that man in Chicago," the President of the United States said. "Timmons's family will be expecting you."

"Mr. President, I'm on my way to pack my bag."

"Reassure the family, Charley, that's the important thing. Make them understand the situation is under control. Get the mayor off my back."

In other words, lie through my teeth.

The situation is anything but under control.

"I'll do my best, sir."

"I've got a number for you to call. Got a pencil?"

"Just a moment, please, sir."

He furiously patted his pockets until he felt a ballpoint pen, dug it out, and knocked the cap off.

"Ready, sir."

Charley wrote the number the President gave him on the heel of his left hand.

"Got it, sir."

The President made him read it back.

"Right," the President said. "Let me know how it goes, Charley."

"Yes, sir."

"Good man!"

The line went dead.

"I don't suppose you've got a piece of paper, do you?" Charley asked the driver.

"There's a clipboard with a pad and a couple of ballpoints on a chain on the back of the other seat, Colonel."

Castillo looked. There was.

"Shit," he muttered.

He took the clipboard, wrote the number on the pad, tore the sheet off, and put it in his pocket. He then tried to erase the number from the heel of his hand with his handkerchief. He couldn't even smear it.

"Shit," he said again.

[TWO]
7200 West Boulevard Drive
Alexandria, Virginia
1005 2 September 2005

"You're dangerous, Charley," Colonel Jake Torine said after Castillo had related what had happened in the presidential apartment. "If I could figure out how, I'd get and stay as far away from you as possible."

Castillo raised an eyebrow. "It's damn sure not intentional. And whatever you do, don't call me Magnet Ass."

"Why not?"

"That one's been taken a long time, by one of you Air Force types. Fred Platt flew forward air controller covert ops over Laos as a Raven. He earned the name Magnet Ass drawing fire in supposedly unarmed Cessnas—0-1 Bird Dogs—and damn near anything else with wings."

"Platt? Didn't we just call him for—?"

"Yeah," Castillo interrupted before he could say anything more, "yeah, we did."

"I ask this because I don't know anything about the drug trade," Edgar Delchamps said, "and also because I am much too old to play John Wayne, but wouldn't I be of more use here working on the oil-for-food maggots?"

"No question about it," Castillo said. "It never entered my mind to bring you or Doherty in on this."

"Next question," Delchamps said. "Do I get to live here?"

"For as long as you want. The only thing I'd like you to do is keep an eye on Eric Kocian and Sándor."

Delchamps gave him a thumbs-up gesture.

"A good spook always takes good care of his sources. You might want to write that down, Ace." He stood up and said, "It's been fun, fellas. We'll have to do it again sometime. Let's keep in touch."

And then he walked out of the living room.

"What about me, Karl?" Alfredo Munz asked.

"I brought you along so you could be with your family and take them home," Castillo said. "But having heard all this, how would you feel about coming to work for us? We could really use you."

Munz didn't reply, and seemed uneasy.

"What is it, Alfredo?"

"I need a job," Munz said. "As much as I would like to do whatever I can to help you, I just can't support my family on my SIDE pension."

"I told you a long time ago we'd take care of you," Castillo said. "So that's not a problem. You've been on the payroll of the Lorimer Charitable & Benevolent Trust as a senior consultant ever since we took that chopper ride to Shangri-La."

"Why do I suspect you are lying, my friend?"

"Because I am," Castillo said. "But the only reason you haven't been on the payroll is because I'm stupid. You may have noticed."

"No," Munz said, emotionally. "The one thing you are not is stupid."

"Well, I *have* noticed, Colonel," Miller said. "I've known him a long time. And with that in mind, I brought the question up to Mrs. Forbison—you met her last night?"

Munz nodded.

"And Agnes decided that since you are, or at least were, a colonel, we should bring you on board as a Lorimer Charitable & Benevolent Trust LB-15, which is the equivalent of a GS-15 in the Federal Service. And, according to Army Regulation 210-50, a GS-15 is regarded as the equivalent of a colonel. The pay is $89,625 a year to start. Would that be satisfactory to you?"

"You are fooling with me, right?"

"Not at all."

"That much? My God, that's two hundred and seventy thousand pesos!"

Castillo thought, surprised: *Miller isn't just making all that up. He and Agnes have given this thought, done the research, and come up with the answer.*

"The Internal Revenue Service will take their cut, of course," Miller said. "But that's the best we can do."

"I don't know what to say," Munz said.

" 'Yes' would work," Castillo said.

"If I retire, Charley," Torine said, "will you hire me?"

"If you're serious, Jake, sure," Castillo said.

"Let me give that some thought," Torine said seriously.

"I myself go on the payroll the first of October," Miller said, "as an LB-12, at $64,478 per annum."

Oh, God, that means they're physically retiring him. Involuntarily.

"Sorry you took a hit. So long, and don't let the doorknob hit you on the ass on your way out."

"What's that 'LB' business?" Castillo asked.

"Lorimer Bureaucrat," Miller said. "An LB-12 is equivalent to a major and a GS-12." He looked at Castillo. "After I gnashed my teeth in agony while rolling around on the floor at Walter Reed begging for compassion, the Medical Review Board gave me a seventy-percent disability pension. Permanent."

"You all right with that?" Castillo asked softly.

"I'd rather have my knee back," Miller said. "But with my pension and my salary as an LB-12, I'll be taking home more than you do. Yeah, I'm all right with it. And somebody has to cover your back, Colonel, sir."

"I hate to tell you this, but I already have a fine young Marine NCO covering my back."

"Don't laugh, Charley," Torine said, chuckling.

"I'm not laughing at all; I owe him," Castillo said. He paused, then said, "Well, before we went off on this tangent, Jake was saying something about me being dangerous."

"And I wasn't joking, either. Only you could get us into something like this. You *are* dangerous."

"I thank you for that heartfelt vote of confidence," Castillo replied. "And moving right along, what shape is the airplane in?"

"If you had read the log, First Officer, you would know that we're pretty close to a hundred-hour."

"Jesus!"

"Not a major problem," Torine said. "We can get it done when we're in Vegas."

" 'When we're in Vegas'?" Castillo parroted, incredulously. "You want to tell me about Vegas?"

"I guess I didn't get around to mentioning that," Miller said.

Castillo looked at him.

Miller explained: "Aloysius is going to replace the avionics in the G-Three. The communications and global positioning portions thereof. Plus, of course, a secure phone and data link."

"You told him about the Gulfstream?"

"Hey, he's one of us."

He's right. He just told Casey we have the Gulfstream, not how we use it.

And Casey really is one of us, and knows we're not using it to fly to the Bahamas for a little time on the beach.

"Point taken," Castillo said.

"Signature Flight Support's got an operation at McCarran," Torine said. "I called them—in Baltimore—this morning, and got them to agree to tell the people in Vegas to do the hundred-hour in the AFC hangar. Somehow I suspected we were going to need the airplane sooner than anyone thought. Wrong move?"

"No. Just something else that comes as a surprise," Castillo said. "Okay, how about this? We go to Chicago and 'assure the family,' and then we go to Midland and either leave Alfredo there or—why not?—pick up Munz's wife and daughters and take everybody to Las Vegas. We get the avionics installed and the hundred-hour done. How long is that service going to take?"

"Twenty-four hours, maybe forty-eight. It depends on (a) what they turn up in the hundred-hour and (b) how long it takes Casey's people to install the avionics."

"Not long, I would think," Miller said, "as I suspect we can count on Aloysius either putting it in himself or standing over whoever else does."

"If it takes more than forty-eight hours, I'll just go to New Orleans commercial to try to talk the ambassador out of going to Shangri-La."

"Where the hell have you been, Charley?" Torine asked. "Louis Armstrong is closed to all but emergency traffic—they're picking people off the roofs of their houses with choppers, using Louis Armstrong as the base. And Lakefront is under fifteen feet of water."

"Keesler?" Castillo asked.

"Wiped out."

"Okay. Moving right along, if they can't do the airplane in forty-eight hours,

I'll go to Atlanta commercial and then Fort Rucker and borrow something with revolving wings and fly that to Masterson's plantation."

"That may not work, either," Miller said.

"Hey, I'm drunk with the power I've been given. You were awake, weren't you, when I said the President said he was going to tell the secretary of Defense to give me whatever I think I need."

"That presupposes Rucker has a chopper to loan you," Miller said. "I suspect that their birds are among those picking people off rooftops in New Orleans."

"Then I'll rent one in Atlanta."

"Same reply," Miller said.

"I think they'd loan you a helicopter at Rucker, Charley," Torine said, "even if they had to bring it back from picking people off roofs in New Orleans." He paused. "You sure you want to do that?"

"No, of course I don't. Okay. So scaling down my grandiose ambitions to conform with reality, I'll fly to Atlanta, take a taxi to Fulton County, and rent a twin Cessna or something. That's probably a better solution anyway."

"It probably is," Torine agreed. "I just had another unpleasant thought. Even if Masterson's airstrip is not under water and long enough for us to get the Gulfstream in there, it's probably being used by a lot of other airplanes."

"Yeah," Castillo agreed. "Okay. Correct me where I'm wrong. The priority is to get to Chicago and, quote, assure the mayor, unquote. I suppose I could do that commercial. But we are going to need the Gulfstream, and with the hundred-hour out of the way."

"And, better yet, with the new avionics," Miller said.

"Right. We have enough time left to go to Chicago, then, with a stop in Midland, to Las Vegas, right?"

"Probably with a couple of hours left over," Torine said.

"So that's what we'll do. And wing it from there, so to speak," Castillo said. "Where's Lorimer? Does he have a uniform?"

"Upstairs and yes," Miller said.

"Okay. Everybody but Jake and Miller go play with the dogs or something while we deal with Lieutenant Lorimer," Castillo said.

Miller started to get up.

"Keep your seat, Dick," Special Agent David W. Yung said. "I'll get him."

"This is where I'm supposed to say, 'I'm perfectly able to climb a flight of stairs,' " Miller said. "But what I am going to say is 'You will be rewarded in heaven, David, for your charity to this poor cripple.' "

Tom McGuire came into the living room first.

"Agnes told me," he said. "Jesus!"

"I only took the job because I knew how you hungered to see the natural beauty and other wonders of Paraguay," Castillo said. "You okay to leave right away for three, four days?"

McGuire nodded and asked, "Where we going? Paraguay?"

"First to Chicago, then to Las Vegas. It's kind of iffy after Vegas."

"I am always ready to go to Las Vegas on a moment's notice, but what's going on in Chicago?"

Castillo told him of the President's call.

". . . And," Castillo finished, "I think a distinguished Supervisory Secret Service agent such as yourself can help reassure this guy's family, who are all cops."

McGuire nodded his understanding but said, "I think I should fess up right away, Charley. I have been successfully avoiding the drug business since I joined the service, and the only thing I know about it is what I read in the papers."

"I think, then, that this is what they call the blind leading the blind," Castillo said.

The door opened and a uniformed First Lieutenant Edmund Lorimer, Intelligence, U.S. Army, stepped in the room, came almost to attention, and waited.

Castillo thought he looked like a Special Forces recruiting poster, and remembered what the President had said about the First Lady saying that about him.

He's even wearing jump boots, Castillo thought, which triggered a mental image of a highly polished, laced-up Corcoran boot from the top of which extended a titanium pole topped by a fully articulated titanium knee.

"Good morning, Lorimer," Castillo said. "Come on in and sit down. We don't do much standing at attention or saluting around here."

"Good morning, sir. Thank you, sir."

"Colonel Torine you know, and Major Miller. This is Supervisory Special Agent Tom McGuire of the Secret Service."

McGuire wordlessly offered Lorimer his hand.

"Before these witnesses, Lorimer," Castillo said formally, "I am going to tell you—again—that anything you see, hear, or surmise here, or at any place at any time about what we're doing or have done, or plan to do, is classified Top Secret Presidential. Is that clear in your mind?"

"Yes, sir."

"Any questions about that?"

"No, sir."

"The President of the United States has tasked the Office of Organizational Analysis, under the authority of an existing Presidential Finding, with freeing Special Agent Timmons from his kidnappers," Castillo said.

"Jesus H. Christ!" Lorimer exclaimed. "Wonderful! Colonel, I don't know how to thank you!"

Castillo looked at him coldly until Lorimer's face showed that he understood that his response had not been welcomed.

"If you have your emotions under control, Lieutenant, I will continue with the admonition that any further emotional outbreaks will not be tolerated."

"Yes, sir. Sorry, sir. It won't happen again."

"Lorimer, to clear the air, have you ever been given an order that you were sure you were not equipped to carry out?"

"Yes, sir."

"And what did you do when you were given an order you knew you were not equipped to carry out?"

"Sir, I told him I didn't know how to do what he was ordering me to do."

"And then?"

"And then I tried to do it."

"Were you successful in carrying out the order?"

"No, sir. I wasn't. But I tried."

"That's the situation here, Lorimer. We have been given an order that is in our judgment beyond our ability to carry out. But we are going to try very hard to obey that order. You have absolutely no reason, therefore, to thank me. Clear?"

"Yes, sir."

"So long as you remain useful—and, more important, cause me and OOA no trouble of any kind—I am going to permit you to participate in this operation."

"Yes, sir. Thank you, sir."

"To say this is probationary would be an understatement. There will be no second chances. Phrased another way, Lieutenant, you fuck up once and you're dead meat. Clear?"

"Yes, sir."

"We are going to Chicago just as soon as I can change into uniform. Our mission, at the personal order of the President, is to assure Timmons's family that everything possible is being done to get him back. Since I don't have a clue about how to get him back, that's probably going to be difficult. One thing we can do, however, is produce you."

"Sir?"

"With a little bit of luck, they'll know who you are, that you were Timmons's buddy."

"Timmons's family knows who I am, sir."

"Then they'll probably believe you when you tell them what happened down there."

"I think they will, sir."

"On the other hand, they may suspect we're blowing smoke. 'What's this guy doing up here when he should be in Asunción looking for . . .' "

"Byron, sir," Lorimer furnished. "His name is Byron Timmons, same as his father."

"In any event, while you are delivering the after-action report, you will look at me every two seconds. If I shake my head slightly, or if you *think* I'm shaking my head, you will stop in midsentence and change subjects. Clear?"

"Yes, sir."

"Timmons's family will certainly have questions. Before you answer any question, you will look at me to see if I shake my head or nod. If I shake my head, your answer to that question will be something intended to assure them. It doesn't have to be true. You understand?"

"Yes, sir."

"If you cannot carry out this instruction satisfactorily, Lorimer, I will conclude that you will not be of any value to this operation and we'll drop you off at Fort Bragg on our way back here. Clear?"

"Yes, sir."

"Are you packed?"

"No, sir. I sort of thought I'd be staying here."

"Go pack. You may well not be coming back here. When you're packed, put your bag in my Denali and wait there."

"Yes, sir," Lorimer said. He stood up and walked—with a just-noticeable limp—out of the living room, closing the door after himself.

As soon as it had closed, Miller said, "I'd forgotten what a starchy prick you can be, Charley."

"My sentiments exactly," Torine said. "What were you trying to do, Charley, make that kid hate you? Couldn't you have cut him some slack?"

"I was actually paying him a compliment, Jake," Castillo said. "And thank you for *that* vote of confidence."

"Compliment?"

"Pegleg is obviously as bright as they come; at least as smart as I am. Before I called him in here, I gave a lot of thought to how I should treat someone I admire, and who is probably as dangerous as you say I am. If that offended you two . . ."

"Okay," Torine said. "You're right. He reminds me of a lot of fighter pilots I've known."

"I would agree with that, Jake, except I'm pretty sure Lorimer can read and write."

Torine gave Castillo the finger.

Castillo took a small sheet of notebook paper from his pocket.

"Call that number, please, Jake, and tell them when we're going to be in Chicago, and how we can get from which airport to where we're going."

"They used to have a nice little airport downtown, right beside the lake," Torine said. "Meigs Field. Supposed to be one of the busiest private aviation fields in the world. But the mayor wanted a park there, so one night he sent in bulldozers and they cut big Xs on the runways."

"Really?" Miller asked.

"Yeah. There were a dozen, maybe more, light planes stranded there. They were finally allowed to take off from the taxiways. And the mayor got his park. He's . . ."

"Formidable?" Miller suggested.

"In spades," Torine said.

[THREE]
Atlantic Aviation Services Operations
Midway International Airport
Chicago, Illinois
1425 2 September 2005

"There's a guy walking toward us, Tom," Castillo said, as he tripped the stair-door lever in the Gulfstream III.

"I saw him."

"Looks like an Irish cop. You want to deal with him?"

McGuire gave Castillo the finger, then pushed himself off the couch on which he'd ridden—slept—from Baltimore, and walked to the door.

The man, a stocky six-footer with a full head of red hair, came up the stair as soon as it was in place.

"I'm Captain O'Day," he announced, as if supremely confident that no one could possibly mistake him for, say, an airline captain or anything but what he was, a Chicago cop. "I'm looking for a Colonel Costello."

Castillo came back into the cabin from the cockpit, and was putting on his green beret.

"Well, you weren't hard to find," O'Day said. "God, you've got more medals than Patton!"

Castillo shook his hand.

"It's *Castillo*, Captain."

"Sorry. You don't look like a Castillo."

"I'm in disguise. Say hello to another Texican, Tom McGuire of the Secret Service."

"If you're . . . whatever he said . . . McGuire, then I'm a . . ."

"Irish cop?" Castillo said, innocently.

"He's a real wiseass, isn't he?" O'Day asked, smiling.

"And he's barely warmed up," McGuire said.

"People are waiting for you. How many are going?"

"Five," McGuire said.

"I knew that. That's why I called for another car," O'Day said.

He gestured for everyone to get off the Gulfstream.

There were two cars, both solid black and brand-new, and looking like any other new Ford Crown Victoria except for little badges on the trunk reading POLICE INTERCEPTOR and, just visible behind the grille, blue and red lights.

"You can ride in front with me, Colonel," O'Day said. "I guess you're senior."

"Actually, Captain, the skinny guy's a full colonel," Castillo said. "But only in the Air Force, so that doesn't count."

"Go to hell, Costello," Torine said.

O'Day took a cellular telephone from his shirt pocket, pushed an autodial key, then after a moment said, "On the way. There's five of them. Maybe twenty minutes." He pressed the END key and put the phone back in his shirt pocket.

"How far is police headquarters?" Castillo asked, several minutes later.

"Why?"

"Isn't that where we're going?"

"No, it isn't," O'Day said, and changed the subject. "I'll forget what you tell me in thirty seconds. But what's the real chances of getting young Byron Timmons back from those bastards? And not hooked on something?"

"You heard about that, huh?"

"His father and I go back a long way," O'Day said. "He showed me Junior's letters. A good kid. I shouldn't have said that. *Young Byron's* a good man."

"All I can tell you is that we're going to try like hell," Castillo said. "With a little luck . . ."

"Yeah. I get the picture," O'Day said. "I was afraid of that. Thanks."

A few minutes later, Castillo realized they were not headed downtown. Instead, they were moving through a residential area, and he guessed from that that they were going to the Timmons home. Proof seemed to come several minutes after that, when they turned one more corner and then stopped before a simple brick house on a side street.

There was a police patrol car parked half up on the sidewalk, and three more cars—unmarked but rather obviously police cars—parked in the driveway beside the house.

"Here we are," he said. "I don't envy you, Colonel."

Castillo got out of the car and waited for the second car, which was carrying McGuire, Munz, and Lorimer. He wordlessly indicated that he and Lorimer would follow Captain O'Day up to the door and the others were to follow.

Before the door chimes finished playing "Home Sweet Home," the door was opened by a gray-haired, plump, middle-aged woman wearing a cotton dress and a pink sweater.

She looked at Castillo and then at Lorimer.

"You're Eddie," she said. "I've seen your pictures."

"Yes, ma'am," Lorimer said.

"Is it okay if I kiss you?" she asked.

"Yes, ma'am."

She hugged and kissed him.

"Honey," she called. "Junior's buddy Eddie is here."

A large man in the uniform of a police captain walked up to them and put out his hand.

"I'm Junior's—Byron's—dad."

"Yes, sir, I know," Lorimer said. "I've seen your pictures, too."

Captain Byron Timmons, Sr., looked at Castillo.

"Sir," Lorimer said, "this is Colonel Castillo."

Timmons crushed Castillo's hand in his massive hand.

"Colonel, I can't tell you how happy I am to see you," he said. "The President told the mayor that if anybody can get my son back from those bastards, you're him."

"I'm going to try very hard, sir," Castillo said.

"Well, just don't stand there in the door," Mrs. Timmons said. "Come in and meet the others. There's coffee and cake."

Captain Timmons took Castillo's arm in a firm grasp and led him through a short corridor to a living room. There were two women there, who looked like Mrs. Timmons, and half a dozen men, two in police uniform and four in casual clothes, who, Castillo decided, might as well have had POLICEMAN painted on their foreheads.

"This is Colonel Castillo," Captain Timmons announced. "The man the President says can get Junior back. The lieutenant is Eddie Lorimer, Junior's pal down there in Paraguay. I don't know who the others are. Colonel, what about identifying the others, and then I'll introduce everybody?"

"Yes, sir," Castillo said. "This is Colonel Jake Torine, U.S. Air Force, that's Tom McGui—"

"They've got their own Gulfstream airplane," Captain O'Day furnished.

"I wondered how they got here so quick," one of the cops said.

". . . Tom McGuire," Castillo went on, "who's a Supervisory Special Agent of the Secret Service, and this gentleman is Colonel Alfredo Munz, who before his retirement was Chief of SIDE in Argentina. SIDE is sort of our CIA and FBI rolled into one. Munz now works with us."

"I thought Junior was in Paraguay," one of the cops said.

"Paraguay and Argentina share a border, sir," Castillo said.

"Okay, now it's my turn," Captain Timmons said, motioning for Castillo to follow him to the people sitting on a couch, two matching armchairs, and two chairs obviously borrowed from the dining room.

"This is Captain, retired, Frank Timmons, Junior's grandfather, known as Big Frank."

"And I'm the goddamned fool, Colonel, God forgive me, who told Junior to go federal."

Castillo shook Big Frank's hand, then Lorimer and McGuire and Munz followed suit.

"And this is Sergeant Charley Mullroney, Junior's sister Ellen's husband— that's her over there. Charley works Narcotics on the job."

Castillo shook Mullroney's hand, then smiled and nodded at Mrs. Mullroney across the room.

"And this is Stan Wyskowski, of the DEA, Charley's pal."

"And I'm the guy who got Junior in the DEA, Colonel."

Castillo shook Wyskowski's hand.

Wyskowski, I admire your balls for being here. That has to be tough.

"And this is the mayor," Captain Timmons said.

Jesus H. Christ! I thought he was another cop-relative.

"The President speaks very highly of you, Colonel," the mayor said as he shook Castillo's hand. "I'm happy to meet you, and that you are here."

"An honor, sir," Castillo said. "I'm sorry I have to be here under these circumstances."

"Well, Colonel, I've always found the way to deal with a problem is get it out in the open and then start working on it."

"Yes, sir," Castillo said.

"And this," Captain Timmons said, moving to the third man on the couch. "is . . ."

Castillo shook that man's hand, but his name—or those of the others—failed to register in his memory.

His mind was busy thinking of something else. . . .

The mayor, who the President has made perfectly clear is to get whatever he wants from me, is not just doing a friend of the family a favor.

He's part of this family.

"And that's about it, I guess," Lorimer said when he had finished telling everybody what he knew of the situation.

He did that about as well as it could be done, Castillo thought.

"Would it be all right if I called you 'Eddie'?" Captain Timmons asked.

"Yes, sir, of course."

"That was a good job, Eddie," Captain Timmons said. "I don't have any questions. Anybody else?"

"I got a couple," Big Frank said.

"Sir?" Lorimer asked politely.

"That Irish Argentine cop, Duffy, Junior was on his way to see when these slimeballs grabbed him. Are there a lot of Irish cops down there? And is this one of the good ones? And what's the Gendarmería Nacional?"

Lorimer glanced at Castillo, who nodded just perceptibly.

"I know Byron trusted Comandante Duffy, sir," Lorimer said. "But maybe Colonel Munz can speak to that?"

"I know Comandante Duffy," Munz said. "Not well, but well enough to know that he's a good man. I haven't spoken to him since this happened, but he's about the first man I'm going to talk to when we get down there. I'm sure he's almost as upset about Agent Timmons as you are."

Big Frank nodded.

Munz went on: "So far as Irish people in Argentina, the ethnic mix in

Argentina—and Uruguay and Chile, but not Paraguay—is much like that in the States. My family came from Germany, for example. There are more people from Italy than from Spain. And many Irish. There are many Irish police, especially in the Gendarmería Nacional."

"Which is what?" Big Frank said.

"A police force with authority all over Argentina," Munz said. "They are a paramilitary force, more heavily armed than the Federal Police. They wear brown rather than blue uniforms, and enjoy the trust of the Argentine people."

"What does *that* mean?" Big Frank asked. "The other cops aren't trusted?"

"Can we agree, Captain, that dishonest police are an international problem?" Munz asked reasonably. "And that the problem is made worse by all the cash available to drug people? Or, for that matter, the criminal community generally?"

"I'd have to agree with that," the mayor said.

"Let me put it this way," Munz said. "When the Jewish Community Center was blown up in Buenos Aires several years ago—"

"Blown up?" Captain Timmons asked. "By who?"

"Most of us believe the Iranians had something to do with it," Munz said. "But the point I was trying to make was, when it became obvious that protection of synagogues, etcetera, was going to be necessary, the Jewish community—there are more Jews in Argentina than any place but New York—demanded, and got, the Gendarmería Nacional as their protectors."

"Meaning they didn't trust the other cops?" Captain Timmons asked.

"Meaning they trusted the Gendarmería more," Munz said.

"You're slick, Colonel," Big Frank said. "Take that as a compliment."

"Thank you."

"What was it you said you did for Colonel Castillo?"

"Whatever he asks me to do, Captain."

"Slick, Colonel," Big Frank said, smiling.

"Well, these bastards were waiting for Junior when he went to the airport, which means somebody told them he was going to the airport," Captain O'Day said.

"Or they set up their roadblock in the reasonable belief that some American agent was probably going to be on the Buenos Aires flight," Munz said. "It may have had nothing to do with Agent Timmons going to see Comandante Duffy."

"And your gut feeling?" Big Frank asked softly.

"That Agent Timmons was specifically targeted."

Big Frank nodded in agreement. Special Agent Timmons's mother inhaled audibly.

"Well, these bastards don't seem to mind whacking people," Wyskowski said. "They didn't have to kill Junior's driver, for Christ's sake."

This is going to drag on for a long time, Castillo thought, *and probably turn into a disaster.*

"They were sending a goddamn message, Stan—" one of the others, whose name Castillo had forgotten, began but was interrupted by His Honor the Mayor, who apparently was thinking the same thing Castillo was.

"Well, I think we've learned everything that's known," the mayor said. "My question is what happens next, Colonel Castillo? You're going right down there?"

"There are some things we have to do here first," Castillo said. "Ambassador Montvale, the DNI—"

"The what?" Sergeant Mullroney asked.

"The director of National Intelligence," Castillo replied. "He's going to have all the experts in this area—from the various intelligence agencies—waiting for us when we get back to Washington."

"Well, that should be helpful," the mayor said. "And with help in mind, Colonel, I thought Sergeant Mullroney, with his experience in Narcotics, might be useful to you, and I asked the commissioner to put him on temporary duty with you."

Oh, Jesus!

What's he going to be useful doing is keeping the family aware of how we're stumbling around in the dark!

His Honor apparently saw something in Castillo's face.

"I thought of that immediately after I last spoke with the President," the mayor said. "Do you have the authority to take him with you, or would it be better for you if I suggested this to the President?"

Talk about slick! No wonder he's the mayor for life.

"Welcome aboard, Sergeant Mullroney," Castillo said. "Glad to have you."

"I sort of thought that you'd have the authority," the mayor said. "The President told me that he places his absolute trust in you. So I told Charley to pack a bag—and his passport—before coming over here. So you're going right back to Washington?"

"No, sir. We've got to make a couple of stops first."

The mayor stood up, obviously to leave.

"Really?" he asked.

The translation of that is "And where are you going to waste time instead of getting to work on this immediately, as I expect you to?"

Oh, what the hell. When in doubt, tell the truth.

"Las Vegas, Mr. Mayor. The airplane needs some maintenance, and we're having radios installed that will permit us to communicate—securely—with the White House no matter where we are."

The mayor examined him carefully, then smiled.

"Just like Air Force One, huh?"

"Almost, Mr. Mayor."

"When my plane is in for work, it takes them forever and a day," the mayor said. "I suppose for you things go a little quicker, don't they?"

The translation of that is "And how long is that going to take?"

"They expect us, sir. They'll work through the night to get us out as quickly as they can."

The mayor nodded, then went through the room, shaking all the men's hands and kissing the women on the cheek. Then he walked out of the living room with Captain O'Day following closely.

Mrs. Timmons kissed Lorimer, then grabbed Castillo by both arms.

"I'll pray for you, Colonel, to get my son back soon. Before . . . before anything happens to him."

"Thank you. We'll do our best."

Then everybody shook hands with everybody else.

The mayor was standing on the sidewalk—surprising Castillo—when he and the others came down the stairs.

Castillo then thought he understood why when a black Lincoln limousine turned the corner.

"Oh, there it is," the mayor said, and turned to Castillo. "If there's anything you need, Colonel, give me a call. Sometimes—I'm not without influence—I can be helpful."

"Thank you very much, sir."

Captain O'Day opened the door of the limousine.

"You'll have to use the jump seats," the mayor said. "And someone will have to ride up front, but there'll be room for all of you." He nodded at the others. "It's been a real pleasure to meet all of you."

Then the mayor of Chicago got in the front seat of one of the black Crown Victoria Police Interceptors, and Captain O'Day drove him away.

[FOUR]
Pilots' Lounge
Atlantic Aviation Services Operations
Midway International Airport
Chicago, Illinois
1635 2 September 2005

Castillo motioned to Munz to come with him. They walked out of earshot of the others.

"I've just had more proof that I'm stupid, Alfredo," Castillo said.

Munz looked curiously at him but didn't reply.

"Would you really rather be with your family at the Double-Bar-C, or with us standing around a hangar in Las Vegas?"

"Wherever I would be most useful, Karl," Munz said in German.

"That's not what I asked."

"With my family."

"And not in Vegas?"

Munz nodded.

"That's what I thought. And I should have thought of it right away. That's what I meant by proof of stupidity."

"You have nothing else on your mind, of course," Munz said.

"So what we'll do is just drop you at the ranch and worry about getting together later. I wish you had one of our cellulars."

Munz reached into his jacket pocket and held up a cellular telephone.

"Miller gave me this," he said, "and this." He held up a thin sheaf of one-hundred-dollar bills held together with a Riggs National Bank band. "He said he's working on the credit cards."

"Make sure you get receipts for everything you spend," Castillo said. "Agnes flips her lid if you don't." He reached for the cellular. "Let me put your number in mine."

After he had done that, he started to push an autodial button on his cellular. He stopped and looked at Munz.

"And now for proof that I am an unprincipled sonofabitch, watch as I lie to my grandmother."

He pushed the autodial button.

"This is Carlos, Juanita," he said in Spanish a moment later. "Is Doña Alicia available?"

He turned to Munz. "She is, damn it."

"Abuela," he said a moment later. "You remember that story you told me about George Washington and the cherry tree?

"Well, neither can I.

"We're in Chicago. Alfredo Munz is with us.

"Yesterday.

"We're going to drop him off at the Double-Bar-C. And I can't do anything more than just that. I really can't. That's the George Washington So Help Me God Boy Scout's Honor Truth. I have to be somewhere else as soon as I can get there.

"I was afraid you'd ask. Las Vegas. But it's business. Believe me.

"Of course I'll have time to give you a kiss. We should be there in a little over two hours.

"I love you, Abuela," he said, and turned to Munz.

"Great lady," Castillo said. "She believed me. Didn't give me any static at all."

"So my wife says," Munz said. "I'm looking forward to meeting her."

Castillo pushed another autodial button, then the LOUDSPEAKER key.

"I want you to listen to this one. You should know about Aloysius Francis Casey."

"What?" a thin, somewhat belligerent voice demanded over the phone's loudspeaker a moment later.

"This is Charley Castillo, Dr. Casey."

"Ah, the boy colonel. How many goddamn times do I have to tell you to call me Frank?"

"Another couple hundred times might do it."

"I hear you're headed out here. When?"

"We're leaving in a couple of minutes—we're in Chicago—and we have to make a stop in Midland, Texas. Say two hours to Midland, and another hour and forty-five minutes to get from Midland to Vegas. We should be on the ground about twenty-thirty or thereabouts."

"Who's 'we'?"

"Jake, of course, and a young Green Beanie who took a pretty bad hit in Afghanistan. And Tom McGuire—"

"He gets a pass because he's a Boston Irishman. Who else?"

"How about a pass for a Chicago cop named Mullroney? He's Irish, too."

"Who the hell is he?"

"I'll tell you when I'm there. Could you get us rooms near McCarren?"

"You'll stay with me."

"There's five of us!"

"There's room. Tell me about the Green Beanie who took the hit."

"Rocket-propelled grenade. One of his legs is titanium from the knee down."

"He need anything special?"

"No."

"He's working with you?"

"Yes."

"I've been working on stuff to set off those goddamn IEDs before they can cause anybody any harm, but those goddamn RPGs . . ."

"Yeah, I know."

"Okay, I'll see you when you get here."

[FIVE]
Double-Bar-C Ranch
Near Midland, Texas
1845 2 September 2005

As the Gulfstream taxied back toward the hangar, Castillo saw four women standing by a silver Jaguar XJ8. Fifty yards away, near an enormous, slowly bobbing horse-head oil pump, several horses and maybe a dozen Santa Gertrudis steers stood watching.

There had been horses and Santa Gertrudis cattle grazing on the Double-Bar-C long before the first automobile had bounced over the West Texas prairie, and long before the first well had tapped the Permian Oil Basin beneath it.

The first time Castillo had been shown the ranch—he was twelve at the time—his newly discovered grandfather, Don Fernando Castillo, had told him, "We were comfortable, Carlos, before they put the first hole down. I often think we were happier—life was certainly simpler—before they found the oil."

And seeing the pump now, he had the same reaction to it he'd had to the first pump he'd ever seen:

Every time that thing goes up and down, it's fifty cents in his pocket.

And there're a lot of those pumps.

The only difference between then and now is that today West Texas sweet crude brings fifty bucks a barrel.

That, and Abuela left the Double-Bar-C to me.

The women waiting for the Gulfstream were Castillo's grandmother—his abuela—and Colonel Alfredo Munz's wife and two daughters.

The warmth of his memory of Don Fernando turned to cold anger with the sight of the Munzes . . . and the reason they were at the ranch.

Goddamn the miserable bastards who go after a man's family.

Munz's family had come to the Double-Bar-C because of a very real threat to their lives in Argentina.

"Wake up, First Officer," Jake Torine said. "We are, no thanks to you, safely on the ground."

Castillo unfastened his shoulder harness and went into the cabin.

Alfredo Munz was already out of his seat, waiting for the stair door to be opened. Castillo worked it, and then waved Munz off the plane first.

Castillo saw that Munz had not taken his suitcase with him. He picked it up and went down the stairs with it. He saw the younger girl running toward her father, followed by the older girl, and then, moving more slowly, Señora Munz. In a moment, Munz had his arms around all of them.

Castillo looked at Doña Alicia and saw that she had a handkerchief to her eyes.

And mine aren't exactly dry, either.

He went to his grandmother. She put her arms around him.

"Hey, Abuela, how's my favorite girl?"

"Very annoyed with you, as usual," she said, and kissed him.

She looked at the Munzes.

"How long is he going to stay?" she asked.

"Until I need him, and that will probably be soon. A couple days."

"And when will it be safe for his family to go back to Argentina?"

"Not for a while yet."

"And when are you going to come and stay longer than ten minutes?"

Divulgence of any detail of any operation conducted under the authority of a Presidential Finding to persons not holding the specific Top Secret Presidential security clearance is a felonious violation of the United States Code, punishable by fine and imprisonment.

"A drug enforcement agent in Paraguay has been kidnapped by drug dealers," Castillo said. "The President wants us to try to get him back, and I have no idea how to do that."

She looked at him but did not reply.

"I don't have to tell you to keep that to yourself, do I?"

She shook her head to show the admonition was entirely unnecessary.

"I don't know whether I'm very proud of you, my darling, or very sad for you," she said. "I guess both."

Five minutes later, the Gulfstream III broke ground.

[SIX]
McCarren International Airport
Las Vegas, Nevada
2055 2 September 2005

A tug stood waiting outside the AFC hangar, and as a ground handler signaled for Castillo's Gulfstream III to shut down its engines, the doors of the hangar began to slide open.

Inside the hangar, Castillo saw that a glistening new Gulfstream V, three older Lears, a Beechcraft King Air and an old but nicely refurbished Cessna 150 had been moved to one side to make room for his G-III.

And then he saw there was a Cadillac Escalade in the hangar. Dr. Aloysius Francis Casey, chairman of the board and chief executive officer of AFC, Inc., was sitting sideward in the driver's seat, the driver's door open. He was wearing his usual baggy black suit.

The tug hooked up to the nose gear of the G-III and dragged the aircraft into the hangar. Two men in white coveralls with the AFC logotype on the chest hooked up an auxiliary power cable.

Castillo opened the stair door and went down it, with Torine following.

Casey pushed himself off the seat of the Escalade and walked to them.

"How are you, Charley?" he asked, shaking his hand, then Torine's.

"Always good to see you, Colonel," Casey said.

"Always good to see you, too, Dr. Casey," Torine said. "And we really appreci—"

"Goddamn it! I keep telling you and the Boy Colonel here that it's Frank," Casey said. "I'm starting to get pissed off about that!"

"Sorry, Frank," Torine said.

Casey looked toward the men in coveralls and raised his voice: "Get the luggage off of that, and put it in my truck."

The men hurried to do his bidding.

Tom McGuire, Ed Lorimer, and, bringing up the rear, Charley Mullroney came down the stairs and somewhat hesitantly walked to them.

Casey put out his hand to Lorimer and said, "Any Special Forces guy is always welcome. My name is Frank Casey. Call me Frank. I did some time as a commo sergeant on an A-Team in 'Nam. Mostly over the fence in Laos and Cambodia."

"Yes, sir," Lorimer said.

"You call me sir one more time, and you can sleep on your airplane. Clear?"

"Yes, s— *Frank.*"

"You're learning," Casey said, then pointed his right index finger at Castillo and Torine. "Which is more than I can say for these two."

He turned to McGuire and Mullroney and said, "Usually I have as little as possible to do with cops, but since you two are Irish and with these guys you get a pass."

He shook their hands, then said: "Come on and get in the truck. We'll go out to the house and hoist a couple and burn some meat."

They had turned off U. S. Highway 93 a few minutes before, and were driving down a macadam two-lane road toward the mountains. Castillo, sitting beside Casey in the front seat of the Escalade, was wondering what electronics were behind the dashboard to power the two telephone handsets and a large liquid crystal display screen—now displaying the AFC logo and STANDBY—mounted on the dash.

Casey suddenly said, "Before we get to the house, I think I should tell you the wife passed. . . ."

"I hadn't heard that, Frank," Castillo said. "I'm very sorry."

"Yeah, well, we all have to go sometime, and, thank God, Mary Alice went good. She took a little nap by the pool and never woke up."

"I'm sorry, Frank," Castillo repeated.

"Me, too, Frank," Jake Torine said.

"Anyway, I got a couple taking care of me at the house. Good people, but you probably want to be careful what you say when they're around."

"Thanks," Castillo said, and then, as much to change the subject as anything else, asked, "What's this stuff?"

Casey looked and saw where Castillo was pointing.

"Oh, that stuff," he said, as if he welcomed the chance to change the subject. "The left handset is an encrypted tie to my communications. The right one, and the display, is pretty much what they're putting in your airplane."

"Is it working?" Castillo said.

"It damned well better be."

"I could get my office on that? The White House switchboard?"

"You can get anybody on your net but the White House," Casey said. "I didn't think I'd better put a link in there. When the new stuff is in the airplane, you'd be linked to the White House, just like your truck. But your office can patch you through to the White House."

I don't want to talk to the White House.

I want to talk to Nuestra Pequeña Casa. I really have to start things moving down there.

But is the radio still up? Or did Sergeant Kensington shut down when we left?

There's only one way to find out.

"Can I try it?"

"Help yourself."

"How does it work?"

"Pick it up, say your name, give it a couple of seconds for the voice identification to work, and then say who you want to talk to."

"There's an operator?"

"There's a little black box."

"And it's encrypted?"

"Not even NSA will know what you're saying."

Castillo picked up the handset. The AFC logo on the display screen disappeared, and then STANDBY went away. ACTIVATING appeared, and then ENCRYPTION ACTIVE, and then VOICE IDENTIFICATION ACTIVE and finally ALL FUNCTIONS OPERATIONAL.

"No more little green and red LEDs," Casey said.

"Clever," Castillo said.

"No recognition," a metallic voice came over the handset speaker.

"Jesus!"

"No recognition," the metallic voice repeated.

"Castillo."

"Go ahead, Colonel Castillo."

"Nuestra Pequeña Casa."

"No recognition."

"Argentina."

"No recognition."

"Safe House."

There was a moment's delay, then Sergeant Robert Kensington's voice came cheerfully over the speaker in the handset: "How's things in Vegas, Dr. Casey?"

"Colonel Castillo, Bob. How's things where you are? And where are you?"

"In the quincho, sir."

"I was afraid that all might be shut down."

"Mr. Darby decided it would make more waves if everybody suddenly vanished, so we're still here."

"Who's we?"

"The Sienos, Ricardo Solez, and me."

"Darby's at the embassy?"

"No, sir. He went to Asunción. He said if you called to tell you he and Tony Santini were going to make sure the cork was back in the bottle."

"We don't have a secure link to Asunción, do we?"

"No, sir. And Mr. Santini said not to send any messages unless we had to."

"What about Ricardo. Is he there?"

"He went grocery shopping in Pilar. I can get him on his cellular, if you want."

"No. Here's what I want you to do. Get through to Darby or Santini, and tell them the situation has changed. They are to stay there until Solez can get there to explain, and then to act accordingly. And then get Solez back from the supermarket, tell him we have been tasked to get back that DEA agent who got himself kidnapped, and to get on the next plane to Asunción to tell Darby and Santini. Nobody in the embassy there—*nobody*—is to be told about this."

"Yes, sir. Well, that's good news, Colonel. That DEA guy is a pretty good guy, according to Solez."

"It is the opposite of good news, Bob. I haven't a clue about how to get him back."

"You'll think of something, Colonel," Kensington said. "You always do."

Well, there's a vote of confidence.

The trouble is it's completely unjustified.

"And tell Solez to ask Darby and Santini, both, to get on a secure line to me as soon as they can."

"You're with Dr. Casey?"

"Right."

"Can I ask what you're doing, sir?"

"Drinking, gambling, and chasing naked women," Castillo said. "What else does one do in Las Vegas? Get right on this, please, Bob."

"I already have Solez on his cellular."

"Okay. Breaking down," Castillo said. He covered the mouthpiece with his hand and turned to Casey. "How do I do that?"

"Say 'Finished' or 'Break it down.' "

"Break it down," Castillo said.

"Disconnecting," the metallic voice said in his ear.

V

"Yeah, I know it's almost two in the morning back there," Sergeant Charley Mullroney said into his cellular phone. "I got a watch. This is the first chance I had to call."

He was standing on a small patio carved out of the mountain about fifty feet below and fifty yards from his room in the house. Small dim lights lined the path leading to the house and were mounted on a low stone wall at the edge of the patio.

He had peered over the edge of the wall. The lights didn't illuminate much, but there was enough light to see it was almost a sheer drop from the patio wall for at least fifty feet, and probably more.

"Not *in* Vegas, Byron. Maybe twenty-five miles outside of Vegas. On the side of a mountain—

"You want to keep interrupting me, or do you want me to tell you what happened?

"Okay. First we landed in the middle of nowhere where that German or Argentine or whateverthefuck he is colonel got off.

"No. There was no sign anywhere. This was a private field. I think Castillo's got something to do with it. He got off the airplane and kissed some old lady.

"Then we come to Vegas. They parked the airplane in a hangar and some little guy named Casey drove us out here in a Cadillac Suburban or whateverthefuck they call them.

"Did I learn anything on the airplane? No. McGuire, the Secret Service guy, did a pretty good job of pumping me to find out what I do on the job. But when I asked him, like, 'Where are we going?', or when we landed in the middle of nowhere, 'Where was that? What was that?', he turned into a clam. And when I asked him what he did for Castillo, he said, 'This and that.'

"Okay, so we got here and this Casey character brings us out here in his white Escalade—that's what they call those Cadillac Suburbans, *Escalades*—

"Great big fucking house on the side of a mountain. Great big fucking swimming pool. The room they gave me is about as big as my whole downstairs. Jacuzzi *and* a shower that's so big it don't even need a door. But the cellular says 'no signal,' so I couldn't call, so I figured I'd wait until later.

"So this guy Casey's got a barbecue set up. With a cook, and great big steaks. And enough booze to take a bath in. So Castillo cooks the steaks and they start in on the booze and I figure maybe now I'll learn something.

"Didn't happen. All they did was talk about the Army. The Special Forces. I don't know how much is bullshit, but this Casey guy, to hear him tell it, practically won the Vietnam War by himself.

"I don't know if they believed it or not, Byron. I think so, but nobody's going to call a guy a bullshitter in his own house. Especially since he's putting free radios in your airplane.

"Because Castillo told him he's got a bunch of money in something called the Lorimer Charitable & Benevolent Fund and can pay for them. Casey said, 'You know your money's no good here, Charley.'

"I don't know what Casey's angle is, and if there's any connection with this Lorimer Charitable Whatever and Junior's buddy Lorimer, I don't know what it is.

"Okay, so finally I said I had a long day and was going to turn in. So I went to my room and then out onto a little patio, whatever, outside it. You can see just about all there is to see in Vegas from there. And, for the hell of it, I tried the cellular again. I got maybe a bar and a half, so I see another patio down the mountain, about fifty yards from the house, walked to it, and the fucker works here. So I called you.

"Yeah, Byron, I know it ain't much, but you just got all I have.

"I have no fucking idea what's going to happen tomorrow. They don't pass out a schedule, for Christ's sake.

"Yeah, I'll call you whenever I have something."

Mullroney took the cell phone from his ear and looked at it.

"You sonofabitch," he said, "you hung up me!"

"Perhaps he didn't hang up on you, Sergeant Mullroney," Castillo said.

Mullroney jumped.

"Perhaps you just lost the connection," Castillo went on, evenly. "Cellulars are not very reliable out here."

"You scared me, Colonel," Mullroney said after a moment. "I didn't hear you come up."

I didn't scare you, I don't think.

But I think I embarrassed you.

"Was there something wrong with the telephone in your room, Sergeant Mullroney? Couldn't get a dial tone?"

Mullroney didn't reply.

"Or was it because you didn't want us to know you were making your report to Captain Timmons? Is that why you sneaked out here to use your cellular?"

Mullroney looked at him almost defiantly.

Not really "fuck you" defiant. He's worried.

Now let's see how far I can push him.

Castillo held out his hand and wiggled the fingers in a *Give it to me* gesture.

Mullroney looked at Castillo's hand and then his face and back at the hand.

"Give me the phone," Castillo ordered.

Mullroney looked again at Castillo's face, as if trying to understand.

So what do I do now? Try to take it away from him?

"Give me the phone," Castillo repeated.

Mullroney didn't move or respond.

"Give the colonel the fucking phone, asshole, or I'll throw you and it off the mountain."

The voice in the dark startled Castillo. He hadn't heard anyone walking up on them. He now saw that Lorimer was standing beside him.

"I'm not going to tell you again," Lorimer said.

Mullroney put the cellular in Castillo's hand.

Castillo threw it down the mountain.

"What the fuck?" Mullroney protested, incredulously.

"You are not permitted to have a cellular telephone," Castillo said calmly.

"Who the fuck do you think you are?" Mullroney demanded.

There wasn't much conviction in that indignation.

"The next time you say something like that to the colonel, I'm going to break your arm before I throw you down the mountain."

"Fuck you, soldier boy," Mullroney said.

Five seconds later, Sergeant Mullroney found himself on his stomach.

His arm was twisted painfully behind him, his cheek was pressed into the rough ground, and Lieutenant Lorimer's knee—the titanium one, Castillo saw—was pressed painfully into the small of his back.

He howled in pain.

"Permission to dislocate his shoulder, sir?" Lorimer asked.

Castillo waited five seconds—long enough, he judged, for Mullroney to have time to consider that he might actually be about to have his shoulder dislocated—before replying: "Put him on his back, Lieutenant. If he even looks like he's considering trying to get up, kick some teeth out."

"Yes, sir."

Ten seconds later, Sergeant Mullroney was lying absolutely motionless on his back. Lieutenant Lorimer was squatting at his head, pulling Mullroney's chin back with one hand, and holding the eight-inch blade of a knife against his throat with the other.

"Permission to speak, sir?" Lieutenant Lorimer said.

"Granted."

"Let me toss him down the mountain, sir."

"I don't want to kill him unless I have to," Castillo said.

"Just let him get busted up a little, sir," Lorimer argued. "Break an ankle, a leg, an arm."

"How would we explain his accident?" Castillo asked reasonably.

"Well, everybody knows he's a boozer. I'll call Captain Timmons and tell him he got drunk, was wandering around the mountain and fell off."

"Is that a credible scenario?"

"Yes, sir, I think so. Who are they going believe? The family drunk, or you and me?"

"The problem with that is they would just send somebody else to snoop on us," Castillo said.

"That's true, sir," Lorimer acknowledged. "But we could deal with that situation as it came up. And we could probably be long gone before they could send someone else."

"True. Okay. Sergeant Mullroney, you have ten seconds to tell me why I should not permit Lieutenant Lorimer to throw you down the mountain."

"You people are out of your fucking minds!" Sergeant Mullroney said.

"Possibly," Castillo said. "But I don't see that as a reason not to send you down the mountain. Five seconds."

"I'm a cop, for Christ sake! You can't get away with this!"

"Time's up," Castillo said. "Carry on, Lieutenant."

"What we're going to do now," Lieutenant Lorimer said, touching the tip of the knife blade to the throat to discourage any sudden movement, "is very slowly get to our feet. . . ."

"Jesus, what the fuck do you want from me? You don't want me to call Chicago? All right, I won't call Chicago. I swear to God! I swear on my mother's grave I'll never call Chicago! Jesus Christ! Please! I've got a wife—Junior's sister—and kids . . ."

"He doesn't get the picture, does he, Lieutenant?"

"No, sir. It would appear he doesn't have a clue."

"Explain it to him, please."

"Yes, sir. Asshole, we don't care if you call Chicago every hour on the hour. But what we can't have is you running at the mouth to somebody else who'll run at the mouth and blow this operation and get people—including my pal Byron—killed."

"I wouldn't do that," Sergeant Mullroney said, more than a little right-eously. "Junior's my brother-in-law, for Christ's sake. My wife's brother."

"I've always wondered what a brother-in-law was," Castillo said. "Thank you for clearing that up for me."

"What?" Mullroney asked, visibly confused.

"Have you anything else you want to say to us?" Castillo asked.

"What the fuck do I have to say to make you understand I'd never do anything to hurt Junior?"

"Byron told me he told you not to call him 'Junior' and you wouldn't stop until he knocked you on your ass," Lorimer said. "And we have a similar situation here, wouldn't you say, Colonel?"

"I'm afraid it looks that way to me," Castillo said.

"I don't know what the fuck you're talking about!"

"Exactly as it was necessary for Byron to knock you on your ass to get you not to say the wrong thing, it looks to me that I'm going to have to put you down the mountain now to keep you from saying the wrong thing. We're talking about people getting killed because of your runaway mouth."

"I'd never say . . ." Sergeant Mullroney began, then he had a sudden inspiration. "What if I told you what I was going to say to Jun . . . *Byron's* father before I said it. I mean, before I called. And you could tell me if there was something I shouldn't say. And I wouldn't. And you could listen to me making the call. . . ."

When there was no reaction from either Castillo or Lorimer, Mullroney added, somewhat plaintively, "Jesus, guys, we're on the same side here."

"You don't call the colonel 'guy,' Asshole," Lorimer said.

"Sorry, Colonel, sir."

"That might work, sir," Lorimer said. "Operative word *might*. On the other hand, I don't want to have to kill him unless it's really necessary."

"Give me a chance, and I promise you'll never regret it," Mullroney said.

"What do you want to do, sir, flip a coin?" Lorimer asked, his tone serious.

"As he points out, Lieutenant, he is Special Agent Timmons's *brother-in-law.* If it could be avoided, I would prefer not to get Special Agent Timmons back only to tell him that we had to terminate his *brother-in-law* in order to guarantee the security of the operation. . . ."

"For your consideration, sir, Special Agent Timmons is not all that fond of the asshole."

"Nevertheless, I think that we should take the chance."

"Yes, sir," Lieutenant Lorimer said, his voice showing his deep disappointment.

"Let him up, Lieutenant," Castillo ordered. "Get him on his feet."

"You heard the colonel, Asshole. Stand up."

"Sergeant," Castillo then said, "I want you to understand that I am authorizing your immediate termination should you ever get close to a telephone without Lieutenant Lorimer or myself being present. Understood?"

"Yeah."

Lorimer barked, "Say 'yes, sir' when you're talking to the colonel!"

"Yes, sir."

"You are dismissed, Sergeant. Please stay in your room until you are called for breakfast."

"Yes, sir."

Castillo made a motion as if brushing away a fly, and Sergeant Mullroney started quickly walking up the path to the house.

Fifteen seconds later, Colonel Castillo whispered, "If you are about to have the giggles, Lorimer, and Asshole hears you, *I'll* throw *you* down the mountain."

Lieutenant Lorimer acknowledged the order by bobbing his head.

He didn't trust himself to open his mouth, the bottom lip of which he was biting as hard as he could.

[TWO]

Lieutenant Colonel Castillo leaned over Lieutenant Lorimer, who was sprawled on a chaise lounge by the side of the swimming pool, and very carefully topped off Lorimer's glass of Famous Grouse with more of the same.

"Lieutenant Lorimer," Castillo said, "I am a lieutenant colonel."

"Yes, sir."

"And, you may have noticed, I wear a green beret."

"Yes, sir, I did notice that."

"And, as I am sure you know, while some lieutenant colonels sometimes make mistakes, and some Special Forces officers sometimes make mistakes, when a Special Forces lieutenant colonel makes a mistake, it is truly a cold day in hell."

"So I have been led to believe, sir."

"That being understood between us, there is sometimes an exception to the rule just cited."

"I find that difficult to accept, sir."

"Nevertheless, I think perhaps—as difficult as this may be for you to accept—I made a mistake about you."

"Yes, sir?"

"Frankly, Lieutenant, when you approached Mullroney and me with stealth worthy of the finest Comanche, I really had no idea how to deal with the son-ofabitch."

"With respect, Colonel, sir, I believe his name is Asshole. And I think the asshole is now under control, sir."

"The knife at his throat when you rolled him over, Lieutenant—don't let this go to your head—was masterful. I would not be surprised to learn that Sergeant Mullroney soiled his undies."

"I would be disappointed to learn that he didn't, Colonel."

"The problem of a police officer being embedded with us having been solved—I devoutly hope—let us now turn our attention to the big picture. How do we get your friend back?"

"Yeah," Lorimer said, and exhaled audibly. "How the hell do we do that?"

"To get him back, we have to know a lot of things, starting with who has him. And where. Your thoughts, please?"

"May I infer from the colonel's question that I am now regarded as part of the team, so to speak?"

"From this moment on, you may regard yourself as the psychological warfare officer of the team. You seem to have some skill in that area."

"I am humbled by that responsibility, sir, and will try very hard to justify your confidence in me."

"Where do these bastards have him, Eddie?"

"Well, he could be in Asunción, but I don't think so. If I had to bet, they've got him in the boonies somewhere. Either in Paraguay or across the river in Argentina."

"Bearing in mind that you're betting with a man's life, why?"

"That's boonieland up there, Argentina and Paraguay. You can raid a house in a city a lot easier than you can in the boonies."

"Meaning that if you're holding somebody in a remote farmhouse, you can see the good guys coming?"

"If there's only one road going someplace, they know you're coming long before you get there. You've got somebody in the bag, you just march him off into the woods, and look innocent when somebody shows up at the door."

"So what we have to do is not only find where he is—I'll get back to that in a minute—but come up with some way to get enough people in there with the element of surprise."

"Yeah," Lorimer said. "And that won't be easy."

"I'm going off at a tangent here, Eddie."

"Yes, sir?"

"Something was said about Timmons's driver being taken out by these people. I want to make sure I heard it right. Tell me about that."

"They found the embassy car parked against the fence of the airport. It's called the Silvio Pettirossi International Airport—you want all the details like that?"

Castillo nodded.

"Anything that comes into your mind, Eddie. My data bank is pretty empty."

"Typical Third World airport," Lorimer went on. "It used to be called the Presidente General Stroessner Airport, and you can still see signs with his name on them. He was the president, read dictator, for thirty-five years. Apparently a world-class sonofabitch—"

"Presidente General *Alfredo* Stroessner," Castillo interrupted, "was exiled to Brazil in 1989 after a coup by General Andrés Rodríguez. I don't know where the hell I got that, but the data bank apparently isn't completely empty. And, I just remembered, he was cozy with the Nazis, the ones who fled to South America after World War Two. Interesting."

"Why? Is that important?"

"I'll tell you in a minute. And the next time we have a little chat like this, I'll have to remember to bring the laptop so I can write all this down. I tend to forget things I hear when I'm drinking. Go on, please, Eddie."

"The embassy car was parked against the fence across the field from the terminal. The driver was on the floor of the backseat choked to death."

"Strangled, you mean?"

"I don't know if that's the word. He had a gizmo around his neck, like those plastic handcuffs the cops use, but metal."

"With a handle?" Castillo asked, quietly, and mimed how the handle would be used.

Lorimer nodded.

"It's called a garrote," Castillo said. "One of them was used to take out a friend of mine, Sergeant First Class Sy Kranz, who was a damned good special operator, when the Ninjas jumped us at Estancia Shangri-La."

"I never heard that you lost anybody."

"We lost Sy Kranz," Castillo said. "And taking him out wasn't easy, which told us right off that the Ninjas we took out were pros."

"How much about that operation are you going to tell me, Colonel?"

"We later found out that one of the people we took out was Major Alejandro Vincenzo of the Cuban Dirección General de Inteligencia. We think the others were probably either ex-Stasi or ex-ÁVO or ex-ÁVH, probably being run by the FSB."

"Colonel, except for the FSB, I don't know what you're talking about. Who was the FSB running? Jesus, what was going on at that farm?"

"*Estancia,*" Castillo corrected him without thinking. "*Estancia* Shangri-La. This much we know: Jean-Paul Lorimer, an American who worked for the UN, was a—probably *the*—bagman in that Iraqi Oil for Food cesspool. We know he set himself up with a phony identification and name on the estancia. We know he had sixteen million dollars. Whether he earned that as the bagman or stole it, we don't know. We know that a team of pros was sent to the estancia. We *think* their basic mission was to whack him to shut his mouth. They *may* have been after the money, too. And we're pretty sure the others were ex-Stasi. . . ."

He stopped when he remembered Lorimer didn't know what he was talking about.

"Stasi, Eddie, was the East German Ministerium für Staatssicherheit—Ministry for State Security. ÁVO—Államvédelmi Osztály—and later ÁVH—Államvédelmi Hatóság—did about the same thing when Hungary was still under the communists."

"And they were involved in that oil-for-food business?"

"They were hired guns, *we think*, for people who were involved in it," Castillo said.

"Like who?"

Castillo ignored the question.

"The one thing the Stasi and the Hungarians had in common, Eddie—aside from being some very unpleasant people very good at what they did—was using the garrote as the silent whacking weapon of choice."

"You're saying you think these people are involved with what happened to Timmons?"

"I'm saying it's very interesting that Timmons's driver was garroted with the same kind of garrote they used on Sergeant Kranz, and tried to use on Eric Kocian."

Lorimer considered what he'd heard, then said, "I don't think anyone in Asunción thinks we're dealing with anything but drug dealers."

"And maybe we're not," Castillo said. "But to finish filling you in on what happened at Shangri-La, the official version—the Uruguayan government version—is that it was a drug deal gone wrong. They know better, but apparently have decided it's best for them to sweep what really happened under the rug. This is made somewhat easier for them by our ambassador, who can't believe that a special operation could happen without his knowing about it. He decided that Lorimer was shipping cocaine in antique vases and a deal went wrong. The Uruguayans decided to let it go at that."

"So you came out clean?"

"For a while, I thought we had."

"But?"

"We were at the safe house in Pilar, just about to wind up putting things together—Inspector Doherty called it 'an investigation to determine what has to be investigated'—when Max caught you sneaking through the bushes."

"Oh."

"Opening the possibility that others may have put together what you did. So we quickly folded the tent and came home. And I again thought we'd come out clean. And then the President said, 'Go get Special Agent Timmons.' So now we're going to have to go back down there, and the whole thing is back at risk of being compromised."

"You don't have to go back to Uruguay, do you?"

"I wouldn't be surprised that as we try to do this, we'll have to go to Uruguay. And there's something else."

"What?"

"Lorimer's father is a retired ambassador. Apparently a very good guy. He lost his house in New Orleans to the hurricane. And he's decided that until things settle down, he wants to take his wife and go to Estancia Shangri-La, which he now owns."

"Uh-oh."

"Yeah. And—since he has a serious heart condition—the secretary of State thought it would be best if he didn't learn what a miserable sonofabitch his son was. He thinks the bastard was killed by roving bandits. Among the other impossible things I have to do, one is talk him out of going to Uruguay. Not only would it be dangerous for him and his wife—"

"Why?"

"The money, for one thing."

"What money?"

"The sixteen million. We have it, but they don't know that."

"You have it?" Lorimer asked, surprised.

Castillo nodded. "It's now the Lorimer Charitable & Benevolent Fund."

Which also now has forty-six million of illegal oil-for-food profits that Philip J. Kenyon of Midland, Texas, thought he had safely hidden from the IRS and the Justice Department—and everybody else—in the Caledonian Bank and Trust Limited in the Cayman Islands.

I don't think Lorimer has to know about that. I've already given him enough to think about.

Which means I've already told him too much.

"That's how we pay for everything," Castillo went on.

"I wondered about that," Lorimer said. "So what happens now?"

"Now we go to bed," Castillo said. "Not only is my tail dragging, but I've learned—painfully—that the brilliant thoughts I have at one o'clock in the morning with half a bag on turn out to be stupid in the morning."

[THREE]
Valley View Ranch
North Las Vegas, Nevada
0835 3 September 2005

When Castillo, wearing a polo shirt and khaki slacks, walked out of the house to the pool, he found Tom McGuire, Jake Torine, and Lorimer, all in sports shirts and slacks, sitting at a table drinking coffee. He saw Casey's cook standing by an enormous stainless steel gas grill that apparently also functioned as an ordinary stove, and decided they were politely waiting for their host to show up before eating.

Jake nodded at Castillo but didn't speak.

"Eddie," Castillo ordered, "why don't you ask Sergeant Mullroney to join us for breakfast?"

Lorimer wordlessly got out of his chair and went into the house.

"Is he—the cop—going to be a problem, Charley?" Torine asked.

"I think that's been taken care of. I'll tell you later. Here comes Frank."

Aloysius Francis Casey came out of the house.

"Jesus, you didn't have to wait for me," Casey said. "Just tell Walter what you want."

He motioned for the cook to come to the table and poured himself a cup of coffee.

"Feed my friends, Walter," he ordered. "You name it, Walter can make it."

"Pheasant under glass," Torine said. "With beluga caviar on toast corners on the side."

Casey chuckled. "The fish eggs aren't a problem, but catching the bird and plucking it may take Walter a little time."

"Bacon and eggs would satisfy this old man's hunger," Torine said.

"Walter makes his own corned beef hash," Casey said.

"Even better," Torine said.

"Me, too, please," Castillo said.

"Make it three, please," McGuire said.

"Where's that nice kid and the cop?" Casey asked.

"The former went to get the latter," Castillo said.

"You never told me about the cop," Casey said.

"He's been embedded with us," Castillo said.

"You don't seem to be very happy about that."

"I'm not. But Lorimer has him under control."

Sergeant Mullroney, wearing a coat and tie, came out of the house, followed by Lorimer. Lorimer pointed to one of the chairs at the table. Mullroney followed the orders and sat down.

"Good morning, Sergeant Mullroney," Castillo said. "We're about to have corned beef hash and eggs. Sound all right to you?"

Mullroney smiled wanly and nodded.

"I see what you mean," McGuire said.

Casey smiled at him, then announced: "I just talked to the guys in the hangar. The new gear is up and running in your airplane. And Signature Flight Support has finished doing whatever they had to do to the G-Three."

"Great!" Torine said. "Thanks, Frank."

"I suppose that means you're not going to hang around for a day, a couple of days? Take in a couple of the shows?"

"We'll have to take a rain check, Frank," Castillo said.

"Yeah, I figured. Is there anything else I can do for you?"

"Now that you mention it . . ."

Casey made a *Give it to me* gesture.

"To get this guy back, we're going to need a team," Castillo said. "Maybe more than one. But at least one. And choppers to move them around. Choppers equipped with both a good GPS and one of your wonderful radios."

"Well, now that they've started giving the 160th what they need," Casey said, "they've got pretty good GPS equipment—"

"What's the 160th?" Mullroney interrupted.

"I'll tell you when you can ask questions, Charley," Lorimer said.

"The 160th is the 160th Special Operations Aviation Regiment, Mull-roney," Castillo said, and turned to Casey. "But the problem there is I can't use their helicopters."

"Why not?" Lorimer asked.

"I'll tell you when you can ask questions, Lieutenant," Castillo said seriously, waited for that to register on Lorimer's face, then smiled. "Hold the questions, Eddie, until your leader is finished."

"Yes, sir."

"The 160th has all the latest equipment," Castillo said. "Which we would have trouble getting into Paraguay and/or Argentina—just physically getting them down there—and even if we could do that, they would stick out like sore thumbs. We're going to have to do this black."

Castillo saw that Mullroney had opened his mouth as if to ask a question and then after a quick glance at Lorimer had changed his mind.

"Black means secretly, covertly, Mullroney. Nobody knows about it," Castillo explained. "Which means we're going to have to use Hueys."

"Where are you going to get Hueys?" Torine asked. "And how are you going to get them down there black?"

"Moving right along," Castillo said. "While I am figuring out where to get Hueys, and how to get them down there black, I thought I would send Munz, Lorimer, and Mullroney down there right away—"

"I guess I don't get to go?" McGuire interrupted.

"Tom, you'll be more useful in Washington," Castillo said.

"I guess," McGuire said, sounding disappointed.

"But keep your bag packed," Castillo said. He went on: "And on the airplane, if I can keep abusing Frank's generosity, there will be two—preferably three—ground versions of the radios. There's two—old models—down there already, and we're going to need at least two more in Paraguay. Plus, I just thought, op-erators for same. You'll probably have to stop by Bragg to pick them up, Jake."

"Not a problem," Torine said.

"The ones you have in South America still working?" Casey asked.

"You heard me talk to Argentina yesterday," Castillo said.

Casey nodded, then offered, "I think there's a half-dozen new models wait-ing to be shipped to Delta, to General McNab, at Bragg—"

"Think about that, Frank," Castillo said, stopping him. "Maybe there's only three waiting to be shipped to General McNab. The other three have mys-teriously disappeared. If that was the case, I won't have to get on my knees and beg him for any."

"If he finds out, he's not going to be happy."

"I devoutly hope he never finds out," Castillo said. "But a bird in hand is worth two in the bush." He looked at Lorimer. "You may want to write that down, Lieutenant."

"Yes, sir," Lorimer said, and took a notebook from his pocket and started writing in it.

Torine and McGuire shook their heads. Mullroney appeared to be confused.

Casey chuckled and said, "It'll take me a couple of days to come up with—what did you say, four?—sets of GPS and that many aviation radios, maybe a little longer for them."

"All contributions gratefully—"

"Yeah, yeah," Casey interrupted impatiently.

He took a cellular from his pocket and pushed a speed-dial key.

"Casey," he announced into it. "There's a half-dozen Model 3405s waiting to be shipped to Bragg. Put three of them in the Gulfstream in the hangar."

Then he hung up.

"What are you going to do about the ambassador?" McGuire asked.

"Try to hide from the one in Washington," Castillo replied, "and put the one in Mississippi on hold. What I have to do now is get to Washington."

Mullroney's face showed that he was trying hard to make sense of what had been said and not having much success.

[FOUR]
Double-Bar-C Ranch
Near Midland, Texas
1225 3 September 2005

As Torine lined up with the runway, Castillo saw there was a Bombardier/Learjet 45XR parked beside the horse-head oil pump.

"Look who's here," Castillo said.

"Put the wheels down, First Officer," Torine said. "We can chat later."

Doña Alicia Castillo was again waiting for them, this time beside a Chevrolet Suburban, and this time a heavyset, almost massive dark-skinned man was with her.

Castillo came down the stair door first. He went to his grandmother and kissed her.

"Nice landing, gringo," the large man said. "Jake must have been flying."

Castillo gave him the finger.

Fernando Manuel Lopez and Carlos Guillermo Castillo thought of themselves as brothers—they had been raised together since puberty—but they were in fact first cousins.

"Are you on parole, or are Maria and the rug rats here, too?" Castillo asked.

Doña Alicia shook her head at both of them.

"Now stop it, the both of you, right now," she ordered.

Lopez answered the question anyway.

"They're in Cancún," he said. "Taking a pre-going-back-to-school vacation."

"You are going to have lunch," Doña Alicia said. "That's in the nature of a statement, not an invitation."

"Nevertheless, I gratefully accept, Abuela," Castillo said.

"Eddie," Castillo ordered, "why don't you take Sergeant Mullroney for a walk?"

Lorimer made a *Get up, let's go* gesture to Mullroney, who stood up and followed Lorimer off the verandah where lunch had been served.

"Presumably, you think you have a good excuse for that discourtesy," Doña Alicia said when they were out of earshot.

"There are some things we have to discuss that are none of his business," Castillo said.

"Then why is he here with you?" she demanded. Before Castillo could reply, she said, "I just saw on Colonel Torine's face that he thinks I'm wrong. Sorry, Carlos."

"I'm the one who should be . . . *is* . . . sorry for involving you in the first place," Castillo said. "If I could have thought of someplace else to take Munz's family, believe me, I would have."

She looked at him for a moment. "Thank you, Carlos."

"For what?"

"For bringing them here. And for not reminding me you tried very hard to keep me from coming here."

He didn't reply.

"What do we have to discuss?" she asked after a moment.

"We're all . . . Colonel Munz, Tom McGuire, and me . . . agreed that there's no longer a threat here to Señora Munz and the girls."

"Well, that's good news! Thank God for that."

"So Tom's going to call off the Secret Service," Castillo said. "Which then raises the question what to do with them for the next two, three weeks, however long it takes to be sure they can safely return to Argentina."

"Why, they'll stay here, of course," she said. "Where else would they go?"

"I hate to ask you to stay with them," Castillo said.

"Don't be silly, Carlos," she said. "I enjoy being with them." She paused. "But . . . Mr. McGuire?"

"Ma'am, could I get you to call me 'Tom'?"

"*Tom*, if they would be safe here, would they be safe in San Antonio?"

McGuire considered the question before replying.

"At your home there, you mean?"

She nodded.

"No," Castillo said.

"Actually, Charley, that might be a better solution than leaving them here," McGuire said. "Ma'am, would having a driver for your car raise any eyebrows?"

"Abuela usually has a driver when she goes out at night," Fernando Lopez said. "What are you thinking, Tom?"

"That, to err on the side of caution, instead of just canceling the protection detail, I have it cut from what we have here now . . . twelve, probably?"

"So Mr. Alvarez told me," Doña Alicia said.

"If it's been a twelve-man detail," McGuire said, "that means there were at any given moment three agents on the job, which means that nine agents were lying around the swimming pool at the local motel, or drinking coffee in the snack bar, with people starting to wonder aloud who were all these guys in suits with guns and Yukons."

McGuire looked at Castillo.

"And we're agreed, Charley, that the threat is almost certainly gone, right?"

Castillo nodded reluctantly.

"So we call off the detail here completely, and we set up a three-man detail in San Antonio. Which means one will be available at all times to do the job when necessary—whenever they leave the house, in other words, they have an agent with them. If we call off the detail here, that means no agents, period. And Alvarez can have a word with the San Antonio cops to keep their eyes open. What's wrong with that, Charley?"

Doña Alicia did not give him a chance to answer.

"That's what we'll do," she said. "And I'll have a little party or two for the girls, so they can meet people their own age. They're already bored being here, and I can't say that I blame them."

"I think we should leave it up to Munz," Castillo said.

"I think we should, too, Chief," McGuire said. "Want to know why?"

"Why?"

"Alfredo has a lot of protection experience. Like I do. Who do you think he's going to agree with, you or me?"

"I guess we'll have to see," Castillo said, a little lamely.

"Carlos, I suppose it's important that Colonel Munz go to South America right away?" Doña Alicia asked.

"I'm afraid so, Abuela. And that means right now. I'm sitting here wondering if I can work up the courage to tell him it's time to go."

"I'll go get him," Doña Alicia said, and stood up and walked into the house.

Castillo looked at Lopez.

"All right, gringo," Fernando said, "I'll ride the right seat down there and back. But that's it. And *that* presumes I can be back before Maria comes back from Cancún."

"I didn't ask, Fernando," Castillo said.

"You knew if you asked, I'd tell you to go to hell," Fernando said. "I told you I'm getting too old to play James Bond with you guys."

"Fernando going would solve the problem of having to find another pilot," Jake Torine said. "All we're going to do is drop off Munz and the others with the radios, and come right back. So thanks, Fernando."

"He should be thanking us for the privilege of flying our airplane," Castillo said.

Fernando gave Castillo the finger.

"How do I get back here to pick up the Lear?" Fernando asked.

"Charley," McGuire asked, "what if I stay here, take your grandmother and the Munzes to San Antonio, say, tomorrow, and get things set up there? That'd probably reassure Munz. By the time I have things set up, Jake and Fernando will be back from Buenos Aires. So you send a plane to pick me up, it brings Fernando here, and then picks me up in San Antonio? That'd work."

Castillo considered the suggestion and nodded. "Okay. Then that's what we do."

"God, I feel sorry for them," Castillo said, nodding discreetly at the wife and young daughters of Alfredo Munz, who had just watched Munz get into the Gulfstream III.

"I probably shouldn't tell you this," Doña Alicia said, "but you're the one I feel sorry for."

"Why?"

"Everybody has somebody but you."

"Hey, Abuela. I have you."

"I'm your grandmother. You share me with Fernando and his family."

"You're all I need," Castillo said.

She would not give up.

"Colonel Munz has his family. Mr. McGuire has his family. Colonel Torine has his family. You don't even have a dog."

"If it will make you happy, I'll get a dog."

Now why the hell did I say that?

What the hell would I do with a dog?

The right engine of the Gulfstream began to whine.

Castillo placed his hands gently on Doña Alicia's arms, kissed her on both cheeks, and went up the stair door.

[FIVE]
7200 West Boulevard Drive
Alexandria, Virginia
2340 3 September 2005

"We're home, Colonel," the Secret Service driver of the Yukon said, gently pushing Castillo's shoulder.

Castillo's head jerked up. For a moment he was confused, and then he knew where he was.

In the front seat of the Yukon, in the basement of the house.

"How long was I out?" he asked.

"You dozed off before we were out of the airport."

"You ever hear that only people with nothing on their conscience can go to sleep with no difficulty?"

The Secret Service agent chuckled.

"So what happens now?" Castillo asked.

"There's my relief," the Secret Service agent said, pointing to a man walking up to the Yukon. "I go off at midnight, in twenty minutes."

Max was walking to one side of the man, and looking at the truck.

"In that case, can I offer you a nightcap?" Castillo offered. "I'm about to have one. Which I richly deserve. This has been one hell of a day."

He sensed reluctance on the part of the Secret Service agent.

"If you have moral scruples against Demon Rum, then okay. Otherwise, consider that an order. I always feel depraved when I drink alone."

"I could use a little nip."

"Then come along."

Castillo's door opened as he reached for the handle.

"Good evening, sir," the Secret Service agent who had walked up to the Denali said.

Max effortlessly stood on his rear paws and put his forepaws on Castillo's legs.

"How are you, pal?" he asked, and scratched Max's ears.

Max sat down on his haunches.

"I see you've made a pal of Max," Castillo said to the Secret Service agent.

"He's been meeting every car that's come in here," the Secret Service agent said. "Obviously waiting for you. Until now, he's just taken a look and gone back upstairs."

"I probably smell like hamburger," Castillo said, and then asked: "You're going to be here all night? What did you do wrong?"

The Secret Service agent chuckled.

"Not to go any farther?"

Castillo nodded.

"We bid for the duty. This looked like a much better deal than spending all night sitting in the truck in the White House parking lot. Seniority counts, and I won."

"Well, the only person who can get me out of here tonight is the President, and I heard on the radio that he's on the Gulf Coast looking at hurricane damage, so why don't you find an empty bedroom and catch some sleep?"

"Maybe later, Colonel. Thank you."

"I have to be at the Nebraska Avenue Complex at eight. Is that going to screw up your getting relieved?"

"No, sir. If you're sure about that, I'll have my relief meet me there."

"Why don't you do that?"

He nodded.

The stairway from the garage led into the kitchen, and there was a door from the kitchen to the living room. When Castillo got close to it, Max brushed past him and pushed it open. Castillo motioned for the Denali driver to follow him. When he got inside, he was surprised to see Edgar Delchamps and a somewhat frumpy man Delchamps's age whom he didn't recognize. They were sitting in the leather chairs and couch around the battered coffee table, working on a bottle of Famous Grouse.

"Oh, Edgar, I'm touched," Castillo said. "You waited up for me!"

Neither man seemed amused.

"We need to talk, Ace," Delchamps said.

"Will it wait until we get a drink?"

"Yeah, but he'll have to drink his someplace else," Delchamps said, then looked at the Secret Service agent and added, "Nothing personal."

"Not a problem, sir. And I can pass on the drink."

"Have the drink," Castillo ordered.

Not another word was said until Castillo had poured two drinks, given one to the Secret Service agent, who downed it, then said, "Ah. Thank you, sir. And good evening, gentlemen."

He left the living room, closing the door behind him.

"Say hello to Milton Weiss, Ace," Delchamps said. "He and I go back a long way."

When they shook hands, Weiss's eyes were cold and penetrating. Castillo was reminded of the first time he'd met Aleksandr Pevsner. He wondered now—as he had then—whether the look in the eyes was natural, or whether it had been cultivated.

When you get that look, you know damned well you're really being examined.

Max walked up to Castillo and rubbed his head against Castillo's leg. Castillo scratched Max's ears and looked at Delchamps.

"And where is the master of this beast?"

"In the Monica Lewinsky Motel," Delchamps said.

"What?"

"Okay, Ace," Delchamps said, tolerating him. "Kocian consulted a canine gynecologist who confirmed that Mädchen is in the family way. Which came as no surprise to those of us who watched the happy couple couple happily in the garden of the safe house for hours at a time.

"Said canine gynecologist offered his professional opinion that the lovers should now be separated, as Max cannot seem to grasp that his role in the pro-creation of his species is no longer required, and that Mädchen is very likely going to take large pieces out of him if he continues to try to force his now un-wanted attentions on her. How to do that?

"Kocian—having been advised by Miller that your suite in the Monica Lewinsky is empty but paid for through the end of the month—decided that he had enough of bucolic suburban life and had Miller take him and Mädchen to the Mayflower, leaving Max here, his fate to be decided later."

"Jesus Christ!" Castillo said.

"To answer your unspoken question: Yes, Herr Kocian is being sat upon. Miller will stay with him until we get the Secret Service in place. Have you any further questions, Colonel, or can we get on with this?"

"Get on with what?"

"Please tell Milton what steps you have taken vis-à-vis your little problem in Paraguay."

"I don't know who the hell Milton is."

"Trust me, Ace," Delchamps said sarcastically. "Milton Weiss is not a member of the drug mafia."

Castillo almost said, *So what?* but stopped. Instead, he asked, "Why?"

"Before you begin to apply damage control, Ace, it is convenient to know the extent of the damage."

Castillo looked at Delchamps but didn't say anything.

"Trust me, Charley," Delchamps said, this time very seriously.

If I don't go along with him now, he's entirely capable of telling me to go fuck myself, get up, and walk out of here and the OOA.

And I can't afford to lose him.

"Lorimer says," Castillo began, "and I think he's right, that they have Timmons in the sticks—on an estancia of some kind—in either Paraguay or across the river in Argentina. Not far from Asunción, in other words. Someplace we can't easily—if at all—get to on the ground without being spotted.

"So the problem is, one, to find out where he is, and, two, to stage an operation to get him back.

"One, I hope, isn't going to be much of a problem. A very competent agency guy is already in Asunción—"

"You mean the station chief?" Weiss interrupted.

"No, I mean a guy who works for me. The station chief in Asunción is apparently . . . intellectually challenged. The guy I'm talking about knows his business."

Weiss nodded.

Castillo went on, "My guy is there—the phrase he used was 'To make sure the cork is back in the bottle'—because a very bright young DIA guy in Asunción pretty much figured out another operation we ran down there, and my guy went to Asunción on his own, to make sure nobody else in the embassy talks too much. My guy—"

"Milton and Alex Darby are old pals, Charley," Delchamps said.

Weiss nodded, and there was the hint of a smile on his lips.

Is he laughing at me?

"*Darby* will learn in about nine hours, maybe ten, about this new mission."

"How?" Weiss asked softly.

"From a . . ."

Oh, to hell with it!

"From a man named Munz, who used to run SIDE and who now works for me—"

"Good man, Milt," Delchamps said softly.

"—and is now on his way to Asunción on our airplane. The airplane is also carrying radios—ours, with some incredible capabilities—"

"The ones you get from AFC?" Weiss asked.

Did this guy already know about the radios?

Or did Delchamps tell him?

Castillo nodded. "Which, with a little bit of luck, they'll be able to get into Paraguay. And with a little more luck, Munz and Darby will be able to get up and running.

"The fallback plan there is that if they can't smuggle the radios into Paraguay, Munz will arrange to see that we can get them into Argentina, and from there into Paraguay. And one of my sergeants—who *can* get the radio, *radios*, up and running—will be on the first plane to Asunción tomorrow morning. That's if he couldn't get on the last plane today. And two Delta Force communicators were supposed to be on the 1130 Aerolíneas flight from Miami to Buenos Aires tonight. They're going as tourists, with orders to report to a certain lady at our embassy. . . ."

"Susanna isn't what comes to mind when one hears the phrase 'clandestine service,' is she?" Weiss said, smiling.

I don't think Delchamps told him about Susanna Sieno. And if I'm right, that means he knows a hell of a lot about what's going on down there.

Who is this guy?

"Cutting this short, if Alex Darby and Munz are half as good as I think they are, finding out where these bastards have Timmons won't take nearly as long as setting up the operation to get him back will take."

"Tell Milton how you plan to do that," Delchamps said.

"The only way to do that is with helicopters," Castillo said. "And the problem there is that we're going to have to use Hueys. Nobody in Argentina or Paraguay has Apaches or Black Hawks or Little Birds. The problem there is where to get the Hueys, and crews for them. I don't want to use active-duty Army pilots if I don't have to; same thing with the technical people.

"There used to be a long list of unemployed Huey drivers hanging around China Post . . ."

Castillo stopped and looked at Weiss to make sure he understood what he was talking about. Weiss nodded, just perceptibly, signaling he knew that China Post No. 1 (In Exile) of the American Legion, in addition to providing the camaraderie and other benefits of any Legion Post, also served as sort of an employment agency for retired special operators of the various branches of service.

". . . but when I called there, a friend of mine said most of them are now either back in the service, or working for Blackwater or people like that, or the agency. He's trying to find me some chopper drivers, etcetera, but that may take some time, if it works at all.

"And then, presuming I can pull that rabbit magically from the hat, that leaves the problem of getting the aircraft and the people into Argentina black.

"Taking first things first, I'm going to Fort Rucker right after the briefing tomorrow—"

"What briefing?" Weiss asked.

"Montvale is gathering all the experts in his empire to give me everything they have on what's going on down there."

Weiss nodded. "And you're going to do what at Fort Rucker?"

"They have some Hueys. Montvale is going to have somebody from the secretary of Defense's office call down there and tell them to give me whatever I ask for, and not to ask questions. I'm going to see what's available and what shape it's in. And then I'm going to borrow an airplane and go see Ambassador Lorimer, who lost his house to Hurricane Katrina and wants to move to Estancia Shangri-La until he can get a new house in New Orleans. I've got to talk him out of that."

"I hadn't heard about that," Delchamps said.

"What are you going to do about shooters?" Weiss asked.

Castillo was surprised at first at Weiss's use of the term. Few people outside the special operations community used the politically incorrect term to describe special operators whose mission was likely to require the use of deadly force.

What the hell, he seems to know about everything else.

"My friend at China Post told me I just about wiped out the list of available shooters when I hired them to protect the Mastersons," Castillo said. "That assignment's just about over, but those guys are all getting a little long in the tooth, so I'm probably going to have to get my shooters from Delta at Fort Bragg. I already gave General McNab a heads-up."

"That's about it?" Weiss said.

"I probably could have gotten more done if I hadn't spent all that time playing the slots in Vegas," Castillo said.

Weiss smiled.

"You're right, Ed," he said. "He is a wiseass, but he's also good. Very good."

"Am I supposed to blush at the compliment?" Castillo challenged.

"The station chief in Asunción is not intellectually challenged, Colonel," Weiss said.

"That's not my information," Castillo said. "If he's a friend of yours, I'm sorry."

"Jonathon Crawford's a very good friend of mine, actually," Weiss said. "And for that reason I was delighted to hear your unflattering opinion of him."

Castillo looked at him in confusion, then threw both hands up to signal he didn't understand.

Weiss explained: "If you—and more important, Alex Darby—didn't see through the image Jonathon has painted of himself as a mediocrity sent to an unimportant backwater post to keep him from causing trouble working beyond his limited ability somewhere important, then perhaps that very important deception is working."

Castillo looked at Delchamps.

"This is where you tell me what's going on here, Ed."

"We've got your attention now, do we, Ace?" He looked at Weiss. "Okay. Where do I start? You want to do this?"

"You do it. I don't think the colonel trusts me."

Delchamps nodded, looked thoughtful for a moment, then said: "When I was bringing you up to speed on the Cold War dinosaurs, Ace, I may have led you to believe that we all came out of Europe. Not so. There is a subspecies, Latin American, which is held with just about the same degree of suspicion and contempt by many people in Langley as are those of us who worked Berlin, Vienna, Budapest, and points east. Milton here is one of these. Fair, Milton?"

"Actually, I think of myself more as a chasmatosaurus, rather than a dinosaur, but close enough."

"As a what?" Castillo asked.

"The chasmatosaurus was a crocodilelike meateater from the Triassic period," Weiss said. "Generally acknowledged to be far more lethal than the dinosaur, the proof being that their descendants are still eating dogs and the occasional child in Florida, Australia, and other places, whereas the dinosaurs are no longer with us."

"Whatever the paleontological distinction," Delchamps said, smiling at the look on Castillo's face, "these people recognize each other as noble persons facing extinction at the hands of the politically correct members of what is laughingly known as the 'Intelligence Community.'

"Such was the case when Milton saw me rooting about in the South American files in Langley. He suggested that we have a drink for auld lang syne. And on the fourth drink, he idly inquired what I was looking for. Knowing him as well as I do, I asked him why he wanted to know.

"He said it had come to his attention that I had been in the Southern Cone, and he wanted to know what I could tell him to confirm or deny a credible rumor that Major Alejandro Vincenzo of the Cuban Dirección General de Inteligencia—dressed up as a Ninja at an estancia in Uruguay called Shangri-La—had been whacked by a bunch of special operators operating under a Presidential Finding."

"Jesus Christ!" Castillo exclaimed softly.

"I asked him where he had heard this rumor, and he told me from his pal Crawford, and one thing led to another, and he told me why he was interested, and I told him what we have been up to in Gaucho Land."

"Jesus Christ!" Castillo said again.

"I suppose you are aware, Colonel," Weiss said, "that you would not win any popularity contests held in Langley?"

Castillo nodded. "So I have been led to believe."

"If I were to tell you that you are a burr under the saddle blankets of two distinct groups of people over there, would that come as a shock to you?"

"Two distinct groups?"

"Group One, as I suspect you know, is composed of those annoyed because you (a) found that stolen 727 they couldn't, thereby splattering a good deal of egg on the agency's face, and (b) you—the Office of Organizational Analysis— is operating under the authority of that Presidential Finding, which among other things has seen Ambassador Montvale give this dinosaur"—he pointed at Delchamps—"blanket access to anything he wants at Langley.

"Group Two—which, as hard as you may find this to believe, I don't think you know about—is a bunch of good guys who are running an important operation they feel you are about to fuck up by the numbers while trying to get this DEA agent back."

"What kind of an important operation? And why hasn't Montvale told me about it?"

"Montvale doesn't know about it," Weiss said. "He's almost as unpopular over there as you are. For a number of reasons, the most obvious being that he's now over the agency. The DCI isn't even number two; just one more subordinate chief of agency, like the heads of DIA and DEA."

"What's this important operation?"

"How much do you know about the drug trade?" Weiss asked.

"Virtually nothing," Castillo admitted.

"Okay. Basic Drugs 101. The agency estimates—and this sort of thing is what the agency is really good at—Afghanistan will have half a million acres devoted to the growing of *Papaver somniferum L.*, or the poppy. Opium is obtained from the unripe poppy seed pods, and then converted to heroin. Afghanistan grows more than ninety percent of poppies used in the heroin drug trade.

"Most of the other eight or nine percent is grown—and converted to heroin—in Colombia and Bolivia. This is sold, primarily, in the East Coast cities here. Most of the stuff consumed in Hollywood and other temples of culture on the West Coast is grown and processed in Mexico, and is not nearly as pure as what's sold on the East Coast.

"Quality, as well as supply and demand, determines price. Will you take my word for it, Colonel, that there's a hell of a lot of money being spent on heroin on the East Coast?"

Castillo nodded.

"One—I guess several—of the good guys I mentioned before took a close look at the business and came up with several questions. Some were pretty obvious. Why are the heroin people in Bolivia sending their product south, into Paraguay and then Argentina, when the market's in New York City, in the other direction?

"The Colombians send most of their product into Mexico. The Mexicans don't seem to be able to stop much—if any—of that traffic. It has been suggested that the authorities have been bought. But whatever the reason, getting their product into Mexico and then across the border into the United States doesn't seem to pose much of a problem. Possibly because our overworked Customs and Border Protection people working the border-crossing points just can't inspect more than a tiny fraction of the thousands of eighteen-wheelers coming into the country every day.

"Or an even smaller fraction of the cars of the tourists returning home from a happy holiday south of the border. You have that picture, Colonel?"

"Ed calls me Charley, Mr. Weiss."

"I thought he called you Ace? You don't like being called colonel, Colonel?"

"Not the way you pronounce it."

"That's probably because I'm having trouble thinking of you as a colonel; you don't look old enough to be a colonel. When Ed and I were running around together, the colonels we dealt with had gray hair—if they had hair at all—and paunches. No offense was intended."

"You won't mind, right, Milton, if I don't believe that?"

"You are a feisty youngster, aren't you? Aren't you, *Charley?*"

"Better, Milton. Better."

"Getting back to the subject at hand, *Charley*. On the other hand, Argentina does have a working drug-interdiction program. They even have a remarkably honest—honest by South American standards—police organization called the Gendarmería Nacional.

"So why run the greater risk?

"Looking into it further, the good guys learned a little more about the flow of drugs through Argentina and into the U.S., and the manner of doing business. Normally—you've seen the movies—it's a cash business. The farmers sell the raw material—that stuff that oozes out of the poppy seed pods—to the refiners. They don't get much for it, but they get paid in cash. Next step, normally, is for the refiners to either sell what is now heroin to someone who shows up at the refinery and carries it off. That is also a cash transaction. Or they take it someplace away from the refinery and sell it there. That's where you see those briefcases full of money in the movies.

"Every time the product changes hands, in other words, so does cash. Usually.

"This didn't seem to be happening with the drugs coming out of Paraguay into Argentina, either when it arrived from the refiners, or when the movers got it into Argentina, or when it left Argentina. The first time money changed hands was when the movers had it in the States and turned it over to the wholesalers. Then we had the briefcases full of hundred-dollar bills.

"So what could be inferred from this? That it was being operated in what the Harvard School of Business Administration would call a vertically integrated manner. The whole process—from initial receipt of the product from the refiner, through the movement to Uruguay, to Argentina, to the United States and the sale there—was under one roof.

"The refiners, the movers, the smugglers, and the transporters, rather than being independent businessmen, were all employees."

"What's the purpose of that? What difference does it make?" Castillo asked.

Weiss held up his hand, signaling he didn't want to be interrupted.

"Another problem businessmen involved in this trade have is what to do with the money once they have sold the product. It cannot be dropped into an ATM machine, for obvious reasons. And, to get it into one of those offshore banks we hear so much about, it has to be transferred through a bank; no cash deposits allowed.

"Unless, of course, the bank is also in the vertically integrated system."

"You mean they own the bank?"

Weiss nodded.

"And that raised the question, among many others, in the good guys' minds,

'Where did all this come from?' Drug dealers are smart, ruthless, and enterprising, but very few of them have passed through Cambridge and learned to sing 'On, Fair Harvard!'

"That suggested something very interesting," Weiss went on, "that it was not a group of Colombian thugs with gold chains around their necks who were running this operation, but some very clever people who may indeed have gone to Harvard and were employed by their government. Two governments came immediately to mind."

"Which?"

"The Democratic People's Republic of Cuba and the Russian Federation."

"Jesus H. Christ!"

"Another thing needed to run this operation smoothly, Charley," Delchamps said, "is discipline. The employees—especially the local hires—had to completely understand that any hanky-panky would get them, and their families, whacked."

"Lorimer told me that Timmons's driver—"

"Timmons?" Weiss interrupted.

Just as Weiss had a moment before, Castillo held up his hand imperiously, signaling he didn't want to be interrupted.

Delchamps chuckled, and Weiss, smiling, shook his head.

"—was garroted," Castillo finished, "with a metal garrote."

"Interesting!" Weiss said. "Stasi?"

"And that might explain what Major Vincenzo and the others were doing at Shangri-La," Castillo said. "Maybe he didn't come from Cuba for that. Maybe he—and the others—were already in Paraguay."

"And," Delchamps added, "since Lorimer wasn't involved with drugs—they wanted to shut his mouth about what he knew of the oil-for-food scam—and Vincenzo was, that suggests there's a connection. Somebody who wanted Lorimer dead was able to order Vincenzo and company to do it."

"And we have the two dead FSB lieutenant colonels," Castillo said.

"Ed somehow neglected to mention two dead FSB officers," Weiss said.

"I didn't think you needed to know," Delchamps said.

Weiss rolled his eyes.

"Who were they?"

"One of the colonel's crack pistol marksmen, a chap named Bradley," Delchamps said with a straight face, "took down Yevgeny Komogorov—"

"Of the FSB's Service for the Protection of the Constitutional System and the Fight Against Terrorism?" Weiss asked drily.

Delchamps nodded as he went on: "—in the Sheraton Hotel garage in

Pilar, outside Buenos Aires. Colonel Komogorov was at the time apparently bent on whacking a fellow Russian by the name of Aleksandr Pevsner—"

"Pevsner?" Weiss asked, incredulously.

With an even more imperious gesture than Castillo had given, Delchamps held up his hand to signal he didn't want to be interrupted.

Castillo laughed.

Delchamps went on: "—when Bradley put a .45 round in his cheek"—he pointed to a spot immediately below his left eye—"and then Lieutenant Colonel Viktor Zhdankov was found beaten to death in the Conrad Casino and Resort in Punta del Este."

Weiss's face showed surprise, and perhaps revulsion.

"Not by us, Milton," Delchamps said. "Do I have to tell you that?"

"By who?"

"He was found in the company of a man named Howard Kennedy, who also had been beaten to death. There's a rumor going around that Kennedy was foolish enough to have tried to arrange the whacking of his employer, Mr. Pevsner."

"Either one of them could have been running Vincenzo," Castillo said thoughtfully.

Weiss considered that, then nodded.

"All of this seems to fit very nicely together," Weiss said. "But the bottom line is that nothing is going to be done about it. The Cubans—if they said anything at all—would say that Vincenzo hasn't been in the Dirección General de Inteligencia for years. The Russians will say they never heard of either Zhdankov or Komogorov."

"What's your point?" Castillo asked.

"The name of the game is to make the other guys hurt," Weiss said.

"Okay. But so what?" Castillo said.

"Let me return to Basic Drugs 101," Weiss said, "since bringing these bad guys before the bar of justice just isn't going to happen. Neither of you has any idea what happens to the heroin once it gets to Argentina, do you?"

Delchamps and Castillo shook their heads.

"The intellectually challenged station chief in Asunción has figured that out," Weiss said. "Has either of you ever wondered how many filet mignon steaks are in the coolers of a cruise ship like, for example, the *Holiday Spirit* of the Southern Cruise Line? I'll give you a little clue. She carries 2,680 passengers, and a crew of some twelve hundred."

"A lot, Milton?" Delchamps asked innocently.

"Since she makes twelve-day cruises out of Miami about the sunny

Caribbean, each of which features two steak nights, and filet mignon is an ever-present option on her luncheon and dinner menus, yeah, Edgar, 'a lot.'

"And has either of you ever wondered where they get all this meat—or the grapefruits and oranges from which is squeezed the fresh juice for the 2,680 breakfasts served each day, etcetera, etcetera?"

"Argentina?" Castillo asked innocently.

"You win the cement bicycle, Charley," Weiss said. "And have either of you ever wondered how all those filet mignons make their way from the Argentine pampas to the coolers of the *Holiday Spirit* and her many sister ships?"

Castillo and Delchamps waited for him to go on.

"I left out the succulent oysters, lobsters, and other fruits of the sea sent from the chilly Chilean South Pacific seas to the coolers of the *Holiday Spirit* and her sister ships," Weiss said.

"You're forgiven," Delchamps said. "Get on with it."

"Air freight!" Weiss said. "Large aircraft—some of them owned by Aleksandr Pevsner, by the way—make frequent, sometimes daily flights from Buenos Aires to Jamaica loaded with chilled but not frozen meat and other victuals for the cruise ship trade."

"Jesus!" Castillo said, sensing where Weiss was headed.

"We all know how wonderful Argentine beef is, and how cheap. And most cruise ships—just about all of the Southern Cruise Line ships, and there are four of these, the smallest capable of carrying eleven hundred passengers—call at Montego Bay or Kingston, or both, on each and every voyage. Kingston is served by Norman Manley International Airfield, and Montego Bay by Sangster International.

"While the happy tourists—is there a word for the people who ride these floating hotels? Cruisers, maybe?—are wandering through the picturesque streets of Kingston and Montego Bay, soaking up culture and taking pictures for the folks back home, the hardworking Jamaican gnomes are moving loins of Argentine beef from refrigerator plants, and occasionally—if yesterday's flight from Buenos Aires was delayed for some reason—directly from the airplane to the coolers on the cruise ships."

"And under the ice is that day's shipment of heroin," Delchamps said.

"Edgar, you've always been just terrible about thinking such awful things are going on," Weiss said, mock innocently.

"And how do they get it off the ship in the States?" Castillo asked.

"There are several ways to do that," Weiss said. "One is with the ship's garbage and sewage, which now has to be brought ashore, rather than as before, when it was tossed overboard, thereby polluting the pristine waters of the

Atlantic. Or, in the wee hours of the morn, as the vessel approaches Miami, it is dumped over the side, to be retrieved later by sportfishermen. Global Positioning System satellites are very helpful to the retrievers."

"And where is the DEA, or the Coast Guard, or whoever is supposed to be dealing with this sort of thing while all this is going on?" Castillo asked.

"So far they don't know about it," Weiss said, and Castillo sensed that suddenly Weiss had become dead serious, that his joking attitude had just been shut off as if a switch had been thrown.

And he made some remark before about Montvale—who was supposed to be on top of everything going on in the intelligence community—not knowing about an "important operation."

What the hell is going on?

Weiss met Castillo's eyes for a moment, and Castillo was again reminded of Aleksandr Pevsner.

"And we don't want them to know about it," Weiss went on.

"Are you going to tell me about that?" Castillo asked carefully.

"That's why I'm here, Castillo. I told you, you're in a position to fuck up an important operation. But before I get into that, I want you to understand this conversation never took place."

"I can't go along with that."

"You don't have any choice," Weiss said. "I'll deny it. And so will Delchamps."

"That leaves out the Secret Service guy you ran off," Castillo said. "He saw you here."

"He saw Delchamps and me taking a walk down memory lane. That's all. Paraguay and Timmons never came up."

Castillo looked at Delchamps.

"I gave him my word, Ace. Not for auld lang syne, but because it was the only way I could get him to come."

"I'm not giving you my word about anything," Castillo said. "And that specifically includes me not going to Montvale and telling him you're withholding intelligence I should have."

"Before this gets unpleasant, let me tell you about the important operation," Weiss said. "The bottom line, Castillo, is that it'll be your call."

"Tell me about the operation," Castillo said.

"There's a hell of a lot of money involved here," Weiss said. "A goodly share of the proceeds go to support the Dirección General de Inteligencia, which means the FSB doesn't have to support it as much as it has been. And that's important, because the FSB's ability to fund clandestine operations, Islamic extremists, etcetera, has been greatly reduced since we went into Iraq and cut off their oil-for-food income.

"And the DGI is supporting its sister service in the Republic of Venezuela, which I presume you know is about to become the People's Democratic Republic of Venezuela under Colonel Chávez, whose heroes are Fidel Castro, Josef Stalin, and Vladimir Putin.

"And the profits left over after the DGI gets what it needs go to the FSB's secret kitty, which supports, among other things, all those ex-Stasi and ex-ÁVO people who are causing trouble all over.

"Another way to put this is that if it wasn't for all this drug income they're getting, the FSB would have its operations seriously curtailed."

"Then my question is, why don't you confide in the Coast Guard, the Customs Service, whoever, what you know about this operation and have them stop it?" Castillo said.

Then he saw Delchamps shake his head, and then the look on Delchamps's face. It said, *Not smart, Ace!*

"Because," Weiss said, his face and tone suggesting he was being very patient with a backward student, "even if they did find a cooler full of coke on the *Holiday Spirit*—and their record of finding anything isn't very good— all that would happen is that we would add a dozen or so people to our prison population."

"So what's the alternative?"

"International Maritime Law provides for the seizure of vessels—including aircraft—involved in the international illicit drug trade."

"You want to grab Pevsner's airplanes?"

"That, too, but what we want to grab is the *Holiday Spirit* and her sister ships. Do you have any idea how much one of those floating palaces costs?"

Castillo shook his head to admit he didn't, then asked, "How are you going to do that?"

"Prove their owners were aware of the purpose to which they had put their ships."

"How are you going to that? They're not registered to Vladimir Putin."

"They're registered to a holding company in Panama," Weiss said. "And proving that Putin controlled that would be difficult, but that doesn't matter. All we have to prove is that *the owners* knew what was going on; that it was illegal. The *owners* lose the ship. The *Holiday Spirit* cost a little over three hundred and fifty million."

"And how are you going to prove the owners knew?"

"The operation could not be carried on without the captain being aware of what was going on."

"But the captains don't own their ships, do they?"

"No. But they don't get command of a ship except from the owners."

"Okay."

"The FSB was not about to entrust a three-hundred-and-fifty-million-dollar ship to some stranger. They wanted their own man running things, and they didn't want him to come from the Saint Petersburg Masters, Mates, and Pilots Union because people might start wondering what the Russians were doing running a cruise ship operation out of Miami.

"So they provided reliable, qualified masters with phony documents saying they were Latvians, or Estonians, or Poles."

"That sounds pretty far-fetched."

"You're a pilot, right? You just flew a Gulfstream Three to Argentina and back, right?"

Castillo nodded.

"Anybody ask to see your pilot's license?"

Castillo shook his head.

"Anybody *ever* ask to see your pilot's license?"

Castillo shook his head again.

"You're flying an eight-, ten-million-dollar airplane, you're given the benefit of the doubt, right?"

"Okay."

"You bring a three-hundred-and-fifty-million-dollar ship into port, everybody's going to say he must be an 'any tonnage, any ocean' master mariner, right? And proved this to the owners—otherwise, they would not have given him their ship, right?"

Castillo nodded once again.

"We have proof that the master of the *Holiday Spirit* and four of his officers gained their nautical experience in the submarine service of the Navy of the Union of Soviet Socialist Republics, and are not Latvians, Estonians, or Poles, or using the names they were born with.

"Now, all we have to do is prove that the owners knew this, *and* that said officers were actively involved in the smuggling of controlled substances into the United States. . . ."

"How are you going to do that?"

"By having people on the *Holiday Spirit*. Filipino seamen come cheap. Getting them onto the *Holiday Spirit* took some doing, but they're in place. And they have been compiling intel—including pictures of the ship's officers checking the incoming drugs, and putting them over the side—for some time. When we're absolutely sure we have enough to go to the Maritime Court in The Hague, we're going to blow the whistle.

"Unless, of course, you go down there and start making waves causing the system to go on hold. Which would mean we would have to start all over again from scratch."

"And you don't want me to make waves, is that it?"

"It's a question of priority."

"The President wants Timmons freed."

"So I understand."

"The only person who can call off my operation is the President," Castillo said simply. "And I don't think he will. And talking about waves, if I go to him with this, and he hears the company is withholding intel like this from Montvale, you'll have a tsunami."

"You were listening, I trust, when I told you we never had this conversation?"

Castillo nodded.

Weiss went on: "Montvale will be pissed on two accounts—first, that he's been kept in the dark, and second, that you let the President know he didn't know what was going on under his nose. When the company denies any knowledge of this, where does that leave you with Montvale? Or the President?"

"You're suggesting I go down there and go through the motions, but don't really try to get Timmons back?"

"I'm not suggesting anything, Colonel," Weiss said. "But it's pretty clear to me that if you go down there and pull a professional operation to get this DEA guy back, it's going to tell these people that they have attracted attention they don't want. They'll go in a caution mode, and we don't want that."

He stood up and looked at Castillo.

"See you at the briefing tomorrow," he said. "I've been selected to brief you."

"What you're suggesting, Weiss, is that I just leave Timmons swinging in the breeze."

"People get left swinging in the breeze all the time," Weiss said. "You know that as well as I do. I told you before, this is your call. One guy sometimes gets fucked for the common good."

Weiss looked at Delchamps.

"Always good to see you, Ed. We'll have to do lunch or something real soon."

And then he walked out of the room.

Castillo looked at Delchamps.

"Thanks a lot, Ed."

"If you want me to, Ace, I'll go with you to Montvale. Or the President. Or both."

Castillo looked at him with a raised eyebrow but didn't say anything.

"I said I went back a long way with Weiss. That's not the same thing as saying I liked him then, or like him now. And I don't like the smell of his operation."

He paused to let that sink in.

"That being said, I don't think that Montvale will believe you, or me, and his first reaction will be to cover his ass."

"What if there were three witnesses to that fascinating conversation?" Dick Miller asked, coming into the living room from the den. "I'm a wounded hero. Would that give me credence?"

"How long have you been in there?" Castillo asked.

"I got back here just as the Secret Service guy got booted out," Miller said. "And curiosity overwhelmed me."

"I still don't think that Montvale would believe you, me, or the wounded hero," Delchamps said, "and that his first reaction would be to cover his ass."

"So what do I do?"

"You're asking for my advice, Ace?"

"Humbly seeking same."

Delchamps nodded and said, "Aside from calling off Jake Torine and Munz, nothing. Give yourself some time to think it over. Hear what Weiss says at the briefing tomorrow."

"You better call off Munz and Torine," Miller agreed. "I don't think Darby and Solez are a problem. They don't know you've been ordered to get Timmons back. They went to Asunción to shut mouths; that's to be expected."

"Let's hope Aloysius's radio works," Castillo said. "I told Torine to go right to Asunción. They're probably already over the Caribbean."

He pushed himself out of his chair, picked up his mostly untouched drink, and walked to the den.

Max followed him.

VI

Castillo's cell phone buzzed, and on the second buzz, he rolled over in bed, grabbed it, rolled back onto his back, put the phone to his ear, and said, "You sonofabitch!"

"Good morning, Colonel."

Castillo recognized the voice as that of his Secret Service driver.

"It may be for you," Castillo said, "but I have just been licked—on the mouth—by a half-ton dog."

"I tried to put my head in your door to wake you, but Max made it pretty clear he didn't think that was a good idea."

"I'll be right down," Castillo said, and sat up.

Max was sitting on the floor beside the double bed.

Castillo put his hand on the bed to push himself out of the bed. The blanket was warm. He looked, and saw that the pillow on the other side was depressed.

"Goddamn it, Max, you're a nice doggie, but you don't get to sleep with me."

Max said, "Arf."

Castillo pulled open the door to the front passenger seat of the Denali. Max brushed him aside and leapt effortlessly onto the seat.

"Tell him to get in the back, Dick," Castillo said.

Major Dick Miller gave Lieutenant Colonel Castillo the finger and bowed Castillo into the second seat.

There was a muted buzz and the red LED on the telephone base mounted on the back of the driver's seat began to flash.

Castillo looked at it. The legend DNI MONTVALE moved across the screen. Castillo picked up the handset.

"Good morning, Mr. Ambassador."

"Where are you, Charley?"

"We just pulled into a Waffle House for our breakfast."

"Are you open to a suggestion?"

"Yes, sir, of course."

"Vis-à-vis the briefing this morning: If I sent Truman Ellsworth, representing me, and he announced that you were representing Secretary Hall, I think fewer questions would be raised."

Truman C. Ellsworth was executive assistant to Montvale. He had worked for Montvale in a dozen different positions in government over the years. Montvale had tried to send him to work as liaison officer between the office of the director of National Intelligence and the Office of Organizational Analysis.

Recognizing this as an attempt to plant a spy in his operation, Castillo had declined the offer, and had to threaten that he would appeal it to the President to keep Ellsworth out of OOA. For this and other reasons—as Ellsworth seemed to be personally offended that the OOA did not come under Montvale's authority—Castillo knew he was not one of Ellsworth's favorite people.

His first reaction was suspicion—*What's the bastard up to here?*—but what Montvale was suggesting made sense. The less conspicuous he was, the better.

"That makes sense, Mr. Ambassador," Castillo said.

"I think so," Montvale said, and the connection was broken.

They all ordered country ham and eggs for breakfast. When Castillo was finished with his, he collected the ham scraps and silver-dollar-sized bone and put them onto a napkin.

"For the beast?" the Secret Service driver asked, and when Castillo nodded, added his to the napkin. And then Miller added his. The napkin now was full to the point of falling apart.

In the Denali, Max sniffed the offering. He then delicately picked up one of the pieces of bone. There was a brief crunching sound, and then he picked up another, crunched that, and then picked up the third.

"I wonder," the Secret Service man asked softly, "how many pounds of pressure per square inch that took?"

"Try not to think what he would have done to your arm had you tried to disturb my sleep," Castillo said.

[TWO]
Office of the Chief
Office of Organizational Analysis
Department of Homeland Security
The Nebraska Avenue Complex
Washington, D.C.
0745 4 September 2005

"Good morning, Chief," OOA Deputy Chief of Administration Agnes Forbison greeted Castillo. "And hello again, Max. Where's your sweetheart?"

"That's right," Castillo said. "You've met Max. Mädchen is in the family way, and resting at the Motel Monica Lewinsky. It's a long story . . ."

"What are you going to do with him?"

"I don't really know," Castillo admitted. He switched to Hungarian. "Say hello to the nice lady, Max."

Max looked at him, then walked to Agnes, sat down, and looked up at her. Agnes scratched his ears.

"What did you say to him?" she asked.

"I told him you had a pound of raw hamburger in your purse."

"I don't, Max," Agnes said to him. "But if you're going to be here for long, I'll pick some up at lunch." She looked at Castillo. "Is he? Going to be here for long?"

Castillo told her how he had come into temporary possession of Max. Agnes smiled and shook her head.

"Well, maybe he's just what you need, Chief. Every boy should have a dog. And it looks to me that he's not all that upset about getting the boot from his happy home."

Max had returned to Castillo and was now sitting beside him, pressing his head against Castillo's leg.

"He's an excellent judge of character," Castillo said.

"The intelligence community is gathering in the conference room," Agnes said. "Is there anything you need besides a cup of coffee before you go in there?"

She put action to her words by going to a coffee service on a credenza behind her desk and getting him a cup of coffee.

"Thank you, ma'am," Castillo said, and then asked, "What do we hear from Jake Torine?"

"He called five minutes ago. Over one of those new radios you got in Vegas."

"What did he have to say?"

"They just took off from Buenos Aires. That translates to mean that he'll be in Baltimore in about ten hours."

"I can't wait that long," Castillo said, thoughtfully. "And Jake'll be beat when he gets here."

"Wait that long for what?"

"I have to go to Fort Rucker."

"You want to go commercial—which may be difficult because of the hurricane—or are you in your usual rush?"

"What's the other option?" he asked as Dick Miller walked in.

"OOA now has a contract with ExecuJet," she said, "who promise to provide service at the airport of your choice within an hour, then transport you to any airport of your choice within the United States in unparalleled luxury and comfort."

"Two questions. Isn't that 'unparalleled luxury and comfort' going to be painfully expensive? And how do you think—what did you say, ExecuJet?—feels about dogs?"

"Expensive, yes. But painfully, no. You did hear that there has been a substantial deposit to our account in the Caymans . . . right at forty-six million?"

Castillo nodded. "Ill-gotten gains about to be spent on noble purposes," he said, mockingly solemn.

"You're taking Max with you?"

"Until I figure out what to do with him. Maybe my grandmother'd take care of him for me."

"I don't think that's a viable option, Chief," she said drily.

"And I'll have to take one of the new radios and our Sergeant Neidermeyer with me. Dick can work the radio here until we can get some more communicators up here from Bragg."

"Once more, Colonel, sir," Dick Miller said. "Your faithful chief of staff is way ahead of you. We now have four communicators, five counting Sergeant Neidermeyer. General McNab said to be sure to tell you how much he now deeply regrets ever having made your acquaintance."

"I'll give ExecuJet a heads-up," Agnes said. "Max won't be a problem. When do you want to leave?"

"As soon as whatever happens in there is over," he said, nodding at the door to the conference room. "First, I want to hit the commo room."

There were five young men in the small room off Castillo's office, which had been taken over as the commo room. There was something about them that suggested the military despite their civilian clothing—sports jackets and slacks—and their "civilian haircuts."

No one called attention, but the moment Castillo pushed open the door all of them were on their feet and standing tall.

"Good morning, Jamie," Castillo said to the young man closest to him, gesturing for the men to relax.

"Welcome home, Colonel," Sergeant James "Jamie" Neidermeyer said.

Neidermeyer, just imported from the Stockade at Bragg to run the OOA commo room, was a little shorter than Castillo, with wide shoulders, a strong youthful face, and thoughtful eyes.

"Thank you, Jamie. Unfortunately, I won't be staying. Got your bag packed?"

"Yes, sir."

"You don't have to leave our nation's capital, of course, Jamie. You could send one of these guys."

Castillo put out his hand to the next closest of the young men.

"My name is Castillo."

"Yes, sir. Sergeant First Class Pollman, Colonel."

As he repeated the process with the others, Max went to the near corner of the room and lay down, his eyes on Castillo and the room.

"What do you guys think of our new radios?" Castillo asked.

There was a chorus of "Outstanding, sir!" and "First class, sir!"

"We just talked to Colonel Torine, sir," Neidermeyer said. "He was five minutes out of Buenos Aires."

"Mrs. Forbison told me," Castillo said. "I guess Jamie has brought you up to speed on the new radios? And what we're doing here?"

Another chorus of "Yes, sir."

"Anyone got any family problems—girlfriend problems don't count—with working with us—here and elsewhere—for a while?"

Another chorus, this time of "No, sir."

"And everybody is on per diem, right? Which doesn't look like it's going to be enough for Washington?"

This time it was apparent that all of them were reluctant to complain.

"Mrs. Forbison will get you each an American Express credit card," Castillo said. "They will be paid by the Lorimer Charitable & Benevolent Fund, which understands the problems of a hardship assignment in Washington. Use them for everything—meals, your rooms, laundry—everything but whiskey and wild women. Save your per diem for the whiskey and wild women. There's a threat to go along with that: Make any waves that call any attention whatever to what's going on here and you will shortly afterward find yourself teaching would-be Rangers how to eat snakes, rodents, and insects in the semitropical jungle swamps at Hurlburt. Everybody understand that?"

That produced another chorus, this time with smiles, of "Yes, sir."

"Okay. I'm glad to have you. I know that Vic D'Alessando wouldn't have sent you if you weren't the best." He paused to let that sink in, then asked, "Questions?"

"Sir, what kind of a dog is that?"

"Max is a Bouvier des Flandres," Castillo said. "It has been reliably reported that one of his ancestors bit off one of Adolf Hitler's testicles during the first world war."

That produced more smiles.

"And you, Sergeant Phillips, are herewith appointed his temporary custodian. I've got to go sit around a table with some Washington bureaucrats, and I don't think Max would be welcome. Have we got anything we can use as a leash?"

Phillips opened a drawer in the table holding the radios and came out with a coil of wire from which he quickly fashioned a leash.

He handed it to Castillo, who looped it to the D-ring of Max's collar and then handed the end of it to Sergeant Phillips.

"Max, you stay," Castillo said, in Hungarian, and then switched back to English. "And while I'm gone, Jamie, make up your mind who's going with me."

"Ever willing to make any sacrifice for the common good, Colonel," Neidermeyer said, "I will take that hardship upon myself."

"Your call, Jamie."

"Where we going, sir?" Neidermeyer said. "Buenos Aires?"

"You like Buenos Aires, do you?"

"It is not what I would call a hardship assignment, sir."

"We're going to Rucker, Sergeant Neidermeyer. One more proof that a smart soldier never volunteers for anything."

Castillo raised his arm in a gesture of *So long* and walked out of the radio room and into his office.

Miller was sitting on the edge of his desk.

"They're waiting for you," he said, nodding toward the door to the conference room. "You want me to come along?"

"Please," Castillo said, and went to the door and opened it.

Truman Ellsworth, a tall, silver-haired, rather elegant man in his fifties, was standing at a lectern set up at the head of the conference table.

There were a dozen people sitting at the table, which had places for twenty. There were perhaps twice that number sitting on chairs against the walls, obviously subordinates of the people at the table, and not senior enough to be at the table.

The only person Castillo recognized was Milton Weiss. He was sitting near one end of the table, between a man and a woman, obviously the CIA delegation.

Castillo and Miller took seats halfway down the table across from Weiss, who looked at Castillo but gave no sign of recognition.

"If I may have your attention, ladies and gentlemen," Ellsworth said. "Now that Lieutenant Colonel Castillo, who is the representative of the Department of Homeland Security, has joined us, we can get this under way."

You pompous sonofabitch!

Should I have brought a note from my mommy saying why I'm late?

"My name is Truman Ellsworth. Ambassador Montvale had other things on his plate this morning and sent me to represent him. This is, as I said, an informal meeting, but in view of the sensitive material which may come to light, a Top Secret security classification is in place, and it is not to be recorded.

"As I understand it," Ellsworth went on, "the attorney general and the DNI, Ambassador Montvale, are agreed that there may well be intelligence aspects to the kidnapping of a DEA agent in Paraguay, and that it behooves us to share, informally, what information we have which might shed light on the situation.

"May I suggest that the principals identify themselves? Why don't we work our way around the table?"

He sat down and nodded to a swarthy man on his right.

"John Walsh, DEA," the man said.

"Helena Dumbrowsky, State Department," a somewhat plump, red-haired woman announced.

"Norman Seacroft, Treasury." He was a slight, thin man in a baggy suit.

"Milton Weiss, CIA."

"Colonel K. L. DeBois, DIA." The representative of the Defense Intelligence Agency was tall and wiry, and wore his hair clipped almost to the skull.

"C. G. Castillo, Homeland Security."

"Inspector Bruce Saffery, FBI." Saffery was a well-tailored man in his early fifties.

Castillo thought: *I wonder if he knows Inspector John J. Doherty?*

"Excuse me," Colonel DeBois said, looking at Castillo and holding up his index finger. "But didn't Mr. Ellsworth just refer to you as 'Lieutenant Colonel'?"

Ellsworth, you sonofabitch. I'm not wearing a uniform. You didn't have to refer to me as an officer.

And why do I think that wasn't an accident?

"Yes, sir, I believe he did."

"You're a serving officer?"

"Yes, sir."

"And—presuming I'm allowed to ask—what exactly is it you do for the Department of Homeland Security, Colonel?"

"Sir, I'm an executive assistant to the secretary."

"How much do you know about the Office of Organizational Analysis?"

"Aside from that we're using their conference room, sir, not much."

"The reason I'm asking, Colonel, is that I was ordered to transfer one of my officers, a young lieutenant who was stationed in Asunción, to the Office of Organizational Analysis."

Oh, shit! Lorimer!

Castillo glanced at Truman Ellsworth and saw that he was looking at him. Ellsworth's face was expressionless, but he was looking.

"His name is First Lieutenant Edmund J. Lorimer," DeBois pursued.

"I just can't help you, Colonel," Castillo said.

This meeting hasn't even started and I'm already lying through my teeth to a fellow officer who looks like a nice guy.

"Perhaps you could ask Secretary Hall, Colonel Castillo," Ellsworth suggested, helpfully.

Oh, you miserable sonofabitch!

"Yes, I suppose I could do that," Castillo said. "I'll get back to you, Colonel, if I'm able to find out anything."

"I'd appreciate it," DeBois said. "He's a nice young officer who lost a leg from above the knee in Afghanistan. I've been sort of keeping an eye on him."

"I'll see what I can find out for you, sir, as soon as this meeting is over."

"I'd really appreciate it, Colonel."

"Why don't we start with you, Mr. Walsh?" Ellsworth said. "Exactly what happened in Asunción?"

Walsh took ten minutes to report in minute detail less than Castillo already knew. He didn't mention the garrote with which Timmons's driver had been murdered, just that he had been killed, means unspecified. Castillo decided he either hadn't been told how the driver had been killed, or had and didn't understand the significance.

Without saying so in so many words, Walsh made it clear that he thought the DEA could get Timmons back by themselves, if certain restrictions on what they could do were relaxed.

Mrs. Dumbrowsky of the State Department took the same amount of time to explain the excellent relations enjoyed by the United States with the Republic of Paraguay, expressed great admiration for the Paraguayan law-enforcement authorities, and made it clear without saying so in so many words that she strongly felt it would be a diplomatic disaster if a cretin like Walsh was allowed to destroy the aforesaid splendid relationship by going down there guns blazing and taking the law into his own hands.

Mr. Seacroft of the Treasury Department somewhat jocularly said that while he wasn't much of an admirer of anything French, he did think it was hard to disagree with their criminal investigation philosophy of searching for the money, and announced that he was going to run everything he had through the computers again and see what came out the other end.

Castillo had glanced at Ellsworth several times during Mr. Seacroft's discourse. Castillo had seen from Ellsworth's look of utter contempt that he, too, knew that the French criminal investigation philosophy was *Cherchez la femme*—though their seeking of *femme* meant "women," not "money."

Milton Weiss of the CIA said that he had to confess being a little surprised at the attention the kidnapping of Special Agent Timmons was getting. He had heard—unofficially, of course—that it was a not-uncommon occurrence—perhaps even common—and that in the end the drug thugs usually turned the kidnappee free.

He implied that the agency had far more important things to do than worry about one DEA agent, who, it could be reasonably assumed, had some idea of what he was getting himself into when he first became a DEA agent and subsequently went to Paraguay. The CIA would, however, Weiss said, keep its ear to the ground and promptly inform everybody if it came up with something.

It was Castillo's turn next.

"I'm sorry," he said. "I know nothing about this. I'm just here to listen and learn."

And the truth here, if I'm to believe what I've heard from these people, is that I know more about this than anyone else.

Except, of course, Weiss, and he's lying through his teeth.

Making at least two of us here who are doing that.

Colonel DeBois was next, and he immediately began to prove that he had come to the meeting prepared to share whatever knowledge the DIA had with the rest of the intelligence community.

"I think I—the DIA—has more knowledge of the situation down there than maybe we should," he began. "The background to that is that our people there, the defense attaché and his assistants, are encouraged to report informally on matters that come to their attention that are not entirely defense related but which they feel may be of interest to the DIA.

"Lieutenant Lorimer, to whom I referred earlier, became friends with Special Agent Timmons, and from him learned a good deal about the DEA operations there, which Lorimer passed on to us. Timmons may well have crossed the 'need to know' line there, telling Lorimer what he did, but I think that area's a little fuzzy. If we're here to share intelligence, what's really wrong with our people in the field doing the same thing?"

"It's against the law, for one thing," Milton Weiss said.

"Oh, come on, Weiss," John Walsh of the DEA said. "They all do it, and we all know they do it, and you know as well as I do that there's nothing really wrong with it."

Good for you, Walsh. I think I like you.

"If I'm getting into something here that perhaps I shouldn't?" DeBois said.

"Whatever you heard from your people couldn't really be called reliable intelligence, could it?" Ellsworth said. "It would be, in legal terms, 'hearsay,' would it not?"

"I'd like to hear the hearsay," Castillo said.

Ellsworth flashed Castillo an icy look.

Is that because he doesn't like me challenging him?

Or because he doesn't want DeBois to report what Lorimer told him?

"Please go on, sir," Castillo said.

"I thought you were chairing this meeting, Mr. Ellsworth?" Weiss demanded.

"We're supposed to be sharing intel, so let's share it," Castillo said.

Careful, Charley, you don't want to lose your temper.

After a moment's hesitation, Ellsworth said, "I think if Colonel Castillo wants to hear what Colonel DeBois has to say, then we should. With my caveat that it really is hearsay."

"Actually, rather than hard intelligence," DeBois said, "what Lieutenant Lorimer provided might be called background—his informal assessment of the problems down there, his own opinions, plus what he heard from Special Agent Timmons and others."

"Why don't you get on with it, Colonel?" Weiss said impatiently. "So the rest of us can get out of here?"

"Very well," DeBois said. "Lorimer reported that Timmons said, and he agreed, that the drug operations in Paraguay are more sophisticated than might be expected."

"Sophisticated?" Weiss parroted incredulously.

"The drug people in Paraguay seemed to be taking unusual steps to keep from calling attention to themselves," DeBois said.

"I thought all drug dealers did that," Weiss said.

"If you keep interrupting Colonel DeBois, Mr. Weiss," Castillo said, "we'll all be here a long time. Why not let him finish, and then offer your comments all at once?"

Colonel DeBois looked at Castillo gratefully, then went on: "According to Lorimer, Timmons said they had sort of a system, a *sophisticated* system, of dealing with the Paraguayan authorities. A system of rewards and punishment."

"I'd like to hear about that," Walsh said. "This is all news to me."

"For one example, people approach the children of Paraguayan police on their way home from school. They give them envelopes to give to their mothers. The envelopes contain money."

"I don't understand," Mrs. Dumbrowsky said.

"Well, to Special Agent Timmons, it was pretty clear it was a message. If you don't give us trouble, we will give you money. And if you do, we know where to find your family."

"Mr. Walsh, how experienced an agent was Timmons?" Weiss asked.

"He hadn't been down there long, if that's what you're asking," Walsh said.

"And how long had he been with the DEA?"

"He hasn't been in DEA very long, but if you're suggesting he was—that *he is*—sort of a rookie, I don't think that's right. He was a cop in Chicago. He comes from a family of cops. And he's a lawyer. He was recruited for the DEA by one of our guys in Chicago who met him and liked what he saw. He's fluent in Spanish."

"Go on, please, Colonel," Weiss said, "and tell us whatever else this very bright, very new DEA agent has theorized."

Colonel DeBois nodded and said, "Timmons also saw sophistication in how these people dealt with DEA agents. There were significant differences. For one thing, there were no envelopes with money, which Timmons felt was significant because it meant that the drug people knew the DEA agents could neither be bought nor coerced by threats against their families. Or because the drug people knew that injuring—or killing—the family of an American would bring a good deal of attention."

"But they are willing to kidnap DEA agents?" Inspector Saffery of the FBI asked.

That's the first time he's opened his mouth.

"Oh, yes."

"One would think that DEA agents would protect themselves from being kidnapped," Weiss said. "Wouldn't you, Inspector?"

"Very few FBI agents are kidnapped," Saffery said, chuckling.

"That's what Timmons found interesting," DeBois said.

"Doesn't kidnapping imply a ransom?" Norman Seacroft, of the Treasury Department, asked. "That's interesting! How much did they ask?"

"Kidnapping is taking someone against his or her will," Saffery said, somewhat intolerantly. "There doesn't have to be a ransom element."

"These people don't ask for a ransom?"

"Not so far," Walsh said.

"Then why do they kidnap them? And how do we get them back?" Seacroft asked.

"According to what Timmons told Lorimer, they kidnap them to suggest that working too hard to interdict the flow of drugs is not smart."

"But they turn them loose, right?" Seacroft said.

"As I understand it, all the DEA agents who have been kidnapped have been returned unharmed," Weiss said.

"Mr. Weiss, are you suggesting that becoming addicted to heroin is not being harmed?" Colonel DeBois asked, coldly courteous.

"Addicted to heroin?" Seacroft parroted.

DeBois explained, "I don't know the exact figure—*Timmons* didn't know—but at least two kidnapped DEA agents who were turned free by their captors had become addicted to heroin."

"Four," Walsh said.

"Let me make sure I understand this," Inspector Saffery said. "While these people held the DEA agents, they forced heroin on them? Turned them into addicts?"

"Correct," Walsh said.

"That's hard to believe!" Mrs. Dumbrowsky said.

"The ones who were addicted were released after there had been a successful delivery of a large drug shipment," Walsh said.

"This is the first I've heard of this!" Saffery said, indignantly.

"Inspector," Walsh said, "think about it. If you were a field agent who had become involuntarily addicted, would you like that information to become widely known? Even—perhaps especially—within the FBI?"

"As Mr. Ellsworth has pointed out, this is nothing more than hearsay," Mrs. Dumbrowsky said. "The State Department has heard nothing like this."

"And unless the colonel has some more fascinating hearsay to relate," Weiss said, "I really do have other things to do."

He stood up.

"As a matter of fact, Mr. Weiss, I wasn't quite through," DeBois said, coldly.

Weiss reluctantly sat down.

"Putting everything together, Timmons had been wondering if perhaps the Paraguayan drug-shipment operation was being run by someone other than the Paraguayan/Colombian/Bolivian drug people."

Castillo glanced at Weiss.

You didn't expect to hear that, did you, Milton?

But who is he talking about?

I can't believe that Timmons got into the Stasi/DGI involvement.

"That's absurd!" Weiss said.

"Why is it absurd, Mr. Weiss?" DeBois asked, courteously.

"On its face," Weiss said.

"Wait a minute," Saffery said. "Why not? The drug trade didn't start last week. A lot of these people have lived in the States for years—some of them even legally with Green Cards, even citizenship—"

"Your point, Inspector?" Weiss interrupted.

"What I'm saying is that they've been in the States long enough to figure out what Cousin José back in Colombia has been doing wrong and to tell him how to do it right."

"Define 'right' for me, please, Inspector," Weiss said.

"Don't kill our DEA people," Saffery said. "That draws attention to you. Knock off that macho bullshit—excuse me, Mrs. Dumbrowsky—that doesn't make us any money. Getting the stuff through is what makes us money."

"With all respect, Inspector, I still think that's absurd," Weiss said, and stood up again. "Mr. Ellsworth, if I have to say this, if the agency comes by some solid intelligence, it will be immediately brought to your attention, and that of Ambassador Montvale."

"Thank you," Ellsworth said.

The rest of the CIA delegation was now on its feet.

They followed Weiss to the door.

"Not that one, Weiss," Castillo blurted. "That's the door to my office."

By then Weiss had cracked the door open.

He turned to look at Castillo.

Max, towing Sergeant Phillips behind him, shouldered the door open.

The edge caught Weiss on the side of the face.

"Sonofabitch!" he exclaimed, and backed away, running into the rest of the

CIA delegation and causing further consternation. No one actually fell down, but almost, and two briefcases hit the floor.

Max went to Castillo, sat down, and offered him his paw.

"Colonel, I'm sorry," Phillips said. "I didn't realize how strong he is!"

"Presumably, Castillo, that animal is yours?" Ellsworth said.

"Actually, I'm just minding him for a friend," Castillo said. "You all right, Mr. Weiss?"

Weiss glared at him, then marched to the other door, and the CIA delegation departed.

The others in the room were reacting as if an auto accident had just happened before their eyes. No one moved, or showed any inclination to do so.

"Well, it would appear this meeting is over," Castillo said.

Ellsworth looked at him with a stone face, then turned to those at the table and said, "Yes, it would appear that way. Thank you, all, for coming."

"Colonel," Castillo said to Colonel DeBois. "May I have a moment of your time, sir?"

He gestured toward the open door to his office.

DeBois nodded, stood up, and walked to the door, then through it. Castillo, with Max and Phillips behind him, followed, and then Miller.

"Dick," Castillo said, "close and lock that behind you, will you, please?"

"I thought I heard you say 'my office,' " DeBois said. "Are you going to tell me what's going on here, Colonel?"

Castillo did not immediately respond.

He said, "Take the leash off Max, Phillips, and then see if you can raise the safe house."

"Yes, sir."

Max—as if he had understood what Castillo had ordered—sat down and allowed Phillips to remove the wire leash from his neck. Phillips went into the commo room. Max walked to Castillo and lay down at his feet.

Castillo met DeBois's eyes.

"Sir, with respect, you are not here and never have been here. But if you had been here, everything you might have seen, heard, or intuited is classified Top Secret Presidential."

DeBois's eyebrows rose, but he didn't reply.

Phillips came to the door of the commo room and said, "We're up, sir."

"Sir?" Castillo said, and asked DeBois with his eyes to go ahead of him into the commo room.

Sergeant Neidermeyer handed Castillo the handset.

The screen flashed the legend SUSANNA SIENO.

Castillo pressed the speaker button, then said: "Good morning, Susanna."

"How are things in our nation's capital?"

"I just had an unpleasant session with one of your coworkers, a guy named Milton Weiss. Know him?"

"Unfortunately."

"Is Eddie Lorimer around?"

"Right here, Colonel," Lorimer's voice came over the speaker.

"Colonel DeBois of DIA has been asking about you."

"I guess that was bound to happen. Colonel DB's one of the good guys, Colonel. What did you tell him?"

"Nothing, of course," Castillo said. "Hold one, Eddie."

He put his hand over the microphone.

"I'm sorry, Colonel," Castillo said. "But that concludes your tour of the Office of Organizational Analysis."

DeBois looked at him a long moment before he spoke.

"Thank you, Colonel Castillo. If you ever need anything, anything at all, you know where to find me."

"Thank you, sir. And if you hear anything interesting, I'd be grateful if you'd pass it to Major Miller."

DeBois nodded and walked out of the commo room. Castillo put the handset to his ear and turned off the speaker.

"Susanna, how long will it take to get just about everybody there? Including Darby and Santini? And Munz."

"Probably the better part of two hours."

"Well, it's important. So will you set it up, please? Give me a call when everybody's there."

"Will do," she said.

"Break it down, Neidermeyer," Castillo said, and handed him the handset. "Stay loose. As soon as I'm finished with that call, we're off."

"Yes, sir."

Castillo walked out of the commo room and sat down at his desk.

"You shut off the phones in the hotel?" he asked.

Miller shook his head.

Castillo picked up one of the telephones on his desk and punched one of the buttons on it.

"And how are you this bright and sunny morning, Uncle Billy?" Castillo asked in German.

"I probably shouldn't admit this to you," Eric Kocian said, "but I'm actually feeling pretty chipper. Mädchen and I took our morning constitutional past the White House. I was reminded of what people say about Paris."

"Which is?"

"Beautiful city. If it wasn't for the people, I'd love it. And then I came back to the hotel and had a word with the manager—"

"What didn't you like?"

"I told him that once he provided a decent leather armchair with footrest, the accommodations would be satisfactory. And to continue to send the bill to Fulda."

"Billy, what am I supposed to do with Max?"

"You were the one who sent Mädchen to him. As ye sow, so shall ye reap."

"I've been thinking of sending him to my grandmother."

"His broken heart would be on your conscience, Karlchen. Max took one look at you and—for reasons that baffle me—transferred his affections to you. But dogs choose their masters, you know, rather than the other way around."

Castillo looked across his office. Max was lying on the carpet in front of the couch, his head between his paws, looking at him.

"Where was Sándor Tor when you took your walk this morning?"

"He insisted on going with me. He and an apparently deaf man from the Secret Service. He wears a hearing aid and keeps talking to his lapel."

Castillo laughed, even though he knew he shouldn't.

"You know why he's there, Billy."

"Even as much as they dislike me, I don't think the FSB is going to try to shoot me in front of the White House."

"Never underestimate your enemy. Write that down, Uncle Billy."

"If you have nothing important to say, Karlchen, the hotel has at long last delivered our breakfast. They do a very nice corned beef hash with poached eggs. I suspect Mädchen will like it."

"I've got to go out of town for a couple of days. We'll resume this conversation when I get back."

"Remember not to give Max more than one small piece of chocolate at a time. Too much chocolate gives him flatulence. *Auf Wiedersehen*, Karlchen."

Castillo put the handset back in its cradle. He opened his mouth as if to say something, but didn't. A red LED on another telephone was flashing. Castillo leaned to it to read the legend.

"Montvale," he said, and reached for it.

"That didn't take long, did it?" Miller asked.

"Good morning, Mr. Ambassador," Castillo said. "Why do I think you've just been talking to Mr. Ellsworth?"

"He has a phone in his Yukon," Montvale said. "Did you actually bring that dog to the meeting?"

"Actually, Max invited himself."

"I gather the meeting wasn't all that we hoped it would be?"

"I didn't learn much that I didn't already know."

"So what's next?"

"In case the President asks?"

"In case the President asks."

"Well, I have to go to MacDill to see General McNab, and then to Fort Rucker to see about Hueys, and then to Mississippi to see if I can talk Ambassador Lorimer out of going to Uruguay."

"Your plane is back already?"

"No. I'm going to travel in unparalleled luxury and comfort in an Execu-Jet aircraft."

"Which will not be able to land at either MacDill or Fort Rucker without making waves. Would you like to use my plane?"

"I'd love to use your plane. But what if you need it?"

"I'll get something from Andrews."

"Then I gratefully accept. Thank you."

"It'll be waiting for you in, say, thirty minutes. Keep in touch, Charley."

"Yes, sir. I will."

The line went dead.

"Do you think he's loaning you his airplane because he likes you," Miller asked, "or because he can now tell the President he loaned it to you?"

"You have a suspicious and devious mind, Major Miller. Have you ever considered a career in intelligence?"

"Charley, if you want—it would save you two hours—I can bring the people in Argentina up to speed. Unless there's something I don't know?"

"Bottom line: Make no waves."

Miller nodded.

Castillo stood up and walked to the door of the commo room.

"Come on, Neidermeyer," he said. "We're off."

[THREE]
MacDill Air Force Base
Tampa, Florida
1135 4 September 2005

The ground handlers wanded the Gulfstream V to a stop on the visiting air-craft tarmac. An Air Force master sergeant, who Castillo had decided was a combination of crew chief and steward, moved quickly to open the door.

Max, who had been lying in the aisle beside Castillo's chair, greeted him at the door and went down the steps long before anyone could stop him.

Castillo looked out his window, vainly hoping that no one would be watching.

General Bruce J. McNab was marching toward the aircraft. Two officers, one middle-aged and the other younger, were on his heels. All were wearing the Army combat uniform, a loose-fitting garment of light green, gray, and tan camouflage material, worn with the jacket outside the trousers. All were wearing green berets.

One of McNab's rather bushy eyebrows rose and his head moved toward the nose of the aircraft. Castillo couldn't see what he was watching, but there was a very good chance he was watching Max void his bladder on the nose gear.

"Sorry, Colonel," Neidermeyer said. "That sonofabitch is quick."

"Not a problem," Castillo said, as he pushed himself out of his seat. "General McNab would have found something to criticize anyway."

When Castillo got to the door, he saw Max was sitting at the foot of the stair door, waiting for him. He went down the steps, faced General McNab, came to attention, and saluted crisply.

McNab returned it with a casual wave in the direction of his forehead.

"I was going to compliment you, Colonel," McNab said, "on your recruiting poster appearance. But curiosity overwhelms me. Where did that animal come from?"

"Sir, I'm going from here to Rucker. I thought Class A's would be a good idea."

"And the animal?"

"That's Max, sir. I'm keeping him for a friend."

Neidermeyer came down the stairs.

"Jamie," General McNab said. "Didn't your mother ever tell you that you will be judged by the company you keep?"

"Good afternoon, sir," Neidermeyer said. "Good to see you, sir."

"It won't be afternoon for another twenty-four minutes," McNab said. "But I'm glad to see you, too. Gentlemen, this is Sergeant Neidermeyer, one of the better communicators from the stockade. The splendidly attired officer is Lieutenant Colonel Castillo, and all the terrible things you have heard about him are true."

The colonel walked around McNab and offered Castillo his hand.

"Tom Kingston, Castillo," he said. "And I have to tell you that on the way here, the general told Inman"—he nodded toward the young officer—"that he hopes whatever you have that made you the best aide he ever had is contagious, because maybe he'll get lucky and catch it."

"Colonel Kingston," General McNab said, "who betrays my confidential remarks at the drop of a hat, was wondering what you're doing here, Charley. I couldn't tell him. Are you going to tell him? Or are you going to let him stumble around in the dark?"

"This might not be the best place to get into that, sir."

"Okay. Inman, take Sergeant Neidermeyer—and the airplane crew and that animal—somewhere nice for lunch. Eat slowly. When you're finished, bring them by my quarters. By then, Colonel Kingston, Lieutenant Colonel Castillo, and I will probably be through saying unkind things about enlisted men and junior officers."

"Yes, sir," the aide said.

McNab made a *Follow me* gesture and started marching across the tarmac.

Mrs. Donna McNab kissed Castillo on the cheek before he was completely through the front door.

"Oh, it's good to see you, Charley!"

"For God's sake, don't encourage him," General McNab said. "I'm trying to get rid of him before he gets me in trouble again."

"How long can you stay?" she asked, ignoring her husband.

"Maybe an hour and a half," Castillo said.

"The Naylors will be really disappointed. They won't be back until tomorrow afternoon."

"Me, too. It would have been great to see them."

She looked at McNab and said, "Everything's set up on the patio, darling. I'm giving you the benefit of the doubt that this is important and will leave you alone."

"Thank you. It is," McNab said, made another *Follow me* gesture, and led

Colonel Kingston and Castillo through the house and out back to a walled patio.

There was a gas grill, a side table on which sat a plate of T-bone steaks and another of tomatoes, and a small patio table that seated four and had place settings for three.

"I will now be able to state that my former aide landed here for fuel, and I entertained him at lunch at my quarters," McNab said. "Purely a social occasion."

Castillo nodded his understanding.

"We are having steak and tomatoes," McNab went on, "because I am on a diet that allows me all the meat I want to eat and small portions of fresh vegetables. While I am cooking the steaks, you can bring Kingston up to speed. Or as much speed as you feel appropriate."

"Yes, sir," Castillo said. "Colonel, I have to begin this with the statement that everything I tell you, or you intuit, is classified Top Secret Presidential."

"Understood," Kingston said. "Maybe it would clear the air a little, Colonel, if I told you that the secretary of Defense has called General McNab and instructed him to give you whatever you ask for, and that you would tell us only what you felt was appropriate."

Castillo nodded.

He began, "A DEA agent named Timmons has been kidnapped in Paraguay. The President has promised the mayor of Chicago that he will get this guy back, and tasked me to do so . . ."

". . . and there is one more problem," Castillo said when he had finished explaining what he had planned and the problems he saw in doing it.

General McNab, his mouth full of steak, gestured for him to go on.

"The agency is apparently running an operation down there to catch these people in the act of bringing drugs into the States aboard cruise ships. They intend to seize the ship—*ships,* plural—under maritime law. A guy named Milton Weiss"—he paused to see if either McNab or Kingston knew of Weiss, and when both shook their heads, went on—"came to see me last night and as much as told me to butt out."

McNab held up his hand as a signal to wait until he had finished chewing. That took at least ten seconds.

McNab then said, "That sort of operation, I would think—correct me if I'm wrong, Tom—would be run by the DEA or the Coast Guard or, for that matter, the Navy. They've got an ONI operation in Key West to do just that sort of thing." He looked at Kingston, who nodded his agreement. "So what does Montvale have to say about this?"

"Montvale doesn't know about it," Castillo said.

"The agency is up to something like that and the director of National Intelligence doesn't know about it?" McNab said.

"Maybe doesn't want to?" Kingston asked.

"I don't think he knows," Castillo said. "He was there when the President gave me this job. He didn't think it was a good idea. Neither did Natalie Cohen. I think if he—and now that I think of it—he or Natalie knew about this agency operation, one or the other or both would have used it as an argument to get the President to change his mind."

"Unless, of course, they know the President well enough to judge that he was not in a frame of mind to change his mind," McNab said.

"I don't think he knows," Castillo said. "I don't think either of them do."

"How did this Weiss character know what you're up to?" Kingston asked.

Castillo told them about Delchamps, and then that Miller had eavesdropped on the session with Weiss, and that both were willing to go with him to the President.

McNab thoughtfully chewed another piece of beef, then said: "My advice, Charley, would be to obey the last lawful order you received, which was to go get the DEA guy back."

"I was hoping you'd say that, sir," Castillo said.

"That was advice, Charley. I'm not in a position to give you orders."

"Yes, sir, I understand. But thanks for the advice."

"I hope it didn't change your mind about anything."

"No, sir. It did not."

"Good. Maybe you did learn something after all during all those years you were my canapé passer."

Castillo chuckled. As long as he had been McNab's aide-de-camp, he had never passed a canapé to the general's guests. McNab regarded the primary function of an aide-de-camp to be sort of an intern, an opportunity for a junior officer to see how senior officers functioned and learn from it.

He wondered if the young captain whom McNab had sent to feed Neidermeyer, Max, and the Gulfstream crew understood this.

McNab had never said anything to me. I had to figure it out myself; that was part of the training.

"Okay, Tom. What do you think?" McNab said.

And that's something else I learned from Bruce J. McNab. I'd heard about it at the Point, but I learned it from him.

A wise officer gets—even if he has to force the issue—the opinions and sugges-tions of his subordinates before he offers his own, and, more important, makes any decisions.

That way, they say what they think, rather than what they think the boss wants to hear.

"Nothing, General, but how to get the Hueys down there black," Kingston said, thoughtfully. "That does not pose much of a real problem—except the usual ones, time and money. Castillo wants this done yesterday."

"With respect, sir, it's not me who wants it done yesterday," Castillo said. "But black outweighs time."

"How about money?" Kingston asked.

"You tell me how much is wanted, and where, and Dick Miller will wire it within a matter of hours."

"It would be impolitic of you, Tom," McNab said, "to ask where he's get-ting the money."

"My concern is whether there's enough."

"There's enough," Castillo said.

"Charley has some experience with how much black costs," McNab said. "So how do we get the Hueys down there, and exactly where do we send them?"

"Open for a wild hair?" Kingston asked.

McNab nodded.

"The *Ronald Reagan*," Kingston said.

McNab pursed his lips thoughtfully.

"Excuse me?" Castillo asked.

"It's an aircraft carrier, Charley. Named after the Gipper," McNab said drily.

Kingston added, "And it's sailing around the world, or at least down the east coast of South America, and around the horn, or whatever they call it, and then up the west coast to San Diego.

"Onto *her*, Tom," McNab corrected him. "*She's* sailing around the world."

Kingston nodded. "If we could get those Hueys onto *her* either before *she* leaves, or even after *she* leaves, they could just be flown off. . . ."

"Wouldn't that make waves?" Castillo asked, and then heard what he had just said and, shaking his head, muttered, "Jesus Christ!"

"I don't think so," Kingston said, smiling at him. "We could say they're for the press or something. The Navy probably won't like the idea—"

"The Navy will do what the secretary of Defense tells it to do," McNab said, flatly.

"You have a place where they could be landed black?" Kingston asked.

"I know just the place," Castillo said. "But the last time I was in Uruguay their head cop told me, 'Good-bye and please don't come back.' "

"You want me to set this up with the Navy or not, Charley?" McNab asked.

"Yes, sir, please. I'll find a place to fly them off to before they get there."

"Just the Hueys? Or the Hueys and the shooters?"

"Just the Hueys," Castillo said. "We've got a few days. It would be better to send them down as tourists, or soccer players, a couple at a time."

"No problem with Spanish-speaking A-Teams, Tom?" McNab asked.

"No."

"Get on the horn to Bragg. I want four shooters on their way within twelve hours, different airlines, and six every twenty-four hours thereafter. You have a place for them to go, Charley?"

"By the time they get there, I will."

He wrote several telephone numbers on a sheet of paper and handed the paper to Kingston.

"That's if something happens and Lorimer doesn't meet them at the airport."

Kingston nodded his understanding.

"We could send the weapons and the gear on the Hueys," Castillo said, thoughtfully. "If we can't get the Hueys into the country black, we won't need the weapons. And that'll eliminate having to send them under diplomatic cover, which would open a can of worms."

Kingston grunted his approval.

"Get the weapons and gear moving to Rucker right away," McNab ordered. "There's a buck general there, Crenshaw, I've dealt with before. I'll get on the horn to him and give him a heads-up, tell him to stash the weapons and gear until Charley knows what he wants to do with it."

"Yes, sir."

"I'll also tell him to expect eight Huey pilots—and four crew chiefs—from the 160th at Campbell, same story. I'll get on the horn to Campbell myself as soon as I can."

"Yes, sir," Kingston said.

"Anything else for right now?"

Kingston looked at Castillo.

"The money?" Kingston said.

"You've got a black account here, sir?"

"In the base branch of the Wachovia Bank."

"If you'll give me the number, sir, I'll get on the horn to Dick Miller, and the money will probably be in it by the close of their business day. How much will you need, sir?"

"This isn't going to be cheap, Castillo. We've got—"

"Will a million cover it for openers, sir?"

"More than enough," Kingston said.

"Wrong answer, Tom," McNab said. "Probably not, Colonel Castillo. But we can always come back to you for more, right?"

"Yes, sir."

"That's it, then?" McNab asked.

"I think that covers just about everything for now, sir," Kingston said.

"Yes, sir. Thank you both."

"Why don't we see if Miller is going to have any problems getting the money down here before I start loaning you money from my special funds?" McNab said.

Castillo took his cellular phone from his pocket. Kingston handed him a slip of paper.

Ninety seconds later, Castillo broke the connection.

"Done, sir. Major Miller sends his compliments, sir."

"Story going around is that he's being retired medically. True?"

"Yes, sir. First of the month. He's going to work for me."

McNab shook his head.

"Goddamn shame," he said, and then heard what he had said. "I don't mean his working for you, Charley. I meant . . . his being involuntarily retired."

"Yes, sir. It is."

McNab shook his head and then smiled.

"Okay. Those shrill girlish giggles you may have been hearing are those made by my wife when she is playing with a dog. I suspect everybody's here. Once again, my timing is perfect."

He began to scrape the meat scraps from his plate onto another and then reached for Castillo's plate.

"That animal of yours eats meat, right?"

"Yes, sir. He does."

When they went into house, Mrs. Bruce J. McNab was already feeding Max.

"Charley, he's adorable," she said. "And he really loves chocolate, doesn't he? That's his fourth Hershey bar."

VII

Castillo stuck his head in the cockpit of the Gulfstream V and said, "Thanks, guys."

"Any time, Colonel," the pilot, an Air Force major, said as he offered his hand.

"You've got another general meeting you, Colonel," the copilot, a young captain, said, offering his hand and then pointing out the window.

Castillo saw that the copilot was wearing an Air Force Academy ring.

Another bright and bushy-tailed young man, he thought, not unkindly, *who went through the academy dreaming of soaring through the wild blue yonder in a supersonic fighter jet . . . and wound up in the right seat of a Gulfstream.*

And who by now has realized he's lucky to be there.

Most of his classmates are probably still wingless, flying a supply room desk.

The Air Force had far more academy graduates wanting—and qualified for—flight training than the Air Force had a requirement for pilots. The bitter joke going around the Air Force was "If you really wanted to fly, you should have joined the Army. They have more aircraft than we do."

Castillo looked to where the lieutenant pointed.

Brigadier General Crenshaw, the deputy commander of Fort Rucker and the Army Aviation Center, was standing in the door of the Base Operations building with a young officer.

Oh, shit!

Last time I saw him, I said I was Secret Service.

That was—what?—just three days ago. . . .

When Castillo turned back to the passenger compartment, he saw that the crew chief/steward had already unloaded their luggage, and Neidermeyer was going down the stair door steps cradling the radio suitcase in his arms. Max was standing in the aisle straining against his makeshift leash, which was firmly tied to a seat mount.

Untying the wire leash proved difficult, as Max's tugging on it had really tightened the knot. Castillo finally got it undone, and allowed Max to tow him down the stair-door steps. As he did, he saw that Crenshaw had walked across the tarmac to the airplane.

He saluted as well as he could while allowing Max to make his way to the nose gear, where Max lifted his leg and broke wind. Several times. Loudly.

"Did you have to teach him to do that, Colonel?" General Crenshaw asked. "Or did it come naturally to him?"

Castillo could think of nothing to say but "Good afternoon, sir," so he said that.

"Welcome back to Fort Rucker, Colonel," Crenshaw said. "I have been reliably informed that you did in fact learn how to fly in Texas, and that there was probably a good reason you told me you were in the Secret Service."

Castillo's confusion showed on his face.

General Crenshaw smiled and nodded toward Base Operations. Two familiar faces were now standing outside the building.

One was Lieutenant General Harold F. Wilson, U.S. Army (Retired), wearing Bermuda shorts and a pink golf shirt. The other was Lieutenant Colonel Randolph Richardson, in ACUs. General Wilson waved happily. Colonel Richardson smiled.

Or is he grimacing as he squints in the bright sunlight? Castillo thought.

"When General McNab called to tell me you were coming, I was on the fifteenth hole with General Wilson. I was once his aide, so I knew about his relationship with your father."

"I haven't seen General Wilson for several years," Castillo said. "He retired to Phoenix, I believe."

"That's right," General Crenshaw said.

"And I haven't seen Richardson for . . . I don't remember the last time I saw him."

"Well, he's my very competent assistant G-3, which makes him just the man to get you whatever you came for. Would that be all right with you?"

"Yes, sir. That would be fine. Thank you."

"And this gentleman is?" Crenshaw asked.

"My communicator, sir. Sergeant First Class Neidermeyer. He has to be close to me, so I was going to introduce him as Mister Neidermeyer and smuggle him in a BOQ with me. But I'm a little tired of bending the truth. So I guess it's the Daleville Inn."

Crenshaw offered his hand to Neidermeyer.

"Welcome to Fort Rucker, Mr. Neidermeyer," he said. "I hope you and Colonel Castillo find the Magnolia House comfortable."

Hearing the name Magnolia House brought back fond memories for Castillo. More than a decade ago, his grandparents had stayed in the World War II–era frame housing that had been converted to a cottage for transient VIPs.

"Thank you, sir," Castillo said.

Castillo, Crenshaw, and Neidermeyer started to walk across the tarmac. Two neat young sergeants trotted out to them and offered to take their luggage. Neidermeyer would not part with the radio suitcase.

When Castillo and Neidermeyer got close to the building, General Wilson spread his arms wide.

"How are you, Charley?" he called, and wrapped him in a bear hug.

When he let him go, he said, "Bethany talked yesterday to your grandmother, who told her you had made a couple of flying trips to the Double-Bar-C but, as usual, she had no idea where you were. So I'm really glad to see you."

"I've been moving around a lot," Castillo said. "What are you doing here?"

"Oh, we came to see Beth and Randy and the grandchildren. Rucker's hot, but not as hot as Phoenix, and I do like to play golf."

"How is Beth?" Castillo asked, politely, as he put out his hand to Richardson.

"Well, thank you," Richardson said without emotion.

What do I call him?

Randolph? Randy?

"Good to see you, Randy."

"Likewise."

"Your grandmother," General Wilson went on, "told us your promotion finally came through. Congratulations."

"They were scraping the bottom of the barrel," Castillo said. "This is Jamie Neidermeyer, my communicator. Jamie, General Wilson flew with my father in Vietnam. And this is Colonel Richardson. We were classmates at West Point."

They shook hands.

It was fairly obvious from Neidermeyer's "how do you do, sirs" as well as his general appearance that he was military. But Richardson either didn't pick up the significance of his not being identified by rank or didn't want to.

"You're in the service, Neidermeyer?"

Neidermeyer looked at Castillo for guidance.

"He works for General McNab, Randy," General Crenshaw said. "At the moment, he's not wearing his uniform. When Castillo was here the last time, neither was he. He told me he was in the Secret Service. Mysterious indeed are the ways of the Special Operations Command and those in it."

"Well, now that that's out in the open," General Wilson said, "am I sticking my nose in where it's not particularly welcome?"

"No, sir. Not at all," Castillo said. "I'm scrounging things for General McNab, but, if you're free, I'd love to buy you and your bride dinner tonight."

"Beth and her mother are at this moment preparing dinner," Richardson said. "She said she couldn't remember the last time she saw you."

Odd. I remember it with great clarity.

"The invitation of course includes you and Mrs. Crenshaw, General," Richardson went on. "And you, Mr. Neidermeyer."

"I don't want to intrude, Richardson," General Crenshaw said.

"It wouldn't be an intrusion at all, sir. And it would give you and the general more time together."

Crenshaw looked at Castillo to see what he should do.

"And you and I could talk about the terrible things we had to do as aides-de-camp to difficult generals, General," Castillo said, then smiled.

"Who was yours?" Crenshaw said.

"Bruce J. McNab."

"I didn't know that," Crenshaw said. "I'd love to hear what that was like. Yes, Colonel Richardson. Mrs. Crenshaw and I gratefully accept your kind invitation to dinner."

"General Crenshaw, could I have a moment of your and Randy's time?" Castillo asked.

"Certainly."

Crenshaw led them to the pilots' lounge, politely asked the two pilots there if they would mind giving them a few minutes alone, and then looked at Castillo.

"This operation is highly classified, sir," Castillo said. "The fewer people who know I'm here, or have been here, the better. What I need is four H-Model Hueys for an operation—"

"What kind of an operation?" Richardson interrupted.

"If you don't know that, Randy," Castillo said somewhat impatiently, "then you can truthfully swear that I didn't tell you what I wanted them for."

Of all the light colonels at Rucker, I get Righteous Randolph?

Richardson nodded his understanding.

"They have to have GPS," Castillo went on, "and they have to be in very good shape. And, I have to tell you, you probably won't get them back."

Righteous's jaw just now about bounced off the tiled floor.

"We have been directed to give Colonel Castillo whatever he asks for, and that he has the highest priority," General Crenshaw said.

"How do we explain your presence if someone recognizes you?" Richardson asked.

"The cover story is that I'm an executive assistant to the secretary of Homeland Security, and that I'm here because this was the most convenient place for me to come and rent a light aircraft—I'll get to that in a minute—and fly to Pass Christian, Mississippi, on a mission for the secretary."

"Two things, Castillo," General Crenshaw said. "That area was badly mauled by Hurricane Katrina. I don't know if any fields down there are open. Have you considered a Black Hawk?"

"There's an airstrip where I'm going. It's open. And a light airplane will attract less attention than an Army helicopter. Neidermeyer went on the Internet and found a Cessna 206H available for charter at the airport in Ozark—"

"The Flying Hearse," Crenshaw interrupted, chuckling.

"Sir?"

Crenshaw smiled, then explained:

"Actually, it's a T206H—turbocharged. The fellow who owns the funeral home is a flying enthusiast. Flying is expensive—that airplane cost more than a quarter million dollars—but he thought he had the solution. If he had an airplane, he could fly cadavers to where they were going to be buried and charge the same thing airlines do—twice the price of the most expensive first-class ticket. That would be a substantial contribution to the cost of his hobby. He was so enthusiastic that he didn't check to see if a coffin would fit in the airplane. They don't. So, it is reliably reported, he transports—in of course the dead of night, so to speak—the cadavers in body bags, strapped into a seat, and has a casket waiting wherever he's going. I know him. I can call and set that up for you, if you'd like. You can fly a 206?"

"I can fly a 182 and a Citation," Castillo said. "Will that work?"

"I don't think that will be a problem," Crenshaw said. "But he'll probably want to ride around the pattern with you. Anything else?"

"There will be pilots and crew chiefs coming here from the 160th at Fort Campbell."

"General McNab told me," Crenshaw said, and looked at his aide. "Find accommodations for them, Richardson. They should start arriving tomorrow. Eight pilots and four crew chiefs."

"Yes, sir," Richardson said.

"And some supplies from Fort Bragg," Castillo added. "Which will have to be stored somewhere secure until they can be loaded on the Hueys."

"What kind of supplies?" Richardson asked.

"The kind that need someplace secure to store them," Castillo said, pointedly avoiding details.

"General McNab said they're coming by truck tonight," Crenshaw said to Richardson. "They'll probably be here by morning. Have the truck put in the MP impound lot until you can make better arrangements in the morning. And make sure the MPs are guarding the impound lot."

"Yes, sir," Richardson said.

"And as soon as possible, Neidermeyer has to get his radio up," Castillo said.

He saw the questioning look on Crenshaw's face.

"It's in the suitcase," Castillo said, nodding at it. "It doesn't take long, but I'd rather not do it here."

"May I ask what kind of a radio?" Richardson asked.

I am tempted to tell you, "None of your fucking business."

But resuming hostilities with you, Righteous, would be counterproductive.

"It's a rather amazing system developed by AFC," Castillo said. "Bounces signals—voice and data, both really deeply encrypted—off satellites. When we get to Magnolia House, I'll show you how it works."

"I'd like to see that," Crenshaw said. "I just thought of something. How are you going to pay for the Flying Hearse?"

"American Express," Castillo said, reaching for his wallet. "Never leave home without it."

He took his AmEx card from his wallet and handed it to Crenshaw, who examined it. He then looked at Castillo.

"The Lorimer Charitable & Benevolent Fund," the general said.

Castillo nodded and grinned. "Yes, sir."

"I won't ask what that is," the general went on, "but will simply repeat what I said before, that mysterious indeed are the ways of the Special Operations Command and those in it." He paused. "I can call from the car on the way to the post, if you'd like. I'm driving my own car, but Richardson's got a van."

I'll be damned if I'm stuck riding the bus with Righteous.

"If you've room in your car, and I'm not an imposition, that'd be great, sir," Castillo said. "Thank you."

[TWO]

"Would you like a drink, Charley?" General Wilson asked when they were inside the Magnolia House. "Under the circumstances, I'm going to allow myself to have *one*. And I might even allow my dear friend General Crenshaw here a little taste."

"Indeed, I would," Castillo said. "I have been a good boy all day, and it's been a very long day."

And I just drove past the Daleville Inn, which triggered a flood of not at all unpleasantly lewd and lascivious memories.

Neidermeyer came into the living room carrying a DirecTV dish antenna.

"You want a drink, Jamie?" Castillo said.

"Wait 'til I get this thing up, sir. What I need now is a stepladder or a chair, so I can stick this thing on the roof."

"Try the kitchen," General Wilson said, and pointed, then asked, "DirecTV?"

Neidermeyer looked at Castillo for guidance. Castillo nodded.

"Actually, sir," Neidermeyer said seriously, "I have a much better one, but it says Super Duper Top Secret Delta Force Satellite Antenna and the colonel won't let me use it. He says it makes people curious."

The general chuckled.

"It took only a couple of small modifications to this," Neidermeyer said. "Mostly the installation of a repeater, so we don't need the coaxial cable to connect to the box. It ought to be up in a minute or so."

"Need any help, Jamie?" Castillo said.

"No, sir. Thank you."

Richardson came in as Castillo, Crenshaw, and Wilson touched glasses.

"Your man is installing a cable TV dish on the roof," Richardson announced.

"And any minute now, we can get Fox News," General Crenshaw said with a straight face.

Castillo chuckled, and Richardson shot him a look, wondering what that was about. Then Richardson turned his attention back to the general.

"Sir, the field-grade OD has been advised of the truck coming from Bragg. They'll be expecting it at the gate, and there will be an MP escort to guide it to the MP impound lot, where it will be under guard until Colonel Castillo tells me what he wants to do with it."

"First thing in the morning, Randy," General Crenshaw said, "go out to Hanchey Field and take over a hangar large enough for four H-models. Arrange for the MPs to guard it, then move this equipment into it. That sound about right, Castillo?"

"Yes, sir, that sounds fine."

"Sir," Richardson said, "am I to sign a receipt for this equipment?"

"Good question," Castillo said. "I didn't think about that. Well, when the truck gets here"—he stopped as Neidermeyer came back in the house, then went on—"Neidermeyer here will happily get out of bed and sign for it. Right, Jamie?"

"The stuff from Bragg?"

Castillo nodded. "Tonight it goes into an MP lot. In the morning, Colonel Richardson will have it moved to a guarded hangar at Hanchey—one of the airfields."

"Yes, sir. Am I going with you tomorrow, sir?"

"You and the magic box."

"Sir, it might be a good idea if we had our own wheels."

"I didn't think of that," Crenshaw said. "What would you like?"

"Sir, vans are pretty inconspicuous. And I don't think we need a driver."

"Randy?" the general said.

"I'll have one here in fifteen minutes, sir."

"This should take me about ninety seconds, sir," Neidermeyer said to Castillo, and walked out of the room.

Richardson walked to a telephone on a credenza, took a small notebook from his pocket, found what he was looking for, and dialed a number.

"Colonel Richardson, Sergeant. General Crenshaw desires that a van be sent immediately to the Magnolia House. A driver will not be required.

"Yes, Sergeant, I'm aware that it's unusual. But that is the general's desire."

He listened a moment and said, "Thank you," and hung up.

For Christ's sake, Righteous!

You're a lieutenant colonel. You can give orders for a lousy van all by yourself.

You didn't have to hide behind Crenshaw's stars.

Castillo caught General Wilson's watching eye.

And that wasn't lost on him, either.

"A van has been laid on, sir," Richardson announced.

"Thank you."

Neidermeyer walked back into the living room and handed a handset to Castillo.

"They say twenty-five feet max with no wire, but give it a try."

Castillo looked at the handset, saw H. R. MILLER, JR. on its small screen, pushed the loudspeaker button, and said, "So I shamed you into not taking off early?"

"Where are you, Charley?"

"In Magnolia House at Rucker. And guess who's with me?"

"No, thanks."

"General Wilson and Randy Richardson."

"You're on loudspeaker?"

"Yeah."

"Good evening, sir. Dick Miller, sir. Hey, Righteous, how they hanging?"

"Hello, Dick," General Wilson said. "Good to hear your voice."

Restraining a smile, Wilson added softly to General Crenshaw: "That's Dick Miller's son. He's also a classmate of Randy's."

"Hello, Miller," Richardson said without enthusiasm.

"Anything happen?" Castillo asked.

"I made the deposit to the bank where you were earlier," Miller said. "That airplane's back from you know where. The pilot thereof is crashing in suburbia. He says if you need to go anywhere in the next twenty-four hours, take a bicycle. The copilot's on his way you know where, and the plane that took him will bring J. Edgar Hoover, Jr., back here. That's about it."

"In the morning, I'm going to Mississippi to see the ambassador. Then back here."

"How are you going to get to Mississippi?"

"I rented a T206H."

"You'll be flying right over what used to be Pascagoula and Biloxi."

"Yeah, I guess."

"I've been watching that on the tube right now. Incredible. The storm surge picked up a couple of those floating casinos and dumped them two, three hundred yards—maybe more—inland. There are slot machines all over. No damage at Rucker?"

"I didn't see any. Nothing like that."

"Okay, Chief. Keep in touch."

Castillo pushed the OFF button.

"I'll hang this up, Jamie. Make yourself a drink. And while you're at it, see what Colonel Richardson will have."

As he left the living room, he heard Richardson say somewhat piously, "Nothing for me, thank you."

[THREE]
1040 Red Cloud Road
Fort Rucker, Alabama
1735 4 September 2005

"There it is, Jamie," General Wilson said. "One Zero Four Zero."

He and Castillo were in the second-row bench seat of the Army Dodge Caravan, Max having decided he would rather ride in the front passenger seat.

Neidermeyer slowed the van almost to a stop as they approached the house. It was a single-family frame one-story building, identical to the ones on its left and right as far as Castillo could see.

Castillo vaguely remembered that lieutenant colonels and better—*or was it majors and better?*—got separate houses. Lower ranks had to share an interior wall.

Hanging from two eighteen-inch-high posts next to the driveway was a sign: LTC R. W. RICHARDSON, AV.

The carport was full with a Pontiac sedan and a civilian Dodge van. Behind them, on the drive, was a Buick sedan with Arizona license plates and a Mercury sedan pulled up behind the Dodge.

"It looks like the Crenshaws are here," General Wilson.

"Maybe I'd better park on the street," Neidermeyer said.

"It's against the law," Wilson said. "Pull in behind the Mercury."

"Why is it against the law?" Castillo asked.

"About the time of Custer's Last Stand, a child darted out between two cars parked on the street and was run over. You just can't have that sort of thing, and so they passed a law. I tried to change it when I was post commander and was dissuaded by a regiment of outraged mothers."

"What do you do if you have more people coming to dinner than you have room in your driveway?"

"You politely ask your neighbors if the extras can park in their drive," Wilson said. "If your neighbor outranks you, or your wives have been scrapping, you're out of luck."

Neidermeyer pulled the van in behind the Mercury.

The house front door opened. Mrs. Harry F. Wilson looked out at the van.

"What do you say I get out and stagger up to the door?" General Wilson said.

"General, please don't do that to me," Castillo said with a grin.

General Wilson slid the back door open, got out, and walked to the door, holding up an index finger.

"Max, you stay," Castillo said in Hungarian, and followed Wilson.

"What's this mean?" Bethany Wilson asked, more than a little suspiciously, holding up her own index finger.

"It's the answer to your question, dear. 'How many drinks did Charley feed you?' "

"Very funny," she said. "Hello, Charley, how are you?"

Castillo held up three fingers.

"Haven't changed a bit, have you, handsome?" she asked, and kissed his cheek.

Neidermeyer was by then standing outside the van.

"Mrs. W., this is Jamie Neidermeyer," Castillo said.

"Hello, Jamie," she said.

"He and Charley are tied together," General Wilson said. "He's got a radio in that suitcase."

"Hello, Charley," Mrs. Randolph Richardson said from behind her mother. "How nice to see you again."

She's still a looker, still looks like a younger version of her mother.

And why do I suspect she's less thrilled than her father and mother that Good Ole Charley's coming to dinner?

"It's nice to see you, too, Beth," Castillo said. "Beth, this is my communicator—and friend—Jamie Neidermeyer."

"Hello, Jamie," Beth said, offering her hand.

"Jamie's going to need a place to put a small dish antenna," General Wilson said.

"A what?"

"A DirecTV antenna," Wilson said. "Except it's not. It's the satellite antenna for the radio in his suitcase. What about the patio?"

Beth smiled uneasily.

A small, dressed-for-company girl, about six years old, pushed past Beth and called out, "Grandpa!"

Another girl, about eleven or twelve and who looked like her mother and grandmother, came through the door, followed finally by a boy Castillo guessed to be about twelve or thirteen.

"Charley," Beth said. "This is Randy, the Fourth, and Bethany—"

"The third?" Castillo asked.

"Girls don't usually do that," Beth said. "And Marjorie. This is Colonel Castillo. You know who he is?"

None of the three had a clue.

"This is Doña Alicia's grandson," Beth explained.

The boy showed a very faint glimmer of interest; the girls none at all.

"Grandpa Wilson flew with Colonel Castillo's father in Vietnam," Mrs. Bethany Wilson said.

"And Daddy and Colonel Castillo were friends, classmates, at West Point," Beth Richardson said.

This produced the same level of fascination and excitement as had the previous footnotes to history.

They're not being rude, Castillo thought. *They just don't give a damn. And why should they?*

Something did excite Marjorie, the smallest: "There's a dog in Grandpa's car!"

She ran toward it.

Oblivious to her mother's order—"Marjorie, come back here this instant!"—she pulled open the front passenger door.

Oh shit! Castillo thought.

The evening's festivities will begin with Beth's forty-pound daughter being mauled by my one-hundred-forty-pound dog.

He ran to the van.

By the time he got there, Max had leapt out of the van, licked Marjorie's face to the point of saturation, and was sitting down offering her his paw.

She put her arms around his neck.

"Marjorie, it would appear, has found a new friend," General Wilson observed. He had been on Castillo's heels and now was catching his breath.

"Is that yours?" Beth accused from behind her father. She didn't seem surprised when Castillo nodded.

"She really loves dogs," Beth said.

"So did you, honey," General Wilson said. "All your life."

"We've never had one," Beth said, and when she saw the look on Castillo's face, added, "You know how it is, moving around all the time in the Army."

Bad answer, Beth.

Your father always was able to keep one.

Truth is that Righteous probably doesn't like dogs.

They're always a nuisance and a potential source of trouble and might interfere with the furtherance of one's career.

Beth averted her eyes as General Crenshaw and Lieutenant Colonel Richardson came out of the house.

"Look at that, will you? Love at first sight!" General Crenshaw called. "Hey, Max!"

Oblivious to the weight of Marjorie clinging to his neck, Max walked to General Crenshaw and offered him his paw.

Now what, Righteous?

Your general thinks Max and your kid make a great pair.

Think fast!

"Beautiful animal," Richardson said. "You've got a nice one there."

"Yeah."

I guess I might as well face it that you are now mine, Max.

Well, what the hell. I told Abuela when she said I didn't even have a dog that I'd get one.

"Well," Richardson went on, "why don't we put the dog back in the car and then see about having a drink and something to eat?"

"I want to play with him!" Marjorie announced firmly.

"Randy," General Wilson said. "What about putting him on the patio and letting the kids play with him?"

"Good idea!" Richardson said with forced enthusiasm.

Dinner—the whole evening—went better than Castillo thought it would.

Beth was a good hostess.

Why am I surprised?

She learned the profession of Officer's Lady from her mother, who may as well have written the book.

And more than that, Beth was gracious.

She seated Jamie Neidermeyer next to her and across from General Crenshaw, and went out of her way to make him comfortable.

And the kids were remarkably well behaved, even the little one.

Castillo was seated between Mrs. Wilson and Mrs. Crenshaw, who struck him as another first-class officer's lady.

Even Max behaved. He lay outside the sliding glass door to the patio, his head between his front paws, just watching and neither whining nor suggesting that he would really like something to eat.

General Wilson, a little happy but not drunk after two glasses of wine, regaled everybody with stories of Warrant Officer Junior Grade Jorge Castillo, who, Colonel Castillo decided, must have driven his commanding officer nuts.

One of the stories, which Castillo had not heard, was of a middle-of-the-night moonlight requisitioning flight in which a mess-hall-sized refrigerator and a generator to power it were, as General Wilson gaily related, "liberated from a QM dump and put to work for the 644th Helicopter Company."

He sipped his wine, then with a huge grin said: "For the better part of the next day, the old man was torn between socking it to Jorge and me for misappropriation of government property—or enjoying the cold beer. Cold beer won in the end."

Castillo glanced at Richardson, who clearly was not as amused with the story as was his son, whose face showed he thought the idea of stealing things with a helicopter sounded great.

Then Castillo's eyes met Beth's, and he wondered if she was thinking of what had happened in the Daleville Inn.

Hell yes, she is.

That would be natural.

But that was a very long time ago.

The last thing I'd do is try to resurrect anything.

A little after eight-thirty, just after Castillo had turned down a glass of brandy— "I have to fly in the morning"—there was a familiar faint beep and, a moment later, Neidermeyer reached into his lap and came up with the radio handset.

He looked at it, then stood up, said, "Excuse me. It's for you, sir," and leaned across the table to hand it to Castillo.

The legend read GEN MCNAB.

"Yes, sir?" Castillo said into the handset.

"I've got the truck driver on a landline. He's fueling at Benning. Who do I tell him to see when he gets to Rucker?"

"General Crenshaw has named Colonel Richardson as his action officer, sir. But Neidermeyer—and maybe me—will meet the truck at the gate."

"Driver and two shooters," McNab said. "Make sure they're taken care of."

"Yes, sir, of course."

Castillo was aware that everyone was looking at him.

"Crenshaw taking good care of you?" McNab went on.

"Couldn't ask for anything more, sir. As a matter of fact, I'm sitting across Colonel Richardson's dinner table from him. And General Wilson."

"I don't have the time to wander down memory lane. Give them my compliments," McNab said, and a faint change in the background noise told Castillo that McNab had broken the connection.

Castillo pushed the OFF button and handed the handset back to Neidermeyer.

"That was General McNab," Castillo said. "His compliments to you, gentlemen, and his apologies for having to take another call right now. The truck has just refueled at Fort Benning. What is that, an hour, hour and a half from here?"

Both Wilson and Crenshaw nodded.

"He was checking to make sure the truck driver and his crew—total of three—are taken care of."

"I'll take care of that, General," Richardson said before Crenshaw could give the order.

And now, Castillo thought, *I can get out of here.*

"Beth, thank you for a delightful meal," he said. "But I'm afraid that Jamie and I are going to have to be the infamous guests who eat and run. We've got a lot on our plate tonight and a first-light flight tomorrow."

"I understand," she said. "We'll have to do it another time."

"I'd like that. I accept."

And with that exchange of polite lies, I really can get out of here.

"Charley, do you know how to find the airport in Ozark?" General Wilson asked.

"I'm sure I can find it, sir."

"I'll take you," Wilson offered.

"That's unnecessary, sir."

"I'll take you," Wilson insisted.

He's trying to be nice, sure. But there's more to it than that.

Hell, he wants to go. Why didn't I think of that?

"Sir, would you like to go along? What I have to do there won't take long—it just has to be done in person. We should be back here at, say, four or five."

"I don't want to intrude, Charley. But I really would like to see the damage along the Gulf Coast."

"Then you'll go. And there's room for one more in the airplane. Any takers? It would be something to see."

"Can I go?" Randolph Richardson IV asked.

"Of course not, son," Randolph Richardson III said quickly.

The look on Beth's face showed that she firmly supported that parental decision.

"Why not?" General Wilson said.

"This is none of my business, of course," General Crenshaw said. "But think it over, Richardson. It's one hell of an opportunity for the boy. For the rest of his life he'd remember that right after the hurricane, he flew over the area with his grandfather and saw everything."

"Well, viewed in that light," Randolph III said.

"I don't think so," Beth announced. "It would be dangerous."

"But General Crenshaw is right, honey," Randolph III said. "It would be something he would remember all his life. Are you sure of your landing field, Castillo? It's safe to use?"

Castillo nodded.

I don't want to take the kid.

I don't even want to take General Wilson.

I was just being a good guy. No good deed ever goes unpunished.

"Okay, then, it's settled," General Wilson said. "Randy and I will pick you up at oh dark hundred at the Magnolia House. That way you won't have to leave the Army van at the airport."

[FOUR]
Ozark Municipal Airport
Ozark, Alabama
0655 5 September 2005

J. G. Jenkins, the somewhat plump proprietor of the Greater Dale County Funeral Home and Crematorium, Inc., incongruously attired in a loud flowered Hawaiian shirt and powder blue shorts, did insist on taking a ride around the pattern with Castillo before turning over his Flying Hearse to him.

In the end, Castillo was glad he did.

As Castillo turned on final, Jenkins idly mentioned that he was sure Castillo was aware that the Rucker reservation—and Cairns Field—was restricted airspace.

"You're going to have to go to either Dothan or Troy before heading for the beach."

"Yes, I know. Thank you."

And another lie leaps quickly from my lips.

I'd forgotten that. And, if you hadn't reminded me, I would've taken off and flown the most direct route to the Gulf—right over both the base and the airfield.

I doubt they would've scrambled jets to shoot me down. But there damned sure would have been a lot of FAA forms to fill out.

"Explain in two hundred words or less why you have done something really stupid like this."

He set the single-engine, high-wing T206H down smoothly on its tricycle gear, then taxied to the hangar where General Wilson, Randy the Fourth, Neidermeyer, and Max were waiting.

Castillo was a little surprised that Jenkins hadn't at least asked questions about Max getting into his pristine airplane—it was painted a glossy black, like a hearse, and the tan leather interior spotless. He concluded in the end that Jenkins had decided in view of the three hundred fifty dollars an hour that he was charging for the use of his hearse—dry, as Castillo had to fuel it himself—it was necessary to accommodate the customer.

"Well, I guess you're my copilot, General," Castillo said after he'd shut down the engine and his passengers approached the aircraft.

"Charley, I'd be useless in the right seat. I haven't flown in years, and . . ."

General Wilson held up a Sony digital motion picture camera. Neidermeyer had an almost identical one hanging from the lanyard around his neck.

When Castillo looked at him, Wilson said, "I'd really like to get pictures of the damage, Colonel."

Castillo looked at the boy.

"Well, I guess *you're* my copilot, Randy."

"Yes, sir."

Castillo motioned to the double doors on the starboard side of the fuselage and said, "Then hop in and make your way forward to the right seat."

Wilson and Neidermeyer would take the middle-row bucket seats.

The bench seat in the rear was just wide enough for Max to lie down, if he wanted.

"What do I do about a seat belt for him?" Castillo wondered aloud.

"Try to fly smooth and not come to a sudden stop," General Wilson said.

Castillo sensed the boy's eyes on him as he trimmed out the airplane and set the autopilot on a more or less southwesterly course for Pensacola, Florida.

"Back in the dark ages when your grandfather and my father were flying, they had to do this just about by themselves," Castillo explained to Randy over the intercom, his voice coming through the David Clark headsets that everyone wore. "Now we just push buttons and computers do all the work."

He showed him the Global Positioning System, then pointed to the screen with its map in motion.

"Here we are, south of Fort Rucker. There's where we're going, Pass Christian, Mississippi. The computer tells me we have one hundred eighty-four miles to go, that we're at five thousand feet, and making about one hundred fifty miles an hour over the ground."

The boy soaked that all in, then asked, "Wasn't it more fun when you did it yourself?"

Without really thinking about it, Castillo disengaged the autopilot, said, "Find out for yourself," then, imitating the tone of a commercial airliner pilot, raised his voice: "Attention in the passenger compartment. The copilot is now flying."

The boy looked at him in disbelief.

"If you're going to drive, it might be a good idea to put your hands on the yoke," Castillo said. He pointed. "That's the yoke."

"The thing to remember, Randy, is to be smooth," General Wilson said, leaning over his grandson's shoulder. "Don't jerk the wheel. A very little goes a long way."

The boy put his hands on the yoke.

"Can you reach the pedals?" Castillo asked.

The boy tried, then nodded.

This probably isn't the smartest thing I've ever done, but what the hell.

General Crenshaw was right last night: The kid will never forget that he went flying with his grandfather to see what Hurricane Katrina did to the Gulf Coast.

And we have plenty of fuel.

"Keep your feet on the pedals," Castillo ordered. "But don't move them till I say. What you're going to do now is make it go up and down. When you've got that down pat, you're going to turn us dead south."

"Yes, sir," the boy said.

"Just ease the yoke forward, Randy," his grandfather said. "And try to keep the wings level."

The hurricane damage—a lot of it—became worse as they came closer to the coast. When they were over Pensacola Beach, Florida, the damage was so bad that Castillo decided they needed a closer look.

"I'll take it now, Randy. I want to get down for a better look, and I don't think you're quite ready to make low-level passes."

"Yes, sir," the boy said, reluctantly taking his hands off the yoke.

The damage to Pensacola Beach was worse than anyone expected.

General Wilson and Jamie Neidermeyer got their video, then Castillo adjusted the flaps and throttle in preparation for the aircraft to climb.

"I'm going to give it back to you, Randy," Castillo said. "What you're going to do now is climb, slowly, to five thousand feet and steer two seven zero."

"Just ease back on the yoke," Grandpa Wilson said. "You're doing fine."

He is. What the hell, his father and grandfather are pilots.

What was it Don Fernando used to say? "Genes don't teach you how to do any-thing, but they damn sure determine whether or not you can learn."

How big were we when he taught Fernando and me to fly? About as big as this kid, I guess.

God, Fernando and I had flown all over Texas and Mexico by the time we were old enough to get a student's license.

Over Mobile, Alabama, Castillo ordered the boy to turn south and fly to the Gulf, and when they were over it, to turn right and start a gentle descent to fifteen hundred feet.

By the time they reached that altitude, they were over Pascagoula, Mississippi, where the damage was literally incredible. Along the beach, the storm had either destroyed or floated away everything within a quarter- or half-mile of the normal waterline.

"Take it down another five hundred feet, copilot, and then I'll take it."

"Yes, sir."

The damage got worse as they flew along the beach. They saw where two floating casinos had been moved five hundred yards from where they had been moored on the beach.

"Now, Randy, since I don't know where I am, or exactly where it is that I want to go, we will now let the computer take over."

"Yes, sir."

Ten minutes later they were over the landing strip of the Masterson Plantation.

There was clear evidence of hurricane damage—tall pines snapped and huge oaks, some of them obviously hundreds of years old, uprooted—but the airstrip and the house and its outbuildings seemed intact.

There were a number of cars and trucks parked around the house.

Castillo made two low passes over the runway to make sure it was clear. As he pulled out of the second pass to gain altitude to make his approach, he happened to glance at the boy's face. Randy clearly was excited, grinning from ear to ear.

Damned shame the general stopped flying. He could have done this, and the kid could remember that.

Oh, for Christ's sake, stop it!

You're here on business, not to pretend you're the kid's loving uncle.

As Castillo completed the landing roll, he saw three SUVs quickly approaching the field. Then, as he taxied back to the single hangar where a sparkling V-tail Beechcraft Bonanza was tied down, he saw people. He recognized Winslow Masterson and his wife, and their daughter and her three children. There was an older couple standing with them. Logic told him they were the other grandparents, Ambassador Lorimer—the man he had come to see—and his wife.

And logic told him, too, that the two approaching-middle-aged men in business suits were members of China Post No. 1 in Exile, the retired special operators whom Castillo had arranged for Masterson to hire to protect his daughter-in-law and grandchildren.

Winslow Masterson was a tall, slim, elegant, sharp-featured man. He had told Castillo that he suspected his ancestors had been Tutsi.

The men in business suits watched carefully as Castillo parked the airplane, and then one of them nodded—but didn't smile—at Castillo when he apparently recognized him. Both men then leaned against the fender of their SUV as everybody else walked up to the airplane.

"Welcome back to the recently renamed Overturned Oaks Plantation, Major Castillo," Masterson said when Castillo climbed out of the airplane. "This is a pleasant surprise."

"Good to see you, sir," Castillo said. "Anybody afraid of dogs?"

The question seemed to surprise everybody, but no one expressed any concern.

Neidermeyer opened the aircraft's rear double door, stepped out, commanded, "Okay, Max," and let loose of his collar.

At the command, Max jumped out of the plane, headed for the nose gear, and relieved himself.

The older Masterson boy laughed.

"It took months to train him how to do that," Castillo said after everyone else had crawled out of the airplane through the same double door.

Jesus Christ it's hot! Castillo thought. *And the humidity is damn near unbearable. Worse than at Rucker.*

"I'm not going to call you Major," Elizabeth Masterson, a tall, slim, thirty-seven-year-old, said. "You're a friend, Charley."

She advanced on him and kissed his cheek.

"Actually, I'm a lieutenant colonel, he announced with overwhelming immodesty."

"Good for you," she said. "And is this your son, Charley?"

"No. Randy is General Wilson's grandson."

Castillo made the introductions.

"General Wilson," Castillo then went on, "flew with my father in Vietnam. I bumped into him at Fort Rucker, and since we were going to fly over what used to be the beautiful Gulf Coast, and there was room in the plane . . ."

"Welcome to Overturned Oaks, formerly Great Oaks, General," Masterson said. "Any friend of *Colonel* Castillo is welcome here. We're all indebted to the *colonel.* And in that connection, *Colonel,* let me say that whenever your promotion came through it was long overdue."

"I am ready and willing to sign autographs," Castillo said.

Max had already discovered the Masterson children, and they him.

"Where'd you get the dog, Colonel?" J. Winslow Masterson III asked, as he shook Max's paw. "He's awesome!"

"My grandmother told me that since I didn't have a family, I should get a dog. And I always do what my grandmother says."

"Pay attention," Mrs. Winslow Masterson said.

"And speaking of grandparents," Betsy Masterson said. "Dad, Mother, this is Charley Castillo, who took such great care of us in Argentina, and brought us home."

"My wife and I are very grateful to you, Colonel," Philippe Lorimer said. He was a very small, very black man with closely cropped white hair and large intelligent eyes. If there was visible evidence of his heart condition, Castillo couldn't see it.

"How do you do, sir? Ma'am? Mr. Ambassador, the secretary of State sends her best regards to you and Mrs. Lorimer."

"That's very kind of her," Lorimer said. "But why do I suspect that's not all she sent?"

"Sir, in fact, the secretary hopes that you'll be willing to have a private minute or two with me. Perhaps out of this heat?"

"Of course. But why do I suspect that's going to take a lot longer than a minute or two?"

Castillo was aware that General Wilson was taking all this in but had absolutely no idea what anyone was talking about.

Ambassador Lorimer looked at Jamie Neidermeyer, then at Castillo.

"I'm surprised that someone like you, Colonel, needs a bodyguard," Lorimer said.

"Dad!" Betsy Masterson protested.

"The one advantage to being an old and retired ambassador, sweetie," he said, "is that after a lifetime of subtlety, evasion, and innuendo, you can just say whatever pops into your mind."

"The same thing is true of being a retired general, Mr. Ambassador," General Wilson said.

"Actually, sir, Jamie is my communicator," Castillo said. "They keep me on a short leash to make sure I don't say whatever pops into my mind."

Lorimer laughed.

"He's got one of those satellite telephones in that suitcase?"

"Yes, sir."

"With which you have direct contact with the secretary of State?"

"Yes, sir, if you'd like to."

"Don't plug it in yet, young man," Lorimer ordered. "I don't wish to speak to Secretary Cohen until after the colonel and I have had our two-minute chat."

"You have a beautiful home," General Wilson said when they were in the foyer of the house.

Castillo thought the house made Tara, of *Gone With the Wind,* look like a Holiday Inn. Off of the foyer, a curved double stairway rose to the second floor. It was not hard to picture Clark Gable carrying Whatshername, the English actress, up the steps to work his wicked way on her.

"Thank you," Mrs. Masterson said. "It's been here a very long time, and God spared it."

"I told her that was God's reward for her unrelenting battle against the gambling hells of the Mississippi Gulf Coast," Masterson said.

"Don't mock me, Winslow!" she said. "But you'll notice what did happen to the casinos."

"Faulty argument, darling. Katrina also wiped out Jefferson Davis's home, and you know that he was a God-fearing gentleman always battling the devil and all his wicked works."

"That's right," General Wilson said. "I'd forgotten that. My wife and I went to his home twice when I was at Fort Rucker. That was damaged?"

"Wiped out," Masterson said. "Utterly destroyed."

"Then you were very lucky here," Wilson said.

"Yes, we were," Masterson said. "And thanks more to the charm of the salesman than any wise planning on my part, there were diesel emergency generators in place to kick in as they were supposed to when the electricity went off. When my cousin Philip flew in with emergency rations—that's his Bonanza

in the hangar—he found us with Betsy and the Lorimers watching the aftermath of the disaster on television."

Wilson shook his head.

"You were very lucky," he said.

"You're an admirer of Jefferson Davis, General?" Masterson asked, changing the subject.

"We went to the same school," Wilson said. "At different times, of course."
Then he added, very seriously, "Yes, I am."

"That's the right thing to say in this house," Masterson said. "From which
my ancestors marched forth to do battle for Southern rights."

"And just as soon as the history lesson is over," Ambassador Lorimer said,
"I'm sure Colonel Castillo would like to have our little chat."

"Why don't you take the colonel into the library, Philippe?" Masterson said,
smiling tolerantly. "I'll send Sophie in with coffee and croissants."

"This way, Colonel, if you please," Lorimer said.

The library, too, would have been at home in Tara, except that an enormous
flat-screen television had been mounted against one of the book-lined walls and
half a dozen red leather armchairs had been arranged to face it.

And there was an array of bottles and glasses above a wet bar set in another
wall of books.

Ambassador Lorimer headed right for it.

"May I offer you a little morning pick-me-up from Winslow's ample stock?"
he asked.

"No, thank you, sir. I'm flying."

"One of the few advantages of having a heart condition like mine is that
spirits, in moderation of course, are medically indicated," Lorimer said as he
poured cognac into a snifter.

"Churchill did that," Castillo said. "He began the day with a little cognac."

"From what I hear, it was a healthy belt. And he was a great man, wasn't
he? Who saved England from the Boche?"

"Yes, sir, he was."

"In large part, in my judgment, because he put Franklin Roosevelt in
his pocket."

"Yes, sir, I suppose that's true."

Lorimer waved Castillo into one of the armchairs and sat in the adja-
cent one.

A middle-aged maid wearing a crisp white apron and cap came in a moment later with a coffee service and a plate of croissants. Lorimer waited for her to leave before speaking.

"I was trained to be a soldier, Colonel," he said. "Are you familiar with Norwich University?"

"Yes, sir, I am."

"It was one of the few places in the old days where a black man had a reasonable chance to get a regular Army commission. So I went there with that intention. Just before graduation, however, I was offered a chance to join the foreign service, and took it primarily, I think, because I thought someone of my stature looked absurd in a uniform."

"I have a number of friends who are Norwich, sir."

"I remember a pithy saying I learned as a Rook at Norwich: 'Never try to bullshit a bullshitter.' Keeping that and the fact that I spent thirty-six years as a diplomat in mind, why don't you tell me why Secretary Cohen is trying to put me in her pocket?"

"I'm not sure I know what you mean, Mr. Ambassador."

"I think you do, Colonel. Let's start with why she doesn't want me to go to my late son's . . . estancia . . . in Uruguay."

"The secretary believes that would be ill-advised, sir," Castillo said. "She asked me to tell you that."

He nodded. "She sent the same message to me through others. What I want to know is: why? I'm old, but not brain-dead. I don't think it has a thing to do with my physical condition, or for that matter do I swallow whole the idea that the secretary, as gracious a lady as I know she is, is deeply concerned for Poor Old Lorimer. Why doesn't she want me to go down there?"

Castillo didn't reply immediately as he tried to gather his thoughts.

Lorimer went on:

"I have my own sources of information, Colonel. Let me tell you what I've learned. It is the belief of our ambassador there, a man named McGrory, who is not known for his dazzling ambassadorial ability, and that of the Uruguayan government, that my son died as the result of a drug deal gone wrong. I'm having trouble accepting that."

"I don't know what to say, Mr. Ambassador," Castillo said.

"Let me clarify that somewhat," Lorimer said. "Sadly, I did not have the same relationship with my son that Winslow Masterson enjoyed with his son Jack. I didn't particularly like Jean-Paul and he didn't like me. I doubt that Jean-Paul was involved in the illicit drug trade, not because he was my son and thus incapable of something like that, but because it's out of character for him."

He paused, then finished: "So, if he wasn't in the drug trade, Colonel, what was he doing that caused his murder?"

Castillo didn't reply.

"Please do me the courtesy, Colonel, of telling me 'I can't tell you' rather than 'I don't have any idea what you're talking about.' "

"I can't tell you, Mr. Ambassador."

"We are now at what is colloquially known as 'the deal breaker,' " Lorimer said. "You have your choice of telling me, which means I will listen to whatever else you have to say, or not telling me, which means our little chat is over, and Mrs. Lorimer and I will be on the first airplane we can catch to Uruguay. We've been imposing on the Mastersons' hospitality too long as it is."

"Mr. Ambassador, this information is classified Top Secret Presidential."

Lorimer didn't seem surprised.

"To me," Lorimer said simply, "that strongly suggests there has been a Presidential Finding."

Castillo didn't reply.

"I will take your silence to mean that there is a Presidential Finding and you don't have the authority to confirm that. Your choice, Colonel. Get on that satellite telephone and tell the secretary—or whoever has put you in your present predicament—that unless you are authorized to tell me about the Finding, the Lorimers are off to Estancia Shangri-La."

Well, what the hell!

If he goes down there—and there's no way I can stop him—the chances are that he'll do something—not on purpose—to compromise that operation, and thus the Presidential Finding.

And for some reason—which is probably foolish—I trust him.

He's a tough old bastard.

"I have that authority, Mr. Ambassador."

"And you're not going to tell me?"

"The President was at the air base in Biloxi when we returned from Argentina with Mr. Masterson's remains and his family. He informed me there that he had made a Finding. A covert and clandestine organization had been formed and charged with finding and rendering harmless those responsible for . . ."

Tapping the balls of his fingers together, Ambassador Lorimer considered for a good sixty seconds what Castillo had told him before raising his eyes to Castillo.

"So the ever-present silver lining is that Jean-Paul was not a drug dealer," he said. "Hell of a note when you're happy to hear your only son was just a thief from other thieves, not a drug dealer."

"I'm sorry, Mr. Ambassador."

"Why should you be sorry? From what I hear, you've been the knight in shining armor on a white horse in the whole sordid affair."

"That's not an accurate description, Mr. Ambassador."

"It's my judgment to make, Colonel," Lorimer said. "How much of what you have just told me does my daughter know?"

"Very little of it, sir. She doesn't have the need to know. I did tell her— and Mr. Masterson—that I was almost certain that the people who had mur- dered Mr. Masterson—"

"Were 'rendered harmless'?"

"Yes, sir."

"How can you be 'almost certain' of that?"

"You don't have the need to know that, sir."

"You wouldn't have told them that unless you were 'almost certain,' which means you weren't repeating what someone else had told you, but rather that you were personally involved."

Castillo didn't reply.

"All of this except for your possible concern that I would go down and somehow compromise the Presidential Finding—which is absurd—doesn't explain why you—and I mean you, not the secretary—don't want me to go to Uruguay."

"May I go off at a tangent for a moment, Mr. Ambassador?"

Lorimer nodded.

"I understand, sir, why you're anxious to . . . get out from under Mr. Mas- terson's hospitality—"

"Guests, as with fish, you know, begin to smell after three days."

"My grandfather was known to say that, often in more colorful terms," Castillo said. "Mr. Ambassador, what would it take to get you to go someplace—Paris, for example; Mr. Lorimer's apartment is there and available to you—for sixty days before you go to Uruguay?"

"The apartment is no longer available, Colonel. The man from the UN who brought me the check for Jean-Paul's death benefit—one hundred thousand euros—also brought with him an offer for Jean-Paul's apartment. Time and half what it was worth. They obviously wanted to make sure Jean-Paul was forgot- ten as soon as possible; now I know why."

"Mr. Ambassador, I am prepared to offer you fifty thousand dollars a month for two months to lease Estancia Shangri-La."

"Either that's your remarkably clumsy way of offering me a bribe to keep me away from the estancia—which raises again the unanswered question of why you don't want me down there—or you really want to lease the ranch, and that raises the really interesting question of why. What would you do with it?"

"I understand Phoenix, Arizona, is very nice this time of year, Mr. Ambassador."

"So is Bali, but I'm getting a little old for bare-breasted maidens in grass skirts. What do you want with the estancia, Colonel?"

"I'm running another operation down there, sir."

"You going to do it under the nose of this fellow McGrory again?"

Castillo nodded.

"I want to use it as a refueling point for several helicopters I want to get into Argentina."

"You mean get into Argentina black," Lorimer replied. He considered that a moment. "Okay. You're going to fly them off some ship in the middle of the night and under the radar, right? Refuel them in the middle of nowhere in Uruguay, and then on to Argentina?"

Castillo nodded.

"What's the operation?"

"We're going to try to get a DEA agent back from the drug dealers who kidnapped him."

"That sounds like a splendid idea," Lorimer said. "It also sounds like the DEA agent is not an ordinary DEA agent. We lose a lot of DEA agents in Mexico and all we do is wring our hands. We certainly don't send Special Forces teams in unmarked helicopters to get them back."

"This one's grandfather is a friend of the mayor of Chicago."

"That would make him special, wouldn't it? Okay, you can use the estancia, and I will forget that money you offered. If I remembered it, it would make me angry."

Castillo looked him in the eyes a long moment and said, "Thank you, sir."

"You're welcome. And now you can tell me the best way to get from the airport in Montevideo to Shangri-La. Rent a car? Buy one? How's the roads?"

Oh, shit!

I totally misread him . . . he's still determined to go.

"I can't talk you out of going down there, sir?"

"You didn't really expect that you could, did you?"

"I really hoped that I could."

Lorimer held up his hands in a gesture of mock sympathy.

"Look at it this way, Colonel," he said. "If I'm there—Jean-Paul's father, come to look after his inheritance—far fewer questions will be asked than if two or three men of military age showed up there by themselves and started hauling barrels of helicopter fuel onto the place."

Castillo didn't say anything.

"Don't look so worried. I didn't spend all my diplomatic career on the cocktail-party circuit."

"I'm sure you didn't, Mr. Ambassador."

"You ever hear of Stanleyville, in the ex–Belgian Congo?"

"Yes, sir."

"When the Belgians finally jumped their paratroops on it—out of USAF airplanes—to stop the cannibalism on the town square, we did things differently back then. We paid less attention to the sensitive nationalist feelings of the natives than to Americans in trouble. There I was on the airfield with two sergeants from the Army Security Agency who'd been running a radio station for me in the bush. We were waving American flags with one hand and .45s in the other."

Castillo shook his head in disbelief.

"I don't lie, Colonel," Lorimer said. "At my age, I don't have to."

"I wasn't doubting your word, Mr. Ambassador."

"I hope not. Until just now I was starting to like you."

"It was not, sir, what I expected to hear from an ambassador."

"There are ambassadors and ambassadors, Colonel. For example, my daughter tells me we have a very good one in Buenos Aires."

"Yes, sir, we do."

"Are we through here? Can we go deal with her now? She's going to have a fit when she hears you have failed in your noble mission to save the old man from himself."

"Sir, about getting to Shangri-La from the airport. I think I can arrange for several Spanish-speaking Americans to meet you and take you there. Maybe they could stay around and help you get organized."

"These Good Samaritans just happen to be in Montevideo, right?"

Castillo laughed.

"No, sir. They'd actually be shooters from Fort Bragg. . . ."

"That's a very politically incorrect term, 'shooters,' " the ambassador said. "I like it."

"They would have a satellite radio with them. That would be useful. And they would provide you and Mrs. Lorimer with a little security."

"I would be delighted to have your friends stay with us as long as necessary and be very grateful for their assistance."

"Thank you, sir."

Ambassador Lorimer stood up, picked up his now empty cognac snifter, returned to the bottles on the credenza, and poured a half inch of Rémy Martin into it. He raised the glass to Castillo.

"Since you're on the wagon, Colonel: Mud in your eye."

"I suspect there will be another time, sir."

"I hope so."

Lorimer looked at him intently for a moment, so intently that Castillo asked, "Sir, is there something else?"

"I always look into a man's eyes when I'm negotiating with him," Lorimer said. "I did so just now. And while I was doing that, I had the odd feeling I'd recently seen eyes very much like yours before."

"Had you, sir?"

"Yes. I just remembered where. On that nice boy you brought with you. The general's grandson. He has eyes just like yours."

I've seen eyes very much like yours, too.

On Aleksandr Pevsner.

"I didn't notice," Castillo said.

The ambassador drained the snifter, then waved Castillo ahead of him out of the library.

J. Winslow Masterson III and Randolph Richardson IV were kicking a soccer ball on the lawn for Max. The adults and the younger Masterson children were sitting in white wicker rockers on the porch.

Just as Castillo was about to warn them that Max was likely to take a bite from the ball, Max did. There was a whistling hiss, which caused Max to drop the ball, push it tentatively with his paw, and then take it into his mouth and give it a good bite.

"Awesome!" Masterson III cried. "Did you see that?"

"I owe you a soccer ball," Castillo said.

"Don't be silly, Charley," Betsy Masterson said, then turned to her father. "How'd your little chat go?"

"Splendidly," the ambassador said. "Colonel Castillo and I are agreed there's absolutely no reason your mother and I can't go to Uruguay."

"Dad, that's absurd," Betsy Masterson said. "Worse than absurd. Insane."

"That's not exactly what I said, Mr. Ambassador," Charley protested.

"Be that as it may," Ambassador Lorimer said, "for the next several months, Betsy, your mother and I will be using Jean-Paul's home in Uruguay in lieu of our own, which is now, as you may have heard, the dikes having been overwhelmed, under twenty feet of water and Mississippi River mud."

Betsy Masterson looked at him in exasperation, as if gathering her thoughts.

"I am reliably informed," Lorimer went on reasonably, "that the house is quite comfortable, that there is a staff to take care of your mother and myself more than adequately—if not quite at the level of Winslow and Dianne's hospitality, for which we will be forever grateful—"

"You know what happened there, Dad!" she interrupted.

"—and your mother and I both speak, as a result of our service in Madrid, quite passable Spanish."

Betsy Masterson looked at Castillo. "Charley, you didn't encourage him to go down there, did you?

"No, ma'am. More the opposite."

"Can't you stop him?"

"I don't see how," Castillo said.

"I'll call the secretary of State myself!"

"Secretary Cohen has already taken her best shot, sweetheart. She sent Colonel Castillo to dissuade me. He failed."

"You're in no condition to fly all the way down there, Dad," Betsy argued. "You're in no condition to go through the security hassle at an airport, much less get on an airplane and fly that far."

"I have survived going through the security hassles at a number of Third World airports," he said. "The one in Addis Ababa comes to mind as the worst."

Despite herself, she smiled.

General Wilson stood up.

"I think I'll take a little walk," he said.

"Please keep your seat, General," Winslow Masterson said. "This is not a family argument. Philippe doesn't have family arguments. He politely listens to whatever anyone wishes to say, then does what he had planned to do in the first place."

"My wife does much the same thing," General Wilson said.

"Thanks for the support, Father Masterson," Betsy said, then turned to her father.

"I'm not talking about down there, Dad, and you know it. I'm talking about here. New Orleans is closed. You'd have to go to Miami. And how are you going to get to Miami?"

"We'll manage. May I suggest we change the subject?"

"Mrs. Masterson . . ." Castillo began.

"I've asked you to call me Betsy, Charley," she snapped.

"Sorry. *Betsy,* since the ambassador is determined to go down there, what I can do is arrange to fly your parents down there in a Gulfstream. I could arrange to have them picked up in New Orleans, and if customs and immigration's not functioning there, stop at Tampa or Miami on the way down."

"I don't know whether to say 'that would be fine, thank you very much' or 'for God's sake, don't enable him!' "

"You could do that, Charley?" Winslow Masterson said.

Castillo nodded.

"And I'll arrange to have some friends keep an eye on your parents."

"The same kind of friends who've been keeping an eye on Betsy and the kids here?" Winslow Masterson asked.

Castillo nodded.

"Darling Betsy," Masterson said. "I agree with you. If I had my way, Philippe and your mother would stay here with us until they can have their house repaired—"

"Winslow, it's *under water,*" Lorimer said. "Everything in it has been destroyed. And you know what they say when someone goes to the hereafter—'I want to remember him as he was, not lying in the coffin.' I want to remember the house as it was. I'm not foolish enough to try to resurrect it."

"—as I was saying, darling Betsy, until they can have their house repaired and a new one can be built for them. Here or in New Orleans—"

"That would be the prudent thing to do," Betsy said. "The intelligent thing. The *only* thing."

"But he's determined to go to Uruguay, and nothing you or I or anyone else has to say will deter him. Just be grateful that Charley can arrange to carry him there in comfort, and that Charley's friends will be available to provide security."

"Can I offer you a taste of Winslow's whiskey, General?" the ambassador asked. "I'm not a drinking man, myself, but a little belt in the morning is medically indicated for someone my age. Our age."

"I've heard that," General Wilson said. He looked at Castillo. "I think *one* would be in order, Mr. Ambassador, thank you."

Max trotted up on the porch with the now deflated soccer ball in his mouth and dropped it at Castillo's feet.

[FIVE]
Ozark Municipal Airport
Ozark, Alabama
1710 5 September 2005

When they walked up to General Wilson's Buick, they found an envelope jammed under the windshield wiper.

General Wilson opened it.

"From Beth," he said. " 'Please call Randy as soon as you land. Charley's friends from Fort Campbell are waiting for him at the Magnolia House.' "

"That was quick," Castillo said.

"So, knowing neither Randy's number nor that of the Magnolia House, what I think I'll do is call Beth, ask her to call Randy, and tell her to tell him we're back, and that we're going to be at the Magnolia House just as soon as we can drop off our copilot at their quarters and get there."

"Thank you," Castillo said.

Mrs. Randolph Richardson III came out of her kitchen door as the Buick drove up the driveway.

"How was the flight?" she asked.

"Colonel Castillo let me fly most of the way over there," Randolph Richardson IV announced, "and just about all the way back. And Max flattened a soccer ball in his mouth."

"How nice of him," she said with some effort.

"And Randy did very well," General Wilson said. "I'll be back right after I drop Charley and Jamie off."

Mrs. Richardson smiled.

"Take care, Randy," Castillo said, and touched the boy's shoulder. "Maybe we can do it again sometime."

"Oh, yeah! Thanks very, very much, Colonel."

The look in her eyes makes it pretty clear she thinks that's about as likely to happen as is our being canonized for a lifetime of sexual fidelity.

"My pleasure, Randy."

"I won't go in, Charley," General Wilson said, as they drove up to the Magnolia House. "But let's try to get together again while you're here."

"I'll try, sir."

"And thank you for the ride. Randy will never forget it, and neither will I."

"I'm glad it worked out."

"Your dad would have been very proud of you, Charley," Wilson said, as he offered his hand.

"Thank you," Castillo said.

I never thought of that before.

What would my father think of me if he were around to have a look?

There were nine men in flight suits sitting at the dining room table of the Magnolia House with Lieutenant Colonel Randolph Richardson III when Castillo and Neidermeyer walked in.

"I would have called 'attention,' Colonel," a barrel-chested, nearly bald man greeted him, "but I knew you would really rather have me kiss your Hudson High ring."

"My God, look what the cat drug in, all the way from Norwich," Castillo said happily.

He put his briefcase on the table, went to him, and wrapped him in a bear hug.

"How the hell are you, Dave?"

Max sat down and looked up at them curiously.

"Where did you get the dog, Charley?"

"Long story," Castillo said. "But he won't tear your leg off if you're polite."

Dave squatted and accepted Max's paw.

Castillo became aware that except for Richardson the other men at the table had stood up.

"And I know who these guys are," Castillo said. "The misfits, scalawags, and ne'er-do-wells the colonel decided he could get rid of when they laid the personnel requirement on him."

"You got it, Charley," a tall, lanky man said, laughing. "Good to see you."

"Where we going, Charley?" another asked.

Castillo didn't reply directly.

Instead, he said, "Has Colonel Richardson gotten you all a place to stay? Chow?"

"They've all been given transient quarters," Richardson said. "We were discussing somewhere to eat when you came in. And there are two vans for their use while they're here."

"I can't stay, Charley," the barrel-chested bald man said. He held up a can of 7UP as proof suggesting that he was about to fly and had not been able to help himself to anything alcoholic.

"The boss," he went on, "is out of town and I'm minding the store. And as the commanding officer, when General McNab said 'ASAP,' I made the command decision that the best way to do that was fire up a Black Hawk and fly these clowns down here. And I knew, of course—being an old buddy who is at least a year senior to you—you would be delighted to tell me what the hell this is all about."

"Nice try, Dave," Castillo said. "But if you're not staying, I can't tell you."

"Nothing?"

"Not one goddamn word, Colonel."

"He just shifted into his official mode, Jerry," Dave said. "So there'll be no arguing with him. We might as well go home."

"Yes, sir," one of the pilots said.

"You understand, Charley, that it's breaking my heart that you don't trust me?"

"Don't let the doorknob hit you in the ass, Dave."

Dave put out his hand.

"Great to see you, Charley," he said, warmly. "You've got four more pilots and two crew chiefs coming. You want them flown down?"

"The sooner they can be here, the better."

"My master has spoken," Dave said. "Not you. McNab. They'll be here for lunch tomorrow. How long are you going to need them?"

"You are tenacious, aren't you?"

"That's why I got promoted eighteen months before you did."

Another of the pilots said, "I thought that had something to do with Charley being out of uniform while flying a borrowed Black Hawk."

The others laughed.

"Come to think of it . . . ," Dave said, which produced more laughter. And then he went on, "And really coming to think about it, he was really much better-looking wearing a beard and Afghan robes, wasn't he? In these civvies, he looks like a used-car salesman."

Castillo gave him the finger.

"Richardson, can we mooch a ride from you out to Cairns?" Dave asked.

"Of course," Richardson said. "Castillo, will I be needed here any more tonight?"

Castillo shook his head. "Why don't you meet us at Hanchey at, say, 0730?"

"I'll be there," Richardson said, then looked at Dave. "Anytime you're ready, Colonel."

"Charley," Dave said, "you take care of my scalawags and ne'er-do-wells, or I'll have your ass."

Castillo nodded.

As Richardson opened the door to leave, Neidermeyer came through it.

"Hey, Jamie, long time no see!" Dave said, offering his hand.

"Good to see you, sir. You going to be in on this?"

"No, goddamn it, I'm not. McNab said, 'Not only no, but hell no!' "

"Remember to send the colonel a postcard, Neidermeyer," Castillo said.

"Yes, sir, I'll do that."

He waited until the door was closed, then went around shaking the hands of the people he knew and was introduced to the others.

"Presumably you have put the antenna back up on the roof?" Castillo said.

"Yes, sir. We should be up."

"Get on it, please, Jamie. Tell Miller and General McNab that we're back and that we have four pilots and two crew chiefs here, and are promised the others by noon tomorrow. And check to see what's going on."

"Yes, sir."

Castillo went to the table, took his laptop from his briefcase, and booted it up.

As the computer hard drive made whirring sounds, he looked up at the others.

"You know the drill," he said. "This is where I tell you the operation is Top Secret and anyone who lets anything out goes to Leavenworth. The only difference this time is that the security classification is Top Secret Presidential. Anyone with a loose lip gets two years as a Phase I Instructor Pilot and *then* goes to Leavenworth."

"A Presidential Finding, Charley?" one of them asked.

Castillo nodded.

"Let me give a quick taste, and then we'll go get something to eat."

From the laptop speakers came the familiar sound of a bugle sounding *Charge!*—Castillo had replaced the annoying out-of-the-box Microsoft tune—announcing that the computer was booted up and ready.

Castillo opened the Google World program and shifted the image of the earth so that it showed the lower half of South America.

"Where in *hell* are we going?" one of them asked.

"Patience is a virtue, Mr. Reston," Castillo said.

Finally, he had what he wanted, and pressed the keys to zoom in on the image.

"That's an estancia, a ranch, called Shangri-La, 31.723 south latitude, 55.993 west longitude."

"What's there, Colonel?"

"A field big enough to take four Hueys at once and refuel them."

"Flying in from where?"

"The USS *Ronald Reagan,* at sea."

"Jesus Christ!"

"And where do we go from there, sir?"

"I'm working on that."

VIII

[ONE]
7200 West Boulevard Drive
Alexandria, Virginia
1115 7 September 2005

Castillo walked into the living room with Max on his heels and, following the dog, an enormous, very black man in a three-button black suit—all buttons buttoned—a crisp white shirt, and a black tie.

Colonel Jake Torine was sitting with Edgar Delchamps at the battered coffee table. They both had their feet up on it, and Delchamps was reaching into the box of Krispy Kreme doughnuts on the table between them.

Special Agent David W. Yung of the FBI and Sergeant Major John Davidson were sprawled in the red leather armchairs, with their own Krispy Kreme box between them on a footstool.

Torine was wearing a blue polo shirt and khaki pants. Yung, Davidson, and Delchamps wore single-breasted nearly black suits. Yung's and Davidson's suits looked as if they were fresh from a Brooks Brothers box. Delchamps's suit looked as if it had been at least six months since it had received any attention from a dry cleaning establishment.

"Welcome home," Torine said, taking a bite of his doughnut. They all looked curiously at the black man.

"Colin," Castillo said. "This is Colonel Torine, Mr. Yung, Mr. Delchamps, and Mr. Davidson."

"Gentlemen," the black man said in a very deep, very Southern voice.

"Every nice house in suburbia needs a butler," Castillo said. "So I got us one. Say something in butler, Colin."

"Yah, suh," the black man said in an even thicker Southern accent. "Can I fix you gentlemen a small Sazerac as a li'l wake-me-up?"

Delchamps's eyebrows rose. A smile crossed Davidson's face. Yung looked baffled. Torine looked confused, and then recognition came.

"I'll be damned," he said, getting to his feet and putting out his hand. "I didn't recognize you in that undertaker's suit. How the hell are you, Sergeant Major?"

"You are speaking, sir," the black man said, now sounding as if he was from Chicago or somewhere else in the Midwest, "to Chief Warrant Officer Five Leverette."

"When did that happen?"

"I took the warrant a couple of years ago when some moron decided they needed two officers on an A-Team and they wanted to make an instructor out of me," Leverette said. "It's good to see you, too, Colonel. Charley said they gave you an eagle. When did you get that?"

"About four years ago. Where did Charley find you?"

"He found me," Castillo said. "I was having my breakfast yesterday at Rucker when in he walked. I thought he was a Bible salesman until he demanded to know what I intended to do with his team."

"You're in on this operation with us, Colin?" Davidson asked.

Leverette nodded. "Somebody's going to have to keep Charley out of trouble, right?"

"Oddly enough, I was just talking to somebody else about that," Torine said. He looked at Castillo. "We need to talk about that, Charley."

"I also need a few minutes of your valuable time, Ace," Delchamps said.

Max walked to Torine and put out his paw.

"Can he have a doughnut?" Torine asked. "I'm not sure he's giving me his paw because he likes me."

"As long as it's not chocolate covered," Castillo said.

"The offer of a Sazerac is still on the table," Leverette said. "Any takers?"

"I thought you couldn't get one outside New Orleans," Delchamps said.

"Today, you can't get one *in* New Orleans. It's under water, as you may have heard." He reached into his jacket pocket and came out with a small paper-wrapped bottle about the size of a Tabasco bottle. "But here you can."

"What's that?" Yung asked.

"What's this, or what's a Sazerac?"

"Two-Gun has led a sheltered life, Colin," Delchamps said. "I accept your kind offer."

" 'Two-Gun'?" Leverette parroted, and then said, "This, *Two-Gun*, is Peychaud's Bitters. I never leave home without it. It is the essential ingredient in a Sazerac cocktail, which I regard as New Orleans's greatest contribution to the general all-around happiness of mankind."

"There's the booze," Torine said, pointing to an array of bottles. "I know there's rye, bourbon, and Pernod. But you need powdered sugar, too, right?" When Leverette nodded, he added: "I saw some in the kitchen, thanks to the ever-efficient Corporal Bradley. I'll go get it." Torine started for the kitchen, then stopped and turned, and added: "About whom we also have to talk, Charley."

Leverette carried bottles of spirits to the table, then began to construct a cocktail shaker full of Sazerac with all the care and precision of a chemist dealing with deadly substances.

Torine returned from the kitchen with a box of confectioner's sugar, a lemon, and a paring knife in one hand, and five glasses in the other.

"Pay attention, Two-Gun," Davidson said. "You will see a master at work."

"It's not even lunchtime," Yung protested.

"They don't drink in the morning in the FBI, Colin," Delchamps said.

"How sad," Leverette said.

"Charley," Torine said. "Where's Jamie and his suitcase?"

"I left him in Rucker. Things went so smoothly down there that any second now the other shoe is sure to drop, and I want to be the first to know what's going wrong. I'm going to need another communicator right about now."

"Does it have to be a communicator?" Torine asked. He stopped, looked down, and saw that Max was again offering his paw. He reached into the Krispy Kreme box and handed Max another doughnut. Then he saw the look of confusion on Castillo's face and added: "I mean a Delta Force guy?"

"Where else would I get one?"

"Lester," Torine said. "He already knows how to work the satellite radio."

"He ask you?" Castillo said.

"No. This is what I wanted to talk to you about. What happened was he went to Davidson and asked him how he thought you would feel about sending him back to the Marine Corps."

He gestured for Davidson to pick up the story.

"I finally pulled it out of him," Davidson said, "that one of the Secret Service drivers asked him one time too many to be a good kid and go get him a cup of coffee."

"You mean *one* of the Secret Service guys asked him too many times, or they *all* have been mistaking him for an errand boy?"

"Many of them, probably most have. You can't blame them, but Lester is

pissed." He looked at Leverette. "The colonel tell you about the Pride of the Marine Corps?"

Leverette shook his head.

"Wait till you see him," Davidson said. "He makes Rambo look like a pansy."

"Well, sending him back to the Marines is out of the question," Castillo said, a touch of impatience in his voice. "We can't afford that. He knows too much, and a lot of jarheads would like to know where he's been and what he's been doing. And then wish *they'd* gone, and *that* would just make the goddamn story circulate wider."

"That's just about what I told him," Davidson said. "I also had a quiet word with a couple of the Secret Service guys."

"Okay. As soon as I have my Sazerac and thus the strength to get off of this couch, I will inform Corporal Bradley that he is now my official communicator."

"Gentlemen," Leverette said, "our libation is ready. You may pick your glasses up, slowly and reverently."

They did so.

"Absent companions," Leverette said, and started to touch glasses.

Yung looked as if he wasn't sure whether he was witnessing some kind of solemn special operator's ritual or his leg was being pulled.

Castillo saw on Leverette's face that he had picked up on Yung's uncertainty and was about to crack wise.

"Two-Gun's one of us, Colin," Castillo said simply. "He was on the operation where Sy Kranz bought the farm."

"I could tell just by looking at him that he was a warrior," Leverette said. "He's bowlegged, wears glasses, and he talks funny."

"I think I like this guy," Delchamps said.

"Sorry, Two-Gun," Leverette said. "I didn't know who the hell you were."

Yung smiled and made a deprecating gesture.

"So was Corporal Bradley," Torine said. "And he probably deserves a medal—for marksmanship, if nothing else—for taking out two of the bad guys with two head shots. But I don't think we ought to call him in here and give him one of these. God, this looks good, Colin!"

"Mud in your eye, Seymour," Castillo said, and took a swallow.

The others followed suit.

Castillo put his glass on the table and exhaled audibly.

"You look beat, Charley," Torine said.

Castillo nodded.

"So beat," he said, "that I forgot that I have to call the secretary of State and tell her I couldn't talk Lorimer—*Ambassador* Lorimer—out of riding out the aftermath of Hurricane Katrina in Uruguay. I should have done that before I had this."

He held up the Sazerac glass.

Torine shrugged. "Well, what the hell, you tried. Miller told me you went to Mississippi just to see him."

"What's bad about it, Jake, is that I'm going to have to lie to her, or at least not tell her the truth, the whole truth, etcetera. And I don't like lying to her."

"Lie to her about what?" Delchamps asked.

"Did Miller tell you I went to see General McNab?"

Delchamps nodded. "But he didn't say why."

"We're going to send two A-Teams—one of them Colin's—to Argentina, a couple of shooters at a time. Then we're going to put four H-model Hueys into Argentina black. Can you guess where we're going to refuel them after they fly off the USS *Ronald Reagan* a hundred miles off the Uruguayan coast before they fly on to I-don't-yet-know-where Argentina?"

"Boy, you have been the busy special operator, haven't you?" Delchamps said. "Does Montvale know about this?"

"No. Not about the *Ronald Reagan.* That idea came from a bird colonel who works for McNab . . . Kingston?"

Delchamps shook his head. Torine and Davidson nodded.

"Tom Kingston," Torine said. "Good guy, Edgar."

"Amen," Leverette said.

"And McNab said he would set that up. If it's possible."

"It's possible," Torine said. "After some admiral tells him not only no, but hell no, he will be told to ask the secretary of the Navy, who will tell him that he's been told by the secretary of Defense that the President told him you're to have whatever you think you need. They call that the chain of command."

Castillo chuckled.

"With that in mind," Castillo said, "and since I couldn't talk him out of going down there, I confided in the ambassador what we want to do with his estancia. He's on board. Good guy. That raised the question of an advance party at Shangri-La, which we damn sure need. One that might have a chance of escaping the attention of Chief Inspector Ordóñez."

"How are you going to handle that? With Two-Gun?" Delchamps asked.

"What Two-Gun is going to do is show up at the embassy in Montevideo and introduce Ambassador Lorimer's butler . . ."

"I wondered what that Colin-the-Butler business was all about," Torine said, smiling and shaking his head.

". . . to Ambassador McGrory," Castillo went on. "Explaining that Colin came down to see what has to be done to Shangri-La before Ambassador and Mrs. Lorimer can use it—which he has decided against advice to do—because his home in New Orleans was destroyed by Hurricane Katrina."

"That just might work, Charley," Torine said.

"Edgar?"

"Why not?" Delchamps said.

"David?" Castillo asked.

"McGrory, like most stupid men in positions of power, is dangerous," Yung said.

"I agree with that, too," Delchamps interjected. "I presume he's to be kept in the dark?"

Castillo nodded. "As is Secretary Cohen, who certainly is not stupid. But there are people around her who might find out, and might tip off McGrory. That's what I meant about having to lie to her. I'm going to tell her Lorimer's going, period."

"She's liable to cable or telephone McGrory and tell him to take care of Lorimer," Yung said.

"I thought about asking her to do just that," Castillo said. "But since I'm not going to tell her about Colin, that would really be lying to her, deceiving her. And I don't want to do that."

"And you're not going to tell Montvale either?" Yung asked.

"More smoke and mirrors, David," Castillo said. "I'm going to tell him that two A-Teams and the Hueys are being sent—but no other details—and that as soon as I firm up the operation, I'll tell him all about it."

The reaction of just about everybody to that was almost identical: Their faces wrinkled in thought, and then there were shrugs.

"Speaking of the director of National Intelligence," Torine said, "or at least his Number Two, I had an interesting chat yesterday with Truman Ellsworth. He even bought me a drink."

Delchamps raised an eyebrow and offered: "And I had one with the DCI, who didn't buy me a drink, but about which we have to talk."

"Ellsworth called you, Jake?" Castillo said.

"I called him."

"Why?"

"What did you think of the crew on Montvale's Gulfstream?"

" 'He asked, going off at a tangent,' " Castillo said.

Torine said reasonably: "I'd really like you to answer the question, Charley."

Castillo grinned. "Well, they were Air Force, so I was pleasantly surprised when they got it up and down three times in a row without bending it."

Delchamps chuckled.

"Screw you, Colonel," Torine said. "What about the copilot?"

"Nice young man. Academy type. I had the feeling he'd rather be flying a fighter."

"Cutting to the chase, that nice young man was naturally curious what a doggie light bird was doing running around in Montvale's personal Gulfstream V. Diligent snooping around revealed that the doggie light bird was doing something clandestine for that Air Force Legend in His Own Time, Colonel Jacob Torine. He found that interesting, because said Colonel Torine was the ring knocker who talked him out of turning in his suit and going to fly airliners. So he called OOA at the Nebraska Complex, finally got Miller on the horn, and Miller transferred the call here."

"What did he want?" Castillo said.

"A transfer to do anything at all for his mentor," Torine said, "so long as it gets him out of flying the right seat in Montvale's Gulfstream."

"What did you tell him?"

"That I'd get back to him. That's when I called Ellsworth to ask him how the ambassador would feel about letting us have him."

"Jesus, Jake, we could really use—we really *need*—another Gulfstream pilot," Castillo said.

"Especially since one of three we have has gone home to wife and kiddies, and the second can count his Gulfstream landings on his fingers."

"Really? I thought you had more landings than that," Castillo said, as if genuinely surprised.

Leverette smiled and shook his head.

Torine gave Castillo the finger.

"So what did Ellsworth say?" Castillo asked.

"He was charm personified. He said he really couldn't talk to me then because he had to meet someone at the Willard, that that would take about an hour, and would I be free to meet him in the Round Robin after his meeting, as he would really like to buy me a drink?"

The Round Robin is the ground-floor bar of the Willard InterContinental Hotel. It usually has two or more lobbyists in it feeding expensive intoxicants to members of Congress as an expression of their admiration.

"And you went?" Castillo asked.

"I even put on a clean shirt and tie. I was prepared to make any sacrifice for the OOA. In the end, I was glad I went. Mr. Ellsworth said all kinds of nice things to me."

"Such as?"

"He told me—in confidence, of course—how happy Ambassador Montvale and he are that I'm in OOA, where I can serve as a wise and calming influence on the brilliant but somewhat impetuous C. Castillo. After all, he said, we all have the same responsibility to make sure the President is never embarrassed."

"That sonofabitch!" Castillo grunted, but there was more admiration in his voice than anger.

"I did admit to having concerns about your impetuousness," Torine said. "And then he told me—as if the thought had just come to him—that 'if something like that came up,' perhaps if he and the ambassador knew about it . . .'"

"And you of course agreed to call him?"

"I was reluctant at first. He didn't push. What he did say was that he thought OOA was going to not only be around for a while, but grow in size and importance. And that being true, it would need someone more senior than a junior lieutenant colonel . . ."

"An *impetuous* junior lieutenant colonel?"

Torine nodded. ". . . to run it. A brigadier general, for example. And wasn't I eligible for promotion?"

"And then you blushed modestly?"

"Uh-huh. And I think we parted with him thinking I thought he and I had an understanding."

"I don't know if I'm amused or disgusted," Castillo said. "But his job is to protect his boss, who, like us, has an obligation to keep the President from being embarrassed. And I am a junior lieutenant colonel. An impetuous one. He really would be happier if you had this job."

"Moot point, Charley. You were there when the President—*before* the Finding—asked me if I would have any trouble working for you. I didn't have any problem working for you then, and I don't have one now. Most important, *your* name is on the Finding setting up OOA, not mine. The commander-in-chief has spoken."

Castillo met his eyes for a moment, but said nothing at first. Then he asked, "So did you get us this Gulfstream jockey you talked into staying in the Air Force?"

"He'll be here at three. I told him to bring a toothbrush, as you would probably want to go somewhere."

"As hard as it may be for any of you to believe, there are several minor but as yet unresolved little problems with my grand master plan. For one thing, I don't know where Special Agent Timmons is being held. Or by who. And once I get the H-models into Uruguay, I don't know what to do with them. And I can't keep them in Shangri-La long. Chief Inspector Ordóñez, I'm sure, has the local cops keeping an eye on it. Which means that I'm going to have to get Munz to get his pal Ordóñez to look the other way, briefly. Even if—*big* 'if'—Ordóñez is willing to do that, he won't do it for long. Which means I will have to get the choppers out of Uruguay quickly. Pevsner has at least one estancia in Argentina. Maybe more than one. *If* I can find him—*another* big 'if'—maybe that'll be the answer.

"And then there's this small problem I have with the agency."

"An old problem," Torine said, "or a new one?"

"The new one. Didn't Miller tell you?"

"Delchamps did. If you're talking about this Weiss guy coming here?"

Castillo nodded.

He went on: "I don't believe for a second, of course, that the agency would even think of fucking up something I'm doing to protect something that they're doing."

"Perish the thought," Torine said in agreement. "What the hell is that all about, Edgar?"

"Which brings us to my little tête-à-tête with the DCI," Delchamps said. "The bottom line of which is that he's either a much better liar than I think he is, or he doesn't know what Weiss and Company are up to in Paraguay."

"How did you come to have a little tête-à-tête with the DCI?" Castillo said.

"Well, there I was rooting around in the bowels of the palace in Langley, and all of a sudden I looked up and there he was.

" 'Ed Delchamps, right?' he asked, and put out his hand. 'I'm Jack Powell.' I picked up right away on that. Here was *John* Powell, the director of Central Intelligence, wanting to make kissy-kissy with a dinosaur-slash-pariah, which I found interesting.

"So I enthusiastically pumped his hand and told him I was really pleased to meet him, Mr. Director, sir."

Leverette chuckled deep in his throat.

"So *Jack* asked me if I had time for a cup of coffee, and I said, 'I always have time for you, Mr. Director, sir,' or words to that effect, thinking we would then take the elevator to his office, where I would either be charmed or terminated.

"Wrong. He takes me to a little room in the bowels, furnished with chrome-and-plastic tables and chairs, and a row of machines offering candy bars, snacks, Coke, and coffee dispensed in plastic cups. It is where the filing cabinet moles go to rest from their labors.

"One look at who had just dropped in and the room emptied of file clerks in thirty seconds flat. There we are alone, holding plastic cups of lukewarm, un-drinkable coffee, two pals-slash-coworkers in the noble, never-ending effort to develop intel against our enemies."

"And he told you how happy he was that you were in a position to restrain the impetuosity of our Charley?" Torine asked.

Delchamps took a sip of his drink, then said: "No. I expected something like that, but that's not what happened. What he said was that he understood there had been problems and disagreements in the past, and that he wasn't going to pretend he wished I hadn't changed my mind about retiring, or that he was happy I was 'in the building with an any-area, any-time pass hanging around my neck, but that's what's happened. More important, that's what Montvale ordered. . . .' "

Delchamps stopped and after a moment went on, "He was even honest about that. He said something about Montvale having ordered him to let me in only because the President had told him to, and that Montvale probably didn't like it any more than he did. Then he said, 'But the point is the President gave that order, and I have taken an oath to obey the orders of those appointed over me, and I don't intend to violate that oath.' "

Delchamps looked at Leverette.

"You don't know me, Uncle Remus, but these guys do. They'll tell you that I am inexperienced in the wicked ways of the world; I have no experience in guessing who's lying to me or not; I believe in the good fairy and in the honesty of all politicians and public servants. They will therefore not be surprised that—in my well-known, all-around naïveté—I believed my new friend Jack.

"And my new friend Jack said that the reason he had come to see me was to personally ensure the President's order was being carried out, that there were those in the company who sometimes decide which orders they will obey and which they won't, justifying their actions on the basis that obedience is sometimes not good for the company. 'I want to make sure that's not happening here and now with you.' "

"Jesus!" Castillo said.

"He asked me if I had even a suspicion that I was being stiffed by anyone, if I suspected that anyone was not being completely forthcoming.

"I could have given him a two-page list, but the truth was that I had modestly decided that no one had kept me—they'd tried, of course—from looking at whatever I wanted to see. And, in their shoes, I probably would have done the same thing. But nothing, I decided, was to be gained by being the class snitch.

"So I took a chance. I said, 'Mr. Director, I have been led to believe you're aware that the President has tasked Colonel Castillo with rescuing a DEA agent who has been kidnapped in Paraguay?'

"To which he replied, 'I'd rather you called me Jack.' "

"Giving him time to think?" Yung asked.

"I don't think so, Two-Gun," Delchamps said. "Could be, but I don't think so. The next thing he said, almost immediately, after he nodded, was 'I also hear the mayor of Chicago was kind enough to send a detective along with him to help him do so.' "

"I'd love to know how the hell he found that out," Castillo said.

"The point is, Ace, he knew about Paraguay. I wasn't springing it on him."

"The point there?" Castillo asked.

"I said, 'Jack, what I'm really concerned about is that Castillo's going to go down there like John Wayne and get this guy back, and in the process upset one of your apple carts.'

"And he looked surprised, and asked, 'One of ours?' and I nodded and he said, 'I don't know of anything we have going on down there that could possibly have a connection with Colonel Castillo's operation.'

"And then I guess he saw the look on my face, which he could have interpreted as surprise or disbelief. He stabbed himself in the chest with his index finger . . ."—he demonstrated—". . . and then he said, 'I'm in the coffee shop on level three. Please join me.'

"Two minutes later, in walks A. Franklin Lammelle, the deputy DCI for operations. 'Frank, Edgar here wonders if we have any operation going in Paraguay or Argentina that in any way could bear on the OOA operation to free the DEA agent. Or, the other way around, can you think of anything Colonel Castillo could do that would in any way interfere with anything we're doing down there?'

"A. Franklin thinks this over very carefully and says, 'Aside from getting caught getting the DEA agent back, no, sir.' And, being the naïve and trusting soul I am, I believed him, too."

"Which means?" Torine asked.

Castillo said: "Weiss told us—right, Edgar?—that the station agent down there is not as intellectually challenged as people think he is. The implication being that's on purpose?"

Delchamps nodded.

"And that disinformation," Delchamps said, "could not have been put in place without a very good reason to do it, or without the knowledge and permission of the DCI and/or A. Franklin Lammelle."

"Which means he is either really intellectually challenged, or was set up by somebody in Langley who didn't think the DCI had to know."

"It smells, Ace," Delchamps said. "And the odor is not coming from my new friend Jack or Lammelle."

Castillo raised his eyebrows, then asked, "So what should we do?"

"I want to have a long talk with Alex Darby and the other social pariahs down there. And their contacts."

"You mean, you want to go down there?"

Delchamps nodded.

"When?"

"Jake," Delchamps said, "what time did you say our new pilot gets here?"

[TWO]
Headquarters
Fort Rucker and the Army Aviation Center
Fort Rucker, Alabama
1105 8 September 2005

"You're not planning to take that animal in there with you, are you?" Lieutenant Colonel Randolph Richardson III inquired of Lieutenant Colonel C. G. Castillo as Castillo slid open the side door of the van to let out Max.

"I can't leave him in the van in this heat," Castillo said. "And General Crenshaw likes him."

Castillo was more than a little pleased when they marched into Crenshaw's office and saluted. General Crenshaw returned the salute, said, "Stand at ease, gentlemen," then clapped his hands together, bent over, and called, "Hey, Max! C'mere, boy!"

Max walked up to him, sat down, offered his paw, then allowed for his ears to be scratched.

"That's one hell of a dog, Castillo," General Crenshaw said, then added, "Please sit down, gentlemen. Can I get you a cup of coffee?"

"No, thank you, sir," Colonel Richardson said.

"If it wouldn't be too much trouble, sir," Colonel Castillo said.

General Crenshaw raised his voice. "Two coffees, please. Black, right, Castillo?"

"Yes, sir."

"Both black."

Castillo thought, *Righteous, you ass-kissing sonofabitch, you're actually wondering if it's too late to change your mind about the coffee.*

If the general is having some, it's obviously the thing for you to do.

"Okay," General Crenshaw said. "What can I do for you this morning, Castillo?"

"Sir, I'm here to make my manners. I'm moving down the road, and it's likely I won't be back. I just wanted to express my thanks for all your support . . ."

Crenshaw waved deprecatingly.

". . . and especially, sir, to let you know how much I appreciate everything Colonel Richardson has done for us. He's really done a first-class job."

That's true, even if he took elaborate precautions to cover his ass every time he did anything.

Crenshaw's secretary delivered two china mugs of coffee.

"You'll notice, Colonel Castillo, that I am not asking how things are going," Crenshaw said, "only if they are going the way you want them to."

"Exactly the way I hoped they would, sir. Colonel Davies sent his S-4 down here yesterday to get the H-models off your books and onto those of the 160th—"

"From which they will drop into the sea, never to be seen again?" Crenshaw asked, jokingly, then quickly added, "I probably shouldn't have said that."

"Into the sea"?

Jesus Christ! Where did he get that?

If he knows about the Ronald Reagan, *we're compromised before we get started.*

Easy, Castillo!

That was a figure of speech, nothing more. He doesn't know about the Ronald Reagan.

"I don't know about them dropping into the sea, sir, but they might wind up on eBay."

Crenshaw laughed.

"I don't mean to pry, Castillo," he said. "Yes, I guess I do. But I understand the ground rules."

"Sir, I regret that . . ."

Crenshaw held up his hand to shut him off.

"You're obeying your orders, Colonel, I understand that."

"Thank you, sir."

"What's going to happen now, sir," Castillo went on, "is that the choppers and their crews will stay here until the word comes for them to move."

"Will that come through me or . . . ?"

"Directly, sir. I have a communicator here, as you know—"

"The man from DirecTV."

"Yes, sir. The execute order will pass through him to Major Ward, the senior pilot. And then they will leave, taking everything with them, and leaving nothing behind but their thanks and the hope that nobody even knew they were here."

"Is there going to be a problem with that, Richardson?" General Crenshaw asked. "Has anyone been extra curious about what's going on in the Hanchey hangar?"

"I don't anticipate any problems in that area, General," Richardson said.

Crenshaw looked at Castillo and asked, "What about my putting out a discreet word that no one is to gossip about what's going on at Hanchey?"

"Sir, I appreciate the offer, but I suggest it would be counterproductive; it might *call* attention to the Hanchey hangar. We have put out the disinformation—when the question *'What are you guys doing here?'* comes up at Happy Hour—that the choppers are being prepared for use as Opposing Force aircraft at the National Training Center at Fort Irwin. We think that's credible."

Crenshaw nodded his agreement.

"You think of everything, don't you, Castillo?"

"Sir, I think of a lot, but there's always something important that gets right past me."

Crenshaw bent over again, and Max gave him his paw again.

"So long, Max," Crenshaw said. "Meeting you has been an experience . . ."—he stood up as he glanced at Castillo—". . . and so has been meeting your boss."

Castillo put his virtually untouched coffee mug down and stood up.

Crenshaw put out his hand to him. "Good luck in whatever you're up to, Colonel."

"Thank you very much, sir. Permission to withdraw, sir?"

Crenshaw nodded.

Castillo and Richardson came to attention and saluted, Crenshaw returned it, then Castillo and Richardson marched out of his office. Max followed.

[THREE]
Aboard Gulfstream III N379LT
33,000 Feet Above the Atlantic Ocean
Approximately 100 Nautical Miles East of
Cancún, Mexico
1630 8 September 2005

Lieutenant Colonel C. G. Castillo couldn't move his legs. He was up to his knees in some kind of muck.

Where the hell am I? What's going on?

He opened his eyes and found himself sitting in the rear-facing seat against the right bulkhead separating the cockpit from the passenger compartment. And saw the reason he had the nightmare in which he couldn't move his legs.

Max was having a little snooze, too, and had chosen to take it in the space between the rear-facing seat and the forward-facing seat, and to rest his weary head on Castillo's feet.

"You big bastard, how did you get in there?"

Max raised his head just enough to look at Castillo—and for Castillo to free his feet—and then laid it down again.

Castillo swung his feet into the aisle, unfastened his seat belt, stood up, and walked down the aisle to meet the call of nature.

He saw that he and Max were not the only ones having a little snooze. Davidson was sitting in the rear-facing seat across the aisle, snoring softly. Delchamps and Leverette were stretched out on the couches, sound asleep.

Yung and Neidermeyer were awake, talking softly, in two of the aisle-facing seats, and Bradley was in one of the forward-facing seats in the rear of the fuselage, looking as if sleep was just around the corner.

When he came out of the toilet, he thought—as he often did—of the fat lady on a transatlantic flight whose rear end had made a perfect seal around the toilet seat, something she found out when she flushed the device, and the vacuum evacuation system kept her glued to it for several hours.

He laughed, then helped himself to a cup of coffee and carried it up the aisle to the cockpit.

"How's it going?" Castillo said to the pilots.

"Our leader is awake," Torine said. "Look busy, Captain!"

Captain Richard M. Sparkman, USAF, glanced over his shoulder and smiled at Castillo, then pointed to a GPS screen in the instrument panel.

"There we are," he said. "About a hundred miles off Cancún. We should make Quito in four-fifteen, give or take."

"There's one of those mounted on the bulkhead in the cabin," Castillo said. "Our benefactor knowing that your revered leader likes to keep an eye on the pilots."

Torine gave him the finger.

Castillo smiled, then did the mental math.

That'll put us in Quito just before eleven. Figure an hour for the fuel, a piss stop, and a sandwich, giving us wheels-up out of there at midnight. And then another five-thirty or six to Buenos Aires, putting us in there about half past five, or six in the morning. Which will be half past three—or four—local time.

Then he had another thought:

*Which means there will be almost nothing doing at Jorge Newbery when
we land.*

People will be curious. . . .

"Jake, how about going into Ezeiza? Jorge Newbery will be deserted at half
past three in the morning. Ezeiza starts getting the FedEx and UPS planes and
some of the European arrivals very early. Maybe we can sort of not be noticed."

"You're right, but they expect us at Jorge Newbery."

"You are forgetting our new commo equipment."

"I stand corrected," Torine said. "And I will get on the horn just as soon as
I'm sure they're all asleep. I don't see why Dick and I should be the only ones
in this group awake all night."

"Fly carefully and smoothly, children," Castillo said. "Your leader is going
to be sleeping."

Torine gave him the finger again.

Castillo went back to his seat, this time carefully lowering his feet onto
Max's chest. Max opened his eyes for a moment, then closed them again.

Castillo sat for a moment, then said, "Oh, shit!"

He then gently tapped on Max with his feet. Max raised his head.

"Sorry, pal," Castillo said. "You have to get up."

Max didn't budge, although he continued to look at Castillo.

"Get up, damn it!"

Max didn't move.

Castillo swung his legs into the aisle, got up, and took a few steps down the
cabin aisle.

"Come on, boy!"

No response.

Castillo clapped his hands together. Once. Twice. A third time.

Max, not without effort, got to his feet and backed into the aisle.

"Good boy!"

Castillo pushed Max backward up the aisle until he had access to the drawer
under his seat. He bent over and pulled it open. Max took two steps and licked
Castillo's face.

"Sonofabitch!" Castillo said, and, pushing at Max to back up, realized the
dog probably thought he was playing.

Castillo reached into the drawer and pulled his laptop from it.

Max kissed him again.

"Aw, goddammit!"

"I think he likes you, Colonel," Sergeant Neidermeyer said.

Castillo looked up at Neidermeyer.

"This is one of those times when I wish I was not a field-grade officer," Castillo said.

"Sir?"

"If we were both sergeants, I could tell you to take a flying fuck at a rolling doughnut," Castillo said.

"With all due respect, Colonel, sir, it is not the sergeant's fault that the animal seems to like you, sir."

"Does the sergeant have something on what is loosely known as his mind?"

"Yes, sir. The sergeant thought the colonel might be interested in some photographs the sergeant took in Louisiana, or, more precisely, Colonel, sir, as we were flying over Mississippi and Louisiana, sir."

He handed Castillo a large manila envelope.

Castillo took it from him and removed the photographs. There were twenty or more eight-by-ten-inch crisp color prints. Just about all of them were photographs of the hurricane damage they had seen from the air.

"Nice, Jamie," Castillo said. "What's the chances of getting a set of these?"

"I made those for you," Neidermeyer said.

"Thanks, Jamie," Castillo said. "I appreciate that."

He was now nearly at the end of the stack of photographs.

The one he had on top of the stack now was of him and the Richardson boy. They had both turned in their seats to look into the rear of the airplane—*Neidermeyer must have done something, called something, to get us to turn and look at him*—Castillo was turned in his seat to his right, and the Richardson boy to his left, the result being their heads were close together.

"Nice kid," Neidermeyer said. "If I didn't know better, I'd think he was yours."

"What?"

"He's got your eyes, Colonel," Neidermeyer said.

"I have so far been spared the joys of matrimony and—so far as I know—of parenthood."

"The eyes, Colonel. They're as blue as yours. That's what I mean."

No, he doesn't look like me.

I'm blond and fair-skinned.

This kid is olive-skinned. He could almost be Latin.

He looks like Fernando looked the first time I saw him. We were about as old then as this kid.

Holy Christ!

Calm down!

How could Richardson's kid possibly be mine?

Castillo suddenly felt a chill down his spine. He had goose bumps.

Dumb fucking question!

"Well, he's a nice kid. I wish he was mine. But he's not, obviously," Castillo said, and put the photographs back in the envelope. "Thanks, Jamie."

"Happy to do it, Colonel," Jamie Neidermeyer said, and walked back to his seat.

Castillo picked up his laptop from the seat, sat down, tucked the envelope of photographs under the laptop, and then opened the computer.

He clicked on a file titled CHKLIST.

A screen full of gibberish appeared.

Why did I bother to encrypt this? No one could make sense out of it if it was on a billboard.

He held down the CTRL key, typed "DEC," and the file decrypted.

The gibberish was replaced by a screen more or less in English.

```
(1)
RRAC???
AV ???????
WHEN????
WHERE???
ETA U??
OR ???


(2)
OO??
C5'S???
C-141S??
HOW MANY??
WHERE LAND??


(3)
PEVSNER??
WHERE??
DRUG CONNECTION??
WHERE HIS BELL???
```

The list of numbered entries—Castillo's system of keeping Things To Do notes numbered according to what he considered was their priority at the moment—ran off the computer screen.

He scrolled slowly down the list, reading each one. There were twenty-three.

He scrolled back up the list to (1). He would deal with that first.

The translation of (1) was:

What about the aircraft carrier USS Ronald Reagan*?*
Is it going to be available?
When is it going to be available?
Where will it be when/if it is made available?
What will its Estimated Time of Arrival off of Uruguay—or
someplace else—be?

He made the necessary corrections based on his current knowledge.

General McNab had sent Colonel Kingston to Tampa International Airport, where they had taken on fuel and gone through the customs and immigration formalities.

Kingston had told him the USS *Ronald Reagan* had been ordered through Navy channels to be prepared to receive four (possibly as many as six) UH-1H helicopters that were engaged in a clandestine operation classified Top Secret. The Task Group Commander and the captain of the *Ronald Reagan* would be advised when and where the helicopters were to be brought aboard. The senior officer of the flight detachment would advise the Task Group Commander and the captain when and where the helicopters were to be launched from the *Reagan.*

The cover story for the operation was that the helicopters were being ferried to an unspecified Latin American country as part of a military assistance program. In this connection, the *Ronald Reagan* was to be prepared to strip the helicopters of their existing U.S. Army paint scheme and identification numbers and repaint them in a paint scheme and numbers to be furnished by the senior officer of the flight detachment.

Castillo deleted the question marks after RRAC??? as there was no longer any question that the USS *Ronald Reagan* would be the means by which the helicopters would go to South America, and he deleted AV??? because he now knew that the ship would be available.

He left the question marks after When??? and Where??? and ETA U??? as he and Colonel Kingston had agreed there was no sense in guessing when the choppers would go aboard the *Reagan,* or where, or when the *Reagan* would be off the coast of Uruguay. The choppers would be flown as soon as possible from Rucker to SOCOM at MacDill, and from MacDill to the *Reagan*. They would have a communicator with them. He would be in touch with both Castillo and McNab—and Kingston and everybody else with one of the AFC radios—and his information would be up to date.

Castillo deleted Or??? because that entry asked at what other location the choppers could be flown off the *Ronald Reagan* if they found for whatever reason that they could not do it off the coast of Uruguay. That was settled. Off the coast of Uruguay was the only place it could be done.

Castillo turned to (2), the translation of which was:

Other Options?
Maybe C-5
Maybe C-141s
How many 141s would be necessary?
Where could they land?

Now that the *Ronald Reagan* was going to ferry the choppers, it was no longer necessary to give consideration to using a C-5 Galaxy or two—or more—of its little brothers, the C-141 Starlifter transport aircraft, to get them to South America. That would have posed all kinds of problems—including coming up with a cover story to hide where a C-5, one of the largest aircraft in the world, was headed and why.

Castillo deleted all of (2) and turned to (3), the translation of which was:

What about Aleksandr Pevsner?
Where is he?
Does he have any connection with these drug people?
Where's his Bell Ranger helicopter?

He renumbered (3) to (2), then shook his head and sighed audibly.

Then he held down the CTRL key, typed "ENC," and thus encrypted the file. He saved the file, then closed the top of the laptop.

He took the manila envelope containing the photographs from beneath the computer. He pulled the image of Randolph Richardson IV and himself from the envelope.

He looked at it.

Problems don't go away by ignoring them.

And, oh boy, do I have a doozie of a problem here.

Perhaps unconsciously, perhaps by habit, he raised the lid of the laptop and began to deal with this problem as he did with most others with many facets. That was to say, as a Staff Study.

But no clever little abbreviations this time.

I can't afford to fuck this up.

He pushed the NEW key and started to type.

```
FACTS BEARING ON THE PROBLEM: THE MALE CHILD KNOWN AS
RANDOLPH RICHARDSON IV IS IN FACT THE BIOLOGICAL CHILD
OF MRS. BETHANY RICHARDSON AND C. G. CASTILLO, HAVING
BEEN CONCEIVED OUT OF WEDLOCK SHORTLY BEFORE THE THEN-
MISS WILSON MARRIED RANDOLPH RICHARDSON III, WHOSE NAME
PRESUMABLY APPEARS ON THE BIRTH CERTIFICATE.

DISCUSSION: CONSIDERING THE RAMIFICATIONS OF THE ABOVE,
AND INASMUCH AS THE HUMAN ANIMAL IS CAPABLE OF
UNLIMITED SELF-DECEPTION, THE FOLLOWING MUST BE TAKEN
INTO CONSIDERATION:

(1) BWR PROBABLY HAS CONSIDERED THE STRONG POSSIBILITY
THAT HER FIRST CHILD WAS CONCEIVED IN THE DALEVILLE INN
WITH CGC RATHER THAN WHEREVER THE HELL SHE WAS ON HER
HONEYMOON AND BY RRIII. SHE HAS DECIDED THAT:
    A. HER LIAISON WITH CGC DID NOT OCCUR DURING HER
    FERTILITY VULNERABILITY AND HER HONEYMOON WITH
    RIGHTEOUS DID, AND THAT THEREFORE, RRIII IS THE FATHER
    OF RRIV. OR,
    B. MORE LIKELY, THAT LITTLE WOULD BE GAINED, AND
    THERE WOULD BE A GREAT DEAL TO BE LOST, BY FESSING UP.
    C. WHY DIDN'T SHE TELL ME?
        I. BECAUSE THAT WOULD BE FESSING UP
        II. BECAUSE SHE KNEW THERE WAS A GOOD CHANCE I
        WOULDN'T GIVE A DAMN (WOULD I HAVE?)
```

III. BECAUSE I MIGHT HAVE RUSHED IN AND ANNOUNCED I WANTED TO DO THE "RIGHT THING," WHICH MEANS EVERYBODY WOULD HAVE KNOWN WHAT HAPPENED; THAT, FOR ONE, THERE WAS A CERTAIN HYPOCRISY IN HER VIRGINAL WHITE BRIDAL GOWN

IV. AND HER PARENTS WOULD HAVE KNOWN OF HER LITTLE INDISCRETION

(2) WHO ELSE KNOWS OR SUSPECTS?

A. RRIII WOULD HAVE NO REASON TO SUSPECT ANYTHING AND PROBABLY WAS PROUD AS HELL WHEN PEOPLE THOUGHT THAT HE MADE HIS BRIDE PREGNANT ON THE HONEYMOON.

I. IF HE SUSPECTED LATER (CHILD DOESN'T LOOK LIKE EITHER OF THEM) IT WOULD BE HARD FOR HIM TO ACCEPT.

II. IF HE SOMEHOW FOUND OUT (INCLUDING IF BWR WAS OVERWHELMED WITH GUILT; OR GOT PLASTERED AND LET IT OUT IN A FIGHT; ETCETERA) HE WOULD EITHER HAVE TO KEEP HIS MOUTH SHUT OR BE FACED WITH THE HUMILIATION OF HAVING IT WHISPERED UP AND DOWN THE LONG GRAY LINE THAT CGC HAD IMPREGNATED HIS VIRGIN BRIDE. SINCE THAT WOULD AFFECT HIS CAREER, HE WOULD KEEP HIS MOUTH SHUT.

III. OR, EQUALLY POSSIBLE, BWR TOLD HIM, AND THEY DECIDED BETWEEN THEM THAT THE BEST WAY TO DEAL WITH THE PROBLEM WOULD BE TO PRETEND IT HAD NEVER HAPPENED. (BUT IS IT POSSIBLE FOR ANYONE TO SIT ON SOMETHING SO EMOTIONALLY CHARGED FOR THAT LONG — 13 YEARS, MORE OR LESS, DEPENDING ON WHEN SHE TOLD HIM?????)

B. GEN & MRS. WILSON — UNLIKELY. NEITHER OF THEM WOULD SUSPECT THAT THEIR PRECIOUS LITTLE GIRL COULD POSSIBLY DO SOMETHING LIKE THIS.

C. HER FRIENDS — UNLIKELY. THERE ARE SECRETS AND THERE ARE SECRETS — AND THIS IS NOT THE KIND TO BE SHARED WITH GIRLISH GIGGLES.

D. ABUELA — OH, GOD!!!

I. IF ABUELA COULD TAKE A TEN-SECOND LOOK AT A

BLACK-AND-WHITE PHOTOGRAPH OF A TWELVE-YEAR-OLD SHE
HAD NEVER SEEN IN HER LIFE AND FIRMLY DECLARE,
"THAT'S MY GRANDSON. HE HAS JORGE'S EYES," OR WORDS
TO THAT EFFECT, THEN . . .

THERE IS ABSOLUTELY NO CHANCE IN HELL THAT ABUELA
DOESN'T KNOW !!!!!!!!!!!!!!!!!!!!!!!!!!!

SO WHY HASN'T SHE SAID ANYTHING?

BECAUSE SHE FIGURES THE KID WOULD BE BETTER OFF WHERE
HE IS???

OR MAYBE SHE HAS SAID SOMETHING — INDIRECTLY — WITH ALL
THAT TALK ABOUT ME NOT HAVING A FAMILY??? AND GETTING A
DOG??? BUT A DOG IS NOT THE KID. . . .

"THE KID"???? HE'S YOUR SON, YOU ASSHOLE!!!! YOUR
BLOOD, THE FRUIT OF YOUR LOINS, THE WHOLE GODDAMN
NINE YARDS!!!!

AND WHAT ABOUT THE BOY??

WHAT'S BETTER FOR HIM??

Castillo stopped typing, looked at what he had written, ran the cursor over everything to highlight it, and then put his finger on the DELETE key.

This is not going to go away by sending it into cyberspace!

Then he held down the CTRL key, then typed "ENC." He saved the now encrypted file as FATHERHOOD and turned off the laptop.

IX

Colonel Jacob Torine, USAF, turned from the left seat in the cockpit of Gulf-stream III N379LT toward Lieutenant Colonel C. G. Castillo, USA, who was standing in the doorway, and pointed his index finger toward the passenger compartment.

Torine ordered, "Sit."

Colonel Castillo complied with the order.

Captain Richard M. Sparkman, USAF, suppressing a smile, then retarded the throttles a tad, waited two seconds more, then greased the aircraft onto the runway.

"Nice," Colonel Torine said to Captain Sparkman over the privacy of the intercom. "Your other option, of course, was coming in hard and/or short or long and having Charley remind you of it for the rest of your natural life."

"What kind of a pilot is he?"

"If you quote me, I will deny it, but he's one of the naturals. Get him to take you for a chopper ride sometime. You'll feel like one of those soaring swallows that fly from Capistrano to Plaza de Mayo here in B. A."

"Stupid question, I guess," Sparkman said. "I saw all those DFCs."

"Three of them," Torine said. "Each for doing something with a helicopter that the manufacturer will tell you is aerodynamically impossible."

Ezeiza ground control directed them to the far left of the terminal building, where ground handlers parked them between two McDonnell Douglas MD-11 cargo aircraft, one belonging to FedEx and the other to Lufthansa, which made the Gulfstream look very small indeed.

"Passengers may now feel free to move about the aircraft," Torine called over the cabin speakers. "Please remember to take your personal items with you. That includes ravenous bears masquerading as lapdogs."

Castillo reappeared in the cockpit doorway.

"How do you want to handle this, Charley?" Torine asked. "Use the valet parking? Or have us stick with it and catch up to you later?"

"There's nothing on here of interest, except the AFC radios, and we'll take them with us. Let's stick together."

"And the weapons?" Torine argued.

"No problem, right, until we try to take them off the airplane? Just leave them."

"I will now go deal with the authorities," Torine said. "When do I tell them we'll need it?"

"On an hour's notice," Castillo said.

"Remember, we're here to fish," Torine said.

Castillo knew that that had come from Darby when Torine had radioed him their arrival time at Ezeiza. Darby had said, "The purpose of your visit is sport-fishing on the Pilcomayo River."

Max took one look at the customs officials at the foot of the stair door and decided he didn't like them. He was, however, now on a leash—Castillo had bought in Quito a hefty woven leather souvenir lariat for that purpose—and thus didn't pose a real problem. Still, the customs officials, smiling nervously, gave Max a wide berth as he towed Castillo to the nose gear.

Inside the terminal, when Castillo's group tried to pass through customs and immigration, there was another problem with Max. They were told that the official charged with ensuring that live animals entering the country had the proper documentation—in Max's case, a certificate from a doctor of veterinary medicine stating he had the proper rabies and other inoculations—had not yet come to work. They would have to wait until he showed up.

Castillo then saw, at about the same time Delchamps did, the two burly men in civilian clothing leaning against the wall across the baggage carousel from them, trying not to conceal their interest in the newly arrived American sport-fishermen.

They might as well have had COP *tattooed on their foreheads.*

When Castillo locked eyes with Delchamps, it was obvious they were both wondering if the official-who-had-not-yet-come-to-work was really late, or whether this was some kind of stall.

Max was not concerned. He had for some reason changed his mind and decided he liked the customs officers who wouldn't let him into the country, and had offered them his paw. They had responded by offering him a thick rope to tug on, and he now was dragging two of them across the baggage room.

Castillo was somewhat concerned that when it came to inspecting their luggage there might be special interest in the AFC satellite telephones in the suitcases carried by Lester Bradley and Jamie Neidermeyer.

There was a cover story ready, of course—that they were ordinary satellite telephones necessary to keep Señor Castillo in touch with the world head-quarters of the Lorimer Charitable & Benevolent Fund in Washington, D.C.—but that sounded fishy to even Señor Castillo, and there might be problems later if the customs officers decided they had best make a record of the entry of the radios into Argentina so that they would leave the country when Señor Castillo did, and not be sold in Argentina without the appropriate taxes being paid.

The problem did not come up. By the time the official charged with mak-ing sure Max was healthy showed up a half hour later, Max had so charmed the customs officials—mostly by being stronger than the two of them tugging on the rope—that as soon as the official had stamped his vaccination certificate they waved them past the luggage X-ray machines and through the doors to the lobby for arriving passengers.

There were no familiar faces waiting for them. But Torine nudged Castillo and nodded toward a man waving a sign with "Herr Gossinger" written on it.

Castillo discreetly signaled the others to wait, then walked over to the man.

Before Castillo could open his mouth, the man with the sign greeted him, in German: "Herr Munz welcomes you to Argentina, Herr Gossinger. He awaits you and your party at the estancia."

"*Danke schoen,*" Castillo replied, and motioned for the others to follow him.

Out of the corner of his eye, he saw that the two cops who had been in bag-gage claim were now in the terminal, and obviously about to follow him and the others wherever they went.

The man with the sign led them out of the terminal to a small yellow Mer-cedes bus with ARGENTOURS painted on its doors. As the driver, eyeing Max warily, stuffed their luggage into it and the two cops watched the process, Torine discreetly nudged Castillo again, this time indicating a BMW with ordinary Ar-gentine license plates.

Castillo saw Alfredo Munz behind the wheel. Alex Darby, the "commercial attaché" of the United States embassy, was sitting next to him. Neither Darby nor Munz gave any sign of recognition.

There were two people in the backseat of the BMW whom Castillo couldn't identify.

Not surprising. I can barely see Darby and Munz through those darkened windows.

But what the hell is this all about?

When the yellow Mercedes bus pulled away from the terminal, Munz's BMW followed it, and when they had left the airport property and were on the highway headed toward downtown Buenos Aires, Munz passed the bus and pulled in front.

That wasn't surprising either, but a minute or so later, Corporal Lester Bradley made his way with some difficulty through the crowded bus to kneel in the aisle beside Castillo.

"Colonel, I may be wrong, but I thought I should bring to your attention the possibility that we're being followed."

Yung heard him. He said, "It's those two cop types who were eyeing us in the terminal."

Castillo looked out over the luggage stacked in the back of the bus. There behind them were four men in a blue Peugeot sedan.

"And two of their friends," Castillo said.

"What's going on, Colonel?" Yung asked.

"I think they're friendlies, bringing up our rear. Munz and Darby are in that BMW in front of us. As to what's going on, I haven't a clue."

Ten minutes later, perhaps five seconds after Castillo had decided they were en route to the safe house in Pilar—they were on the sort of parkway that connects the downtown Buenos Aires–Ezeiza autopista with the Acceso Norte, which turns into Ruta 8—the BMW ahead of them suddenly turned onto an exit road and the bus, tires squealing, followed them.

When Castillo looked out the back, he saw that the Peugeot behind them had come to a stop in the middle of the exit road, effectively blocking anyone who might be following.

They drove three blocks into what looked like a working-class neighborhood—rows of small, wall-sharing, single-family homes built of masonry, broken only by buildings that could have been small factories, or garages, or warehouses—then made another screeching turn, and abruptly slowed before making a left turn off the street and rolling through an opened overhead door into a three-story building.

A stocky man wearing a pistol shoulder holster was standing just inside the door, and as soon as the bus was inside, he pulled on a chain mechanism that quickly lowered a corrugated steel door.

The room had been dimly lit. Now fluorescent lights flickered on, filling the area with a bright, harsh light.

They could see they were in some kind of garage. Vehicles of all descriptions—twenty-five or thirty, perhaps more, including several taxis and a nearly new Mercedes-Benz 220—were parked closely together, noses out, against the walls. There was a ramp at the end of the room leading upward.

"Is this where we go fishing, Colonel?" Chief Warrant Officer Five Colin Leverette asked.

The bus driver opened the door.

Munz stuck his head into the bus.

"We change vehicles here," he announced.

"What's going on, Alfredo?" Castillo asked in German.

"In a moment, please, Karl," Munz replied in German, then said in English, "Would everybody please get off the bus?"

Max needed no further encouragement. Munz ducked out of his way at the last possible second.

Max ran around the area—*In a strange gait*, Castillo noticed, *almost as if he's running on his toes. He's hunting, that's what he's doing. I'll be damned if he didn't sense that just about all us warriors of legendary icy courage on the bus were scared shitless by this mysterious little joyride*—found nothing that worried him and returned to Munz, where he sat down and offered him his paw.

"Max says it's safe to get off the bus, fellas," Davidson said.

"Don't laugh at him," Castillo said. "Remember the last time he went looking for something in a garage?"

"Who's laughing?" Davidson said agreeably.

Everybody piled off the bus.

The driver went to the rear and started unloading the luggage. Two more large men who looked like cops—*the ones who had been in the backseat of Munz's BMW*, Castillo decided—moved quickly to help him.

Castillo caught Munz's eye and wordlessly asked who they were and what was going on.

"I'll explain this all in a minute," Munz said. "We're pressed for time. Lester, could you find Acceso Norte from here?"

"Yes, sir," Corporal Bradley replied. "I am fairly familiar with the area."

"Yung?" Munz asked.

"Yeah. I know my way around B.A."

"Karl, would it be all right with you if Lester and Yung drove everybody not needed here out to Nuestra Pequeña Casa?"

"Who's 'needed here,' Alfredo?" Castillo asked.

"Edgar and Jake should be in on this, Charley," Alex Darby said.

"Okay," Castillo said. "Are we going to need a radio right now?"

Darby shook his head.

"Okay, load the cars that Mr. Darby's going to give you," Castillo ordered. "Neidermeyer, if you ride with Two-Gun, we won't have both radios in one car. Otherwise, suit yourselves. Take all the luggage. Edgar and Jake, you'll stay."

They nodded.

Two minutes later, the corrugated steel door clanked noisily up. Yung drove a Volkswagen Golf out of the building. The door came clanking quickly down again, to rise two minutes later to permit the exit of a Jeep Grand Cherokee with Bradley driving.

When the corrugated steel door had crashed noisily down again, one of the cops who had helped with the luggage raised his hand toward the ramp.

"Please," he said in English.

They started to follow him up the ramp. Max ran past him without difficulty. The others had a little trouble. The ramp was quite steep, not very wide, and had six-inch-wide anti-wheel-slip bumps running across it.

At the next level, they found themselves in an area much like the level they had just left. Vehicles of all descriptions were parked tightly together against the walls.

Max was standing in the middle, looking at a brown uniformed gendarmería sergeant sitting on a folding chair with an Uzi in his lap. The gendarme sat in front of a steel door in an interior concrete-block wall.

As the man led them across the open area toward the door, the gendarme, eyeing Max warily, got quickly out of his chair and had the door open by the time the man got to it.

The man went inside, and there was again the flicker of fluorescent lights coming on.

"Please," he said once more, as he waved them inside.

Max trotted in first.

The room was dominated by an old desk—once grand and elegant—before which sat a simple, sturdy, rather battered oak conference table. There were eight chairs at the table. The wall behind the desk was covered with maps of Argentina in various scales, including an enormous one of Buenos Aires Province. Along both walls were tables holding computers, facsimile machines, telephones, a coffee maker, and some sort of communications radios. All of it looked old.

"Please," the man said again, this time an invitation for everyone to sit down.

"That will be all, thank you," Munz said to the man.

"*Sí, mi coronel,*" the man said, and left the room, closing the door behind him.

Max lay down with his head between his paws and looked at the closed door.

"Okay, Alfredo," Castillo said. "What's going on, starting with where are we?"

"We have a law of confiscation in Argentina, Karl," Munz said. "This building was being used as a warehouse for cocaine and marijuana; it was seized. And so were the vehicles you saw. Comandante Liam Duffy of the Gendarmería Nacional now uses it, unofficially, as an office and base of operations."

"He's the guy who the DEA guy was on his way to see when he was snatched?" Delchamps asked.

Munz nodded.

"So what are we doing here?" Delchamps went on. "And who are all the guys with guns?"

"Comandante Duffy thought there was a good chance that you would be at some risk at the airport. . . ."

"How did he know we would be at the airport?" Torine asked.

"He was with us at the house when you radioed saying you were going to Ezeiza instead of Jorge Newbery," Darby offered.

"You had this guy in Nuestra Pequeña Casa?" Castillo snapped at Alex Darby. "That's supposed to be our safe house!"

"A lot of things have happened, Charley," Darby replied.

"Obviously," Castillo said, thickly sarcastic.

"Easy, Ace," Delchamps said, then looked at Darby. "Like what, Alex? What has happened?"

"The bottom line is that Chief Inspector José Ordóñez, of the Interior Police Division of the Uruguayan Policía Nacional, is back in the game. . . ."

"Jesus Christ!" Castillo exploded. "How the hell—?"

"Let him finish, Ace," Delchamps said reasonably.

Castillo glowered at him but said nothing.

"If I may . . . ," Alfredo Munz began, and when Castillo motioned impatiently for him to go on, Munz picked up the explanation: "The day I came back here, I called José Ordóñez. For several reasons. One, to thank him for what he had done for us. And to tell him that I was back. And, frankly, the primary reason I called was to ask him how well he knew Duffy. I knew we had to deal with Duffy, and I knew Duffy only casually. And I knew Duffy would know that I had been 'retired' from SIDE, and was afraid that he wouldn't want to have anything to do with me."

"And?" Castillo said.

"José told me that Duffy had come to Uruguay to see him, and that as a result of the interesting conversation he'd had with him, he had called Bob Howell and asked him how Duffy could get in touch with me. And, more important,
with you."

Robert Howell, the "cultural attaché" of the U.S. embassy in Montevideo,
was in fact the CIA station chief.

"And what did Howell tell him?" Castillo asked carefully.

"The truth—or what he thought was the truth. That both you and I were
in the United States, but that he would relay the message."

"And what did Howell do?"

"He got on the next plane to Buenos Aires and came to see me," Darby said.
"So I took him out to Nuestra Pequeña Casa to see Alfredo to see if he had any
idea what this was all about."

"Did you?" Castillo asked.

Munz shook his head.

"I don't think we were in the house thirty minutes," Darby said, "when
Duffy showed up at the front door."

"The *front door,* or at the gate?" Castillo asked.

"The front door," Darby said. "Obviously, he had people on me or
Howell—more likely both—and they followed us from the embassy. And no
country club security guard is going to tell a comandante of the gendarmería
he can't come in."

"What did he want?" Castillo asked.

"To talk to me," Munz said. "But especially to you."

"What about?"

"I wanted to show you some photographs, Colonel," a voice behind Castillo said. It sounded not only American, but as if the speaker were a native of
Brooklyn.

Castillo turned to see a tall, muscular, very fair-skinned man with a full head
of curly red hair. He was in the process of taking off his suit jacket, under
which he carried in a shoulder holster what looked like a full-frame Model
1911A1 Colt .45 semiautomatic pistol.

Max was now on his feet, his head cocked to one side, looking at the new-
comer.

So you're Liam Duffy, Castillo thought.

*And how long have you been outside listening to this conversation, Señor
Duffy?*

Duffy walked around to behind the ornate desk. He hung his jacket on the
back of his chair, sat down, and then announced, "I am Comandante Duffy, of
the Gendarmería Nacional."

He really does sound like he's from Brooklyn.
Where the hell did that come from?

"How do you do, Comandante?" Castillo said. "Am I to thank you for the protection we've had since we walked into the terminal at Ezeiza?"

"Alfredo, who I recently learned is a very dear friend of a very dear friend of mine in Uruguay—José Ordóñez—which makes him a very dear friend of mine, thinks we might work together, Colonel. With that in mind, it was in the interest of the gendarmería to guard you and your men against a threat I don't think you knew existed."

"What kind of a threat?"

"Possibly being shot, or perhaps being strangled."

"Now, who would want to do something like that to innocent tourists who came to your beautiful country to fly-fish its rivers of trophy trout?"

"The same people who did this, Colonel," Duffy said.

He tossed a large manila envelope—very skillfully, it landed right where Castillo was sitting—across his desk.

Castillo took from the envelope a thick sheath of color prints. They had been printed on ordinary paper, but the quality told him they had been taken with a high-quality digital camera.

He took a quick look at the first one, then passed it to Delchamps, and signaled that he was to pass it to Torine and the others when he had seen it.

It showed a bullet-riddled body of a man in a brown, military-type uniform. He was lying on his back, eyes open, in a dark pool of blood, on what was probably the gravel shoulder of a macadam country road.

There were, in all, eight photographs of the body. Several fairly close photographs of the head and torso showed the head was distorted. It had been shot several times at close range, including, Castillo judged, once in the mouth. There were more signs of entrance wounds in the body than Castillo could conveniently count, which strongly suggested the use of a submachine gun, with what looked like an entirely unnecessary coup de grâce shot in the mouth.

Next came as many photographs of a second gendarme. He had died of strangulation. A blue metal garrote had been so tightly drawn against his throat that it had cut into the flesh; he had lost a substantial quantity of blood before he had died.

Then there were glossy photographs of two gendarmes sitting in a chair. Both had their wrists handcuffed and showed signs of having been beaten.

Castillo passed along the last of the pictures and the envelope to Delchamps, then looked at Duffy. Duffy locked eyes with him, and Castillo sensed it would not be in his best interests to break the eye contact first.

Castillo didn't look away until Munz touched his arm with the envelope, now again thick with pictures. He took it from Munz, stood up, and walked to Duffy's desk. He put the envelope on the desk, then walked back to his chair, sat down, and looked at Duffy again.

"My gendarmes were manning road checks when the *hijos de puta* did this to them," Duffy then said. "The gendarmería sometimes sets up road checks at random sites and sometimes at sites where we have information about where drugs will be coming down the highway. In both cases here, we had had information that drugs would be coming down two particular highways, which happen to be some seventy kilometers apart."

Duffy paused a moment, then continued: "Killing and kidnapping gendarmes is very unusual. Criminals almost never kill members of the gendarmería, and never before have kidnapped any of them."

"Why is that, Comandante?" Delchamps asked softly.

"Because they know it is unacceptable," Munz said.

"What does that mean, 'unacceptable'?" Castillo demanded.

"It means the gendarmes will take revenge," Munz said. "Killing anyone they suspect may have been involved."

He let that sink in for a moment, then went on: "The gendarmería operates all over Argentina, very often in remote areas and with very few men. They usually operate in two-man teams, and sometimes alone. They are not attacked, because the price for doing so is too high. When this happened—"

"When *did* this happen?" Castillo interrupted. "Before or after Timmons was snatched?"

"A week after Timmons was taken," Munz said. "The day—or the day after—Max found Lorimer in the bushes at Nuestra Pequeña Casa."

"The gendarmería, Colonel," Duffy said, "prides itself on always getting its man. It was not wise to do what these hijos de puta did, and I asked myself why these narcos had.

"The first conclusion obviously to be drawn was that they decided to send the gendarmería the same kind of message they have been sending your DEA people in Asunción—that they will not tolerate interference with their business.

"Then I asked myself why they had suddenly decided to do this. What came to mind there was that they were about to start significantly increasing the flow of product to the point where so much money would be involved that they would think that protecting the shipments was worth the risk of behaving toward the gendarmería in a manner heretofore considered unacceptable.

"If this were true, I reasoned, it was possible—even likely—that my men were targeted by the narcos, rather than it being that they simply had stopped a narco truck and that the narcos had resisted. If the latter were the case, then both men would have been killed—no witnesses—not one of them taken away.

"That posed a number of questions, including how they had learned—that is, who had told them—where the road checks would be. I had some ideas about that, but nothing that I could prove. The most kind was that the hijos de puta offered the farmhands, the *peones,* in the area a little gift if they would telephone a number to report where we had set up a road check. Less kind was the possibility that the narcos offered a little gift to the officers of the Policía Federal in the area to do the same thing.

"But the major question in my mind was what had happened to cause the sudden increase in actions by the hijos de puta that they had to know were not only unacceptable to the gendarmería but would also call attention to them, which was also not in their best interests.

"At that point, I remembered hearing some gossip about something interesting that had happened in Uruguay. It sounded incredible, but I decided it was worth looking into. What I had heard was that a drug deal had gone wrong on an estancia in Tacuarembó Province in central Uruguay. According to this story, six men, all dressed in black, like characters in a children's movie, had been found shot to death.

"I thought that checking out the story would be a simple matter. José Ordóñez is more than a professional associate with whom I have worked closely over the years. As I said, we are dear friends. I thought all I would have to do would be to telephone José—unofficially, of course; I have José's private number and he has mine—and ask him what there was to this incredible story. And also to ask him if he had noticed any sudden increase in the drug shipments into and out of his country.

"So I called him. When I asked him what had happened in Tacuarembó Province, he didn't answer directly. He said that it had been too long since we had seen one another, and that we should really try to have lunch very soon.

"Well, the very next morning, I was on the Buquebus to Montevideo," Duffy went on. "Tourist class, as I was paying for it myself. Getting an official authorization to travel to Uruguay is difficult, takes time, and then only results in a voucher for a tourist-class seat. Is it that way in the U.S. Army, Colonel?"

"Very much so, Comandante. Getting the U.S. Army to pay for travel is like pulling teeth."

"That, then, raises the question of who is paying for the helicopter in which you have been flying all over down here."

Castillo looked Duffy square in the eyes and said evenly, "I have no idea what you're talking about, Comandante."

"If we are going to work together, Colonel, we are going to have to tell each other the truth."

The last three words of the sentence came out: *udder da trute.*

Castillo couldn't restrain a smile.

"You find that amusing?" Duffy asked.

"Colonel Munz didn't tell me you were from Brooklyn, Comandante."

"I don't understand."

"You have a Brooklyn accent, Comandante."

Duffy, visibly annoyed, looked at Munz.

Munz gestured that he didn't understand, and then turned to Castillo and said, "I don't understand either, Karl."

"Okay," Delchamps said, "Cultural History 101. Pay attention, there will be a pop quiz. Sometime around the time of the potato famine in Ireland, the Catholic Church sent a large number of priests—from Kilkenny, I think, but don't hold me to that—to minister to Irish Catholic immigrants in the New World. Many of them went to Brooklyn, and many to New Orleans. Their flocks picked up their accent. Now that I've heard Comandante Duffy speak, I wouldn't be a bit surprised if some of them were sent down here, too."

Now Duffy smiled.

"On the other hand," Duffy said to Castillo, "you sound like a Porteño, Colonel. What did Holy Mother Church in Argentina do, send Porteño priests to New York?"

Castillo laughed.

"Actually, I'm a Texican," Castillo said.

"A what?"

"A Texican. One whose family came from Mexico a very long time ago, before Texas was a state. My family's from San Antonio."

"I am a great admirer of the Texas Rangers," Duffy said.

"I have two ancestors who were Texas Rangers, a long time ago."

"Sometimes we think of the colonel as the Lone Ranger," Delchamps said. "Can I ask what a Porteño is?"

"Somebody from Buenos Aires," Alex Darby offered, "who speaks with sort of a special cant."

"And a hijos de puta?" Delchamps pursued.

"Argentina is a society where people like narcos are held in scorn by men," Darby said, chuckling. "Hijos de puta is a pejorative."

"I believe you would say 'sonsofbitches,' " Duffy said.

"What did you have in mind, Comandante," Castillo asked, "when you said, 'If we are going to work together'?"

"Well, José and I had a very nice luncheon in the port restaurant in Montevideo. Do you know it?"

Castillo shook his head.

"You'll have to try it sometime. It's really excellent, if you like meat prepared on a parrilla. It's right across from the Buquebus terminal."

"Can we get to the point of this?" Castillo asked.

"During which," Duffy went on, nodding, "Ordóñez told me, in confidence, of course, that what really happened at Estancia Shangri-La had nothing to do with narcos."

"Would you believe me if I told you I never heard of Estancia Shangri-La?"

"No. But I certainly understand why you would profess never to have heard of it. If I may continue?"

Castillo made a dramatic, sarcastic gesture for him to do so.

"I also learned from my friend José that his very dear friend, El Coronel Alfredo Munz, formerly the head of SIDE, was associated with you, Colonel. I had only the privilege of a casual acquaintance with El Coronel Munz before the Interior Ministry threw him to the wolves following the murder of Señor Masterson, but I had always heard that he was an honest man, despite the rumors that he was very close to a very bad man named Aleksandr Pevsner."

"Never heard of him, either," Castillo said. "You, Edgar?"

Delchamps shook his head.

Duffy's face first paled, then flushed.

"Enough of this nonsense," Comandante Liam Duffy said angrily. "Let me tell you what I know about you, Colonel Castillo. When the diplomat's wife was kidnapped, you suddenly appeared on the scene and were placed in charge of the situation. But by someone superior to the ambassador, because the ambassador was placed at your orders. You directed the protection of the Masterson family. After Masterson was murdered, you found out who had killed him, and when those hijos de puta went to the estancia of Masterson's brother-in-law, most probably to eliminate him and take possession of some sixteen million dollars, they were surprised to find you and a team of your men waiting for them, having traveled there by helicopter.

"You eliminated all of the bastards and took possession of the sixteen million dollars. You lost one of your men, and Colonel Munz suffered a wound. And these were not ordinary narcos. One of them was Major Alejandro Vincenzo of the Cuban Dirección General de Inteligencia."

He paused.

"Shall I go on, Colonel Castillo?"

"What is it that you want from me, Comandante?" Castillo asked.

"What I *intend* to do, Colonel, is find and deal with the criminales who murdered and kidnapped my men. I will make the point very strongly that this was unacceptable behavior. I'm very much afraid that in your efforts to free Special Agent Timmons, you will interfere with my plans to do this. That is something I cannot—*will not*—permit.

"From what both Ordóñez and Munz tell me about you, you let nothing get in your way of what you consider your mission. So you have the choice, Colonel, between working under my orders or leaving Argentina. You have already broken many of our laws, and are obviously prepared to break whatever of our laws might interfere with your mission.

"Working under my orders will mean that I will have access to your assets, including money, intelligence, equipment, and personnel. More important, it will mean that you will take no action of any kind without my approval.

"On the other hand, you will have access to my intelligence and what few assets I have. Ordóñez has told Munz I am a man of my word. I am. We have a more or less common goal. You want to get your man Timmons back from the narcos. Beyond that, I don't know. We share an interest in interdicting the flow of drugs, of course. But we both know that neither you nor I—or you and I together—can stop the trade. But we can, I believe, cost the hijos de puta a great deal of money. That's something.

"So what you are going to do now, Colonel Castillo, is go out to Nuestra Pequeña Casa—which was rented under fraudulent conditions for illegal purposes—and get on that marvelous radio of yours—the possession and use of which are also offenses under Argentina law—and tell your superior of this conversation. If he is agreeable to our working together, Alfredo knows how to contact me. If not, I will give you twenty-four hours from noon today to get out of Argentina before I notify the Interior Ministry of your illegal behavior, and the foreign ministry of the actions of el Señor Darby, el Señor la Señora Sieno, and others, which I feel certain will merit their being declared persona non grata. Do I make myself clear, Colonel?"

Castillo met Duffy's eyes and nodded.

"I mentioned sharing my intelligence with you," Duffy said. "It has come to my attention that the narcos were aware you were coming to Argentina to deal with Special Agent Timmons's kidnapping. Their solution to that potential problem for them was to kidnap you, and failing that, to kill you. And, of course, your men. It was for that reason that my men were at Ezeiza and escorted you here. I didn't want that to happen to you until we had a chance to talk."

"Thank you very much for your concern," Castillo said with a sarcastic edge.

"It is nothing, Colonel. Have a pleasant day."

Duffy stood up behind his desk and threw the envelope of photographs back across the desk to Castillo.

"You may have those, Colonel," he said as he put on his suit jacket. "In case you might need a reminder that if the hijos de puta are willing to do this to my men, they'll certainly be willing to do the same to Special Agent Timmons."

Then he walked out of the room, leaving the door open.

Max lay down again, watching the door with his head resting between his front paws.

They heard the sound of an engine starting, of a car moving, then the sound of it bumping down over the bumps of the ramp, then the screech of the corrugated steel overhead door opening to the street.

Castillo looked at the others and found they were all looking at him.

"Gentlemen," he said. "Why don't we go out to Nuestra Pequeña Casa and get some breakfast?"

He paused, then went on: "And if you have nothing better to do, please assemble your thoughts vis-à-vis getting your leader out of this fucking mess."

[TWO]
Mayerling Country Club
Pilar, Buenos Aires Province, Argentina
1125 9 September 2005

When Munz slowed the BMW as they approached the striped pole barrier to the country club, he looked over at Castillo, who was sitting beside him. Max had somehow managed to squeeze himself between Castillo's feet, and now had his head on Castillo's lap. Castillo, his head bent, was apparently asleep.

Munz smiled and shook his head.

"We're here, Karl," Munz announced. "Our gendarmería escort has just left us."

Castillo's head immediately jerked erect.

"Would you believe I was thinking?" he asked.

"No," Jake Torine said from the backseat.

Torine was jammed in between Alex Darby and Edgar Delchamps.

"I was trying to make an important decision," Castillo said.

"And did you?"

"I thought I would seek your wise counsel before reaching a final decision," Castillo said. "Based on your vast poker-playing experience."

"What the hell are you talking about, Ace?" Delchamps asked.

"When do I call that Evil Leprechaun sonofabitch and tell him I surrender?"

"Is that what you're going to do?" Darby asked.

Castillo did not reply directly. Instead, he went on, "Do I call almost immediately, as if my superior in Washington immediately caved in? Or in an hour—or two or three—giving Duffy the idea that my superior ordered me to surrender only after solemn thought, probably after he consulted with *his* superiors?"

"I gather you are not going to seek Montvale's sage advice?" Delchamps said. "Or anybody else's?"

"Two problems with that," Castillo said, "the first, of course, being that Montvale is *not* my superior. Second, my asking Montvale would permit him to happily run to the President—who is my boss—then sadly report that, as he predicted, the impetuous young colonel has gotten himself in a bind in Argentina. The idea there being to really put me in Montvale's pocket. So the only 'anybody else' I can call is my boss—'Good morning, Mr. President. The Lone Ranger here. A redheaded Argentine cop has got me by the balls and I really don't know what to do.' "

Delchamps chuckled.

"Make the call in two or three hours, Karl," Munz said, softly but seriously.

"Reasoning?" Castillo asked.

"Liam Duffy would be suspicious if you called him right away, that you did not consult with your superior and were lying to him. He expects that you do have a superior—far down the ladder from your President, but a superior, or superiors. If you wait the several hours, he will probably think that you have been ordered to cooperate with him. And will think that makes you less of a problem to him."

Castillo grunted, then looked at Darby.

"Alex?"

"I think you should follow Alfredo's advice," Alex Darby said. "He tends to be right."

"Jake?" Castillo said, turning.

"That's a decision someone of my pay grade is not qualified to make," Torine said.

"Edgar?"

"I go with Alfredo," Delchamps said.

"Okay. I'll call him in three hours," Castillo said.

"Karl," Munz said, "remember that Duffy said, 'Munz knows how to contact me.' "

"I remember," Castillo said. "So?"

"I suggest it might be better if I was your contact with Duffy."

Castillo was considering the implications of that when Delchamps said, "He's right again, Ace."

"Okay again, then," Castillo said.

He looked out the window. They were almost at Nuestra Pequeña Casa.

"I thought with a little bit of luck I might never see this place again," he said.

Susanna Sieno opened the door of the house as they pulled up to it. Max got out first, climbing over Castillo into the rear seat and then jumping out the rear door as Darby opened it.

Castillo swore.

"Not very well trained, is he, Ace?" Delchamps asked innocently.

There was a man sitting in a straight-backed chair just inside the door. He stood up and came to attention as Castillo entered.

He was short, stocky, olive-skinned, had a neatly trimmed pencil-line mustache and a closely cropped ring of dark hair circling the rear of his skull, the rest of which was hairless and shiny. He was wearing a shiny blue single-breasted suit, a white shirt, and a really ugly necktie, which ended halfway down his stomach.

That Irish sonofabitch has had the balls to put a spy in here!

Confirmation of that seemed to come when the man said, *"Buenos días, mi coronel. A sus órdenes."*

Castillo nodded, and replied in Spanish, "Good day. And you are?"

"Capitán Manuel D'Elia, *mi coronel.*"

Castillo continued the exchange in Spanish: "And what are you doing here?"

"I am here for duty, *mi coronel.*"

"Comandante Duffy sent you?"

"No, *mi coronel.*"

"Then who did?"

"General McNab, *mi coronel.*"

"You're an American?"

"Sí, mi coronel."

"Where are you from, Captain?"

Captain D'Elia switched to English. "Miami, Colonel."

"It's not your day, is it, Ace?" Delchamps said. "He really got you."

Castillo flashed him a dirty look.

D'Elia said, "I sent Colin Leverette to Rucker—he said he knew you, sir— while I got the team moving from Bragg. And I brought up the rear. I got here yesterday morning. Mrs. Sieno brought me out here."

"Your whole team is here?"

"Yes, sir."

"Here here? Or someplace else?"

"I'm the only one here, sir. The others are stashed in hotels around Buenos Aires. Except our commo and intel sergeants who—at Mr. Darby's suggestion—I sent ahead to Asunción."

"Where in Asunción?"

Darby said, "They're in the Hotel Resort Casino Yacht & Golf Club Paraguay, Charley. Gambling, chasing ladies, maybe even playing golf—on your nickel—and incidentally looking around."

"They're not going to attract attention doing that?"

"They're traveling on Mexican passports, Colonel," D'Elia said. "Legitimate ones. They're Texicans."

He looked at Castillo to see if he understood the term.

"You're looking at one," Castillo said.

D'Elia smiled.

"With all possible respect, sir—and I admit you *do* talk the talk—you look like a gringo to me."

"And you don't, fortunately," Castillo said. "What about your sergeants in Asunción?"

"No one will think they're gringos, Colonel."

"And the rest of your team?"

"Everybody but Colin Leverette can pass—has passed—as a native Latino. That's presuming Paraguay isn't that much different from Bolivia or Venezuela. Or Cuba, for that matter, although not everybody on my team has had the chance to see how Castro has fucked up the land of my ancestors."

"Colin told me he'd been to Cuba," Castillo said.

"He did fine in Cuba as a Brazilian," D'Elia said. "In Venezuela—not so many black-skinned folks—he also passed himself off as a Brazilian. He speaks pretty good Portuguese."

"He also speaks pretty good Pashtu," Castillo said.

"So do I," D'Elia said in Pashtu. "Darby and I were talking about that. We must have just missed each other over there, sir."

"You knew Alex there?"

D'Elia nodded.

"And Mrs. Sieno and I have been exchanging Cuban war stories," he said.

"Under those circumstances, welcome, welcome, Captain," Castillo said. "Just as soon as we get something to eat, I'll bring you up to speed on what's going down."

He turned to Susanna Sieno.

"How about mustering the troops in the quincho, Susanna?"

"Everybody?"

Castillo nodded, then understood her question.

"Ask Sergeant Mullroney and Lieutenant Lorimer to come watch us eat first, please. Then muster them in the quincho."

"Sit down, please, Sergeant Mullroney," Lieutenant Colonel C. G. Castillo said politely when the Chicago detective came into the dining room of the main house with Lorimer. "While we talk about what we're going to do with you."

Mullroney sat down across the table from Castillo; Lorimer sat down between Torine and Delchamps.

A plump, middle-aged woman and a younger one began distributing ham and eggs and plates of rolls.

Her daughter? Castillo wondered.

Whoever they are, they wouldn't be here if Susanna didn't trust them.

Castillo pushed a coffee thermos across the table.

"Has Charley here been a good boy, Eddie?" Castillo asked.

"A very good boy, sir," First Lieutenant Edmund Lorimer said.

"Then we mustn't forget to give him a gold star to take home to mommy— I mean, the mayor—mustn't we?"

"No, sir, we mustn't. I'll be sure to do that. May I ask when that will be, Colonel?"

"First thing tomorrow morning," Castillo said. He looked at Mullroney for a long moment, then asked, "No comment, Sergeant?"

"You know the mayor's not going to be happy if you send me home, Colonel," Mullroney said after a moment.

"I guess not," Castillo said. "But the situation here—already bad—got worse about an hour ago, which leaves me with two choices. Making the mayor unhappy by sending you back home, or watching this operation blow up in my face—which, as you know, Sergeant, means in the President's face—which is not really an option."

"Lorimer just told you I haven't been giving anybody any trouble," Mullroney protested.

"That's because *Lieutenant* Lorimer has been sitting on you, under my orders to take you out if you even looked like you were thinking of doing something you shouldn't. So you behaved, and you get to go home—alive—with that gold star I was talking about."

"You really don't want to piss off the mayor, Colonel," Mullroney said.

"No, I don't, and I don't think I will. Making him unhappy and pissing him off are two different things. Do you know what we mean by a Gold Star for Mommy, Sergeant?"

Mullroney didn't reply, and his face showed embarrassed confusion.

"I will send a letter to the mayor with Colonel Torine," Castillo said, "with copies to the President and the director of National Intelligence, saying how much we appreciate his offering us your services, and how hard you have tried to be of use, but that I have reluctantly concluded you just don't have the investigative, analytical, and other skills necessary, and that I decided the best thing to do to ensure the success of the operation was to send you home."

"You sonofabitch!" Mullroney said.

Castillo went on as if he hadn't heard him: "Now, that will almost certainly make the mayor unhappy, but I think if he's going to be pissed off at anybody it will be at you, Sergeant Mullroney, for not being able to cut the mustard. I don't think that will make you too popular with Special Agent Timmons's family, either."

Mullroney locked eyes with Castillo but didn't say anything.

"Permission to speak, sir?" Lorimer asked.

Castillo appeared to be considering that before he made a *Come on with it* gesture.

"Sir, inasmuch as Sergeant Mullroney didn't ask to be sent with us, it doesn't seem fair that he should find his ass in a crack."

From the expression in Mullroney's eyes, ol' Charley did in fact volunteer to come along with us.

Volunteering no doubt scored a lot of points with the mayor.

And there'd be even more brownie points if we—and he—managed to get Timmons back.

"We're not in the 'fair' business, Lorimer," Castillo said coldly. "And therefore, since you are presumed to understand that—"

"Colonel," Delchamps interrupted. "If I may?"

Castillo appeared to be considering that, too, before he gestured for Delchamps to continue.

I don't know what you're going to say, Edgar, but obviously you picked up on where I'm trying to go with Mullroney.

You even called me "colonel."

What's going to happen now, I think, is instead of the ordinary good guy, bad guy scam, we're going to have two good guys saving Mullroney from bad ol' Colonel Castillo.

"I understand your concerns, Colonel," Delchamps went on. "But what I have been thinking is that Detective Mullroney might be useful when we go to Paraguay."

"How?" Castillo asked, his tone on the edge of sarcasm.

"In dealing with both the people in the embassy and the local police. With regard to the former, whether you go there as Colonel Castillo or as Mr. Castillo, you are still going to be the important visitor from Washington, and they are not going to tell you anything that might come around, in that marvelous phrase, to bite them on the ass. As far as the local police are concerned—your command of the language notwithstanding—you are going to be a visiting gringo, and they are not going to tell you anything."

Delchamps paused, then continued, "Now, Detective Mullroney—"

"Actually, I'm a sergeant," Mullroney interrupted.

Delchamps flashed Mullroney a look making it clear that he didn't like being interrupted, then went on, "*Sergeant* Mullroney is a bona fide police officer, low enough in rank so as not to frighten away the people in the embassy but yet to be, so to speak, one of them. I'm suggesting that he might be told—or would see—things they would not tell or show you."

I am now pretending to carefully consider what Delchamps just said.

The funny thing is it makes sense, even if he came up with it just to help Lorimer and me keep Mullroney on a tight leash.

"There may be something to what you say, Delchamps," Castillo said after what he considered to be a suitable pause, "but do you really believe that it outweighs the risk of Mullroney doing something stupid that would blow the operation?"

"Well, you'd have to keep him on a short leash, of course," Delchamps said, "but, yes, Colonel, I do. You might be surprised how valuable he might be."

"Sir, I'll be sitting on him," Lorimer said.

"But you have this odd notion of fair play, Lieutenant," Castillo said.

Castillo put what he hoped was a thoughtful look on his face and kept it there for thirty seconds, which seemed much longer.

"And," Castillo then went on, "to be of any use to us in the manner you suggest, he would have to know what's going on—starting with being present at the briefing I am about to deliver—and I'm uncomfortable with that."

"Sir, I'll be sitting on him," Lorimer said again.

"You've mentioned that," Castillo snapped.

"Sorry, sir," Lorimer said, and looked at Mullroney with a look that said, *Well, I tried.*

"All right," Castillo said. "I'll go this far. You will not return to the United

States with Colonel Torine tomorrow. I will give this matter further thought, and let you know what I finally decide."

"Thank you," Mullroney said softly.

"Take Sergeant Mullroney out to the quincho and tell the others I'll be there shortly. I need a word with these gentlemen."

"Yes, sir," Lorimer said.

He gestured for Mullroney to get up and then followed him out of the room.

When the door had closed, Castillo mimed applauding. The others chuckled.

"May I ask a question, Karl?" Munz said.

"Sure."

"You don't trust him, do you?"

"He strikes me as the kind of not-too-bright guy who, meaning well, is likely to rush off in the wrong direction. And we can't afford that."

"Can I ask why you trust me?"

"Aside from all that money we're paying you, and the bullet you took for us?"

Torine, Darby, and Delchamps chuckled.

"You know what I mean, Karl," Munz pursued.

"Straight answer?"

Munz nodded.

"There are some people I intuitively know I can trust. You're one of them. That may not be professional or even smart, but—the proof being I'm not pushing up daisies—so far it's worked."

"Thank you," Munz said softly, on the edge of emotion. "I had the same feeling about you."

Their eyes met for a moment.

"Hurriedly changing the subject," Castillo said, "pay close attention. Your leader has just had one of his brilliant—if somewhat off at a tangent—thoughts."

"Can you hold it a minute, Ace?" Delchamps asked.

"Sure."

"When I talked about Mullroney being useful in Paraguay, I meant it. Not only for the reasons I gave."

"Okay?"

"Did you pick up on what Duffy said about him being worried about your health?"

Castillo nodded.

Delchamps said, "Somebody—Weiss, probably—has sent the CIA guy in Asunción a heads-up. 'Watch out for Castillo.' "

"I sort of thought he would," Castillo said.

"And did you sort of think his reaction would be 'whack Castillo'? and/or 'whack him and everybody with him'?"

"Who's Weiss?" Darby asked.

Delchamps held up his hand, palm outward, as a sign to Darby to wait a minute.

Castillo shook his head.

"No. I didn't," Castillo said, simply.

"What's your take on the threat, Alfredo?" Delchamps asked. "A little theater on Duffy's part?"

"No. I think he believes there was a threat."

"Which would mean he has somebody in the embassy, or at least somebody in Asunción, who he trusts and who fed him that," Delchamps said.

Munz nodded his agreement.

Delchamps turned to Darby.

"Maybe you know him, Alex," he said. "Company old-timer. Milton Weiss?"

"I don't *know* him. I've seen him around."

"Weiss first came to me, then to Castillo, and told us (a) that the station chief in Asunción is a lot smarter than he wants people to think he is, and (b) that they've got an operation going where they're going to grab a cruise ship, maybe ships—"

"*Cruise ships?*" Darby said, incredulously.

Delchamps nodded, and continued, "Under maritime law, they're subject to seizure if the owners collude in their use to transport drugs."

"How are they going to prove the owners knew?" Darby asked.

"According to Weiss, they have that figured out," Castillo said.

"And they don't want our operation to free Timmons to fuck up that operation," Delchamps said.

"At first it made sort of sense, but then I found out that the agency doesn't know anything about this operation—for that matter, anything—going on down there that we could screw up getting Timmons back."

"You think the bastards in Langley would tell you?" Darby asked.

Delchamps answered with a question: "Alex, do you think an operation like that would or could escape the notice of either John Powell or A. Franklin Lammelle?"

Darby considered that for a moment.

"No. One or the other, probably both, would know about it. The potential for it blowing up . . ."

"The DCI told me he knew of no such operation."

"Told you personally?"

"Yeah. And I believed him. Then he sent for Lammelle, and asked him, and Lammelle said he didn't know anything about it, either. And I believed him, too."

"So what do you think's going on?"

"I don't know. But when I thought about it, putting myself in the Asunción station chief's shoes, if I had come up with an operation anything like what Weiss told us he's got going—and I'm not known for either modesty or my love for the Langley bastards—I'd want all the help I could get. Even if that meant taking it to Langley myself and waiting in the lobby or the guard shack to catch Lammelle or the DCI wherever I could find them."

"Again, Edgar, what do you think's going on?" Castillo asked.

"No goddamn idea, Ace, except that I know it's not what Weiss has been feeding us. But now that we have it on good authority that my fellow officers of the clandestine service want to whack me and the President's agent, I'm beginning to wonder if maybe they've changed sides."

"Jesus Christ," Jake Torine said softly.

"So what do we do?" Castillo said.

"I don't know that either. But I think—what I was saying before about Mullroney being useful—that you and he should go to the embassy in Asunción and let him stumble around."

"Use him as a beard?" Castillo asked.

Delchamps nodded, then asked: "Can I use your 007 radio to make a couple of calls? Like maybe two hundred? There are some questions I can ask some people I know."

"You don't have to ask, for Christ's sake," Castillo said.

"That's the best I can do right now, Ace. I *suggest* you go to Asunción with Mullroney, acting as if you don't think there's anything wrong, but it's your call. You don't have to be a rocket scientist to whack people."

"I want to talk to Pevsner before I go to Asunción."

"They'll expect you two in Asunción as soon as you can get there," Delchamps said simply.

"Let's make that choice after we hear what Duffy has to say," Castillo said.

"Okay. You need me in that meeting, or can I get on the horn?"

Before Castillo could open his mouth, Delchamps went on: "Sorry. We haven't heard your brilliant thought."

"It was brilliant just a few minutes ago," Castillo said. "Now it doesn't seem either very brilliant or especially important."

"Let's hear it," Delchamps said.

"I was worried about the Hueys and the guys from the 160th on the *Ronald Reagan.*"

"Why?" Torine asked.

"There's a two-star admiral on board. Two-star admirals tend to cover their ass. We can't afford not to get those choppers repainted and off the ship, but the senior 160th guy is a major. Majors tend to do what flag and general officers tell them to do."

"I knew a major one time, an Army Aviator, who didn't seem all that impressed by two-stars," Darby said. "He even stole one of their Black Hawks."

"*Borrowed,* Alex. *Borrowed.* I gave it back," Castillo said.

"What are you thinking, Charley?" Torine asked.

"That we need a more senior officer aboard the *Reagan,*" Castillo said. "Like maybe an Air Force colonel bearing a letter from Truman Ellsworth or maybe even Montvale, saying in essence, 'Don't fuck with the Hueys.' "

"God, you are devious!" Torine said. He thought that over a moment, and then said, "What if I got on—what did Edgar call it?—'the 007 radio' and called Ellsworth and said I was a little worried . . ."

"Talk about devious!" Delchamps said.

". . . he would think it was his idea," Torine finished. "When are the Hueys going to leave Rucker?"

"I don't know," Castillo said.

"So you call—*you,* Jake," Delchamps said, "and find out, and then you call Ellsworth and say, 'I just found out the choppers are about to go on board the *Reagan,* and I'm a little worried about something going wrong.' "

"Why do I feel I have just been had?" Torine asked. "Okay, Charley, you're right. Some admiral is liable to feel he can't get in trouble launching black helicopters if something happens—like being too far at sea—that keeps him from launching them."

"Thanks, Jake."

"Don't be too grateful, Ace," Delchamps said with a grin. "Nobody's going to shoot at him on the *Reagan,* which I think explains his sudden enthusiasm."

Torine gave him the finger.

"We can call from right here, right?" Torine asked.

Castillo nodded.

"That will be all, Colonel," Torine said. "You may now go brief the troops."

[ONE]
Nuestra Pequeña Casa
Mayerling Country Club
Pilar, Buenos Aires Province, Argentina
1220 9 September 2005

Castillo rapped a spoon against his coffee mug and waited silently until everybody who had gathered in the quincho was looking at him.

Then Castillo began: "An initial review of our current situation, gentlemen—and lady—suggested the possibility of some minor problems. A more detailed analysis indicates that we are really in the deep do-do."

That got the chuckles he expected.

"Let me trace the events from the moment Max found Lieutenant Lorimer sneaking through our shrubbery. . . ."

Castillo had gotten as far into his recapitulation of what had happened since they had hurriedly left Argentina as the Chicago meeting of Special Agent Timmons's family—and the mayor—when Jake Torine appeared in the door of the quincho.

Castillo made a T with his hands, signaling *Time out,* and walked to the quincho door.

"Sorry to interrupt, Colonel," Torine announced, "but I really need a moment of your time."

Castillo gestured for Torine to follow him outside.

"I called Rucker," Torine said once they were alone. "Major Ward told me they're going to fly to Jacksonville Naval Air Station tomorrow, and then, the day after tomorrow, fly out to the *Ronald Reagan.*"

"Why?"

"Jacksonville, Florida," Torine explained. "East Coast, almost at the Georgia border."

"I know where Jacksonville is, Jake. But why not go to Jacksonville the day after tomorrow, take on fuel, and then fly onto the *Reagan?* Their sitting around Jacksonville for a day will cause questions to be asked."

"Ward says the Navy wants to make sure they're not going to sink the aircraft carrier trying to land on it."

"That's bullshit, Jake. The pilots in the 160th are the best in the Army, the most experienced. And landing a Huey on a carrier is a hell of a lot easier than making an arrested landing with a fighter."

"That's what I told Truman Ellsworth," Torine said. He waited until he saw Castillo's reaction to that, then smiled and nodded.

"I called him," Torine went on, "and reminded him that he had suggested I call him if you had done something impulsive. And then I told him you had arranged to send choppers to South America aboard the *Ronald Reagan,* and I was afraid that the Navy didn't like it—proof being the 'orientation' they were insisting on—and was going to cause trouble."

He paused.

"I was good, Charley. I didn't know I had it in me."

"Maybe because you don't like Ellsworth any more than I do."

"That's a real possibility. My conscience didn't bother me at all."

"And what did our mutual friend have to say?"

"He said he'd call me right back. Five minutes later, Montvale called me. First thing, he asked where you were. I told him you were somewhere between Buenos Aires and Asunción. Which is true. So then he said he would have to deal with this himself. He said it was a pity I wasn't in the States, because what he really would like to do is send me aboard the *Reagan* to keep an eye on things."

"And?"

"I told him I would be in the States tomorrow."

"And?"

"And he said, 'Don't plan on unpacking your bags when you get to Washington, Colonel, you're going for a little voyage.' To which I replied, 'What will I tell Castillo?' To which he replied, "*I'll* deal with *Lieutenant* Colonel Castillo, *Colonel* Torine. You don't have to worry about that.' "

"So the thing to do," Castillo said, "is get you back to the States as soon as possible. Which opens a new can of worms. For one thing, you just got here; you're tired, you don't want to—shouldn't—fly right back. The flip side of that is: What is the Evil Leprechaun going to say when I call him? He may consider the Gulfstream as one of the assets he wants me to share with him. So getting it out of here as soon as possible is probably smart."

"What about me taking Dave Yung and Colin Leverette to Montevideo?"

Torine suggested. "Right now, I mean. Sparkman and I could crash in Two-Gun's apartment for a while—five, six hours, anyway—then leave for the States later today, tonight, or first thing in the morning."

"That'd work. But the worm that pops up there is: How do we get the airplane back here? Ambassador Lorimer, his wife, and the two guys from China Post will be on board."

"I can get another Gulfstream pilot from the Presidential Flight Detachment."

Castillo, visibly thinking, didn't reply.

"Isn't that what you meant?" Torine pursued.

Castillo didn't have time to reply. Edgar Delchamps was walking toward them from the house. Max decided Delchamps had come out to play, intercepted him, and dropped a tennis ball at his feet. Delchamps picked up the ball and threw it as far across the yard as he could, then walked up to Castillo and Torine.

"I just had a brilliant insight of my own," Delchamps announced. "Anybody interested?"

"I'm breathless with anticipation," Torine said.

"We're just spinning our wheels if we can't get the choppers off the *Reagan* and refuel them at Shangri-La. And the key to making that happen is Chief Inspector José Ordóñez. If you can't get Ordóñez to look the other way, we're fucked. And you don't know how much damage your new pal Duffy has done with him."

Castillo considered that a moment. "You're right," he said. "I don't suppose you had a solution to go along with your insight?"

"The obvious one: Go see him."

"Me? Or Alfredo? Or both? You remember the last time we saw Ordóñez he said, 'So long, and don't come back'?"

"Why don't you ask Munz?"

"Jake and I had just about decided that he'd drop off Yung and Leverette in Montevideo on his way to the States," Castillo said. "No reason he couldn't take Munz with him. Or both of us."

He stepped into the quincho doorway and motioned for Alfredo Munz to come out. Then he raised his voice and announced to the others, "Something's come up that we have to deal with right away. Just sit tight."

Munz waited for Castillo to speak.

"Two questions, Alfredo: How much damage did Liam Duffy do to us with Ordóñez?"

"I was about to suggest that we go see him," Munz said. "Until we do that, we won't know how much damage he's caused, and it's important that we know."

"Aren't *we* liable to cause more damage if I go? I just reminded Delchamps that the last time I saw him, he said, 'Good-bye, and don't come back.' "

"He knows you're planning an operation in either Argentina or Paraguay. That's none of his business. What he doesn't want—and will work very hard to prevent—is another operation in Uruguay."

"We're not planning anything in Uruguay," Castillo said, "except the refueling. And done right, that shouldn't take much more than a couple of hours." He paused, then added, "Well, let's go off on another tangent. Probably the best way to get the Hueys ashore is to launch them one at a time from the *Reagan,* one every forty-five minutes or an hour. And have them fly into and out of Shangri-La on different courses."

He looked at Torine for any input.

"You're the expert, Charley," Torine said.

"Four Hueys, or even two, flying overhead is going to attract more attention than just one," Castillo said.

"True," Torine agreed.

"Whatever you decide to do, Karl," Munz said, "Ordóñez would be more assured if he heard it from you than from me. Like me, José believes you can tell if a man is lying by looking into his eyes."

"I've got to ask this," Castillo said. "Would a little gift—hell, a great big gift—make any difference?"

"The very offer would probably kill any chance at all of him being willing to look the other way," Munz said. "What you're going to have to do, Karl, is convince him that his permitting your helicopters to enter—even secretly—Uruguayan airspace and using Shangri-La as a refueling place is in the best interests of Uruguay. That it won't cause any problems for Uruguay."

"Okay. So we go to Uruguay," Castillo said. "And right now."

He gestured for the others to follow him back into the quincho.

"Comandante Duffy's going to be annoyed when he finds out we've left here," Castillo explained. "But I will deal with that later when I call him from Montevideo. What I don't want to do is have any friction with him *as* we leave that might cause trouble about us going to Montevideo.

"I regard his threat to have us kicked out of the country—or arrested—as valid. But I think he's very interested in what he calls our assets, and I don't think he's going to blow that whistle until I tell him no, or until I do something suspicious.

"I am also convinced that the arrogant bastard thinks he's got me really scared. Which, as a matter of fact, he does. So we're going to go with exactly that—I'm scared and I'm leaving.

"What we're going to do is load in the van everybody who's going to Uruguay—that's Yung, Leverette, Sparkman, Munz, Torine, Bradley, and me—and have Neidermeyer drive us out to Ezeiza, where we will file a flight plan to Montevideo, then clear immigration and customs, and leave."

Castillo glanced at the others, who would remain at the safe house. Alex Darby, D'Elia, the Sienos, and Lieutenant Lorimer showed no signs of having any problem with that. But Castillo thought he saw questions in Sergeant Mullroney's eyes.

Questions, Castillo thought, *that he's learned not to ask, thanks no doubt to our little incident in the mountains outside Vegas.*

Maybe he's not completely stupid. . . .

Castillo went on: "I think we can presume Duffy has a car—maybe two—sitting on us at the gate. We are *not* going to try, à la James Bond, to lose them in traffic. If they can't keep up, much better, but we're not going to look as if we're running away.

"We can also presume that if they have managed to follow us to Ezeiza, they'll follow us inside the terminal and learn what we're doing and tell Duffy. With a little luck, they'll also tell him we haven't tried anything sneaky.

"That'll give him the choice between letting us leave or trying to stop us, and he'll have to make that choice in a hurry. I think he'll decide, 'Okay, good riddance,' possibly because keeping us from leaving might be hard for him to do anyway. If we're brazen, he'll reason that's because we've destroyed everything—the radios, for example—that could get us in trouble. And he doesn't want the stink that would be made if a bunch of American tourists were stopped without cause. So I think we can make it to Uruguay.

"Once we're airborne, we'll call on the radio. If you don't hear from us, or if somebody comes knocking at the door, be ready to use the thermite grenades to torch the radios and anything else that's incriminating."

He looked at everybody and added, "If anybody has any better ideas, I'm wide open."

There was a moment's silence.

"What about Max?" Delchamps asked.

"What about him?"

"If you don't take him, Ace, that might give Duffy the idea you plan to come back. But if you do, what are you going to do with him? How are you going to get him back here from Uruguay? The Gulfstream's going to the States."

Castillo looked down at Max, who was lying with his head between his paws, his big eyes looking up at him.

"Max goes," he said after a moment. "You're right. Duffy would expect me to take him with me if I was leaving."

Did I say that because I believe it? Or because, quite clearly, I just again heard Abuela saying, "You don't even have a dog"—and I don't have the heart to just leave the big sonofabitch here not knowing if I am coming back.

He's saved my life, once for sure in Budapest and probably in the garage of the Sheraton Pilar, and I could hide behind that.

But the truth is, Castillo, that you're a goddamned softie.

You like the way he looks at you with those big, soft eyes.

"Okay, Lieutenant Lorimer, sound 'Boots and Saddles,' " Castillo ordered.

[TWO]
Suite 2152
Radisson Montevideo Victoria Plaza Hotel
Plaza Independencia 759
Montevideo, República Oriental del Uruguay
1720 9 September 2005

Special Agent David W. Yung was smiling and shaking his head as he watched Jake Torine toss peanuts to Max, who snapped them from the air.

Chief Warrant Officer Five Colin Leverette, holding a bottle of beer, stood up from the minibar, looked at Yung, and announced, "Two-Gun is thinking about sex. He's shaking his head in disbelief and smiling."

"Close," Yung replied. "I'm thinking I can't believe the general manager believed Charley's yarn—*'I'm an epileptic and this dog has been trained to alert me when he senses a seizure coming on.' "*

"I was counting on him having seen that malady on Fox News," Castillo said, solemnly. "You always have to have an answer prepared, David."

"What our dog lover here was actually counting on working was that hundred-dollar bill he slipped the manager," Torine said.

"Max is up here, isn't he, despite those 'No Pets' signs in three languages on the door?" Castillo said.

"And a good thing for you that he is, Charley," Torine said. "You're going to need him to protect you from that cop when he learns you're back."

The telephone buzzed. Castillo signaled for Yung to pick it up.

"Thank you," Yung said in Spanish into the receiver. "We'll be right down." He hung up, looked at Castillo, and switched back to English: "The car from the embassy is here."

"That was quick," Leverette said.

"The embassy's only a couple of blocks from here," Yung explained, and then added, "Maybe I better take Max with me to protect me from Ambassador McGrory. I don't think he's going to be happy to see me."

"Nonsense," Castillo said. "He'll be thrilled. The secretary of State called him personally to tell him you're coming."

"That's what I mean," Yung said.

"Okay," Castillo said. "You get the keys to your apartment for Jake and Sparkman. And the keys to your car, if that's been fixed. All McGrory has to know about Jake and Sparkman is that they're pilots from the Presidential Flight Detachment, and will be leaving as soon as they get some rest. But tell him that, even if he doesn't ask; he's liable to be impressed with that. And then come back here and let us know how he reacted."

"Yes, *sir,*" Yung said.

Castillo picked up on something in Yung's tone, something just shy of sarcasm.

"Dave," he said, "I learned a long time ago that it's better to piss off one of your guys by telling him again and again how to do something he already knows how to do than to take the chance he misunderstood you. If I didn't think you could handle McGrory, I wouldn't be sending you to the embassy."

Yung met his eyes, then smiled and shrugged.

"Yeah," he said simply.

Castillo raised his right arm and hand in the manner of a priest blessing one of the faithful. "Go forth and do good, Two-Gun," he said solemnly.

Yung smiled, shook his head, and started for the door.

Castillo waited until they had left, then turned to Munz.

"Let's get it over with," he said. "Call Ordóñez."

Munz punched an autodial number on his cellular telephone. When it began to ring, Munz pushed the SPEAKER button.

"Ordóñez," the familiar voice came over the speaker.

"Alfredo Munz, José."

"I've been waiting for your call, my friend."

"We're in the Victoria Plaza. 2152."

"I know. Stay there."

Munz exchanged glances with Castillo, who raised his eyebrows.

"Where are you?" Munz said into the phone.

"Sixty kilometers out of Punta del Este. I should be there in about an hour. Did you hear what I said about staying where you are?"

"Yes."

"That includes Colonel Castillo."

"Understood," Munz said, looking at Castillo again.

"They weren't supposed to permit Castillo or anyone with him to enter the country," Ordóñez said. "When I pointed this out to them, they wanted to arrest you. I think I stopped that, but I would not try to leave the hotel."

"Yung and three others were with us; they were just picked up by an American embassy car."

"I know. Stay in the Victoria, Alfredo."

"Very well."

There was a change in the background noise, and Munz pushed the phone's END CALL button.

Munz said, "He apparently meant it when he said, 'Good-bye, and don't come back.' I don't know what to think, Karl."

Castillo silently raised his hands in a gesture of helplessness.

The door chimes sounded pleasantly almost exactly an hour later, and Munz went to the door and opened it.

Uruguayan Policía Nacional Chief Inspector José Ordóñez, a trim, well-dressed, olive-skinned man in his late thirties, stepped into the room. He was visibly surprised to see Max—who sat with his head cocked, as if making up his mind about the visitor—but Ordóñez didn't seem afraid of the dog; he ignored him.

He embraced Munz and kissed the air next to his cheek, then looked at Castillo. After a moment, he put out his hand.

"I won't say that I'm delighted to see you, Colonel Castillo," he said in Spanish.

"Nevertheless, good evening, Chief Inspector," Castillo replied in Spanish.

"Amazing," Ordóñez said. "If I didn't know better, I'd swear he is a Porteño. The accent is perfect."

"Carlos is an amazing man, José," Munz said.

"May we offer you something to drink, Chief Inspector?" Castillo said.

"Yes, thank you," Ordóñez said without hesitation. "Scotch, please, if you have it." He looked at an array of bottles on a credenza. "Some of that Famous Grouse single malt, if it wouldn't be an imposition."

"Not at all," Castillo said.

He remembered hearing that Uruguay consumed more scotch whiskey per capita than any other nation in the world, and that the present head of the family that had had the lock on importing the whiskey for generations was a Dartmouth graduate.

What remote corner of the memory bank did that come from?

He started to open the bottle.

"Just one lump of ice, please," Ordóñez said. "And half as much gas-free water as whiskey."

"Coming up," Castillo said.

He made three identical drinks and handed Ordóñez and Munz theirs.

They clicked glasses.

Ordóñez walked to the window, pushed the curtain aside, and looked out.

"If this hotel had been built in 1939," he said, "Millington-Drake could have watched in comfort from here—for that matter, from the bar in the Arcadia—rather than having to climb all those stairs to stand in the rain over there."

"Excuse me?" Castillo asked.

"The Arcadia restaurant on the twenty-fifth floor. It has a bar."

Castillo's confusion showed on his face.

"You do know who Millington-Drake was, don't you, Colonel?"

"I have no idea who he was," Castillo said.

"Does the name Langsdorff mean anything to you?"

Langsdorff?

Who the hell is he talking about?

What the hell is he talking about?

Oh, hell!

You are a disgrace to the Long Gray Line, Castillo!

"Of course," Castillo said. "He's buried in Buenos Aires, isn't he?"

"Yes, he is," Ordóñez said. "And from the towers of that building—come have a look—"

Castillo went to the window. In a moment, Munz and Max followed. Ordóñez pointed to a tall building across the street, the open ornate masonry towers of which seemed to be fifty or sixty feet below them.

Ordóñez said: "Sir John Henry Millington-Drake, the British ambassador, who was a close friend of my great-grandfather, climbed to the top of the towers you see there—it was raining hard, I understand; he must have gotten soaked—to watch the pocket battleship *Graf Spee* sail out of the harbor and scuttle herself. When the conditions are right, you can make out her superstructure."

"Interesting man," Castillo said, as the memory banks suddenly opened. "After seeing to the burial of his dead, and negotiating the terms of the internment of the rest of the crew, he put on his dress uniform and shot himself to prove that he had scuttled his ship to save the lives of his men; that he personally wasn't afraid to die. He positioned himself so that his body fell on the German Navy battle flag, rather than the Nazi swastika flag."

Ordóñez said, "I thought perhaps you—as a graduate of your military academy—would know who Langsdorff was."

Yeah, I indeed know who he was.

An officer and a gentleman who lived and died by his code, Death Before Dishonor.

The motto that murderers, rapists, drug dealers, and other human scum in prisons now tattoo on one another to help pass the time.

"Of course," Castillo said.

"My great-grandfather told me, Colonel Castillo, that despite the public story that said it was Millington-Drake's eloquence and strong personality that caused the Uruguayan government to scrupulously follow international law and order the *Graf Spee* to leave Montevideo within the seventy-two-hour period required by the law, it was in fact enormous pressure applied by the United States government—which, as I'm sure you know, was, like Uruguay, ostensibly neutral in the war between the English and the Germans—that caused it to do so."

"I hadn't heard that," Castillo said. "But it seems credible."

"So what are you doing here, Colonel? You know—I'm sure you remember me telling you—you're not welcome here. So, again, what is it you're doing here?"

"I'm helping Ambassador Lorimer move onto Estancia Shangri-La."

"Ambassador Lorimer?"

"Jean-Paul Lorimer's father. He's a retired diplomat. You didn't know?"

Ordóñez did not reply directly, instead asking: "Why on earth would he want to move to a remote estancia in Tacuarembó Province?"

"The Lorimers lost their home in New Orleans to Hurricane Katrina," Castillo said. "It is—or at least was—under fifteen feet of water."

"I understand that Mr. Lorimer—the late Mr. Lorimer—had an apartment in Paris. Wouldn't that be more comfortable for Ambassador Lorimer?"

"The ambassador told me the United Nations took his son's Paris apartment off his hands. At a very good price. He said he had the feeling they would rather he didn't go to Paris."

"So he decided to come here."

Castillo nodded.

"What are Yung and the others doing at your embassy?"

"The State Department—actually the secretary of State herself—called Ambassador McGrory to tell him to help Ambassador Lorimer in any way he can. They're going to see him about that."

Ordóñez took a notebook from his pocket, read from it, then asked, "Who are Sparkman and Leverette?"

"Sparkman is the copilot of the Gulfstream. Leverette is the ambassador's butler. He's going out to Shangri-La and set things up. As soon as that's done, we'll fly the ambassador and his wife down here."

"All right, Colonel, that's your cover story, and it's a good one." He paused as he looked him in the eyes. Then he added: "Now let's get to the truth. Why are you here?"

"I just told you—" Castillo began, but when he saw Ordóñez hold up his hand and was about to interrupt him, went on: "And . . . and . . . I need your help."

"To do what?" Ordóñez asked matter-of-factly.

"I need to secretly move helicopters into Uruguayan airspace, refuel them, and fly them out of Uruguay."

"Using Estancia Shangri-La?"

"Using Shangri-La," Castillo confirmed.

"And what would the helicopters be used for?"

"One of our DEA agents in Paraguay is being held by drug dealers. My orders are to get him back from the people who have kidnapped him."

"You know who they are?"

Castillo shook his head.

"Or where they are holding this man?"

Castillo shook his head.

"Not even in which country?"

Castillo shook his head again.

"Then this man whom you have been ordered to rescue could be in Uruguay?"

"That's possible, but unlikely."

"Have you had the opportunity to meet Comandante Duffy of the Argentine Gendarmería Nacional, Colonel?" Ordóñez asked. "I know he was hoping to talk to you."

"I met Comandante Duffy this morning."

"Did he tell you that two of his men have been murdered, and two kidnapped, presumably by the same people who have taken your man?"

Castillo nodded.

"Did he tell you what he intends to do to the people who have done this? Or who he *thinks may* have done this?"

"He didn't spell it out in so many words, but he made it pretty clear that he intends to take them out."

"He intends not only to kill them, but to leave their bodies where they fall, as an example of what happens to people who murder gendarmes."

Castillo nodded.

"Much as you did with the people at Shangri-La," Ordóñez added.

Castillo met his eyes for a moment.

Castillo then softly but angrily said, "Sorry, Ordóñez, I can't—*won't*—let you get away with equating what happened at Shangri-La with the cold-blooded murder of Duffy's gendarmes."

"You're not going to deny that there were six bodies—seven, counting Lorimer's corpse—left lying in pools of blood at Estancia Shangri-La, are you, Colonel?"

"Actually, eight men died at the estancia," Castillo said, his voice rising. "I lost one of my men, and we damn near lost Alfredo. But we acted in self-defense. They opened fire on us, without warning. We returned it. They died. What the hell were we supposed to do, call a priest, give them the last rites, and bury them?"

"José," Munz said evenly. "Colonel Castillo went to Estancia Shangri-la with plans to take Lorimer back—alive—to the United States. Violence was neither planned nor expected."

"And you went with him, Alfredo, fully aware that kidnapping is just as much a crime in Uruguay as it is in Argentina," Ordóñez said.

Munz, his eyes narrowed, nodded.

"And was making off with Lorimer's sixteen million dollars planned or expected?"

"We didn't know about the money until we went into Lorimer's safe," Castillo said.

"So you're admitting you stole the money?"

Neither Castillo nor Munz replied.

"What did you do with the money?"

"Alfredo and I spent most of it on whiskey and wild women," Castillo said.

Ordóñez stared at him coldly.

"So tell me, Ordóñez, what happens now?" Castillo asked after a moment. "You escort us to the Buquebus?"

"Excuse me?"

"Well, obviously, our coming here has been a waste of time; you're not going to help us. But on the other hand, we've given you no reason to arrest us; we've broken none of your laws."

"Not today," Ordóñez allowed. "Except, of course, the small matter of trying to get a senior police official to acquiesce in your violation of the laws of his country."

"We came to ask your help, José," Munz said with an edge in his voice. "Help in getting a fellow police officer—who happens to be an American—back from the hijos de puta who kidnapped him."

"The hijos de puta who have him also have two of Duffy's gendarmes," Ordóñez replied evenly. "And have brutally murdered two of his gendarmes. And that's what worries me, Alfredo. That's *who* worries me."

"The narcos or Duffy?" Munz asked.

"You and I both know, Alfredo, that these people are not ordinary narcos. If they were, I'd probably be hoping—may God forgive me—that Duffy would be leaving bodies not suitable for viewing in their caskets all over Corrientes and Entre Ríos Provinces and, for that matter, Paraguay. He's right that the kidnapping—and the murder—of police officers cannot be tolerated, and that leaving bullet-riddled bodies on the side of the road, or at narcotics refining plants, would send that message far more effectively than running them through a justice system where, sadly, justice is often for sale."

Ordóñez paused a moment.

"But," he went on, "as I say, these are not ordinary narcos. Major Alejandro Vincenzo of the Cuban Dirección General de Inteligencia is proof of that."

Castillo thought: *How the hell does he know that—and how the hell much more does he know?*

"Excuse me?" Castillo asked.

"Certainly someone of your background, Colonel, has considered that Vincenzo was here—possibly, even probably, in Paraguay—long before Lorimer went missing in Paris. And as 'their' man on the scene was available to supervise the very professional kidnapping of Mrs. Masterson and the subsequent murder of her husband, when they wanted to locate Lorimer. And their sixteen million dollars."

"Can you define 'they' and 'their'?" Castillo asked.

"Obviously, Vincenzo was a Cuban. But what is the connection between the Russian FSB and the Cuban Dirección General de Inteligencia? There are two possibilities: One, no connection here in this instance; Vincenzo was here to (a) make money from the drug trade and (b) cause what trouble he could in the interests of Cuba. Or, two, the Russians are involved, for the same purposes—making money and causing trouble. I place more credence in the latter in no small measure because of the murder of Lieutenant Colonel Viktor Zhdankov of the FSB in Punta del Este, and the presence of your friend Aleksandr Pevsner."

"So far as I know, Pevsner is not under the FSB," Castillo said. "And, as a matter of fact, he as much as admitted to me that he had Zhdankov and Kennedy eliminated in Punta del Este."

"I suspected that, of course. And I appreciate your candor. Which leads us right now to what I was going to come to eventually. From this point on, we will tell each other the truth. Duffy has lied to me—"

"About what?" Munz asked.

"It doesn't matter, Alfredo. But it is one more reason that I am worried about him and this situation. I want to have nothing whatever to do with him as he goes after these narcos."

"Does that bring us back to my question about you escorting us to the Buquebus terminal?" Castillo asked.

"Listen to what I am saying, please, Colonel. I said I wanted to have nothing to do with Duffy in what he's going to do. I am prepared, with the understanding that we will tell each other the truth, to help you with your helicopters. The truth about everything, and that includes el Señor Pevsner."

Castillo met his eyes.

"So far as I know," Castillo repeated, "Pevsner is not under the FSB. That's the truth. He almost certainly has flown things around for them, but he has also flown things around for the CIA. But, again, so far as I know, he is no more an asset of the Federal'naya Sluzhba Bezopasnosti than he is an asset of the Central Intelligence Agency."

Munz added: "And—other than what Carlos has just said—I found no connection between him and the FSB when I worked for him."

Ordóñez looked at Munz a moment, nodded, then said, "I have to ask you something, Alfredo."

Munz made a *Go on* gesture.

"When you worked for him," Ordóñez said, "who were you working for?"

"Argentina," Munz said. "But, since we're telling the truth, I never turned the money Pevsner paid me over to SIDE."

"One more indelicate question, old friend, I have to ask. Who are you working for now?"

"I am working for Carlos," Munz said, met Castillo's eyes, then looked back at Ordóñez. "But we have the unspoken agreement between us that I am not working—and will not work—against Argentina. In this case, it should go without saying that these hijos de puta—or whoever else, the Dirección General de Inteligencia and/or the FSB—are working against the best interests of my country. My conscience is clear, José. Before God, I have not, *will not,* sell out my country."

"Thank you," Ordóñez said. "The problem we have here—I'm sure you will agree—is that Duffy also believes he's working for his country. And can't—or doesn't want to—understand that his duty to Argentina is to turn over what he has to SIDE, and not embark on this mission to murder whoever killed and kidnapped his men." He let that sink in for a moment, then added, "I don't want you—by you, I mean you and Colonel Castillo—working with Duffy."

"And you think I want to?" Castillo said. "What if I have to?"

"Then I can't permit you to bring your helicopters into Uruguay."

"All I want to do is refuel helicopters at Estancia Shangri-La. They would be on the ground less than an hour, and they would not be coming back."

"An hour or two, plus whatever time it took them to reach the estancia, and then to leave Uruguayan air space," Ordóñez corrected him.

"That's right," Castillo said.

"If I had your word, and Alfredo's, I could arrange it so that you will not be working with Duffy."

"I can't give you my word," Castillo said. "It's going to be hard—impossible—for me not to work with Duffy. Duffy's told me that unless I can get my superiors to order me to work under his orders and share my assets with him, I will have to leave Argentina within twenty-four hours. And I have to say this: If you hadn't run at the mouth, I wouldn't have that problem."

Ordóñez considered that a moment, then almost visibly decided not to take offense.

"I 'ran at the mouth'—an interesting phrase—before I understood what Duffy was planning to do. And before I discovered that he had lied to me."

"But the cow's out of the barn. It doesn't matter who opened the barn door or when or why. The damage has been done."

"And have your superiors ordered you to work with Duffy?"

Castillo hesitated before replying.

"Okay. Truth time. I have not asked my superior. But I'm going to call Duffy, very soon, and tell him that I have been ordered to do whatever he wants me to do."

"You're taking that responsibility on yourself?"

"I have been ordered to get an American Drug Enforcement Administration agent back from his kidnappers. The order carried with it the authority to do whatever I have to do to get him—his name is Timmons—back. There is no point in me calling my superior when I know his answer will be to do whatever I have to do."

Ordóñez nodded.

"Colonel," he said, "let me tell you about my superior, *superiors*. Nominally, I am under the authority of the minister of the interior. But when a situation has international implications, I get my directions from the foreign minister as well. Actually—for purposes of credible deniability—I get them from Deputy Foreign Minister Alvarez.

"It was Alvarez who decided with me that it was in the best interests of Uruguay to ascribe the murder of Lorimer at his estancia, the murders of Lieutenant Colonel Viktor Zhdankov of the FSB and Howard Kennedy in Punta del Este, and of course the deaths of Major Vincenzo and his five friends at Shangri-La to internecine warfare in the drug business.

"I don't know—and don't want to know—what, if anything, Alvarez told the foreign minister about what we had done, but there was no pressure from either the Foreign Ministry or the Interior Ministry on me to zealously pursue the people responsible for all those deaths." He paused, then added, "Which, of course, would have included you and your men.

"It seemed to be the best solution to the problem. While murder is a terrible crime, no Uruguayans had been murdered. Kennedy and Zhdankov were buried beside Vincenzo and the others in graves marked 'Unknown' in the Sacred Heart of Jesus church cemetery in Tacuarembó.

"David Yung—through the American embassy—was repatriating the remains of Lorimer, and it seemed unlikely that the Russians or the Cubans would ask questions about Zhdankov or Vincenzo. And you and I had the little chat in which I suggested you should leave Uruguay and not come back soon. When you agreed to do so, I thought the matter was closed.

"I was wrong about that, of course. The day before Duffy called me—two days before he came here—Alvarez told me our ambassador in Washington had called him to report that Senator Homer Johns . . ."—he paused and looked at Castillo to see if he knew who he was talking about, and when Castillo nodded, went on—". . . to ask him what he could tell him—officially or otherwise—about the death of Lorimer, or if he had heard anything about your Special Forces having conducted an operation in Uruguay."

"And what did the ambassador tell him?" Castillo asked.

"That Lorimer was involved in the drug trade, and that he had heard nothing about Special Forces operating secretly in Uruguay. The senator then asked him to discreetly inquire again, and the ambassador agreed to do so.

"As it happens, the ambassador and I are old friends—Uruguay is a small country, and we have a saying, *'Don't worry if you don't know someone, he'll marry into your family by the end of the week.'* But the ambassador and I are friends from school, and you'll remember it was he who I turned to for help in identifying the 7.62mm National Match cartridge case we found at Shangri-La.

"So, unofficially, I called him to see what else Senator Johns had had on his mind. He told me that the senator had told him he'd gone to see Ambassador Charles W. Montvale, who as your director of National Intelligence could be presumed to know about such things, and that Montvale had denied any prior knowledge of Lorimer's involvement in the drug trade and denied any knowledge of a Special Forces operation in Uruguay."

Ordóñez looked more intensely at Castillo.

"I've always suspected Montvale is the man you answer to, Colonel. Do you?"

Castillo shook his head.

"I thought we were agreed to tell one another the truth," Ordóñez said.

"I don't work for Ambassador Montvale."

"For whom, then? The secretary of Defense?"

Castillo shook his head again.

"Ah, then, the secretary of State," Ordóñez said, clearly pleased with himself. "Of course. I should have thought of that. It explains a great deal. The authority you wielded in your embassy in Buenos Aires; the decision to keep Ambassador McGrory in the dark about your operation."

"I don't work for Secretary Cohen, either," Castillo said.

Ordóñez's face showed that not only did he not believe that, but that the denial offended him.

Munz caught that, and said, "He doesn't, José."

"Well, who *does* he work for? Do you know?"

Munz was quiet a moment, then laughed.

"Yes, I do," he said. "But if I told you, I'd have to kill you."

"What did you say?" Ordóñez asked incredulously.

"It's a useful phrase I've learned working for Carlos," Munz said.

"It's not said seriously?"

"You never know, José," Munz said. "You're not going to put it to the test, are you?"

"I may not be Sherlock Holmes," Ordóñez said to Castillo, "but after we eliminate Montvale and your secretaries of State and Defense, there's not many people left, are there, from whom you could be taking orders?"

"What else did you learn from your old pal the ambassador?" Castillo asked, ignoring the question.

Ordóñez looked at him for a long moment, as if deciding whether or not to pursue the question of who gave Castillo his authority and orders. Finally, he said: "He said that he had the distinct feeling that Senator Johns would like nothing more than proof that there had been a secret Special Forces operation in Uruguay and that Montvale had lied to him about it."

"Perhaps he doesn't like Ambassador Montvale. A lot of people don't," Castillo said. "I don't like him much myself. But I would hate to see him embarrassed by Senator Johns."

"And so would I," Ordóñez said. "Because that would mean the decision Alvarez and I made about everything would come to light. The Cubans—and probably the Russians, too—would go to the United Nations to righteously denounce Uruguay—"

"I get the picture," Castillo interrupted. "And you're right, of course."

"—for not only permitting the imperialist Yankees to send their infamous Special Forces to murder innocent Cuban tourists and Czechoslovakian businessmen on Uruguayan soil, but then to shamelessly deny it."

Castillo was silent for a moment, then he said: "Just for the record . . . oh, hell."

"Go on," Ordóñez said.

"I was going to split a hair," Castillo said. "My people at Shangri-La were not all Special Forces. It was not an SF unit that was sent here."

"I don't think, whatever the legalities, that anyone will believe that."

"That's what I decided. And the people who came here now to rescue Timmons are bona fide Special Forces."

"They're already here?"

"Just about all of them," Castillo said. "And the helicopter pilots are from the 160th—the Special Operations Aviation Regiment."

"And the helicopters, too, presumably?"

"No. I got the helicopters from a graveyard. By the time they get here, they'll be cleaned and black—"

" 'Cleaned and black'?" Ordóñez parroted.

"Anything that could indicate they belong to the U.S. Army will be removed. And they'll be painted in the color scheme used by the Argentine Army. They'll be more or less identical to the Hueys the Argentines are flying."

"And if nothing goes wrong and you manage to rescue your man without murdering everyone whoever so much as talked to the narcos, how do you plan to get your men and the helicopters out of Argentina or Paraguay?"

If he's not going to let me use Shangri-La to bring the choppers in, Castillo thought, *what the hell does he care about the details of what's-not-to-happen?*

What the hell is he hinting at?

"The men will leave the same way they came in, as tourists. I haven't given much thought to the helicopters."

"You weren't planning on flying them back to where they came from?"

"The 'field' from which they will have been flown into Uruguay is an aircraft carrier—the USS *Ronald Reagan*. By the time I can get Timmons back, it will have sailed around Cape Horn and be halfway up the Pacific coast to Valparaiso, Chile."

"So?"

"I understand some of the lakes in Argentina are very deep," Castillo said.

"You're not suggesting that you intend to . . . *sink* four helicopters in an Argentine lake?"

What the hell's going on here?

Why the curiosity? And it's damned sure not idle curiosity!

"What else would you suggest I do with them? I can't just leave them in a field somewhere. Or, for that matter, destroy them, torch them. They have to disappear. My orders are to come down here quietly, get Timmons back quietly, and leave quietly."

"Tell me, Colonel, are helicopters of this type readily available on the commercial market?"

"Sure."

"But wouldn't there be some means of tracing their history? All the way back to the factory?"

"The communists captured several hundred of them when Vietnam fell. Many of those have appeared at various places around the world."

Ordóñez nodded and asked, "Involved with criminal activity of some sort?"

Castillo nodded.

I'll be a sonofabitch.

Does Mr. Clean, who Munz warned me was above taking a bribe, want my birds?

Confirmation of that wild theory came immediately.

"It would then be credible, if your helicopters somehow made their way to a field somewhere in Uruguay, for me to find them and announce that they probably had been in the use of drug dealers. Criminals who arrived at the field to refuel them, found no fuel, and had to abandon them."

"Whereupon they would enter the service of the Policía Nacional?" Castillo said.

Ordóñez nodded, then asked, "Parts would be available for them?"

"Ordóñez, if you let me refuel the choppers at Shangri-La, I'll fly them anywhere in Uruguay you say when I'm finished my operation. Even if I have to fly them there myself."

When Ordóñez didn't immediately reply, Castillo added: "And I will get you all the parts you need for them. Either through government channels, or black."

"This 'black' would be better," Ordóñez said. "It would continue to keep Ambassador McGrory out of the picture. Also, it would be better if you had someone other than yourself bring them back into Uruguay, Colonel."

"Then we have a deal?" Castillo asked.

Ordóñez nodded and exhaled audibly.

"But let me clarify it, Colonel. I don't think it's quite what you're thinking. You haven't bribed me with a gift of helicopters for which you will no longer have a need and which in fact give you a disposal problem. What they represent is a sugar pill for me to accompany the bitter one I have to swallow—that of assisting you in an operation which is really none of my business and which I am really afraid is going to end in a disaster.

"I realized that I was going to have to help you, not because I want to, but because I have no choice but to hope—even pray—that you are successful. Your failure would be a disaster for me. Do we understand each other?"

Castillo nodded.

Ordóñez went on, "You mentioned the Buquebus. Why don't you fly back to Buenos Aires?"

Castillo pointed at Max, who was lying beside him with his head between his paws, and said, "Yung told me that taking him on Austral or Aerolíneas would be very difficult."

Ordóñez considered that, then said: "And even if I helped you overcome the difficulties, it would still attract attention. Let me make a suggestion: If you could arrange to have someone meet you at the customs house at the International Bridge at Fray Bentos–Gualeguaychús, I'll fly you there in one of the Policía Nacional Hueys. We have four very old ones, two of which are flyable. It will perhaps make you understand why I am so interested in yours."

"That's very kind of you, José," Munz said.

"You, Alfredo, and your animal. Anyone else?"

"My communicator."

"Give me an hour to set it up," Ordóñez said. "Call me when you're ready to go." He stood up. "I presume Alfredo will keep me advised of what's happening?"

Castillo nodded.

"Thank you for your hospitality," Ordóñez said, offering Castillo his hand. He embraced Munz, went through the hug-and-kiss rite, and walked out of the room.

[THREE]
Embassy of the United States of America
Lauro Miller 1776
Montevideo, República Oriental del Uruguay
1835 9 September 2005

The Honorable Michael A. McGrory, the ambassador extraordinary and plenipotentiary of the President of the United States to the Republic of Uruguay,
was a small and wiry, well-tailored man of fifty-five with a full head of curly
gray hair. His staff referred to him as "Napoleon" and "Señor Pomposo." Mc-
Grory looked across his highly polished wooden desk at Special Agent David
W. Yung, who sat beside Colin Leverette. Robert Howell, the embassy's cultural
attaché, stood near the door.

McGrory smiled and said to Yung, "If you'll be good enough to give me a
minute alone with Mr. Howell—I need to speak with him on another matter—
you can be on your way."

"Thank you, Mr. Ambassador," Yung said.

"And it's been a pleasure meeting you, Mr. Leverette. If you need something
for Ambassador Lorimer—anything at all—that either Mr. Yung or Mr. Howell can't arrange, please feel free to come see me at any time."

"Thank you very much, sir," Leverette said.

Yung and Leverette stood up, shook the ambassador's hand, and walked out
of the ambassador's office, closing the door behind them.

"Well, Howell, what do you think?" McGrory asked.

"What do I think about what, Mr. Ambassador?" Howell replied.

While officially the cultural attaché of the embassy, Howell was in fact the
CIA's Uruguay station chief.

"What do we really have here?"

"Excuse me?"

"You don't see anything odd in Lorimer's father coming down here to live
on that estancia in the middle of nowhere? With a butler?"

"I thought that was pretty well explained when Yung told us the ambassador
lost his home in Hurricane Katrina, sir."

"And the presence of Yung? That didn't strike you as unusual?"

"I can think of a likely scenario, sir."

"Let's have it."

"It could very well be that the secretary, who I think has known the ambassador a long time, went out of her way to do what she could for the

ambassador. She knows he has a heart condition. His son-in-law was murdered, and right after Mr. Masterson's remains were repatriated, the hurricane struck and destroyed the ambassador's home."

"Huh!" the ambassador snorted.

"And Yung, who was on the secretary's personal staff—"

"We learned after the fact," McGrory interrupted. "Nobody knew that when he was here."

"Yes, sir. Well, he was available. He was still accredited diplomatically down here. Yung probably struck her as the obvious choice to come here and set things up."

"Traveling in a private Gulfstream jet airplane. I wonder what that cost?"

"I don't like to think, Mr. Ambassador. But on the other hand, we know the ambassador's daughter came into her husband's money. And we know how much of that there is. It poses no financial strain on her to charter airplanes. Or, for that matter, to pay for the private security people who will be coming here with the ambassador."

"And none of this strikes you as suspicious?"

"I don't know what to suspect, Mr. Ambassador."

"Years ago, Howell, there was a terribly racist saying to the effect that one suspected an African-American in the woodpile."

"I'm familiar with the expression, sir, but I don't know what Ambassador Lorimer could be concealing."

"I'm not referring to Ambassador Lorimer," Ambassador McGrory said impatiently, stopping himself just in time from finishing the sentence with *you idiot!*

"You're referring to the butler, sir? Leverette?"

McGrory stared at Howell and thought, *I can't believe this. This man works for the Central Intelligence Agency?*

If he's typical, and I suspect he is, they should call it the Central Stupidity Agency.

"No," Ambassador McGrory said carefully, aware he was on the edge of losing his temper. After a moment, hoping his contempt wasn't showing, he went on, "That was a figure of speech, Howell, a figure of speech only. I was suggesting that there's something about this whole sequence of events that doesn't seem . . ."—he stopped himself just in time from saying *kosher*—". . . quite right."

"And what is that, Mr. Ambassador?" Howell asked.

"If you've been in this business as long as I have, Howell, you develop a sense, a feeling," McGrory explained somewhat smugly.

"I understand," Howell said. "How may I help, Mr. Ambassador?"

"You can keep a close eye on Yung and that man Leverette. See if they do anything suspicious; see who they talk to."

"Yes, sir."

"I think the best way to handle this is just report everything you see or hear."

"Yes, sir."

"Any time of the day or night."

"Yes, sir."

Ambassador McGrory dismissed Howell with a wave of his hand, then rose from his desk and walked to the window. It provided a view of the Rambla, the road that ran along the Atlantic Ocean beach.

The water was muddy because it bore all the silt—and God only knows what else—from the River Plate. It didn't become clear—really become the Atlantic Ocean—until Punta del Este, a hundred-odd kilometers north.

McGrory stood at the window for perhaps three minutes, debating whether or not to call his brother-in-law. He really didn't like Senator Homer Johns. While McGrory admitted that his brother-in-law had had a lot to do with his being named ambassador to Uruguay, it was also true that Homer not only reminded him of this entirely too often, but accompanied the reminder with some snide observation about McGrory's slow movement up the ranks of the foreign service.

McGrory didn't *know* why Homer bitterly hated the director of National Intelligence, Ambassador Charles W. Montvale, but he suspected it was because Montvale and not Homer had gotten that job when it was created after 9/11. Homer was on the Senate intelligence committee and thought the job should have been his.

Homer hadn't been at all sympathetic when McGrory had called him and told him how the deputy foreign minister, Alvarez, had as much as called him a liar in his own office when he had told him that there were no Special Forces teams operating in Uruguay; that anything like that could not take place without his permission.

And the senator hadn't been at all impressed when McGrory told him that he had figured out what had really happened with Lorimer at his estancia—that Lorimer had been a big-time drug dealer on the side, using his United Nations diplomatic passport whenever that helped.

The first time he'd told that to the senator, the senator's reply had been "Mike, that's the most absurd bullshit you've ever tried to hand me."

And Homer hadn't even apologized when McGrory had called him to report (a) the Uruguayan cops had finally figured out what had happened, a drug deal gone bad, just as McGrory had said, and (b) that he had gotten this from Deputy Foreign Minister Alvarez, together with an apology for what Alvarez had said to him in the beginning.

He'd gotten back a little at Homer—he didn't want to go too far with that, of course; there were more important diplomatic posts than Uruguay, and his brother-in-law could be helpful again in that regard—the last time Homer had called.

Homer said he'd just gotten word from a good source—a woman who had been canned by the CIA and was highly pissed—that Montvale had indeed sent a Special Forces team to Uruguay to keep Lorimer from running off at the mouth. Homer said she'd also supplied the name of the guy in charge: Castillo.

McGrory had smiled knowingly at the purported news.

"Homer," he'd said, "I know all about Castillo. He works for the Department of Homeland Security, and he just happened to be in Argentina and was put in charge of protecting the Masterson family until they could get out of Argentina. That's all. He's a lousy major, is all. I think your source is full of shit."

"You know about this Castillo, do you?"

"Yes, I do. Lorimer was killed by drug people, not by Special Forces."

"I don't know, Mike, my source sounded pretty sure of herself."

"Why did she come to you, Homer? As an outraged citizen? Or a disgruntled employee trying to make trouble for the CIA? Why'd she get fired?"

"She didn't tell me that," Homer had said, and then added: "She does have a reputation around town for sleeping around."

"Well, there you have it, Homer."

"Maybe. But what I want you to do anyway, Mike, is keep your eyes and ears open. I want to hear of anything at all that happens down there that's out of the ordinary. Let me decide whether or not it's important."

Okay, Ambassador McGrory thought, still looking out his window at the muddy waters of the River Plate, *on the one hand, while Ambassador Lorimer coming down here is a little odd, it is true that New Orleans is under water, and that his daughter, Masterson's widow, now has her hands on that sixty million dollars Jack the Stack got when that beer truck ran over him. So having a butler and flying around in a chartered jet airplane isn't so strange.*

What the hell could a retired old ambassador with a heart condition be into but waiting to die?

And on the other hand, Homer said he wants to hear anything out of the ordinary; to let him decide what's important.

So I'll call him and tell him about this.

And he can run it past his source, the lady with the round heels reputation who got canned from the CIA, and see what she has to say.

And when some other post—Buenos Aires, for example—comes open, he can re-member how useful I have been to him whenever he asked for something.

McGrory went to his desk, picked up the telephone, and told the oper-ator to get Senator Homer Johns—and not anyone on Johns's staff—on a secure line.

[FOUR]
Suite 2152
Radisson Montevideo Victoria Plaza Hotel
Plaza Independencia 759
Montevideo, República Oriental del Uruguay
1915 9 September 2005

"How'd it go, Dave?" Castillo asked as Yung, Howell, and Leverette came into the room.

"I didn't tell McGrory that Jake and Sparkman were from the Presidential Flight Detachment—"

"Jesus Christ!" Robert Howell suddenly said as Max walked toward him. "Where'd that dog come from?"

"I keep him around to eat people who don't do what I tell them," Castillo said. "Why didn't you, Dave?"

"I thought it would be better to let him think the Gulfstream was a charter."

Castillo considered that a moment.

"Good thinking. You were right and I was wrong," he said. "And he bought that?"

Yung nodded. "But after that, I wondered if he was going to wonder why I had sent the pilots of a chartered aircraft out to my apartment and not to a hotel."

"And you think he will?"

"I don't know. But it's too late to do anything about it."

"Even if he actually comes looking for them, it's not a problem," Munz said. "While you were telling the manager about your seizure problem, Jake gave them his credit card for this room; it's in his name."

" 'Seizure problem'?" Howell asked.

"Don't ask," Yung said. "It will make you question the sanity of our leader."

"I asked how it went," Castillo said.

"I don't think there's a problem," Howell said. "So how'd you make out with Ordóñez?"

"We get to use the estancia . . . Dave told you what's going down?"

Howell nodded.

"Ordóñez gets the choppers when we're through with them. But, and this is important, he gets them—what did he say?—as a sugar pill to accompany the bitter one he has to swallow of helping us to help Duffy in something that's none of his business. In other words, it wasn't a bribe."

Howell nodded.

"So what happens now?" he asked.

"How are you planning to go to the estancia, Dave?" Castillo said.

"My car is fixed. I really can't believe it. The last time I saw it, it was full of double-aught buckshot holes."

"Okay. That means you can take the radio with you. Colin'll need communication, but not a communicator, right, butler?"

Leverette replied with a thumbs-up gesture.

"I don't see any need for you to drive all the way out there and then back, do you, Bob?"

Howell shook his head.

"Ordóñez is going to chopper us to the international bridge at—what's the name of that place, Alfredo?"

"Gualeguaychú," Munz furnished, making it sound like *Wally-wha-chew.*

"Where someone—one of us—will meet us and drive us into Buenos Aires."

"Not to the safe house?"

"I'm going to the Four Seasons, where I will entertain Comandante Duffy at breakfast. But on the way to . . . wherever the international bridge is."

"Gualeguaychú," Munz repeated.

"How do you spell it?"

Munz spelled *Gualeguaychú.*

"No wonder I can't pronounce it," Castillo said. "On the way to *Wally-wha-chew* I'm going to suggest to Ordóñez that he go home by way of the estancia. A couple of words from him to the local cops who are sitting on the place will make Colin's job easier and get them accustomed to helicopters dropping in unannounced."

Yung nodded.

"You seem to be in pretty good spirits, Charley."

"Compared to this morning, you mean?"

Yung nodded.

"This morning, after meeting with the Evil Leprechaun, I thought this operation had no chance at all of succeeding. Now I think the odds are one in, say, eight or ten that we can carry it off. That's a hell of an improvement, wouldn't you say?"

XI

[ONE]
Presidente de la Rua Suite
The Four Seasons Hotel
Cerrito 1433
Buenos Aires, Argentina
0700 10 September 2005

"Fuck it," Castillo said, more or less to himself. "We can either carry this off or we can't. And I don't think the Evil Leprechaun would be dazzled by uniforms. Yours or mine or both of ours. So it's civvies, Pegleg. Go change back."

Wrapped in a plush, ankle-length, terry-cloth robe with the Four Seasons logo embroidered on the chest, Castillo was in the large sitting room, standing by the plateglass windows that offered a view of the Retiro railway station and, at a distance, the River Plate.

First Lieutenant Eddie Lorimer, wearing a Class A uniform complete to green beret and ribbon decorations—and there was an impressive display of ribbons—stood between Castillo and the others in the room, the latter seated on couches and chairs and at the dining table.

Edgar Delchamps, reclined in one of the armchairs with his legs stretched straight before him, cleared his throat.

"For what it's worth, Ace," he began, "I agree with you. But that leaves unanswered the question of how *do* we dazzle the bastard?"

"Looking at the beautiful Mrs. Sieno just now, I realized how," Castillo said, and gestured at Susanna Sieno, who was sitting at the dining table. Her husband was on one of the couches, seated beside Tony Santini.

"Why do I think I'm not going to like this?" Susanna Sieno asked.

"Females are masters of deception," Castillo said. "They're born with the ability, which is why they run the world."

Mrs. Sieno gave Lieutenant Colonel Castillo an unladylike gesture, extending her center finger from her balled fist in an upward motion.

Castillo gestured dramatically toward her.

"Exactly! Right there the lady proves my point. Complete control. And how do they do that? They wing it, that's how. And that's what we're going to do."

When there was no response, save for several raised eyebrows, Castillo went on: "Think about it, lady and gentlemen. What we have in here are spooks, cops, soldiers, and, of course, a Marine."

He smiled at Corporal Lester Bradley, USMC, who was sitting at a small desk on which sat an AFC Corporation communications console. Bradley wore a dark gray Brooks Brothers suit—one of two identical garments, the first suits he had ever owned. Dick Miller told Castillo that he had taken Lester to Brooks Brothers in Washington as a morale booster after the Secret Service agents at the house kept treating him like an errand boy. Max, lying at Bradley's feet, had one paw on his highly polished black leather loafers. Due to the peso exchange rate, Bradley had acquired them for next to nothing— "Thirty bucks U.S.," he'd told Castillo, "for what would've run me more than a hundred back home—at one of the luxury leather-goods stores in downtown Buenos Aires.

"None of us are actors," Castillo went on in explanation. "And even if we were, we don't have time before Comandante Duffy shows up to write a script and memorize our lines. And even if we did that, sure as God made little apples we'd either forget them or blow them trying to deliver them. And it would look rehearsed. So . . . we'll wing it."

There was some nodding of understanding around the room.

"What we should do, I think," Castillo then said, "is make sure we're all on the same page, so herewith a recap: We've got the helicopters as far as Estancia Shangri-La, presuming of course there's no tropical storm off Montevideo to keep them from flying, and the Navy doesn't push them over the side or sail too far from the coast to cover their buttocks.

"One of the reasons Ordóñez came through for us on that is because Duffy lied to him. I don't know about what, but he lied to Ordóñez and that pissed Ordóñez off. Right, Alfredo?"

El Coronel Alfredo Munz, who was sitting in the armchair facing Delchamps with his legs also stretched out, nodded.

Castillo continued: "We should keep Duffy's lying in mind. Then the question of what to do with the choppers—how to get them near Asunción, how to refuel them en route, etcetera—comes up. We need Duffy to do all those things for us plus, of course, reassure any authorities who might spot the choppers that Argentina is not being invaded by the gringos.

"Then we get to the snatch-and-grab itself. We need Duffy not only to help but to do it our way. I want this op to go down as quietly as possible, which means I'm going to have to dissuade him from leaving bodies all over the place. I'll figure out how to do that later. Right now, getting him under control is the thing." He paused. "I can't think of anything else. Anyone . . . ?"

He looked around the room to see if someone had a better idea. No one did.

"Okay, then," Castillo said. "Edgar, how about you sitting out the confrontation in my bedroom? What I'm thinking is that if we've done something stupid and are about to blow it, you can come in. That would surprise Duffy, take his mind off what we did wrong. And if you pick up on how we screwed up, you'll probably have a fix."

Delchamps nodded his agreement.

"Okay, Eddie and I will go change clothes. While we're gone, Alfredo, will you check on the Aero Commander? We may not need it if we screw this up, but if we don't, the sooner we get to Bariloche the better."

"It'll be waiting for us at Jorge Newbery, Karl," Munz said. "The owner owes me several large favors."

"Susanna, if you realize we're screwing up, you might consider flashing some thigh at him."

Susanna smiled, shook her head, and gave him the finger again.

The door chime bonged discreetly fifteen minutes later.

Castillo, now wearing a business suit and sitting on the couch as he sipped at a cup of coffee, signaled first with his right index finger for Eddie Lorimer to open the door and then, his eyebrows raised, signaled to all by holding up his right hand with the index and middle fingers crossed.

Everyone in the large sitting room took his meaning: *Hope like hell we get away with this!*

Lorimer pulled the door open. Comandante Liam Duffy of the Gendarmería Nacional, in civilian clothing, looked somewhat disapprovingly at Lorimer and then at the others in the room.

Tony Santini and Manuel D'Elia were sitting at the dining table, on which a room service waiter was arranging tableware around chrome-dome-covered plates. Alfredo Munz was standing at the plateglass windows, drinking a cup of coffee.

"Well, good morning, Comandante," Castillo called cheerfully. "You're just in time for breakfast."

He pointed at the dining table.

Duffy, who did not look at all pleased with what he saw, ignored Castillo, eyed Max warily, looked curiously at the others, then crossed the room to Munz.

"So, Alfredo," Duffy said stiffly, and went through the hug-and-kiss rite.

Munz did not respond with anything close to warmth.

"Liam," he said simply.

"So what's going on, Alfredo? Who are these people?"

"Right now, Comandante," Castillo replied for him, "you don't have to know that."

"I thought you understood that if we are to work together, I am to know everything," Duffy said.

Castillo didn't immediately reply. Instead—with a grunt—he pushed himself off the couch and walked to the dining table. He sat down and waved for Duffy to take a seat.

"I've had my breakfast," Duffy said curtly.

"Well, have a little more," Castillo said. "As my much-loved abuela is always saying, 'Breakfast is the most important meal of the day. It gives you the strength to attack the day's problems.' "

"I asked who these people are," Duffy said.

"Maybe we can get to that a little later," Castillo said.

"I want to know who they are and what they're doing here," Duffy said, his voice rising.

"Or?" Castillo asked, quietly.

"Or what?" Duffy responded.

"I didn't detect some sort of a threat in that request, did I? I really don't like to be threatened."

"What's going on here, Colonel?"

"Well, everybody but you is having their breakfast."

"You remember our conversation yesterday morning, I presume?"

"Yes, of course. Actually, I've given it a lot of thought."

"The twenty-four hours I gave you to leave the country unless your superiors authorize you to place yourself under my orders is about over, Colonel. And I am not amused by this . . . this whatever it is."

"Oh, come on, Duffy," Castillo said. "You didn't really think that little act of yours was going to work, did you?" He looked up at Duffy. "You're sure you don't want to sit down and have some of these scrambled eggs? They put little chopped up pieces of ham in them. Delicious!"

"Coronel Munz, you had best advise your Yankee friend that I'm serious!"

"So is Colonel Castillo serious, Comandante," Munz said.

"Actually, Duffy, I'm more of a *Texican* than a Yankee," Castillo said. "Wouldn't you agree, Manuel?"

"I would say that's so, Colonel," D'Elia said.

Duffy glared at D'Elia, as if trying to identify his accent, and then looked at Castillo.

"On the telephone you said that you had contacted your superiors and—"

"What I actually said," Castillo interrupted, "was 'I've been in touch with Washington.' And then I suggested we have breakfast. And you agreed. But then you come and say you've already had yours."

"All right, enough," Duffy said. "I am a man of my word, Colonel. I will not have you arrested if you leave the country by midnight tonight."

He walked to the door.

"At midnight tonight, I'll be somewhere in Patagonia," Castillo said. "When I know in which hotel . . ."

"The Llao Llao, Colonel," Munz furnished. "Confirmation came when you were in the bathroom."

"What an odd name," Castillo said. "The hotel *Llao Llao,* then, in San Carlos de Bariloche. I don't think we have our room numbers yet, but I'm sure the management will be able to tell you where we are when your people come to arrest us."

Duffy turned and looked at him in disbelief and anger.

"Duffy, you're not going to have me or anyone else arrested, and we both know that," Castillo said unpleasantly.

"I'm not?" Duffy flared. "You are under arrest for possession and use of an unauthorized radio transmitter."

"You don't give up, do you?" Castillo said. "Tell him about the radio, Tony."

"Just to make sure, Comandante," Santini said, "I checked with the communications ministry. They tell me that a radio telephone such as that is perfectly legal."

"We'll see about that at the police station," Duffy said. "You may also consider yourself under arrest, señor."

Santini forced back a grin.

"There's a small problem with that, Comandante," Santini said, straight-faced. "I've got one of these things." He waved a small plastic carnet. "I'm an assistant legal attaché at the U.S. embassy. You have no authority to arrest me."

When Duffy didn't reply, Santini went on: "I also called the foreign ministry and told them that we were registering Nuestra Pequeña Casa at the Mayerling Country Club in Pilar as the official residence of el Señor la Señora Sieno, which of course—as they also enjoy diplomatic status—gives the house and grounds diplomatic status and makes it inviolate to search."

Duffy looked at Castillo.

"You sonofabitch!" Duffy said.

"I'll tell you this one time, Duffy," Castillo replied coldly. "You can call me just about anything you want *but* a sonofabitch. If you *ever* call me a sonofabitch again, I'll break both of your arms."

Duffy shook his head in disbelief.

"Alfredo, this man is crazy," he said. "He has threatened violence—before witnesses; you, if no one else—against a comandante of the Gendarmería Nacional."

"I didn't hear any threats, Liam," Munz said. "But if you ever hear one, pay attention. The colonel doesn't make them idly."

"Duffy," Castillo announced, then realized that all of Duffy's attention—confused or outraged or both—was focused on Munz.

"Duffy," he repeated more forcefully.

Duffy finally looked at him.

"Are you going to continue with this nonsense," Castillo went on, "or shall we start all over again?"

After a very long moment, Duffy asked, "What do you mean, 'start all over again'?"

"Well, I say, 'Good morning, Comandante. You're just in time for breakfast.' And then you say, 'How nice. I'm starved.' And then you come and shake my hand and sit down. And we have our breakfast, and we start talking about how we can help each other. You want to try that, Duffy, or do you want to cut your nose off to spite your face?"

They stared at each other for a long moment.

"Good morning, Comandante," Castillo said. "You're just in time for breakfast."

"I will listen to what you have to say," Duffy said finally.

"Well, that's not exactly what I hoped to hear you say," Castillo said, "but it's a start, and I'm willing to bend a little."

He waved Duffy into a chair and offered him a plate of scrambled eggs and ham. When Duffy shook his head, Castillo passed the plate to D'Elia.

Then Castillo put several spoonfuls of the egg and ham onto another plate. There was a basket of hard-crusted baguettes. Castillo took one, broke off a piece of the bread, then forked egg onto that. He generously applied salt and pepper, shook several drops of Tabasco on it, then popped the open-faced sandwich into his mouth and chewed appreciatively.

"Por favor, mi coronel?" D'Elia asked as he motioned with his hand for the bottle of hot sauce.

Castillo passed the Tabasco to him.

D'Elia then made a little sandwich much like Castillo's. Except that D'Elia was far more liberal with the application of Tabasco. When he had it in his mouth, his face showed his satisfaction with his efforts. He handed the Tabasco back to Castillo as Castillo finished constructing another little egg sandwich. When he had that one in his mouth, he passed the Tabasco to Duffy, who had been watching impatiently, but who took the bottle as a reflex action.

"I'd be careful with that," Castillo said. "They make it in Louisiana, and some men find it a little too spicy."

Duffy rose to the challenge. After he made himself a chopped ham and scrambled egg open-faced sandwich, he began to liberally polka-dot it with Tabasco.

"Be careful," Munz warned.

Duffy popped the little sandwich in his mouth. He chewed and smiled . . . but then his lips contorted and his face broke out in a sweat.

"La puta madre!" he exclaimed, spitting out the sandwich into a napkin.

"I told you to be careful, and so did Alfredo," Castillo said, smiling and shaking his head sympathetically.

Duffy ignored that.

"What is it you wish to say, Colonel?" he said impatiently after taking a sip of water. "You said we should 'start talking about how we can help each other.' "

As Castillo began making himself another sandwich, he said, "Pegleg, why don't you tell Comandante Duffy what you told us about where you think these people are holding Special Agent Timmons? And the problems of extracting him?"

" 'Pegleg'?" Duffy said without thinking.

"Show the comandante your leg, Pegleg," Castillo ordered.

"Yes, sir," Lorimer said, and hoisted his trouser leg.

"The knee is fully articulated," he said. "And it's titanium, so light I hardly know it's on there." Then, without breaking his cadence, he went on: "They're more than likely holding Timmons at a remote farm, most likely in Paraguay, but possibly in Argentina. Another possibility is that he's being held on a watercraft of some sort on the Río Paraguay. Wherever it is—"

"Then you *don't* know where he's being held, I gather?" Duffy interrupted sarcastically.

"Not yet," Castillo answered for Lorimer. "Let him finish, Comandante."

"Wherever Timmons is being held, it will be difficult to approach without being detected. The moment they suspect that there will be visitors, they will take Timmons into the bush or put him in a small boat and hide it along the shore of the river. A variation of this scenario—a likely one because of their changed modus operandi—is that they've got Timmons at a plant where they refine the paste into cocaine hydrochloride. That sort of place would also be difficult to approach without detection—"

"Difficult? Impossible!" Duffy snorted.

"—as it will almost certainly be approachable over only one road. In this latter scenario, furthermore, there would probably be additional, better-armed and more-skilled guards, better communication, and a generator, or generators, to provide the electricity necessary for the refining operation in case the local power grid goes down. The availability of electricity would probably allow them to have motion-sensing and other intrusion-detecting devices."

"May I ask a question, Colonel?" Duffy said.

Castillo gestured that he could.

Duffy looked at Lorimer and said, "Where did you acquire this information, señor . . . ? I didn't get your name."

"I didn't give it," Lorimer said. He looked at Castillo, and when Castillo just perceptibly nodded, Lorimer went on, "Special Agent Timmons and I were close in Asunción. We talked."

"I was not aware that you were friends," Duffy said. "So were we."

"If that's so," Castillo put in, "then perhaps you might consider devoting more of your effort to the problem of getting Timmons and your two men back, instead of planning for the massacre of those who took them."

Duffy gave him a dirty look but didn't respond directly.

"How would you deal with the problems you see?" he asked Lorimer. "Starting with locating precisely where Timmons and my men are, presuming they're together?"

Castillo answered for him: "We're working on that as we speak."

"I'll let that pass for the moment," Duffy said to Castillo, then turned back to Lorimer. "How would you go about rescuing Timmons and my men?"

Lorimer looked to Castillo again for permission. Castillo nodded, and Lorimer replied, "A simple helicopter assault operation."

"Like the one staged at Estancia Shangri-La?" Duffy said, more than a little sarcastically.

"Not quite," Castillo said. "Shangri-La was supposed to be a passenger pickup, not an assault. We were really surprised when those people shot at us. We'll go into this one expecting resistance. And act accordingly."

"How many helicopters do you think you can borrow from Pevsner, Colonel? How many does he have? Enough for even a 'simple helicopter assault operation'?"

"Excuse me?"

"Isn't that why you're going to Bariloche?" Duffy asked, almost triumphantly. "To borrow a helicopter again from that Russian criminal Aleksandr Pevsner?"

"No, that's not why I'm going to Bariloche, not that that is any of your business. The helicopters involved in this operation will begin to arrive somewhere around midnight on the eighteenth of September. In one week, plus one day, plus however many hours between now and midnight. This is tentative; I haven't had much time to plan. And, frankly, I need your help with the planning."

Castillo noticed that that got Duffy's attention.

"Between now and then—this is where you come in, Comandante—we are going to have to set up refueling stations for the helos, a landing field between where I plan to initially land the aircraft—which is on the playing fields of the Polo Association in Pilar—and then somewhere near Asunción. The landing field will need to be big enough for a JP-4 fuel cache for each helo every three hundred kilometers. And be an isolated field, of course. And we need a base of operations in Argentina, also isolated, where we can conceal the helicopters from anyone flying over, and from which we can operate into Paraguay."

Duffy considered all of this a moment.

"How many helicopters will you have?"

"Four, at least."

"And you think you'll be able to fly four U.S. Army helicopters across a thousand—fifteen hundred—kilometers of Argentina and get away with it? Undetected?"

"U.S. Army helicopters? No. But I don't think one or two Argentine Army helicopters flying anywhere—across the pampas or up the Río de la Plata or the Río Paraguay—are going to attract attention from anybody."

"Your helicopters will be painted like ours," Duffy replied, "is that what you're saying?"

Castillo nodded, and thought, *Now I really have his attention.*

I just have to sink the hook.

"Except maybe other Argentine Army helicopters?" Duffy pursued. "Their pilots might say, 'I wonder who that is?' "

"Mine will be flying nap of the earth, very low—"

"I know what nap of the earth means," Duffy protested.

"—and will have radar on board, which will permit my pilots to take evasive action should they detect any other aircraft in the vicinity."

"Like a sudden turn of course which will take them right over an airfield, or a city?"

"They're equipped with satellite navigation systems to keep that from happening," Castillo said. "And the pilots do this sort of thing for a living."

"You seem very sure of yourself, Colonel."

"This is what *I* do for a living, Comandante," Castillo said evenly. "Now, would you like to hear our very preliminary plans for the actual assault? I really need your input on this."

Duffy nodded without hesitation.

Got him!

Castillo glanced at Munz, who nodded just perceptibly. Castillo then motioned at D'Elia.

"This is Captain D'Elia, Comandante," Castillo said. "He will be in charge of the actual assault."

Duffy offered his hand.

"Mucho gusto, mi comandante," D'Elia said, then glanced at Castillo. "With your permission, *mi coronel?"*

"Go ahead," Castillo said.

"Generally speaking," D'Elia began, "as I understand we not only intend to rescue our men but plan to take prisoners—and if we determine our people are being held at a refinery, or transfer point, to either seize or destroy both the drugs and the plant itself—"

"You are an Argentine, Capitán?" Duffy interrupted.

"No. But thank you, *mi comandante,* for your error. I have worked hard on the Porteño accent."

"Well, you could have fooled me," Duffy said.

We all fooled you, Duffy, Castillo thought.

And thank God for that!

I don't know what the hell I would have done if you had stormed out of here in a rage right after you came in.

"If I may continue?" D'Elia asked politely, then went on: "If we are to take prisoners and seize drugs, etcetera, the fact that Lieutenant Lorimer has told us these places are accessible only by one road works in our favor."

Duffy's face was expressionless.

"If there's only one way in," D'Elia explained, "there's only one way out."

Duffy nodded knowingly.

"That's where your men will come in, Comandante," D'Elia continued. "At the moment the assault begins—we call that 'boots on the ground'—the road will have to be cut. Not a moment before, which would alert them, nor a moment after, as it has been my experience that an amazing number of rats can get through even a very small hole in a very short period of time when they are frightened. And we intend to do our very best to badly frighten them."

Duffy again nodded his understanding.

Castillo looked at Munz, who very discreetly gave him a thumbs-up signal.

Castillo smiled at him, but thought, *Why am I waiting for the other shoe to drop?*

[TWO]
Above San Carlos de Bariloche
Río Negro Province, Argentina
1755 10 September 2005

"There it is," Alfredo Munz said, pointing.

Castillo, in the pilot seat of the Aero Commander 680, looked where Munz was pointing out the copilot side window, then banked the high-winged airplane to the right so that he could get a better view below.

Darkness was rising, but there was still enough light to see a red-tile-roofed collection of buildings—the Llao Llao Resort Hotel—sitting on a mountainside sticking into and several hundred feet above the startling blue waters of a lake.

Lakes, Castillo corrected himself. *Lake Moreno and Lake Nahuel Huapi.*

Well, it looks like we cheated death again. The airport is only twenty-six clicks from here.

And I'm only half kidding.

He straightened the wings, then put his hand, palm upward, over his shoulder.

"Let me have the magic black box, navigator," he said.

Corporal Lester Bradley very carefully laid a small laptop computer in his hand, and Castillo very carefully lowered it into his lap.

He was navigating using a prototype AFC Global Positioning System device connected to the laptop. Aloysius Francis Casey himself had warned him that it was a prototype, its database incomplete, and he really shouldn't rely on it.

"It'll take me three, four days to come up with a good data chip for Argentina and that part of the world, Charley," Casey had told him in Las Vegas. "You got somebody down there I can FedEx it to?"

Since Aloysius Francis Casey was a man of his word, presumably the data chip was on its way—or shortly would be—to Mr. Anthony Santini, Assistant Legal Attaché, Embassy of the United States of America, Colombia 4300, Buenos Aires, Argentina.

But the bottom line was that it hadn't arrived.

Still, what Castillo had—the prototype—looked a helluva lot better to him than the navigation system he'd found in the cockpit of the Aero Commander when they'd gone to Jorge Newbery.

There had been a bigger problem than aged avionics when they first went to get the airplane at Jorge Newbery. The Commander's owner had presumed that when Munz had told him he needed to borrow the aircraft, Munz had meant using the owner's pilot, and he had shown up with his pilot in tow.

Ordinarily, Castillo was a devout believer in the aviator's adage *"There are old pilots and there are bold pilots, but there are very few old, bold pilots."* And, accordingly, he really would have preferred a pilot experienced in (a) flying "his" own Aero Commander and (b) flying it around Argentina. Particularly since Castillo himself had not flown an Aero Commander for a long time.

But the unspoken problem was that after Bariloche, Castillo planned on going on to Asunción . . . and intended en route to take the opportunity to make what the U.S. Army called a low-level visual reconnaissance of the area.

For some wild reason, Castillo believed that (a) the owner would not be too fond of such an activity and (b) even if the owner gave his blessing, the pilot would not be experienced in such low-level visual reconnaissance techniques.

After considerable discussion, the Aero Commander's owner had apparently decided that the "several large favors" he owed to el Coronel Munz outweighed his enormous reluctance to turn over his airplane to some gringo friend of Munz, even if that gringo sounded almost like a Porteño.

The owner's agreement had come with a caveat: that the owner's pilot take the gringo friend for "a couple of touch-and-goes," what was tactfully explained as being helpful "to familiarize one with the aircraft."

And what that familiarization flight had done was convince Castillo that while the airplane was obviously scrupulously maintained, most of its navigation equipment had been in its control panel when the aircraft was first delivered— some forty-odd years earlier. Clearly, none of it was going to be as reliable as what Aloysius Francis Casey had given Castillo in the form of a prototype laptop computer and was worried about his using.

All of this had taken time, of course, and it was quarter to one before Castillo finally managed to get Colonel Munz, Lieutenant Lorimer, Sergeant Mullroney, Corporal Bradley, and Max aboard and could take off on what he announced to the Jorge Newbery tower as "a local area flight, visual flight rules, destination private field near Pilar."

As Castillo retracted the landing gear, he suddenly remembered that another U.S. Army lieutenant colonel—the most decorated soldier of World War II, Audie Murphy, who later became a movie star—had been flying in an identical Aero Commander in 1971 when its wing came off in a thunderstorm over Roanoke, Virginia. Murphy, also a skilled aviator, crashed to his death.

"Right on the money, Alfredo," Castillo said, pointing to the GPS satellite map on the laptop screen. "The airport's twenty-odd clicks thataway."

"Pevsner's place is on the other side of the lake—Moreno," Munz replied, and pointed again. "I don't see how we can get over there tonight. It'll be dark by the time we get to the hotel."

"You'll think of something, Alfredo. You always do."

Then he reached for the radio microphone to call the Bariloche tower.

[THREE]
The Llao Llao Resort Hotel
San Carlos de Bariloche
Río Negro Province, Argentina
1955 10 September 2005

The general manager of the Llao Llao was about as unenthusiastic with the notion of providing accommodations to Max as the owner of the Aero Commander had been about turning his airplane over to a rich gringo. But as Castillo, holding Max's leash in one hand and his briefcase in his other, watched Munz discussing this with him, he knew that Munz was going to prevail.

And at the precise moment Castillo reached this conclusion, the problem of how to meet Aleksandr Pevsner at his home across the lake now that it was dark—really dark; there was no moon—solved itself.

"Mama!" a young female voice said enthusiastically in Russian. "Look at that dog!"

"Stay away from him!" a mother's voice warned.

Castillo turned.

Twenty or thirty feet down the wide, high-ceilinged, thickly carpeted lobby, there stood a tall, dark-haired, well-dressed man in his late thirties. With him was a striking blond woman—"Mama"—and a girl of thirteen or fourteen whose own blond hair hung down her back nearly to her waist—*My God, Elena's about as old as Randy!*—and two boys, one about age six, and the other maybe ten.

Behind them stood two burly men. One of them Castillo knew, but only by his first name, János. He was Pevsner's primary bodyguard. And János knew him, even if there was no sign of recognition on his face. Proof of that came when the other burly man put his hand under his suit jacket—and got a sharp elbow in the abdomen followed by the slashing motion of János's hand.

"It's all right, Anna," Castillo said to the mother in Russian. "Max only eats the fathers of pretty girls named Elena."

Simultaneously, János and Aleksandr Pevsner said, "It's all right."

Pevsner looked at Castillo and added: "I thought I saw you—I even asked János—but we decided, 'No. What would my friends Charley and Alfredo be doing in Patagonia with a dog the size of a horse?' "

"Can I pet him?" Elena asked. "Does he speak Russian?"

"He speaks dog, Elena," Castillo said, "but he understands Russian."

She giggled and went to Max, who sat down and offered his paw. She scratched his ears, and when he licked her face, she put her arms around his neck.

"So what *are* my friends Charley and Alfredo doing in Patagonia with a dog the size of a horse?" Pevsner asked.

"Would you believe we came to see the fossilized dinosaur bones?" Castillo said.

"Knowing that you never lie to me, I would have to."

"How about we heard you would be here and decided to buy you dinner?"

"It would be a strain, but I would have to believe that, too."

"We need to talk, Alek," Castillo said.

"*That* I believe. That's what I was afraid of," Pevsner said. "All right, to-morrow morning. I'll send the boat for you at, say, half past nine?"

"How about tonight?" Castillo said. "I'm really pressed for time."

Pevsner obviously didn't like that, but after a moment, he said, "We came for dinner. We could talk about what you want to talk about after dinner, if you like."

"That would be fine," Castillo said. "Thank you. And you'll be my guests at dinner, of course."

"That's not what I meant, as I suspect you know full well, friend Charley. But faced with the choice between the long face of Elena over dinner—having been separated from her newfound friend—or breaking bread with you, I opt for the less painful of the two."

"Alek!" his wife protested.

"It's all right, Anna," Castillo said. "What are friends for if not to insult?"

"I'm afraid that after dinner I will learn what you really think friends are for," Pevsner said. "Shall we go in?" He gestured toward the dining room.

"Elena, the dog goes with the understanding he does not get fed from the table, understood?"

"Yes, Poppa."

"I don't think they'll let him in there, Alek," Castillo said. "This isn't Budapest."

"Yes, I know," Pevsner said. "In Patagonia, you have to have a substantial financial interest in the hotel if you want to bring a dog into the dining room."

Castillo smiled and shook his head.

The maître d'hôtel appeared, clutching menus to his chest.

"These gentlemen," Pevsner ordered, indicating Castillo and Munz, "will be dining with us. Their friends"—he pointed to Lorimer, Mullroney, and Bradley—"will dine with mine."

His Spanish was good, even fluent, but heavily Russian-accented.

"Bradley," Castillo ordered, "go to your room and see if I have any telephone calls. If it's important, tell me. Otherwise, just come down here and have your dinner."

"Aye, aye, sir," Bradley said.

A waiter arrived with a tray of champagne glasses almost as soon as the headwaiter had laid their menus before them. Two of the glasses held a bubbling brown liquid that Castillo decided was Coca-Cola for Sergei and Aleksandr. He was surprised when Elena was offered and accepted one of the champagne stems.

I don't need champagne if I'm going to be flying. I'll just take a sip when we get to the inevitable toast.

That came almost immediately.

Pevsner got half out of his chair, picked up his glass, and reached out with it to touch Castillo's.

"To dear and trusted friends," Pevsner said, and then moved his glass to tap the rims of the others, including his daughter's.

When that was over, Pevsner just about emptied his glass. Elena didn't do that, but she took a healthy ladylike sip.

They let her drink? Maybe she is older than Randy.

"When were you born, honey?" Castillo asked her.

"Sixteen November 1992, by the Western calendar," Elena said.

Jesus Christ! She is almost exactly *as old as Randy. Thirteen.*

"And her drinking champagne shocks you?" Pevsner said.

"Do you always think the worst of people, Alek?" Castillo asked, and then he turned to Elena and his mouth went onto autopilot: "What I was thinking, honey, is that you're just about the same age as my son."

Jesus Christ!

I just said "my son" out loud for the first time.

"I didn't know you had a family, Charley," Anna said. "You never said anything."

Castillo was aware of Munz's eyes on him.

"I have a grandmother, a cousin who is more of a brother, and his family. And a son—Randy—who was also born in November of 1992. He lives with his mother and her husband."

"You don't get to see him?" Elena asked, sympathetically.

"I saw him just a few days ago," Castillo said. "I gave him flying lessons as we flew over the Gulf Coast looking at the damage Hurricane Katrina had done."

"Was it as terrible as we saw on television?" Anna asked.

"If anything, worse. Unbelievable."

"Have you got a picture?" Elena asked.

"You're interested?"

She nodded.

"In my son? Or the hurricane damage?"

She giggled and blushed.

"Both," she said.

Castillo reached under his chair and picked up his soft leather briefcase.

"What's that?" Pevsner asked.

"My American Express card. I never leave home without it."

Pevsner exhaled audibly, smiled, and shook his head.

Castillo took out the envelope of photographs that Sergeant Neidermeyer had made for him and handed it to Elena.

"Show these to your father and mother when you're finished," Castillo said.

"He's beautiful, Charley," Pevsner said some moments later. "His eyes are just like yours."

So much for the question "Does Abuela know?"

"Boys are 'handsome,' Alek," Castillo said, then glanced at Elena. "Girls are 'beautiful.' "

She smiled as she flipped to another photo.

"My boys are beautiful," Pevsner said. "And so is yours."

The waiter approached, excused his interruption, and said, "A cocktail before dinner?"

"Ginger ale for the children," Pevsner ordered. "Very dry vodka martinis, with onions, for my wife and myself. Alfredo?"

"I would like scotch," Munz said. "Single-malt Famous Grouse?"

The waiter nodded, and looked at Castillo.

"Nothing for me, thanks, I'm driving."

"Have one, friend Charley," Pevsner said. "I never trust a man who doesn't drink when I do."

"You never trust a man, period," Castillo said.

What the hell.

I'll just get off the ground in the morning a little later.

"I'll have what he's having," he said to the waiter. "Except hold the vegetables and vermouth."

[FOUR]

Corporal Lester Bradley appeared at their table about the same time as the appetizers of prosciutto crudo with melon and pâté de foie gras.

"Major Miller would like to speak to you, sir," Bradley announced. "He said it's really important."

I knew I shouldn't have had that martini.

"Excuse me, please," Castillo said, and stood. "I'll try to cut this as short as possible. C'mon, Max."

He signaled for Bradley to lead the way.

Castillo and Max followed him down the lobby to an elevator, which took them up to the second floor, then down a corridor almost to the end. Bradley unlocked a hotel room door, waved them ahead of him, and then followed them inside.

The control console was nowhere in sight, but Castillo saw a DirecTV dish fastened to the railing of the small balcony and remembered that there was a repeater mounted in the antenna; no cable was required.

Bradley took the control console from the shelf of a small closet and put it on a small table barely large enough to hold it.

For a five-star hotel, this room is pretty damn small.

He looked around the room and saw that the only furniture beside the bed and tiny table was a small chest of drawers and a small upholstered armchair. The chair was across the room from the table, with the control console now sitting on it.

"Will that work in my room without moving the antenna, Lester? This room's pretty small."

"This *is* your room, sir," Bradley replied. "Mine is even smaller."

A moment later, Bradley announced, "We're up, sir," and handed Castillo what looked very much like an ordinary wireless telephone handset.

"Why don't you sit, sir?" Bradley asked, nodding at the armchair.

When Castillo settled in the armchair, he learned that it was not only small but also uncomfortably close to the ground. His head was now as far off the ground as Max's, which Max interpreted to mean Castillo wanted to be kissed. Which he did.

Is this damn place designed for dwarfs?

Castillo looked at the handset. The AFC logo was discreetly molded into the plastic. He also saw that there was a thin soft black cushion on the earpiece.

Not for comfort. That's to muffle the incoming voice. Bradley won't be able to hear what Miller's saying, but needs to.

"Put it on speaker, Les," Castillo said, as he put the handset to his ear.

"Aye, aye, sir," Bradley said, and when he had pushed the appropriate button, went to the corridor wall and leaned on it.

It was either that or sit on my bed.

"Hello?" Castillo said into the handset.

"Where the hell have you been, Charley?" Major Richard Miller announced. "I've been trying to raise you for two hours."

"What's up?" Castillo replied, and then hurriedly added: "Are we secure?"

"According to my indicators we are."

"Okay, so what's so important?"

"Now you've got me worried, Charley. I therefore will talk in tongues. Four of the birds managed to land where they were going without sinking it. The reason I know this . . . Oh, to hell with it. I think this may damned well be blown anyway."

"What may be damned well blown?"

"The reason I know they're on the carrier is because a bluesuit—a commander—showed up here to personally deliver to you an Info Copy of an Urgent from the captain to the CNO. It took me five minutes to get the bastard to give it to me."

"What did it say?"

There was a rattling at the door to the hotel room, and it suddenly swung open.

"What the hell?" Castillo said, and then, "Hold one, Dick."

Castillo saw that the manager of the hotel was holding the door open for Pevsner and János.

"I don't recall inviting you up here," Castillo said angrily, in Russian.

"We have to talk, friend Charley," Pevsner said, matter-of-factly, also in Russian.

"It won't wait until after dinner?"

Pevsner shook his head, thanked the manager in Spanish, then closed the door on him. He turned to Castillo and, switching back to Russian, asked, "Do you have a weapon?"

"No, but Bradley does," Castillo said, and pointed at Corporal Bradley.

Bradley held his M1911A1 .45 pistol in both hands, its hammer back and the muzzle aimed at the floor at János's and Pevsner's feet.

He didn't understand a word of the Russian, but he saw the look on my face, and he's taking no chances.

Neither is Max. He's on his feet and inching toward Pevsner and János.

"That's the pistol, János," Castillo said, almost conversationally, "that Bradley used to take down Colonel Komogorov in the hotel garage in Pilar after Komogorov put a bullet in you."

"We mean you no harm, friend Charley!" Pevsner said.

For some reason, I don't think that tone of anguish is phony.

"Put it away, Lester," Castillo ordered in English. He switched to Hungarian— "Down, Max!"—and then to Russian. "People who come barging into my room are likely to get shot. You might want to write that down, Alek."

"We came to make sure you had a gun in order to do just that," Pevsner said. "János, give it him."

János—very carefully, using his thumb and index finger—took what looked like a Model 1911 Colt pistol from his jacket's inside pocket and handed it to Castillo.

"That's an Argentine copy of your .45," Pevsner said. "Almost identical. A Ballester Molina stolen, I'm told, from the Argentine Army ten years ago."

In almost a Pavlovian act, Castillo ejected the magazine and worked the pistol's slide. A cartridge flew through the air and landed on the bed. Castillo picked it up, put it in the magazine, then put the magazine back in the pistol and dropped the hammer.

"What the hell is going on there, Charley?" Major Richard Miller's voice demanded over the speaker circuit.

"Turn the speaker off, Lester," Castillo ordered, and picked up the handset.

Pevsner looked as if he was going to leave the room.

Oh, what the hell!

"Stay, Alek," Castillo said.

He'll be able to hear only one side of the conversation.

And he already knows I work for the President.

Castillo spoke into the handset: "Excuse the interruption, Richard. The maid wanted to turn down the bed. You were saying?"

"I was about to read the message the bluesuit didn't want to give me."

"Please do."

"Skipping the address crap at the top . . . *'(1) Pursuant to verbal order issued by DepSecNav to undersigned in telecon 1530 6 September 2005, four US Army HU1D rotary-wing aircraft were permitted to land aboard USS* Ronald Reagan *at 1305 10 September 2005.*

" *'(2) Senior officer among them, who states he is a US Army major but declines to further identify himself with identity card or similar document, also has refused to inform the undersigned of the nature of his mission, stating it is classified Top Secret Presidential, and neither the undersigned nor RADM Jacoby, USN, the Task Force Commander, is authorized access to such information.' "*

"Good for him," Castillo said.

"It gets better," Miller replied. " *'(3) US Army major was denied permission by undersigned to communicate with US Army LtCol Costello of Dept of Homeland Security using a non-standard satellite radio he brought aboard. He said LtCol Costello could quote clarify unquote the situation. He refused use of* Reagan*'s communication services, stating he could not be sure of their encryption capabilities.*

" *'(4) US Army major has also refused inspection of cargo aboard helicopters, again citing classification of Top Secret Presidential.' "*

"And, again, good for him," Castillo said. "Who screwed up and didn't clue the Navy in on what's happening?"

"I'm not finished," Miller said. "Get this: " *'(5) Helicopters and their crews are presently on flight deck in what amounts to a standoff between members of my crew and the Army personnel.'*

"Oh, shit!" Castillo said.

"Continuing right along," Miller replied, " *'(6) Further action was not taken because the US Army personnel are obviously American and they pose no threat to USS* Ronald Reagan *that cannot be dealt with.*

" *'(7) Urgently and respectfully request clarification of this situation and existing orders. It is suggested that contacting LtCol Costello, only, might be useful.'* That's why the bluesuit didn't even want to give me this."

"Jesus Christ!" Castillo said.

"And we conclude with, *'(8) USS* Ronald Reagan *proceeding.'* The signature is *'Kenton, Captain USN, Captain, USS* Ronald Reagan*'* and below that it says, *'Rear Admiral K. G. Jacoby, USN, concurs.' "*

"What did Montvale have to say?"

"That's why I called you, Charley. I can't get through to Montvale."

"What do you mean you can't get through to him?"

"Your buddy Truman Ellsworth, who answers his line, says he's not available."

"He does?" Castillo said, coldly. "Get me the White House switchboard."

He saw Pevsner's eyes light up when he heard "White House."

Miller said, "Before you charge off in righteous indignation, would you be interested in hearing my probably somewhat paranoid assessment of the situation?"

"As long as it doesn't take longer than sixty seconds."

"What happened, I submit, is that General McNab went to the secretary of Defense and told him he had to move the Hueys down there black, under the authority of the Presidential Finding. So far, so good, as the secretary of Defense knows about the Finding and that he's being told, not asked. So the secretary of Defense got on the horn to the secretary of the Navy and told him to do it." He paused. "I don't know if the secretary of the Navy knows about the Finding. Do you?"

"No."

"Okay," Miller said. "I don't think he does, but it doesn't really matter. I'm pretty sure that the deputy secretary of the Navy doesn't. Agree?"

"He probably doesn't."

"The Urgent says the bluesuit captain got his orders to land the Hueys on his ship from the deputy on the phone. I think it's very reasonable to assume the bluesuit captain asked the deputy what the hell was going on, and the deputy couldn't tell him, because he didn't know any more than he was told, which was essentially, just do it, explanation to follow."

"Okay," Castillo agreed.

"Which causes the bluesuit captain to shift into cover-my-ass mode. So he goes and tells the admiral, who is in charge of the whole carrier group. Which causes the admiral not only to be pissed, because *he's* the admiral, and the deputy should have called him, not the captain, but also causes him to shift into his cover-my-ass mode."

"Probably," Castillo agreed.

"So the admiral says, 'There's nothing we can really do except wait for the Army choppers to land. Whoever's in charge of them probably will explain what's going on, and based on that we can decide how to best protect our beloved Navy from the fucking Army.

"And then the birds land on the carrier, and good ol' Major Bob Ward, in the sacred traditions of the 160th, ain't gonna tell nobody nothing—or show anybody anything, not even a bluesuit with stars—without permission from the guy running the operation, one C. G. Castillo. He is willing to get this permission, providing they let him set up his nonstandard radio which—for reasons I don't know; they were in their cover-my-ass mode, which may explain it—they were unwilling to do.

"So there's the standoff and why they sent the Urgent."

"Very credible," Castillo said, "but what's it got to do with Ellsworth not letting you talk to Montvale?"

"Let me finish," Miller said. "Montvale knew you were worried about the Navy giving us trouble because Jake Torine called him, right?"

"So?"

"And Montvale is going to get Jake on the carrier to make sure there's no trouble caused by the aforementioned impetuous light colonel Castillo, right?"

"So, again?"

"So, if you were Montvale and had NSA at Fort Meade in your pocket, and wanted to stay on top of the situation, wouldn't you task NSA to look for—'search filter: Army choppers on Navy ships, any reference'—and immediately give him any and all intercepts? Of course you would. And I'll bet that sonofabitch had the Urgent before I did."

"Where are you going with this, Dick?" Castillo asked.

I think I know, he thought, *but I'd like confirmation.*

"Montvale doesn't give a damn whether or not you get Timmons back, Charley. We both heard him say as much. He wants to protect the President, I'll give him that much, and he thinks your operation is going to blow up in everybody's face, including the President's. And Truman Ellsworth, for sure, and probably Montvale, would love to see you fuck up and embarrass the President, which would happen if you can't run the snatch-and-grab successfully. Which you can't without the choppers. That's why he was so helpful in arranging to get Jake onto the *Gipper.* Montvale, not you, would have sent him. That means Jake works for Montvale, which cuts you out of the picture.

"Then, and you know the sonofabitch is good at this, he whispers in the admiral's ear that no serious harm would be done if something happened to keep him from launching the choppers, and an embarrassing-to-the-Navy situation might well be avoided."

"Sonofabitch!"

"And he knows you're out of touch. And he knows, that being the case, when I got the Urgent, I would try to call him. So he tells Ellsworth that he's not available to me. I think he's betting that I wouldn't call the President. And if I did, so what? All that would mean was that the Lunatic's Chief of Staff is as loony as he is. And if the President asked him what the hell's going on, Montvale could pull the rug out from under you—for this operation and generally."

"Yeah, except the lunatic found out and is perfectly willing to get on the horn to the President."

"Permission to speak, sir?" Miller said.

Castillo sensed that Miller was not being clever. He had used the phrase a subordinate officer uses when his superior officer is about to do something the subordinate thinks is wrong.

"Granted."

"Sir, how often do you think Admiral Jacoby gets phone calls from the White House switchboard?"

It was a moment before Castillo answered.

"Where's Torine now?" he asked.

"Forty minutes ago, he was about to land at MacDill."

"As soon as we get off here, contact him, bring him up to speed on what's happened. Tell him Montvale is not to know we're onto him, and to call me once he's on the *Gipper.*"

"Okay, but what's happened? I must have missed something."

"Stay on the line while I brighten Admiral Jacoby's dull daily routine with a call from the White House."

"White House," the pleasant professional female voice answered. "What can I do for you, Colonel Castillo?"

"I need Rear Admiral K. G. Jacoby on a secure line. He's aboard the USS *Ronald Reagan,* which is somewhere between Norfolk and Key West."

There was a moment's pause, then the operator replied: "The difficult we do immediately, sir; the impossible takes a little longer. I'll have to go through the Navy. That'll take a little time. Can I call you when it's set up?"

"Can I stay on the line?"

"Certainly."

"Navy."

"White House. We need a secure encrypted voice connection to the USS *Ronald Reagan.* It's in the Atlantic some—"

"We know where *she* is, thank you very much, White House."

"*Reagan.*"

"Navy. Establish secure encrypted voice connection."

"Hold one, Navy."

"Navy, *Reagan.* This connection is encrypted Class Two."

"*Reagan.* The White House is calling. Request upgraded encryption."

"Hold one, Navy."

"Navy, *Reagan*. This connection is now encrypted Class One."

"White House, Navy. You read?"

"Reagan, this is the White House. We're calling Rear Admiral K. G. Jacoby."

"White House, *Reagan*. Ma'am, the admiral is in his cabin. He has only Class Two encryption on that line. It will take a minute to get him to the secure voice communication room."

"We'll wait. Thank you."

"Radio, voice commo room."

"Go."

"We have Admiral Jacoby. Encryption status Class One."

"White House, Navy. You read?"

"Admiral Jacoby?"

"Speaking."

"This is the White House. Please hold for Colonel Castillo. Go ahead, Colonel."

"We have verified Class One encryption?"

"Yes, sir, we do."

"Good evening, Admiral. My name is Castillo."

"Yes, sir?"

"Sir, I'm a lowly lieutenant colonel."

"What's this all about, Colonel?"

"Sir, I am in receipt of your Urgent referring to the Army helicopters you now have aboard. Your message referred to me as 'Costello.' "

"Sorry about that."

"Sir, getting my name wrong apparently is not the only communications problem we are having."

"Is that so?"

"Sir, it was intended by the secretary of Defense that you or Captain Kenton receive your orders regarding the helicopters from the secretary of the Navy. According to your Urgent, Captain Kenton spoke with the deputy secretary."

"That is correct, Colonel. Frankly, I wondered why the deputy secretary didn't call me."

"Sir, I had nothing to do with that call. But I am calling to do what I can to straighten out the mess. Let me begin by saying the helicopters are involved in an operation classified Top Secret Presidential."

"I've heard nothing of the kind, Colonel."

"Yes, sir. I understand. But that being the case, it is the reason the Army officer in charge was unable to explain what he's doing or permit inspection of his helicopters. Unless I'm mistaken, there is no one aboard the *Reagan* with that security clearance."

"Excuse me, Colonel, is there some way I can verify what you're telling me? This is highly unusual."

"Yes, sir, it is. May I suggest, sir, that you contact the secretary of Defense? Or, alternatively, wait until Colonel Jacob Torine, USAF, arrives on the *Reagan.*"

"What did you say?"

"The director of National Intelligence, Ambassador Montvale, as we speak, is arranging for Colonel Torine, who is my deputy, to be put aboard the *Reagan*—"

"Your deputy? You gave me to believe you are a *lieutenant* colonel."

"I am, sir. And Colonel Torine is my deputy. We have both been detached from our respective services, sir, for this duty, and normal military protocol does not apply."

"I will be damned!"

"I admit it often causes some confusion, sir. But as I was saying, sir, Colonel Torine will arrive on the *Reagan* probably within a matter of hours, and he'll tell you what he can about what is being required of you. In the meantime, sir, I would be grateful if you could do several things."

"Such as?"

"Sir, please permit the major to establish communication with us using the equipment he has with him. That is so much simpler for us than going through the White House switchboard."

"Well, I can't see any reason why that can't be done."

"And, Admiral, the sooner you have the helicopters moved to the hangar deck and the paint stripping started, the better."

"I don't know anything about any paint stripping, Colonel. What's that all—"

"Colonel Torine will explain what has to be done, sir, when he comes aboard." He paused, crossed his fingers, and went on: "Sir, with respect, I suspect you're having trouble accepting all this. May I ask, sir, that you immediately communicate with the secretary of Defense to get his assurance?"

There was a moment's silence, and then Admiral Jacoby said, "I think we can hold off, Colonel, until your deputy comes aboard. But in the meantime, I'll have the aircraft moved to the hangar deck and the paint stripping started."

"Yes, sir. Thank you, sir. Break it down, White House."

Admiral Jacoby just had time to say "shit" before a hissing announced the connection was gone.

"How'd I do, Dick?"

"I think you ruined the admiral's day."

"He was about to ruin mine. You know what to tell Jake, right?"

"He just took off from MacDill. That's next."

"Thanks a hell of a lot, Dick," Castillo said, then signaled to Lester to break the connection.

Castillo looked at Pevsner.

"Now that that's done, you want to tell me about the pistol?" Castillo said.

"People are trying to kill you, friend Charley."

"You mean right here and now? Or can we go finish our dinner?"

"We will talk after dinner," Pevsner said.

Castillo picked up the Argentine .45, slipped it into the waistband at the small of his back, and gestured for Pevsner to precede him out of the room.

XII

[ONE]
The Llao Llao Resort Hotel
San Carlos de Bariloche
Río Negro Province, Argentina
2035 10 September 2005

They all crowded into the elevator and rode to the lobby floor. When the door opened, Pevsner touched Castillo's arm and motioned everyone else out.

"I need a moment with my friend Charley," he announced, waving toward the dining room. "The rest of you go in."

Everyone obeyed but Max, who simply sat down and looked to Castillo for instructions. The others made their way around him, and when they all had left the car, Pevsner pushed one of the upper-floor buttons. The door closed and the elevator started to rise.

Pevsner somehow managed to stop the elevator as it ascended; Castillo wondered if an alarm bell was about to go off.

"I don't want to scare Anna and the children," Pevsner said, "so don't say anything at the table."

"What's going on, Alek?"

Pevsner didn't respond directly.

"I will arrange for your baggage to be taken to the boat," he said. "You can spend the night at the house. Among other things, that'll give us the opportunity to talk."

"I can't get far from the communicator," Castillo said, thinking aloud.

"And the boy who operates it?"

Castillo nodded, then said, "He's the communicator, and he's young, Alek, but don't think of him as a boy."

Again, Pevsner didn't respond directly. After a moment, he said, "All right, everybody goes. That'll take a little longer to arrange." He smiled. "That's probably better anyway. A gun battle would disturb the guests."

"There's a possibility of that?"

Pevsner nodded.

"What's going on, Alek?"

"About an hour and a half ago," Pevsner said, "Gellini called and said you were back in Argentina—"

"Gellini?" Castillo wondered aloud, then made the connection: "The SIDE guy?"

Pevsner nodded.

"The man who replaced Alfredo when he was relieved," he confirmed.

"And who now works for you?" Castillo asked.

Pevsner seemed unable to answer that directly, too.

"He admires you, friend Charley. The way you stood up for Alfredo when he was relieved."

Alfredo Munz had been chief of SIDE when J. Winslow Masterson was murdered. He had been retired—in fact, fired—in order to be the Argentine government's scapegoat. Castillo, who had found Munz not only unusually competent and dedicated, thought that the Argentine government's action was inexcusable and had told his replacement, Coronel Alejandro Gellini, so much in less than tactful terms.

"Alfredo was screwed, Alek, and you know it. I told Gellini what I thought of it. And him."

"Gellini could not protect Alfredo from the foreign minister, and neither could I. But there was a silver lining to that cloud: Alfredo now works for you, and Gellini admires you."

"And what did my admirer have to say besides telling you that I was back down here?"

"That people are trying to kill you."

"A lot of people have been telling me that lately. He didn't happen to say who?"

"This is serious business, friend Charley," Pevsner said, smiling and shaking his head in exasperation.

"Gellini didn't happen to say who?" Castillo asked again.

"What is that word you use? 'Bounty'? Gellini said there is a bounty on you."

"I think he probably meant 'contract,'" Castillo said. "Meaning: whoever would whack me would get paid."

Pevsner nodded. "What is a 'bounty'?"

"A price the good guys put on the head of a bad guy," Castillo explained. "Or on some bad guy who jumps bail. Who put out the contract on me?"

"Gellini knows only that the gangsters know about the *contract*; he didn't know who issued it. It could be something the FSB has done in addition to their own plans for you, but I don't know. They usually like to do that sort of thing themselves."

"What're the FSB's plans for me?"

"What do you think, friend Charley? First you took out the Cuban, Vincenzo—"

"Major Vincenzo was shooting at me at the time."

"—and then Komogorov of the FSB."

"Colonel Komogorov was shooting at you at the time. And I didn't take him out, Lester did."

Pevsner shook his head in exasperation again.

"As you well know, when something like that happens, what the FSB wants to hear—what Putin himself wants to hear—is not some excuse or explanation. They want confirmation that whoever has killed one of them has himself been killed."

"I know an Argentine cop who has much the same philosophy of life."

Pevsner looked at him curiously.

"I don't understand," he said, finally.

"It's too long a story to be told in an elevator. It will have to wait until after dinner."

This time Pevsner expressed his exasperation by exhaling audibly. He pushed a button on the control panel and the elevator began to descend.

[TWO]

The dinner was first class, which did not surprise Castillo. But he was surprised at how hungry he was and how much he ate, including all of an enormous slice of cheesecake topped with a strawberry sauce he thought was probably a hundred calories a spoonful.

Afterward, Pevsner led the group back to the elevator bank and they filled both elevators. This time, the elevators went down and the doors opened on a corridor in the basement.

At the end of the corridor, a door opened to the outside, where a Peugeot van and three men—obviously armed—waited for them. They climbed into the van and were driven maybe a kilometer to a wharf on the lakeshore.

This has to be Lake Moreno, Castillo decided.

Munz said, "Pevsner's place is on the other side of the lake—Moreno."

Floodlights came on as they stepped onto the wharf. Castillo saw a cabin cruiser, what looked like a thirty-five- or forty-foot Bertram sportfisherman tied to the pier, and had a mental image of the boat being hauled along some narrow provincial road on a trailer, dazzling the natives.

There were no lights on the boat, but as they approached the vessel he heard its exhaust burbling. As soon as they were on the boat, in the cockpit aft, the floodlights on the pier went on and the cabin lights on the boat illuminated.

Pevsner asked with a gesture whether Castillo wanted to go into the cabin or up to the flying bridge. Castillo opted for the flying bridge, despite the fact that the air was chilly. These were the Andes Mountains, and springtime would not come to Argentina for several weeks. But Castillo—perhaps as a reflex response—wanted to see what could be seen and began climbing the ladder fashioned of heavy-gauge aluminum tubing toward the flying bridge.

Max barked his protest at not being able to follow him up the ladder. Elena appeared at the cabin door and called to him. He looked to Castillo for guidance.

"Go with Elena," Castillo ordered, and after a moment's thought Max walked into the cabin.

The man who had been with Pevsner when Castillo had first seen them was at the helm, his hands on the controls. As soon as Pevsner was on the flying bridge, the boat began to move.

Set into the panel were radar and GPS screens, and the man used the latter to navigate.

Meaning, of course, that he's pretty sure nothing is out there, on the surface or below.

Wrong. I hear other engines.

A moment later, as Castillo's eyes adjusted to the darkness, he saw first the wake of a boat ahead of them and then the boat itself, a twenty-odd-foot inboard. The three men who had been waiting for them outside the Llao Llao were in it.

The small inboard boat picked up speed and began to turn, obviously intending to circle the sportfisherman.

"Nice boat, Alek," Castillo said, raising his voice over the sound of wind and the rumble of twin diesels. "How did you get it here?"

"By truck," Pevsner replied. "The first try was a disaster. They went off the road and turned over."

"Jesus!" Castillo said, sympathetically.

"Always look for the silver lining, friend Charley. It took another month to get another boat from Miami—this wouldn't fit in any of my airplanes—but I now have spare parts for everything but the hull."

Twenty minutes later, a light appeared almost dead ahead. The radar screen showed something that had to be a pier extending into the lake from the shore. The engines slowed. A minute later, floodlights on a pier came on and the inboard boat came out of the darkness and tied up. A twin of the Peugeot van at the Llao Llao was backed up onto the pier.

Three minutes later, they had tied up to the wharf and were in the van, which started down the pier. As soon as the vehicle reached the foot of the pier, the floodlights went off.

It was a five-minute drive along a steep, curving, gravel road, and then they passed through a gate in a ten-foot-tall stone wall and came to a stop before an imposing house.

Pevsner led them all inside.

Anna and the boys and the girl—*Elena, who is almost exactly as old as my son*—said a polite good night.

Castillo looked around. There was an enormous room off the entrance foyer. A crystal chandelier hung from what was probably a thirty-foot-high ceiling, illuminating a wall on which hung probably fifty stuffed deer and stag heads. On either side of a desk, two stuffed, snarling pumas faced each other.

This is familiar.

Why do I recognize it?

The memory bank produced an image of a large, fat, jowly man standing at the entrance to the room, dressed in lederhosen and a Bavarian hat with a pheasant tail feather stuck in it, and holding a bow and arrow.

I'll be goddamned!

Pevsner said in Russian: "My people will take care of your bags, friend Charley. Does the boy—*your communicator*—have to be present while we talk?"

"No, but he has to be close," Castillo answered in Russian. "And he'll need some place to set up his radio."

"Will he require help?"

Castillo shook his head.

"Then let's go in there," Pevsner said, pointing to the enormous room and taking Castillo's arm.

Castillo switched to German and asked, "Are you sure it will be all right with the *Reichsforst und Jägermeister*?"

"You are amazing," Pevsner said in Russian. "How are you familiar with that, with Carinhall?"

Castillo continued to speak German: "My grandfather had a book—a large, leather-bound book—that Göring gave him when he was a guest. I used to look at it when I was a kid."

"Your grandfather was a Nazi?"

"He was an Army officer who was badly wounded at Stalingrad and evacuated just before it fell. With Billy Kocian, incidentally. He told me Göring used to receive busloads of wounded senior officers at the place, and everyone got a book. The first picture inside, so help me God, was of Göring in lederhosen holding a bow and arrow.

"But, no, to answer your question, my grandfather was not a Nazi. My mother told me—when she knew she was dying; she said she thought I should know—that he was on the SS's list of those officers known to be associated with Claus von Stauffenberg in the bomb plot, and they were looking for him until the end of the war."

"What kind of a senior officer, Karl?" Pevsner said, now speaking German.

"Infantry, detailed to Intelligence. He was a lieutenant colonel at Stalingrad; they promoted him to colonel while he was recuperating."

"And now the German senior officer's grandson is an American senior officer detailed to Intelligence, and the descendants of the SS, now in the employ of the Russians, are looking for him in order to kill him. Blood really does run deep, doesn't it, friend Charley?"

Castillo realized that Pevsner's observation made him uncomfortable and wondered why.

"I think you mean, 'History does repeat itself, doesn't it?' " Castillo said, then went on quickly before Pevsner could reply: "I had a couple of days off one time in Berlin and went to see Carinhall. It's in Brandenburg, in the Schorfheide Forest—*was* there; Göring had the place blown up to keep the Russians from getting it. They did a good job. The gates are still there, but aside from that not much else is left."

A maid rolled a cart loaded with spirits and the necessary accoutrements into the room, cutting off the conversation. After she had positioned the cart, she looked at Pevsner.

"That will be all, thank you," Pevsner said, and waited to continue speaking until she had left them alone.

"Would you have me serve you, friend Charley? Or . . . ?"

"Wait on me, please. I find that flattering. Some of that Famous Grouse single-malt will do nicely, thank you very much."

Pevsner shook his head and turned to making the drinks.

Pevsner began: "The fellow who built this place—I bought it from his grandson—was German. Nothing much is known about him before he came here—and I have inquired and have had friends inquire. There is no record of a Heinrich Schmidt having ever lived in Dresden, which is where his Argentine Document of National Identity says he was born.

"Of course, the records may have been destroyed when Dresden was fire-bombed. What's interesting is that there is no record of his having immigrated to Argentina, or having been issued a DNI. Or of Herr Schmidt becoming an Argentine citizen. What I did learn was he bought this place—it was then four hundred sixteen hectares of forestland—and began construction of the house two months after it was alleged that a German submarine laden with cash and jewelry and gold had discharged its cargo near Mar del Plata and then scuttled itself at sea."

Pevsner handed Charley a glass, held his own up, and tapped rims.

"To friends you can really trust, friend Charley."

"Amen, brother. May their tribe increase."

"Unlikely, but a nice thought," Pevsner replied, took a sip, then went on: "Such a submarine was found eighteen months ago off Mar del Plata, incidentally. Probably just a coincidence."

"I know that story. There were three of them loaded with loot. One was known to have been sunk in the English Channel. The second is known to have made it here. I thought the third one just disappeared."

"It did. But—from what I have learned—only after it unloaded its cargo here in Argentina. Anyway, Herr Schmidt lived very quietly—one might say secretly—here with his family—a wife, a daughter, and a son—until his wife died. Then he passed on. Under Argentine law, property passes equally to children. The son—no one seems to know where he got the cash—bought out his sister's share, and she went to live in Buenos Aires, where she met and married an American, and subsequently moved to the United States.

"The son married an Argentine, and aside from shopping trips to Buenos Aires and Santiago, Chile—never to Europe, which I found interesting—lived here with his wife and their only son—the fellow from whom I bought the place—much as his father had done. I understand that the father—and, later, the son—were silent partners in a number of business enterprises here.

"When the son passed on, the widow did not want to live here alone, so she moved to Buenos Aires. The property sat unused for some years, until at her death it was finally put on the market and I bought it. Interestingly, they reduced the asking price considerably on condition I pay cash. More specifically, in gold. And that payment take place in the United Arab Emirates."

"What are you suggesting, Alek? That the guy who built this place was a Nazi?"

"I'm suggesting nothing, friend Charley. But I, too, noticed the architectural similarity to the reception hall at Carinhall, and went to some lengths to check that out. Between you and me, friend Charley, if Hermann Göring walked in the front door, he would think he was in Carinhall. I wouldn't be surprised if Herr Schmidt used the same architect. For that matter, the same drawings.

"That led me to look into which business associates of Göring—not party members or people like that—had gone missing during and after the war. No luck in making a connection with Herr Schmidt."

"What you are suggesting is that some Nazi big shot did in fact get away with running off to here."

"That has happened, you know. Just a year or so ago, they found that the owner of a hotel here in Bariloche, a man named Pribke, had been an SS officer deeply involved in the massacre at the Ardeatine Caves outside Rome. He was extradited to Italy. And actually, friend Charley, there is an interesting legend that one of the founders of this area was an American, from Texas, who was here because the authorities were looking for him at home."

"Butch Cassidy? The Sundance Kid?" Castillo asked, sarcastically.

Pevsner shook his head. "They were in Bolivia."

"I didn't know you were such a history buff, Alek."

Pevsner looked into Castillo's eyes for a long moment.

"What I am, friend Charley, is a man who would like to build a future for his children that would be unconnected with their father's past. I am more than a little jealous of Herr Schmidt."

Castillo looked at him but didn't reply.

Jesus Christ, he's serious.

Where's he going with this?

"You're a father, you will understand," Pevsner went on.

Actually, Alek, I'm having a hard time accepting that I am a father.

But, yeah. I understand.

"I think so," Castillo said.

"I never thought—I am a pragmatist—that I could do what Herr Schmidt did. These are different times. But I did think that I could perhaps do something like it. Did you see *The Godfather*?"

Now what?

Castillo nodded.

"I thought I could do something like young Michael Corleone wanted to do: Go completely legitimate. You remember that part?"

Castillo nodded again.

"I reasoned that if I gave up the more profitable aspects of my businesses—really gave them up—and maintained what you would call a low profile here—"

"I get the picture," Castillo interrupted.

"Not quite, I don't think, friend Charley. And I think it's important that you do."

"Go ahead."

"I have been using you since you came into my life, sometimes successfully, sometimes at a price. You recall how we met, Herr Gossinger?"

"On the Cobenzl in Vienna," Castillo said. "I thought you had stolen an airplane."

"You came very close to dying that night, friend Charley. When I heard that you wanted to interview me, I thought I would send a message to the press that looking into my affairs was not acceptable and was indeed very dangerous."

I believe him.

But why is he bringing that up now?

"But then Howard found out that you were really an American intelligence officer—Kennedy was very good at what he did; it's sad he turned out to be so weak and greedy—and you were using the name Karl Gossinger as a cover.

"I found that interesting. So I decided to meet you in person. And when you suggested that—I love this American phrase—we could scratch each other's back, I went along, to see where that would go—"

"Cutting to the chase," Castillo interrupted, "I would never have found that 727 without you. And I made good on my promise. I got the CIA and the FBI off your back."

"So you did, proving yourself intelligent, capable, and a man of your word."

"I'm going to blush if you keep this up."

"You'll remember certainly that the Southern Cone, especially Argentina, never came up in Vienna. You found the 727 where I told you it would be, in Central America."

"Yeah, I remember."

"When that transaction between us was over, I thought it had gone extraordinarily well. You got what you wanted. And I got what I wanted, the CIA and the FBI to leave me alone. Which was very important to me, as I was already establishing myself here and—being pragmatic—I knew that if they were still looking for me, they would have inevitably found me."

"And then I showed up here," Castillo said.

Pevsner nodded.

"Now that we both know who Howard Kennedy really was," Pevsner went on, "I don't think it is surprising that when you bumped into Howard in the elevator at the Four Seasons, his first reaction was to suggest to me that we had made a mistake in Vienna and it was now obviously the time to rectify that omission."

You mean, whack me.

"He suggested we could have our Russian friends do it, so there would be no connection with me. My initial reaction was to go along—I naturally thought that you had turned on me, and had come here to demand something of me.

"But, again, I was curious, and told Howard that that would wait until we learned what you wanted from me. So I told Howard to put a bag over your head and bring you out to my house in Buena Vista in Pilar. The bag offended you. I understood. So I told Howard to bring you anyway. You could be dealt with at Buena Vista.

"While I was waiting for you, I realized that I was really sorry I had misjudged you and regretted that I would have to deal with the problem. The strange truth seemed to be that I liked you more than I knew I should."

Giving me an "Indian beauty mark" in the center of my forehead with a small-caliber, soft-nose pistol bullet . . . that's how you were going to "deal with the problem."

"If you try to kiss me, Alek, I'll kick your scrotum over the chandelier."

"You are . . . impossible!" Pevsner said.

"But lovable."

Pevsner shook his head in disbelief.

"I often function on intuition. I knew when I looked into your eyes that you were telling me the truth about your reason for being in Argentina, that not only didn't you want anything from me but you had no idea I was in Argentina."

"Oh, but I did. I wanted to borrow your helicopter."

"That came later," Pevsner said, somewhat impatiently. "What happened at the time was that I decided we were friends. I have very few friends. Howard was a trusted employee—my mistake—but I never thought of him as my friend. I trust my friends completely. So I introduced you to my family. Anna liked you from the moment you met. So I decided to help you find—and possibly assist in getting back—the kidnapped wife of the American diplomat. Alfredo was then working for me; it wouldn't take much effort on my part.

"That night, I asked Anna whether she thought I had made a mistake about you. She thought not. She said, 'He's very much like you.' "

"I thought you said she liked me."

"Why do you always have to mock me?"

"Because it always pisses you off?"

Pevsner, smiling despite himself, shook his head.

"The next morning, you met Alfredo on your way to where Pavel Primakov's people had left Masterson's body."

"Whose people?"

"Colonel—I've heard he's actually a colonel general—Pavel Primakov is the FSB's senior man for South America. You did know they were responsible for the murder of Masterson, didn't you?"

"I had no proof and no names. But there was no question in Billy Kocian's mind that the FSB was responsible, trying to cover Putin's involvement in the Iraqi oil-for-food cesspool."

"The proof of that would seem to be what they tried to do with Kocian on the Szabadság híd, wouldn't you say?"

An attempt to kidnap—or, failing that, murder—Eric Kocian on the Liberty Bridge in Budapest had been thwarted by his bodyguard, Sándor Tor, and by Max, whose gleaming white teeth had caused severe muscular trauma to one of the triggermen's arms.

"Point taken," Castillo said.

"Where is the old man now?"

"In Washington."

"The FSB wants him dead—to get ahead of myself—about as much as they do you."

"The last time I talked to Billy, he complained that he was being followed around by deaf men wearing large hearing aids who kept talking into their lapels."

It took a moment for Pevsner to form the mental picture. Then he smiled. "Good men, I hope."

"The best. Secret Service. Most of them are on, or were on, the President's protection detail."

"Getting back where we were, friend Charley," Pevsner went on, "I asked Alfredo what he thought of you and his response was unusual. He said that he felt you were a lot more competent than your looks—and your behavior—suggested, and that, strangely, he felt you were one of the very few men he trusted instinctively.

"You proved your competence almost immediately by finding Lorimer on his estancia, getting there with your men before Major Vincenzo and his men did—and they had been looking for him for some time—and then, of course, by effectively dealing with Vincenzo."

"And losing one of my men in the process. And getting Alfredo wounded. Let's not forget that."

Pevsner ignored the comment.

"And then there are two more things."

"Keep it up," Castillo said, raising his glass in a mock toast, then taking a large sip of the single-malt. "Flattery will get you anywhere."

"What motivates you to always be a wise guy, friend Charley?" Pevsner asked, exasperated, but went on before Castillo could reply. "First, when Alfredo told you he thought I was trying to dispose of him, you took care of him and his family, knowing that was—if the situation was what you thought it was— in defiance of me.

"I was annoyed—very disappointed—with you at the time by that, and worse, by the way you threatened me with turning the CIA loose on me again unless I loaned you my helicopter for your Uruguayan operation. I don't like being threatened."

"Would you break out in tears if I told you that you have the reputation for being a ruthless sonofabitch?" Castillo said. "Helping Alfredo was a no-brainer for me, Alek. I knew that Alfredo hadn't betrayed you—"

"How did you know that?" Pevsner interrupted.

"We were talking a moment ago about there being men you instinctively trust. And you do have that ruthless sonofabitch reputation, Alek. Who should I have trusted? A man like Alfredo, or a man with a reputation like yours? Who, incidentally, had a known ruthless sonofabitch whispering in his ear?"

"And that brings us to that treasonous scum, doesn't it?"

"Does it?"

"A traitor who told my good friend Lieutenant Colonel Yevgeny Komogorov that I was going to meet with you in the Sheraton in Pilar, knowing full well—"

"Well, that didn't happen, did it?"

"If it were not for you, János and I would be dead."

"True."

"And I am grateful."

"Which gratitude you demonstrated by having Howard Kennedy and Viktor Zhdankov beaten to death—slowly, apparently—in Punta del Este. *After* I told you I wanted Kennedy alive so that I could ask him a couple of dozen questions."

"Howard knew too much about me for him to continue to live. And I could not permit it to get around that anyone who attempted to assassinate me would live very long."

After a moment, Castillo asked: "Are we getting near the end of our walk down memory lane, Alek? I'd really like to know who wants me whacked."

Pevsner ignored the question. He took a long, thoughtful sip of his drink.

"And now you are here, friend Charley, presumably to ask me something, or for something. I wanted you to know where you and I stand before you do that."

"Okay. Cutting to the chase, a DEA agent by the name of Timmons was kidnapped in Paraguay. So far as I know, he's still alive. As quietly as possible, I want him back. Alive."

" 'A DEA agent'?" Pevsner parroted, incredulously.

"A DEA agent named Timmons," Castillo repeated.

"How did you get involved in something like that?"

"How would you guess?"

"The President of the United States is involving himself personally in rescuing one drug enforcement agent?"

Castillo didn't answer.

"And how did you think I could help?"

"I thought maybe you could get word through mutual acquaintances to whoever is holding him that if Agent Timmons were to miraculously reappear unharmed, either in Asunción or somewhere in Argentina, I would not only be very happy but would be out of here within twenty-four hours. Otherwise, I'm going to have to come after him, which would make everybody unhappy, including me."

"I think I'm missing something here," Pevsner said. "You don't really think you can load a half-dozen men on my helicopter and just take this man away from these people?"

"Your helicopter is not in my contingency plans, Alek, but thank you just the same."

"Do you even have an idea who has this man? Or where?"

"I'm working on that."

"Or who they are? I don't think they're liable to be Bolivian drug dealers."

"Why would you say that?"

"My information is that Major Vincenzo—who was in charge of dealing with the drug people for Colonel Primakov—has already been replaced by another officer from the Cuban Dirección General de Inteligencia, as have the ex–Stasi people who you also eliminated in Uruguay."

"I'm not surprised."

"You can't be seriously considering dealing with people like that with a handful of men, no more than you can load on my helicopter."

"Weren't you listening when I said your helicopter is not in my contingency plans?"

"Then what?"

"Can you keep a secret, friend Alek?"

"You dare ask me that?"

"Yes or no?"

"My God, Charley!"

"If you'll give me Boy Scout's Honor"—he demonstrated what that was by holding up his right hand with the center three fingers extended; Pevsner looked at him in confusion—"that's Boy Scout's Honor, Alek. Very sacred. Meaning that you really swear what I'm about to tell you will not leave this room."

Castillo waved his right hand with the fingers extended and gestured with his left for Pevsner to make the same gesture. Pevsner looked at him in disbelief, then offered a somewhat petulant philosophic observation.

"Maybe you behave in this idiotic and childish manner to confuse people," he said, "to appear to be a fool so that no one will believe you're as competent as you are."

"Yes or no, Alek?"

Pevsner raised his right hand, extended three fingers, and waved it angrily in Castillo's face.

"Thank you," Castillo said, solemnly. "Alek, you're a betting man. Tell me, who do you think would come out on top between Señor Whateverhisname is—Vincenzo's replacement—and his stalwart men and two Delta Force A-Teams dropping in on them with four helicopters armed with 4,000-round-per-minute machine guns?"

Pevsner looked at him for a long moment.

"You're serious," Pevsner said. It was a statement, not a question.

"And other interesting lethal devices," Castillo continued. "Said force backed up by a hundred or so gendarmes argentinos who want not only to get back two of their number also kidnapped by these people, but also to seek righteous vengeance for two of their number who were murdered."

Pevsner looked at him intently.

Castillo nodded knowingly and went on: "And their orders will be—I know, because their commanding officer told me, and I believe him—to leave as many bodies scattered over the terrain as possible and then to blow everything up."

Pevsner looked at him curiously but didn't say anything.

Castillo answered the unspoken question.

"He wants to send the message that kidnapping or murdering members of the gendarmería is unacceptable behavior and is punished accordingly."

"Your president is going to do all this over one drug enforcement agent?"

"A lot of people, Alek, and I unequivocally count myself among them," Castillo said evenly, "believe in the work of these drug enforcement agents and do not consider them expendable."

"You're a soldier, friend Charley. You know men die in wars."

"We don't shoot our own men in the back. Or write them off when they're captured."

"My God, there's no way something like this could happen without it getting out."

"And that is why I was hoping you would pass the message through your mutual acquaintances to these bastards that I would much prefer that Timmons miraculously reappear unharmed instead of me having to come after him."

"That is wishful thinking. I am surprised you even suggested it."

"All they can say is 'no.' Give it a shot, please."

"I will not be talking to mutual acquaintances about this man," Pevsner said. "It would not only be a waste of my breath, but—and I'm surprised you didn't think of this, too—it would warn them that action is contemplated."

Castillo shrugged, hoping it suggested Pevsner's refusal didn't matter.

He instead was thinking, *Now what the hell do I do?*

Pevsner took a moment to drain his glass and think.

"You couldn't possibly get four helicopters and all the men you say you have into Argentina without at least the tacit approval of the Argentine government," Pevsner went on.

"The Argentine government knows nothing about this," Castillo said, "and if I can work it, never will. And, yes, I can. I already have most of the shooters in country; the rest will be here in a day or two; and so will the helicopters. I'm going to get Agent Timmons back. I hope I can do it without the Evil Leprechaun carrying out the bloodbath he wants, but if that happens . . ."

" 'The Evil Leprechaun'?"

"Reminding you that you're still bound by the Boy Scout's oath of secrecy, his name is Liam Duffy. He's a comandante in the Gendarmería Nacional. You know him?"

Pevsner shook his head.

"I think I'll have another drink, friend Charley. You?"

Castillo emptied his glass and held it out. "Please."

As Pevsner made the drinks, Castillo heard him say, as if he was thinking aloud, "I almost wish I had given you a beauty mark in Vienna."

"Oh, Alek, you don't mean that! You love me!"

A moment later, Pevsner turned and handed Castillo the drink.

"Unfortunately, I do," he said, sincerely. "But I never dreamed how expensive that would be."

"There's no reason you have to be involved in this," Castillo said, seriously. Pevsner snorted.

"You had better pray your Evil Leprechaun does what he says he wants to do," he said.

"Meaning what?"

"Meaning that's the only way your noble rescue mission can succeed without bringing yourself down—and me down with you."

"You're going to explain that, right?"

Pevsner raised his glass toward Castillo's and touched rims.

"Oh, God, friend Charley. You do cause me problems."

"That's what friends are for, right?"

Pevsner shook his head and exhaled audibly.

"You're sure that the Argentine government is not involved? Either with you? Or that they're not winking at this man Duffy?"

"The Argentine government has no idea what I plan. And I don't think they know what Duffy plans," Castillo said.

"Why do you say that?"

"When I got here, he had men waiting for me. He knew I was coming, which means he has someone in the U.S. embassy in Asunción."

"Someone in your embassy knew you were coming?"

"That's another whole story."

"I should know it, if I'm to help," Pevsner said.

That's really none of his business.

But why not tell him?

Maybe he can fill in the blanks.

"As I understand it, Alek, the drugs are moved to the United States with fresh meat shipped from Ezeiza by air to Jamaica—maybe on your airplanes, although I don't expect you to fess up about that."

"My airplanes make a number of such flights, sometimes every other day," Pevsner said, somewhat indignantly. "But the pilots will not take off until they have in their hand documents from Argentine customs stating that the sealed and locked containers they are carrying have passed customs inspection. There may well be drugs in those containers, but I don't know about it, and neither does anyone who works for me. And my people know what happens to people who do what I have told them not to do."

"Okay. I believe you"—*Strangely enough, I do, especially the part about what happens to people who do what you've told them not to*—"but in Jamaica, they are loaded aboard cruise ships and smuggled into the United States from the cruise ships. The CIA station chief in the Asunción embassy, and maybe the head man from the DEA, has been setting up an operation to seize the cruise ships under international law, which permits the seizure of ships whose owners collude in the shipment of drugs—"

"You believe this story?" Pevsner interrupted.

"What I know is that a CIA guy heard I was being sent down here to grab Timmons and looked me up to tell me—Timmons be damned—that he would be unhappy if my operation interfered with his."

"And you were sent down here anyway? One drug agent is worth more than seizing a cruise ship?"

"To answer the second question first, yeah, Alek, in my book one drug agent is worth more than a cruise ship. And, what's really interesting here, the director of the CIA and his deputy don't know anything about the ship-seizing operation."

"I find that hard to believe."

"I believe that. But that operation smells somehow."

"You don't have any idea what's going on?"

"No. But to get back to the Evil Leprechaun: I told you the only way that he could have known I was coming down here was that he has somebody in the Asunción embassy close to either the CIA station chief or the head of the DEA there. There's no question in my mind that the CIA guy who came to me in Washington—after I told him I didn't care about his operation; I was going to get Timmons back—warned the CIA guy in Asunción that I was coming."

"With the Delta Force people and the helicopters?"

Castillo shook his head. "He didn't know that. And I don't think he's found out. But the Evil Leprechaun told me he had word that there were people intent on whacking me and the people with me. I believe him."

"You don't mean your own CIA people?"

Castillo shrugged, meaning he didn't know.

"Duffy tried to bluff me," Castillo went on, "to get back to your original, original question. He threatened to have me kicked out of the country within twenty-four hours unless I put myself and my assets under his command."

"He knew about the helicopters and—what did you call them?—'the shooters'?"

Castillo nodded as he sipped his single-malt.

"He didn't then," he explained. "I told him this morning, after I called his bluff. He backed down. I don't think he would have backed down from his threat if the government—hell, even his boss in the gendarmería—knew about the massacre he's planning."

"Why did you tell him anything?"

"Because I need his help in getting the helicopters up there around Asunción where I can stage them, and to find out where these people have Timmons."

"You trust him?"

"Not very much. But as long as he thinks I'm on board to get his men back and I'm willing to go along with his plan to shoot everybody in sight and let the Lord sort them out, I don't think he's going to cause me any problems. I left him with one of the A-Team commanders, who'll warn me if he's about to go out of control."

"What have you got against letting him do what he wants to do?"

"I'm an Army officer, Alek, for one thing, not the avenging hand of God. For another, if I let him do that, and this operation blows up in my face, they call that murder."

"Letting him do what he wants is the only chance you have to get away with this, friend Charley."

"Unless you can get these people to let Timmons go."

"I've told you that that is not going to happen. These people are making a point. They can kidnap people. They're not going to turn this fellow loose because you threaten them. And if you just drop in and get him, leaving their men alive—and their refining facility and warehouse full of drugs intact—they would have to send another message. On the other hand, if you—or this fellow Duffy—leave bodies all over the terrain, to use your phrase, and blow up their warehouse and refinery, what do you think will happen?"

"I think you're about to tell me."

"There's no way that could be kept a secret. The word will get out—Duffy's gendarmes will talk. More important, Duffy will want it to get out, to take credit; he got the people who killed and kidnapped his gendarmes. And that will leave the Argentine government with the choice of trying Duffy for murder or saying, 'Congratulations, Comandante, for dealing so effectively with these criminals. It is to be regretted, of course, that so many of them died, but those who live by the sword, etcetera, etcetera. . . .'"

"What about my involvement?"

"Who's going to believe the United States government sent Delta Force shooters and helicopters to carry them down here to rescue *one* ordinary drug agent? I find that hard to believe myself, even coming from you, friend Charley."

Castillo looked at him with a sinking feeling in his stomach.

"All you have to do is get out of wherever they're holding your man as soon as you have him," Pevsner said, then added, as if he had read Castillo's mind, "You know I'm right, friend Charley."

Castillo still didn't reply.

"And Colonel Primakov is wise enough to take his losses; he's too smart to attempt retribution against what he will believe is the Argentine government. He'll lay low for a while, and then start up again. He may even call off the people he sent looking for you. After all, you'll no longer be here, will you?"

"Shit," Castillo said.

"What's next for you?" Pevsner asked, the question implying that a discussion had been held and a conclusion drawn.

"I'm going to Asunción in the morning," Castillo said. "To see what I can find out about who in the embassy ordered me whacked. And I want to see what I can find out about this scheme to seize cruise ships. There's something about it that smells."

"Is there an expression in English to the effect that wise men leave sleeping dogs lie? That's really none of your business, is it, friend Charley?"

Castillo looked at him and thought, *And he's right about that, too.*

"No, it isn't any of my business. Neither, I suppose, is finding out who in the embassy wants me whacked. Unless, of course, they succeed before I can get out of here."

[THREE]
La Casa el Bosque
San Carlos de Bariloche
Río Negro Province, Argentina
0730 11 September 2005

Castillo, Munz, János, and Pevsner were standing on the steps of the house smoking cigars and holding mugs of coffee steaming in the morning cold. Max was gnawing on an enormous bone.

They had begun smoking the cigars at the breakfast table but had been ordered out of the house by Anna's raised eyebrow when Sergei, the youngest boy, had sneezed.

"He and Aleksandr both have colds, poor things," she had said, and then raised her eyebrow directly at her husband.

"Gentlemen, why don't we have our coffee on the verandah?" Pevsner had suggested.

Once there, he had said, not bitterly, "There is a price one must pay for children. It generally has to do with giving up something one is fond of. True, friend Charley?"

"Absolutely," Castillo agreed.

I think.

I have been a father about a week, and I'm still not familiar with the price . . . or the rules.

He heard a cry, a strange one, of a bird and looked around to find the bird. He didn't see the bird, but as he looked up he saw a legend carved into the marble above the massive doors.

"I'll be a sonofabitch," he said, and read it aloud: "House in the Woods."

"That's what Schmidt called it," Pevsner said.

"It's what our family calls the house in Germany, Haus im Wald," Castillo said.

"Where you grew up?"

Castillo nodded.

"Don't tell me it looks like Carinhall."

"No, it looks like a factory," Castillo said. "Or maybe a funeral home."

"Bad memories?"

"Quite the contrary. Good memories, except when my grandfather and uncle killed themselves on the autobahn, and then my mother developed pancreatic cancer a couple of months later. Haus im Wald was—is—ugly, but it's comfortable. And interesting. From the dining room window, I could look out and see the Volkspolitzei—and every once in a while, a real Russian soldier—running up and down the far side of the fence that cut across our property, and the stalwart troops of the 14th Armored Cavalry Regiment running up and down on our side of the fence. I decided right off that I would rather be an American."

"You didn't know you were an American?" Pevsner asked, confused.

"Not until I was twelve. I had a number of surprises in my twelfth year."

"But your son doesn't live there? You said something about his living with his mother."

"I didn't know I had a son until last week, Alek."

Castillo met Munz's eyes.

There's more than idle curiosity in those eyes.

Jesus, did he make the connection with the pictures? Does he know?

He can't know, but he damned sure suspects.

After a perceptible pause, Pevsner said, "And you'd rather not talk about it?"

"I didn't know I had a son until one of my men gave me the picture I showed you last night. The boy doesn't know about me, about our connection."

"A youthful indiscretion, friend Charley?"

"That's what they call a massive understatement," Castillo said. "His mother—five days before she married a West Point classmate of mine—had so much to drink that what began as a deep-seated feeling of revulsion toward me was converted to irresistible lust."

"But she must know . . ."

"I don't know if she does or not. I'm sure her husband doesn't, and I'm certain Randy, the boy, doesn't. The problem is her father does, I'm sure. He flew with my father in the Vietnam War—was flying with my father when he was killed. Randy looks just like my father."

"He has your eyes," Pevsner said. "The photo was clear."

Castillo nodded. "Worse, I'm sure my grandmother knows. For the same reason. The eyes. She took one look at my eyes in a picture—and I was then a twelve-year-old, blue-eyed, blond-headed Aryan—and announced that I was my father's son. Subsequently confirmed by science, of course, but she knew when she saw my eyes."

"Karl," Munz said. "This is none of my business . . ."

"But?"

"There is a picture of the boy at the Double-Bar-C. On a table next to your grandmother's chair in the living room. With pictures of your father and your cousin and you, all as boys. The boy looks like your father as a boy. I asked who he was, and she said that he was General Wilson's grandson and told me who General Wilson was, and then she said, 'He's an adorable child. I often wish he was my grandson.' And there were tears in her eyes, Karl." He paused. "She knows."

Castillo shook his head.

"How terrible for you!" Pevsner said. "What are you going to do?"

"I don't have a fucking clue, Alek."

Pevsner gripped Castillo's shoulder firmly in what Castillo recognized as genuine sympathy.

The left of the double doors to the house opened and Corporal Lester Bradley came out. He held the radio handset.

"Saved by the Marine Corps once again," Castillo said.

"Sir?"

"What have you got, Lester?"

"Colonel Torine, sir. He's on the *Gipper*."

Castillo gestured for him to give him the handset. The legend on the small screen flashed: COL TORINE ENCRYPTION ENABLED.

"And how are things on the high seas, Jake?" Castillo said into the handset.

"You wouldn't believe how big this mobile airfield is, Charley."

"And how are you getting along with the admiral?"

"I'm going to have breakfast with him shortly. He's a little confused."

"How's that?"

"He somehow had the idea that I was bringing a letter to him from Ambassador Montvale, for whom I work."

"And you didn't have a letter? I guess you talked to Miller?"

"I seem to have misplaced the letter, but I didn't want to admit that to the admiral. But I did clear up his misunderstanding about who I work for."

"How'd you do that?"

"I told him that I worked for you. And who you work for. And under what authority."

"That was necessary?"

"I thought so, Charley. Wrong move?"

"I guess it couldn't be helped. Did he believe you?"

"Not until I suggested he could get that confirmed at the source."

"You called the President?"

"I got as far as getting the White House switchboard on here. When the admiral heard the White House operator say, 'Good evening, Colonel Torine,' the admiral said he didn't think it would be necessary to disturb the President."

"Good move, Jake."

"I also told the admiral my orders were to keep you advised of our position every four hours. Aside from coming right out and telling the admiral not to launch the birds—which I don't think Montvale would dare do—I think that's the end of the Montvale problem."

"And there goes the star he promised you for changing sides, Jake."

"Yeah, well, what the hell."

"Jake, I want you to take a close look at the pilots."

"What will I be looking for?"

"Any of them who would be uncomfortable with a really dirty operation."

"Ouch! That's likely?"

"It looks that way. I don't want you to explain the operation and then ask for volunteers. I'll do that here. But if there's somebody who strikes you as . . . being reluctant . . . to do what has to be done, just leave him on the carrier."

"These are all 160th pilots, Charley. I don't think I'll find anybody . . ."

"You never know. I knew a 160th guy who turned in his suit and became a Catholic priest after Kosovo."

"Anything else?"

"Don't put the Argentine insignia on the birds until the last minute; this operation still may get called off."

"Done."

"And keep me posted."

"Will do."

"Give the admiral my regards when you have breakfast," Castillo said. "Out."

Castillo held out the handset to Bradley, who didn't make any effort to take it.

"Sir," Corporal Lester Bradley said, "Mr. Darby wants to talk to you. I'll have to set that up at the console. Just watch the legend, sir, until you see his name."

Castillo nodded, and Lester trotted back into the house.

He held the handset in his palm until the legend read ALEX DARBY ENCRYPTION ENABLED.

"What's up, Alex?"

"D'Elia had an interesting telephone call from some friends vacationing in Paraguay."

"Really?"

"They asked him to send them a couple of dozen golf balls."

"You don't say?"

"They said they were completely out, and they'd had to spend a lot of time looking for balls in the rough, and although they'd found a bunch they found only one really good one. They said they were watching that one very carefully."

"Bingo!"

"I don't see what else they could mean, Charley."

"Neither do I."

"You going over there?"

"Just as soon as I can get to the airport."

"When you find out for sure, do you want me to tell the Irishman?"

"I'll tell you that when I call from there."

"Pevsner been any help?"

"In a manner of speaking. I'll explain that later. Thanks, Alex."

"Talk to you soon, Charley."

Bradley came back onto the verandah.

"You want to speak to anyone else, sir?"

"Call Major Miller and see what the schedule for the Lorimers coming down is. And then break it down, Lester."

"Aye, aye, sir."

Castillo looked at Munz and Pevsner.

"Since you could only hear one side of that conversation, I suspect you're curious."

" 'Bingo!'?" Munz said.

"The shooters in Paraguay have apparently found where they've got Timmons," Castillo said. "Or that's what I think a message about golf balls meant. We'll know as soon as we get there."

" 'A really dirty operation'?" Munz then asked.

"Alek says he thinks the only way we can get out of here with Timmons without appearing on the front page of *The New York Times* and other newspapers around the world is to let the Evil Leprechaun do what he wants to do."

Munz considered that.

"I know you don't like that, Karl, but I'm afraid Alek is right."

"Why did I think you were going to say that?" Castillo said. "Okay, thank you for your hospitality, Alek, and will you now arrange for us to get to the airport?"

"You're all going to Asunción?"

"Yeah, why?"

"Well, I'm going to Buenos Aires, and if someone has to go there, I could take him in the Lear."

"Why are you going to Buenos Aires?" he asked, greatly concerned.

"To see what I can turn up that might be helpful to you. I've got a good deal at stake here if you can't do what you want to do."

"Just don't do anything to help unless you tell me first. Okay, Alek?"

"I wouldn't dream of it," Pevsner said, mockingly.

"I mean that, Alek."

"I know, friend Charley," Pevsner said, seriously.

XIII

[ONE]
Silvio Pettirossi International Airport
Asunción, Paraguay
1830 11 September 2005

It was winter here, and night came early, making moot Castillo's worry that maybe he should have made a low-level reconnaissance anyway, even after learning the shooters had located where Timmons was being held.

I wouldn't have been able to see anything, even if I knew what I was looking for.

It had been a long flight; they had been in the air almost eight hours, with an hour and a half on the ground at the Taravell airport in Córdoba, where they'd gone through Argentine customs and immigration.

There almost had been a dogfight at Córdoba. Max had taken an instant dislike to a large black Labrador retriever—a drug sniffer for the Policía Federal—when the Lab had put his curious nose in the Commander the moment the door opened—and found himself facing a visibly belligerent Max determined to protect his airplane.

After considering his situation for perhaps twenty seconds, the Lab concluded that there was only one wise course of action to take when faced with an apparently infuriated fellow canine twice his size.

The Lab took it . . . and rolled over on his back, putting his paws in the air in surrender.

Max examined the Lab for a moment, gave him a final growl, then exited the aircraft and trotted—*Somewhat arrogantly,* Castillo thought—to the nose gear of the Commander for what had become his routine postlanding bladder voiding.

The Lab's handler was mortified. Thus Castillo was not surprised when he and his fellow officers subjected the cabin and the baggage compartment to a very thorough inspection. As they were doing it, however, Munz softly told him it was probably routine and they could expect a similar close inspection when they landed in Asunción.

"A lot of drugs are brought across the border in light aircraft like this one," Munz said. "They don't take off or land at airports with their contraband, of course, but they sometimes—when empty—put down at airfields like this one to take on fuel or whatever. Sometimes, the sniffer dogs pick up traces of heroin or cocaine or marijuana, and that lets the police know that the aircraft is involved in the trade and they thereafter try to keep an eye on it. It's about as effective as trying to empty the River Plate with a spoon, but . . ."

He shrugged, and Castillo nodded.

They landed at Pettirossi International immediately after an Aerolíneas Argentinas 727 set down.

"That's the last flight today from Buenos Aires," Munz said. "And it will return. What that means is we're going to have to wait until the authorities deal with both flights before they turn their sniffer dogs loose on this airplane."

"Wonderful! More delay," Castillo said, disgustedly.

Standing on the tarmac waiting for the Paraguayan officials, Castillo saw on the terminal building that it was possible to still make out the lettering of AEROPORTO PRESIDENTE GEN. STROESSNER under the fresh paint of its new name.

For some reason, the wait wasn't as long as they feared. They got lucky.

And when they finally made it through customs and were in the unsecured area of the terminal, they saw that a van with HOTEL RESORT CASINO YACHT & GOLF CLUB PARAGUAY painted on its side was waiting for guests.

"Alfredo, why don't you take Lester out there, get us rooms, and—without asking—see if you can't find my shooters? I'm ashamed to admit I don't have their names, which they almost certainly aren't using anyway."

When Castillo arrived with Lieutenant Lorimer, Sergeant Mullroney, and Max at the U.S. embassy at almost eight o'clock, an officious Paraguayan security guard at the well-lit gate informed Castillo and his party that the embassy had closed for the day.

"Get the Marine guard out here," Castillo ordered, angrily, in English.

As Castillo listened to the security guard speak into his radio in Spanish, he pretended not to understand the unkind things the guard said under his breath about Americans in general and this one in particular.

The Marine guard who came to the guardhouse several minutes later recognized Lorimer.

"Hello, Lieutenant," he said.

"We need to get inside."

"I can let you in, but I can't let your friends in—"

"We're American," Castillo offered.

"—without getting one of the officers to pass them in."

"Well, then, Sergeant," Castillo said. "Get an officer. Preferably Mr. Crawford."

The Marine guard now examined him more closely.

"Mr. Crawford, sir? Our commercial attaché?"

"Mr. Jonathon Crawford, whatever his title," Castillo said.

"May I ask who you are and the nature of your business with Mr. Crawford, sir?"

Castillo handed him the credentials identifying him as a supervisory agent of the United States Secret Service.

The sergeant examined the credentials very carefully.

"And this gentleman, sir?"

"He is Detective Sergeant Mullroney of the Chicago Police Department. Show the sergeant your tin, Sergeant."

Mullroney did so. The sergeant examined the leather folder carefully and then handed it back.

"I guess I can let you gentlemen in as far as Station One, sir," the sergeant said. "I mean to the building, but not inside. I'll call Mr. Crawford from there, sir."

"Thank you."

"But you can't bring that dog into the building, sir."

"Why don't we take Max as far as Station One and then see what Mr. Crawford has to say about that?"

"I don't know, sir . . ."

"That was more in the nature of an order, Sergeant," Lorimer said, "than a question."

"Yes, sir," the Marine sergeant said.

There was a row of chrome-frame plastic seats in the lobby of the building, and two sand-topped, chrome-can ashtrays despite the ABSOLUTELY NO SMOKING! signs on two walls.

Mr. Jonathon Crawford, "commercial attaché" of the embassy, appeared thirty minutes later. He was a nondescript man in his fifties whose only distinguishing characteristic was his eyes. They were deep and intelligent.

"You wanted to see me?" he asked, without any preliminaries.

"If you're Crawford, I do," Castillo said, and handed him the Secret Service credentials.

Crawford examined them and looked at Mullroney.

"Show Mr. Crawford your badge, Charley," Castillo said, then turned back to Crawford. "I think you know Lieutenant Lorimer?"

Crawford examined the credentials and handed them back, but said nothing to—or about—Lorimer.

"This wouldn't have kept until morning? I have guests at my house."

"If it would have kept till morning, I would have come in the morning," Castillo said.

"That your dog?"

Castillo nodded.

"No dogs in the embassy, sorry."

"What do you want me to do, Crawford, call Frank Lammelle—or, for that matter, John Powell—and tell him that you find it impossible to talk to me right now because you have guests and don't like dogs?"

"I don't think I like your attitude, Castillo."

"Well, then we're even, aren't we? I don't like being kept waiting for half an hour while you schmooze your guests and finish your drink. Frank sent you a heads-up that I was coming. You should have been expecting me."

Crawford looked at him a long moment with tight lips.

"Make a note in your log, Sergeant," Crawford ordered, "that—over my objections—Mr. Castillo insisted on bringing his dog into the embassy."

Then he gestured for the sergeant to open the door. There came the sound of a solenoid buzzing, and then Crawford pushed the door open.

He led them to an elevator, waved them onto it, then punched in a code on a control panel to make the elevator operable. It rose two floors. He led them down a corridor to an unmarked door—also equipped with a keypad—punched in the code, and then pushed open that door.

They entered an outer office, and he led them through that to a larger office and then gestured for them to sit in the leather-upholstered chairs.

"I'm sorry I kept you waiting," he said. "The cold truth of the matter is my wife flipped when I told her I had to come down here. I was not in a very good mood. Can we start all over?"

"My name is Castillo, Mr. Crawford. How are you tonight?"

"Thanks. I think I just told you how I am. How are you, Lorimer?"

"I'm fine, thank you."

"You're now working for the Office of Organizational Analysis, I understand. What's that all about? What *is* the Office of Organizational Analysis?"

Castillo answered for him.

"And that transfer, Mr. Crawford," he concluded, "was already in the works when Special Agent Timmons went missing," he said. "I brought Lorimer with me because he had been stationed here. I've never been in Paraguay."

"Do you speak Spanish?"

Castillo nodded. "I'm a Texican."

"A what?"

"A Texan with Mexican roots. I speak Mexican Spanish."

I also can pass myself off as a Porteño, and after I'm here three days, people will swear that I sound just like whatever they call the natives here. Asunciónites?

But the less qualified you think I am, the better.

"I heard you were coming here, Mr. Costello . . ."

"Castillo," Castillo corrected him.

"*Castillo.* Sorry. But not from Deputy Director Lammelle. Actually, it was back-channel."

"You want to call Lammelle and check my bona fides before this goes any further?"

"No. I understand you're here officially; there's no need to bother Deputy Director Lammelle. But I don't know exactly why you're here."

"There's unusual interest in Special Agent Timmons. My boss sent me down to find out what I can."

"And your boss is?" Crawford asked, casually.

"And to report to him what I find out," Castillo went on.

"You didn't say who your boss is."

"No, I didn't."

"Are those Secret Service credentials the real thing?"

"About as real as your 'commercial attaché' diplomatic carnet. If somebody were to call the Secret Service, they would be told there is indeed a Supervisory Special Agent by the came of Castillo."

"Exactly what is it that you want from me, Mr. Castillo?"

"I want you to give Lieutenant Lorimer and Sergeant Mullroney access to all information regarding this incident, and that means I want them to have access to your people. Alone."

"What exactly is Sergeant Mullroney's role in this?"

"Personal and professional. Professionally, he works drugs in Chicago. Personally, he's Special Agent Timmons's brother-in-law."

"That's not a problem. But is that all?"

"That's all I'm going to do for now," Castillo said. "I'll write my report, then see if these people turn him loose or not. Or if he dies of an overdose."

"Well, I don't think that's going to happen. Timmons will more than likely be turned loose. Maybe tonight. Maybe two weeks from now. But, for the sake of knowing . . . what do you plan to do if he isn't released?"

"Bring some people and other things down here to help you get him back."

"Other things? For example?"

"For example, a couple of helicopters. Ambassador Montvale is working on that now."

Crawford's eyebrows went up. "The Paraguayan government is not going to let you try to get Timmons back," he said, "much less bring people and helicopters into the country to do it."

"Ambassador Montvale is a very persuasive man," Castillo said. "And, besides, that wasn't my decision. I will just implement it."

"How are you going to do that?"

"I'm sure I will be told what to do, and how, and when."

"I understand you met Milton Weiss," Crawford said.

Castillo nodded, then said, "Is that who gave you the back-channel heads-up about us coming down here?"

Crawford nodded.

"Milton," he said, "led me to believe he let you know a little about an interesting operation we're planning here."

"Grabbing the cruise ships?" Castillo said.

Crawford didn't reply.

"Well," Castillo went on, "I told Weiss I was not a DEA agent and my paycheck doesn't come from Langley, so that was none of my business, and I would—if possible—stay out of your way so I won't compromise your operation."

" 'If possible'?"

"I'm not prescient, Crawford. I don't know what my orders will be if Timmons isn't turned loose and turns up dead. At that point, someone will decide what's important and I'll be told what to do. If this cruise-ship-grabbing operation of yours is so important, maybe you should start doing more than you have so far to get Special Agent Timmons back."

Crawford sat up in his chair.

"Just who the hell do you think you are, Castillo, to waltz in here and question what I've done or not done?"

Castillo did not immediately reply. He thought, *That took me a little longer than I thought it would to make him lose his temper.*

"Like you," Castillo then said, "I'm just a simple servant of the public, hoping I can make it to retirement. So tell me, what *have* you done, Crawford, to get Timmons back? Anything at all? Or have you placed your faith in the honesty and competence of the Paraguayan law enforcement community?"

With a little luck, he will now say, "Fuck you, Castillo."

Crawford glowered at him for a long moment, then said, "Is there anything else I can do for you tonight, Mr. Castillo? I really have to get back to my guests."

"By ten o'clock tomorrow morning, Crawford, I need a list of the things you've done to get Special Agent Timmons back. My boss said I was to get that to him as soon as possible. Give it to Lorimer."

Maybe now a "Fuck you!" or a "Kiss my ass!"?

"Very well, Mr. Castillo," Crawford said. "But you'll really have to excuse me now."

He stood up and smiled, then gestured toward the door.

"I'll have to check you out with the Marine guard," he said.

[TWO]
Hotel Resort Casino Yacht & Golf Club Paraguay
Avenida del Yacht 11
Asunción, Paraguay
2120 11 September 2005

Just as the elevator door was closing, a tall, good-looking, olive-skinned young man stopped the door and got on. He wore his shiny black hair long, so that it covered his shirt collar. And on his hairy chest—his yellow shirt was unbuttoned almost to the navel—there gleamed a gold medallion the size of a saucer.

"Thank you ever so much," he said, smiling broadly. "*Muy amable.*"

Castillo, who had automatically classified the Spanish as Mexican, managed a smile, but not without effort.

I don't feel very amiable, asshole.

The last thing I need right now is a Mexican drunk breathing charm and booze fumes all over me.

The door closed and the elevator started to rise.

As Pevsner had done in Llao Llao, the Mexican manipulated the control panel and stopped the elevator.

Castillo felt a rush of adrenaline, and then the Mexican drunk said in English, "Welcome to the Hotel Resort Casino Yacht and Golf Club Paraguay, Colonel. Master Sergeant Gilmore, sir."

"*Gilmore?*" Castillo asked, incredulously.

"Yes, sir. My mother's the Texican. She married a gringo. If the colonel will give me a look at his room key?"

Castillo held it up.

"Sir, if the colonel will wait until they deliver his luggage, and then flick his lights three times, and then leave the lights off, repeat off, and unlock the balcony sliding door, Technical Sergeant Bustamante and I will be able to report properly without attracting attention."

"You don't just want to walk down the corridor and knock on the door? Who are we hiding from?"

"There have been some unsavory characters, Colonel, who seem fascinated with Bustamante and myself. Bolivians, maybe. Maybe Cubans. But what would Cubans be doing here?"

"I'll explain that when you surreptitiously appear in my room. But give me a couple of minutes. I've got some people with me. I want them to be there."

"Yes, sir. Corporal Bradley told me."

"He did?"

"Mean little sonofabitch, isn't he?" Master Sergeant Gilmore said, admiringly. "I was having a surreptitious look at what looked like an AFC case in his room, when all of a sudden there he was, with his .45 aimed at my crotch. He got me hands down, Colonel. It was five minutes before he'd let me get off the floor. If I hadn't been able to tell him who Sergeant Major Jack Davidson was, I'd probably still be there."

"Never judge a book by its cover, Sergeant. You might want to write that down."

"Should I call him and the German guy and tell them you want to see them right now?"

Castillo nodded.

"And I'll call Lorimer and Mullroney," Castillo said.

"Okay," Castillo ordered when everyone was in the room, "unlock the sliding door, then flick the lights three times and leave them off."

Then he firmly grasped Max's collar. He didn't want to surprise the shooters when they came into the darkened suite.

"I'll be curious to see how they do this, Charley," Munz said as the lights blinked. "These places are supposed to be burglar-proof. And we're on the third floor."

"I have no idea," Castillo confessed.

Corporal Bradley's voice in the darkness explained, "They're using a rubber-covered chain with loops every foot or so for handholds. And it has a collapsible grappling hook at the end, sir. Sergeant Gilmore showed me when he came to my room. I'd never seen a system like that before."

Ninety seconds later, there was the sound of the sliding door opening and then closing.

"The drapes are in place," Master Sergeant Gilmore said. "Somebody can hit the lights."

When the lights came on, Castillo didn't see any kind of a chain on either Gilmore or Technical Sergeant Bustamante, who looked like Captain D'Elia's younger brother.

"You used a chain, Sergeant Gilmore?"

Gilmore pulled a thin chain from a deep pocket on the hip of his trousers.

"Clever," Castillo said.

"Well, you know how it is when you're in the stockade, Colonel. You've got nothing to do but think up things like this."

Castillo laughed.

The Army's elite Delta Force—and some other, even more secret units—were housed at Fort Bragg, North Carolina, in what at one time had been the post stockade.

"Isn't a stockade a military prison?" Sergeant Mullroney asked.

"Yes, it is, Mullroney," Castillo said, mock seriously. "It's where we keep people like these two chained up when they're not working."

He went to Bustamante and offered his hand.

"My name is Castillo, Sergeant. We're glad to have you."

"I'm glad to be here, sir."

"That's because you don't know what's going to happen," Castillo said.

"Can I ask another dumb question?" Mullroney asked.

Castillo thought, *Not "no" but "hell no,"* and was about to say exactly that when Mullroney asked anyway.

"Maybe I'm out of line, Colonel, but was pissing off that CIA guy the way you did smart?"

You bet your ass you're out of line.

Who the hell do you think you are, calling me on that?

But, actually . . .

"Actually, I'm glad you brought that up. What I was trying to do with Crawford was make him think I'm a wiseass out of my league." *Much like you, Mullroney.* "I think I managed to do that, but I couldn't make him lose his temper, and I tried. Okay?"

Mullroney nodded.

Castillo looked at the others and went on: "Crawford is dangerous. I still don't know what he's up to, but he's not on our side. Everybody got that?"

There were nods.

"Okay, the burglars are Sergeants Bustamante and Gilmore, from Captain D'Elia's team. This is Colonel Munz, who works for me; Lieutenant Lorimer, who also works for me; and Sergeant Mullroney, who is a Chicago cop and Timmons's brother-in-law. And Corporal Bradley, our designated marksman."

Castillo looked at Gilmore.

"So what have you got?"

"I don't know if it's what you're looking for, Colonel," Gilmore said. "But there is a very strange setup on the river a couple of miles downstream from the hotel. You have a laptop, sir?"

"What are you going to do, Google Earth it?"

"Yes, sir. I've got the coordinates on this, sir." He held up a USB flash memory device that recorded data. It was the size of a small disposable butane lighter. "I thought I'd start with the big picture."

Within a minute, everyone was looking at the laptop computer screen, which now showed a composite aerial photograph of the river south of Asunción as it would appear from an airplane at five thousand feet.

"What exactly are we looking at?" Castillo asked.

"I finally learned how to add my own data to the imagery, Colonel. Hold one, sir."

He plugged the flash memory device into one of the USB ports on the side of the laptop. An icon of it immediately popped up on the screen. Thirty seconds later, after he touched several keys, a more or less circular ring of tiny flashing spots appeared on the map on the Paraguayan side of the river.

"I still don't know what I'm looking at," Castillo said.

"Bustamante found it, sir. We were fishing."

"Fishing?"

"Yes, sir, I even caught a couple," Gilmore said with a grin, then sighed. "We had covered *a lot* of water before we came across it. We noticed something wasn't right."

"How's that?" Castillo said.

"There was something about the riverbank, sir," Bustamante offered.

"What?" Castillo said, gesturing *Give it to me* with the fingers of his right hand.

Bustamante, anticipating the reaction his answer was going to cause, shrugged. "The grass was too green, Colonel. Twelve feet or so of green grass. The rest was all brown."

"Suggesting?" Castillo asked.

"I didn't know, sir. Maybe it was near a stream. Maybe somebody was watering it. But I figured it was worth a look, so we took one as soon as it was dark."

"How?

"*He* swam, sir," Gilmore said.

"You brought wet suits with you?"

"No, sir. We have night goggles."

"It was a little chilly," Bustamante admitted.

"Why Bustamante?"

"He found the green fucking grass, Colonel," Gilmore said, reasonably.

"And what did you find?"

"It was planted," Bustamante said. "Plastic boxes, maybe three feet by a foot, four of them, and all mounted on a heavy timber, so they could be moved out of the way and put back easy. I figured somebody wanted access to the river and didn't want anybody to see it."

"And farther inland?"

"Well, there was also a motion sensor on the boxes of grass—I almost set it off—so I went kind of slow. I called Gilmore and told him he ought to have a look, so he came in with the boat."

"You have radios?"

"We bought throwaway cell phones in the airport," Gilmore said. "They work fine."

"And?"

"Well, we reconnoitered, Colonel," Bustamante said. "The place is crawling with detection devices, and put in by somebody who knows what he's doing." After a moment, he added: "Damned near got caught."

Castillo turned quickly and looked at him.

" 'Caught' ?" Castillo parroted. "By who?"

Bustamante shrugged. "I don't know, sir."

"Some big sonofabitch moving like a cat," Gilmore offered. "At least one guy, maybe more." He shrugged. "If he was a perimeter guard, he sure as hell didn't act like one."

Oh, shit! Castillo thought. *Is this a repeat of our run-in at Estancia Shangri-La?*

Who the fuck can this guy be—another ex-Stasi?

Or . . . maybe one of Duffy's goons going in ahead of us?

Who the hell knows?

With drugs and money, anything is fucking possible.

"I swam the hell out of there just the same," Bustamante said. "I was more afraid this guy was going to trigger one of the sensors."

Gilmore moved the cursor on the screen to one of the blinking dots, the one closest to the river. An inset appeared, a photo.

"You can barely see the device," Bustamante said, "but if I had stepped over the grass boxes—or even touched them—it would have gone off."

Gilmore moved the cursor to another of the flashing dots and another inset photo appeared, this one of a trip wire.

"I couldn't tell if it would do anything but set off a Claymore," Bustamante said. An inset of a concealed, barely visible Claymore mine appeared. "But I guess that would be like an alarm bell, right, a Claymore going off?"

"That's about all we were able to do, Colonel," Gilmore said. "We worked our way around their perimeter. I figure there's probably five, six acres of protected terrain. We just didn't have the stuff to try to penetrate it. Sorry."

"You couldn't penetrate it?" Castillo asked, in mock shock. "A couple of trip wires and some Claymores and you just quit? Turn in your Ranger tabs. You're a disgrace to the Hurlburt School for Boys." Then he smiled and finished: "Great job, guys. I never expected anything like this."

"You think that's the place you're looking for, sir?"

"Unless it's some pig farmer worried about piglet rustlers," Castillo said. "What else could it be?"

"The Claymore was made in East Germany," Bustamante said. "I thought that was sort of interesting."

"Roads?"

"One. A couple of clicks from this highway," Gilmore said, pointing. "You want us to have another shot at penetration, Colonel?"

"Absolutely not," Castillo said. "As clumsy as you two are, that would let them know we plan to do terrible things to them."

Both smiled. Neither spoke, but there was a question in their eyes.

"Are we up, Lester?"

"Yes, sir."

"Get me Major Miller."

"Aye, aye, sir."

"Put the GPS coordinates on the screen so I can read them," Castillo ordered.

The legend on the handset read: AGNES FORBISON.

"I was beginning to worry that you'd been stolen by gypsies," she said as she opened the conversation. "Where are you, Charley?"

"In Paraguay. Where's Dick?"

"He's arranging Ambassador Lorimer's trip down to the estancia. Oh, hell, I cannot tell a lie, Charley. He decided he's up to flying the Gulfstream as co-pilot, and in the absence of the only one who could have told him no, that's what he authorized himself to do. Shall I call him and tell him you said no? They probably are still in the country."

Castillo considered that for a moment.

"No. He would know you ratted on him. It'll be all right; all he'll have to do is work the radios. But it poses a problem right now."

"What do you need?"

"Continuous satellite surveillance starting yesterday—using every sensing technique they have—of a small piece of Paraguayan real estate."

"You found where they have this guy? God, that was quick."

"Where we strongly believe he is," Castillo said. "Two very good shooters from the stockade did it. I was going to have Dick set up the surveillance—"

"You don't think I can?"

"I think we have to go through Montvale, and I'm not at all sure that Montvale will produce what he promises to produce. I was going to send Dick to Fort Meade or Langley—wherever this stuff will come in—to watch what he does and make sure that it doesn't slip through the cracks *and* that no copies are passed around the intelligence community. I can't afford any tracks, either."

"I can go to Meade or Langley and do that as well as Dick could. And he's not here. Unless you don't want me to . . ."

"With profound apologies for not remembering that you are, of all of the merry band, the best one to deal with the ambassador, Agnes, get the SOB on the line. And listen in, of course."

"You're forgiven," Agnes said.

"White House."

"Colonel Castillo needs Ambassador Montvale on a secure line, please."

"Yes, ma'am."

"Ambassador Montvale's line, Truman Ellsworth."

"This line is secure. Colonel Castillo calling the ambassador."

"The ambassador's not immediately available. Will the colonel talk to me?"

"Ellsworth," Castillo jumped in, "when the ambassador becomes available, tell him that when I couldn't get him, I called the President and that he'll probably be hearing from him."

"Hold one, Castillo."

"And how are things in the Southern Cone, Charley?"

"Looking up, Mr. Ambassador."

"What can I do for you?"

"Got a pencil? I want to give you some coordinates."

"Coordinates of what?"

Castillo began to read the coordinates from the laptop screen.

"Wait, wait a moment, Castillo . . . okay, I'm ready. Start again."

Castillo did, then said, "Would you read those back to me, please, so we know we have them right?"

Montvale's exasperation was evident in his voice as he read back the coordinates.

"Okay?" Montvale asked, finally.

"Okay. Now what I need, starting immediately, is satellite surveillance of that area. I want everything: photographs, infrared, electronic emissions of all kinds, everything those clever people have and I probably don't know about."

"What are they looking for?"

"Whatever they can find."

"What's there, Colonel?"

"I think Special Agent Timmons is there, but before I go after him, I want to make sure."

"Go after him?"

"That's what I've been ordered to do, you'll remember. But I've been thinking about the sensitivity of the operation."

"I'm glad to hear that."

"So what I want you to do, please . . ." His voice trailed off in thought, then he said, "Where is the first place the imagery will go? Langley or Fort Meade?"

"I'm surprised you don't know. It goes to Meade, then is linked to Langley."

"Okay . . ."

"Do you have any idea what you're asking? How difficult it will be to shift satellites? How much it will cost?"

"I didn't think it would be easy, Mr. Ambassador. And I'm sure it will be expensive. Would you rather I ask the President to authorize it?"

"What's in the back of my mind . . . are you interested? And can I say what I have to say without you taking offense?"

"Of course."

"*If* you have found Timmons and *if* those helicopters you're trying to send down actually get there and you can stage a successful operation, fine. But you're not *sure* you've found Timmons. And something—God knows, any-thing—can interfere with those helicopters getting down there—"

"I'd love to have them, the helicopters, of course, but I have a Plan B in case something goes wrong. And didn't you get Colonel Torine onto the *Ronald Rea-gan* to ensure that everything possible is being done, will be done, to get them to me?"

"Yes, I did. But to continue, if something goes awry, questions will be asked, especially about the satellite surveillance. People are going to know that happened."

"I have a Plan B for that, too, Mr. Ambassador."

"Do you really?"

"When you order the surveillance, I want you to have the analysts at Meade taken off all other duties until this is over. I want them told this is classified Top Secret Presidential. And I want the automatic link to Langley cut off."

"What are you going to do with the data at Meade?"

"Mrs. Forbison will be there. She will forward to me what the analysts tell her."

"Your office manager?"

"Actually, she's the deputy chief of OOA for administration," Castillo said. "And she's been cleared for the Finding."

"You're going to send her to Meade?" Montvale asked, incredulously.

"And by the time she gets there, I hope you'll have ordered that no one but she—or whichever of my men with a Finding clearance she designates—is to get any of the material generated by the surveillance."

"When is she going to Meade?"

"Just as soon as we get off the phone. Right, Agnes?"

"Yes, sir," Mrs. Forbison said.

"Good evening, Mrs. Forbison," Montvale said, icily. "I wasn't aware you were on the line."

"Standard office procedure, Mr. Ambassador," Agnes said, sweetly. "Whenever the chief is speaking with you or the President. You didn't know?"

"No, I didn't."

"Unless you've got something for me, Mr. Ambassador, that's all I have," Castillo said.

"I'll get right on this, of course," Montvale said. "And you will keep me up to speed, right, Colonel?"

"Absolutely," Castillo said. "Break it down, Lester."

"It's broken down, Lester?"

"Yes, sir."

"Get Agnes back for me, please."

"Aye, aye, sir."

"Yes, Chief?"

"Who won that one, Agnes?"

"You did. Hands down. You couldn't tell?"

"I thought I did. So why am I worried?"

"What happens now?" she asked.

"I'm going to Buenos Aires first thing in the morning. There's a lot to be done. I'm going to leave Lester's radio here, so you'll be able to send the data to the shooters here. How do I get them into the voice-recognition circuit?"

"You identify yourself—it has to be you, me, or Miller—and say, 'Adding voice-recognition personnel.' Then you have them give their names and say a few words."

"Stand by," Castillo said, and motioned for Sergeants Bustamante and Gilmore to join him.

"You heard that?" he asked, and they nodded.

"Colonel Castillo. Adding voice recognition personnel. Master Sergeant Gilmore."

He looked at Gilmore and said, "Repeat after me: 'Master Sergeant Gilmore.' "

"Master Sergeant Gilmore," Gilmore said.

Castillo nodded and went on: " 'When I failed reconnoitering as a Ranger, I had to become a Green Beanie."

Gilmore automatically began, " 'When I failed' . . ." Then he paused. "With all possible respect, Colonel, sir, screw you."

An artificial voice joined the conversation: "Sufficient data. System recognizes"—the voice now changed to Gilmore's—"Master Sergeant Gilmore."

Castillo nodded appreciatively.

"Colonel Castillo," he went on. "Adding voice-recognition personnel. Technical Sergeant Bustamante."

He looked at Bustamante, and said, "Repeat after me, 'Technical Sergeant Bustamante.' "

"Technical Sergeant Bustamante," Bustamante began, then quickly added, "Thank you, Colonel, for all those very kind things you have said about me. While I'm normally a modest—"

"Sufficient data," the artificial voice broke in. "System recognizes"—and Bustamante's voice added—"Technical Sergeant Bustamante."

"Wiseass," Castillo said.

"Okay, Agnes, they're on. The communicator will be able to help you pick what data to send down."

"I wasn't going over there by myself."

"If they say something about the radio, tell them to check with Montvale. But don't let it out of your hands. Entirely separate from this, those NSA guys would really like a look at the encryption circuits."

"I will guard it as I would my virtue."

"That's the best you can do?" Castillo said with mock shock.

There was a moment's silence, then Agnes said, with laughter in her voice, "Screw you, Charley!"

"Break it down, Lester."

"Okay," Castillo said. "In the morning, Lester, Max, and I are going to go to Buenos Aires. Lorimer and Mullroney are going to go to the embassy and nose around, half for show, half to see if they can come up with something."

Lorimer and Mullroney nodded.

Castillo went on: "Colonel Munz will do whatever he thinks makes the most sense. You two will start writing the ops order, based on what you know and what intel we get from the satellite or anybody else. Number them. Whenever one is complete, based on what you have, send it to me. To the safe house. There's a radio there, and probably some others have caught up with us by now. Between now and oh dark hundred—I want to leave as early as possible; it's a long way to Buenos Aires—Lester will check you out on the radio and procedures. Any questions?"

Heads shook.

"Good. Let's go."

[THREE]
Nuestra Pequeña Casa
Mayerling Country Club
Pilar, Buenos Aires Province, Argentina
1345 12 September 2005

"Duffy and D'Elia just came in the gate," Susanna Sieno announced as she hung up a telephone in the quincho.

"If I were not a modest man, I would say we are about to blow the comandante's mind," Castillo said.

"This is pretty impressive stuff, Charley," Susanna said.

"I meant with our drapes," he said, gesturing toward drapes now closed over the plateglass windows. "Lavender and pink stripes, with gold highlights. Really chic!"

She gave him the finger.

"Next time, you buy them," she said. "More important, *you* look soulfully into the eyes of the drapes-hanger, or whatever the hell he's called, to get him to hang them right now, not mañana sometime."

The lavender-and-pink-striped drapes—with gold highlights—were thick enough to shut out all light from the outside and, of course, ensured that no one could see into the quincho.

The quincho was now the command post, at least for the time being, for what had been jokingly dubbed Operation GGT—Go Get Timmons.

Four sixty-four-inch flat-screen LCD television monitors sat on a low table against the new drapes.

One was tuned to the Fox News Channel, with the sound barely audible.

Another monitor was connected to the AFC console and showed the data coming in from Fort Meade as it arrived. The encryption system was fast, but there was an enormous amount of data being sent. The result of this was that the screen first filled with what looked like snowlike static, which then began to take form, until the entire image was clear.

The third monitor was connected both to a large computer server and to Castillo's laptop computer. He could call up any of the satellite images to the flat-screen by pushing a key or two on the laptop. Now, since the decryption process was over, the images appeared almost instantaneously.

The fourth monitor was connected both to the server and to a laptop computer being operated by Sergeant Major Jack Davidson, who Castillo had announced was "going to be our map guy."

His job was to prepare and continuously update the maps that would be issued—either in printed copies or as a computer file—to everyone who would have need of one.

Like Castillo, Davidson could instantly call up on his laptop screen, and the monitor, any of the maps and any other data stored in the database. The difference was that Davidson—and he alone—could change the data.

They were both devout believers in the adage—one that went back to the dark ages, when maps were printed, hung on a wall, covered with a sheet of acetate, and corrections and additions made with a grease pencil—that, *"If more than one man can make changes to a map, said map invariably will soon be fucked up beyond all repair."*

They had worked together before, and they worked together now with a smoothness born of practice.

The first satellite imagery had arrived in Nuestra Pequeña Casa an hour before Castillo and Bradley. It was the first photography of the site, and about all it was good for was to enable Davidson to set up the system he knew Castillo would want to use.

By the time Castillo and Bradley walked into the quincho, the refining data had begun to come in. The first imagery had been much like the imagery provided by Google Earth, but in far greater resolution. It hadn't shown anything but *suggestions* of human activity.

The "refining data" that began to come in about the time Castillo and Bradley walked in used a number of sensing techniques, at first primarily infrared. It sensed differences in temperature between objects in the target area. Computer analyses of these defined what they were.

The easiest to identify were human beings. Their normal temperature was a given. The ambient temperature of the area was known. A difference of so many degrees determined with a great deal of certainty that *that* moving blob was a human being. And *that* one a cow. And *that* one a dog.

Similarly, the heat generated by such things as open fires, stoves, internal combustion engines—making the distinction between gasoline, diesel, and size—was recognized by the computers at Fort Meade and transferred as "refined data."

The blobs were replaced with a symbol—an outline of a truck, for example, or of a man—in which was a number estimating how confident, on a scale of 1 to 5, the computer was of its interpretation.

There would be more refining data as more satellites passed over the target area and the results of more sensing techniques were fed to the computers at Fort Meade. But after Davidson had "laid" the first refining data on top of the aerial photographs, what they had was enough for Castillo to make a decision.

"Bingo!" he said. "That has to be it."

"What that is, Charley, is some sort of a hidden operation," Davidson said, reasonably. "A fairly large one, to judge by the bodies, and probably a refinery, to judge by the large unknown infrared blobs." He paused. "But none of this data has Timmons's name on it."

"So what do we do, Jack?" Castillo had asked. "Send Bustamante or someone else back to penetrate? Running the risk that they get caught? In which case, the best scenario would be that they would move Timmons and the gendarmes someplace we couldn't find them. Or cut their throats and toss them in the river?"

"Don't forget giving them an overdose," Davidson said. He made a face of frustration. "That's why they pay you the big bucks, Charley, to make decisions like that."

"Or we just go in," Castillo went on, "and if Timmons isn't there, we kidnap a couple of them and arrange a swap."

"I don't think you want to do that," Susanna said. "Do you?"

"No, I don't want to do that."

She raised an eyebrow. "Is that the same as 'No, I won't do that'?"

"No."

"Come on in, gentlemen," Castillo called cheerfully as Comandante Duffy and Captain D'Elia appeared in the quincho door. "And I'll . . . oops!"

A third man—stocky, nearly bald, dark-skinned, and in his thirties—had followed them in. Castillo had no idea who he was, and was already phrasing how he would tell Duffy he was not to bring any of his gendarmes to the safe house without prior permission when the man saluted very casually and, in English, introduced himself:

"Captain Urquila, Colonel," he said. "I ran into D'Elia at the embassy, and he said—since I hadn't actually reported in to you—that I probably should come out here and do it; that you were either here or would be shortly."

Castillo returned the salute as casually.

"What were you doing at the embassy, Captain Urquila?" Castillo asked, very softly and politely.

Davidson, who knew what it often meant when Castillo spoke very softly and politely, looked concerned.

"I wanted to ask Mrs. Sieno, sir, when I could expect you to be in country."

"And how long have you been in country, Captain?" Castillo asked again, softly and politely.

Urquila did the math in his head before replying.

"A week, sir. I got here the morning of the fifth. My team was up when General McNab laid this on us. I appointed myself and my medic the advance party, and we were on the LAN Chile flight out of Miami that night."

"You've been here a week, Captain—correct me if I'm wrong—and *today* you went looking for Mrs. Sieno at the embassy?"

"That's right, sir."

"And—curiosity frankly overwhelms me, Captain—how have you passed the time since you arrived in beautiful Argentina?"

"I've been nosing around Asunción, sir, looking for someplace where these people could be holding this DEA guy."

"You and your medic," Castillo said, his tone making it more a question than a statement.

"Just he and I at first, sir. But now my whole team is up there."

"And why did you do that?"

"General McNab briefed me on the problem, sir, and when I came to see Mrs. Sieno before . . ."

Is he saying he saw Susanna before?

Castillo looked at Susanna. She nodded.

". . . right after I got here, and she said she didn't really know where you were, and to hang loose, I figured the best thing to do was start nosing around looking for this place."

"Tony's found something very interesting, Colonel," D'Elia offered.

"Really?" Castillo said. "And what would that be, Captain?"

"Well, there's a sort of hidden compound on the Paraguayan side of the river—right on the river—protected by some really heavy anti-intrusion stuff. Including Claymores. Now, I've never seen this Timmons guy, but these people have three guys chained together to a pole. Two of them are Latinos, wearing some kind of brown uniform. The third is in a suit; he's got light skin, and I'd say the odds are he's Timmons or whatever his name is."

Jesus Christ!

"You've penetrated this compound?" Castillo asked, suddenly very serious.

"Not me, sir. My intel sergeant. Master Sergeant Ludwicz—"

"Skinhead Ludwicz?" Castillo interrupted. "*That* Master Sergeant Ludwicz?"

"Yes, sir. He said you two had been around the block a couple times."

Maybe that's *who Bustamante saw on his intrusion!*

I'll be a sonofabitch!

"Indeed we have," Castillo said.

"Well, he's one hell of a penetrator, as you probably know, so he went in. Alone. I didn't want to take any more chances than I had to, until I knew what was coming down."

"And Skinhead says he saw two brown-uniformed Latinos and a gringo in a suit, all chained to a pole?"

"Yes, sir. Sir, he said they have two bowls. One with water, one with food. And that they . . . this is what Ludwicz said, sir . . . and that they looked stoned, sir."

"As if, for example, they had been injected with heroin?"

Captain Urquila shrugged.

"Personally, sir, I don't know that I'd recognize the signs of someone on heroin, what they'd look like. And Ludwicz didn't say anything about seeing a needle, sir. Just that they looked stoned."

"Put the composite on the monitor, Jack," Castillo ordered.

"Why don't you have a look at this, Comandante?" Castillo said.

The composite appeared a second later.

Duffy's eyes widened.

"What is that?" he asked.

"Your compound look anything like this, Captain?" Castillo asked.

Urquila examined the composite very carefully and shook his head.

"That's not it?" Castillo asked, incredulously.

"Oh, that's it," Urquila said. "I should have known you'd be way ahead of me. Colonel, I hope I haven't fucked anything up by sending Ludwicz in there . . ."

"Come here, Captain," Castillo said, gesturing with his hands for Urquila to move in very close. When he had, Castillo grabbed both of Urquila's ears and kissed him wetly on the forehead.

"Captain Urquila, I love you. I love Skinhead Ludwicz and I love you!"

Captain Urquila and Comandante Duffy both looked somewhat dazed.

"Corporal Bradley!" Castillo called.

"Sir?"

"There is a bottle of Famous Grouse single-malt in my room. I have been saving it for a special occasion. This is it! Go get it!"

"Aye, aye, sir."

Bradley and the Famous Grouse single-malt appeared three minutes later. But Bradley was not alone. Edgar Delchamps and David Yung followed him into the quincho.

"You really should let people know when you come home, Daddy," Delchamps greeted him. "Otherwise, Two-Gun and me will start to think you don't love us."

"Sorry, Ed. I just wanted to see what the satellite—"

"Is that why you're celebrating?" Delchamps asked, and crossed the room so that he could look at the monitors.

He moved quickly, but not as quickly as Sergeant Major Davidson's fingers on his laptop keyboard.

All four monitors now displayed images of provocatively posed naked young females.

Delchamps gave Davidson the finger.

"Me, too, Jack," Susanna Sieno said, disgustedly. "Really!"

Davidson hit more keys and the composite came back up on the center screen.

"What are we looking at?" Delchamps asked.

"That's where these people have Timmons and two gendarmes chained to a pole," Castillo said. "It's a couple of miles south of Asunción. In Paraguay."

"*Believed* to be the location," Delchamps asked, "or *confirmed* to be?"

"We have a visual from a very good man," Castillo said. "Master Sergeant Ludwicz, who is Captain Urquila's intel sergeant." He pointed to Urquila. "First name Tony, right?"

Urquila nodded. "Yes, sir."

"This is Ed Delchamps, known as The Dinosaur, and Two-Gun Yung of the Federal Bureau of Ignorance."

The men nodded at each other.

"For real, Urquila?" Delchamps asked. "You got a man into this place and got an eyes-on?"

Castillo said, "What Ludwicz saw was two guys in brown uniforms and a gringo in a suit. Chained to a pole, and probably doped up. That's what we're going on."

"I asked *him,* Ace, but okay. That's enough really good news to start pouring the sauce, Lester, my boy, but the colonel don't get none."

"Might I dare to inquire why not?" Castillo responded.

"There are several obvious reasons," Delchamps said. "But primarily because you're about to fly Two-Gun and me to Montevideo. And I have this perhaps foolish aversion to being flown about by a sauced-up pilot."

"Curiosity overwhelms me. Why am I flying you and Two-Gun to Montevideo? Why can't you go commercial? And what are the other obvious reasons to which you allude?"

"Well, Ace, if you insist—about three inches, please, Lester, two ice cubes and no water—for one thing, Ordóñez wants to see you before Ambassador Lorimer arrives, which will be about seven P.M. if Miller is to be believed. And what is The Gimp doing flying that airplane? I am wondering. For another, before you slip into your armor and gallop off on your white horse to do battle with the forces of evil, we have to have a long chat about what the CIA is up to in Asunción, and I want you to be sober for that."

"And what evil is the CIA up to in Asunción?"

Castillo was having trouble restraining a smile. Captain Urquila had absolutely no idea what was going on, and it showed on his face.

"When I explain that to you, Ace, I'm sure you will have cause to shamefully remember what you said about Two-Gun being a member of the Federal Bureau of Ignorance."

"Oh, I doubt that!"

"That's because I haven't told you what splendid service Inspector John J. Doherty has rendered to our noble cause."

"Which is?"

"I will tell you on the way to Montevideo, on which journey will we embark immediately after Brother Davidson has explained to me the computer game he is playing. And, of course, after I finish this drink and probably another. I always need a little liquid courage in order to fly with you at the wheel."

He turned a chair around and sat in it backward, facing the monitor.

"You may proceed, Brother Davidson," Delchamps said. "And speak slowly and use itsy-bitsy words, as Two-Gun will also be watching, and I don't want to have to explain everything all over again to him."

XIV

Corporal Lester Bradley was in the copilot seat of the Aero Commander, holding Castillo's laptop, with which Castillo was going to navigate their route to Montevideo. Edgar Delchamps and David Yung sat behind them, trying with little success to get Max to move to the area behind their seats.

"We're up, sir," Bradley announced.

Castillo looked at the laptop screen. There was a representation of an automobile—Casey's programmers had yet to add the option of an aircraft icon—sitting just off the single main runway of the downtown airport.

"You guys ready?" Castillo asked over his shoulder as he reached for the main buss switch.

"Don't wind it up just yet, Ace," Delchamps said. "Daddy has a confession to make."

Castillo turned to look at him.

"Oh, really?"

"Oh, really. And my shame and humiliation is tempered only by the fact that you—once you hear it—are going to have to abjectly apologize for all the unkind things you have been saying about the FBI."

"Time will tell, Edgar," Castillo said.

"You can listen to this, Lester," Delchamps went on, "even though it will probably shatter the childlike faith you have in me. And with the caveat, of course, that once you hear this, I shall probably have to kill you to keep you from spreading this among your friends."

"And you *are* going to make this confession in the next fifteen minutes or so, right?" Castillo said.

"This is very difficult for me, Ace. I seldom make errors of this magnitude. The last time was in 1986, when I erroneously concluded I had made an error."

Bradley giggled.

"Don't encourage him, for God's sake, Lester," Castillo said. "We'll never get to Montevideo."

"My mistake this time was in thinking I had conned Milton Weiss, when the opposite is true," Delchamps said.

He's serious now. This is no joke.

"That whole scenario about how he and Crawford plan to seize cruise ships is pure bullshit," Delchamps said. "And I not only swallowed it hook, line, and sinker, but encouraged you to do the same. Mea culpa, Ace."

"How do you know?" Castillo asked.

"Inspector John J. Doherty of the blessed Federal Bureau of Investigation, those wonderful checkers of fact, told Two-Gun," Delchamps said. "Before Two-Gun could come from Shangri-La to tell me, Doherty—damn his black Irish heart—got on the Gee-Whiz radio himself to break the news to me as gently as a mother telling her child, 'Sorry, there really is no Santa Claus.' He actually was embarrassed to have to tell me what a spectacular ass I'd made of myself."

"You are going to give us the details, right?" Castillo said, softly.

"Not yet. Not until you say something really nice to Two-Gun, who turned over the rock, so to speak."

"Okay," Castillo said, and turned to Yung. " 'Something nice,' Two-Gun. Now, what damn rock did you turn over?"

Yung shrugged. "There was something about that ship-seizure plot that smelled, Colonel," he said. "So I got on the radio to Inspector Doherty, went over all the details we knew of it, then asked him what he thought. It smelled to him, too, so he checked it out. He called me back and said it doesn't work that way. There *are* fines for companies whose ships do something illegal like moving drugs. But it's not like what the cops can do—seize a car, then have the bad guys go to court and try to get their car back."

Delchamps picked up the story: "According to Doherty, the only way these people could lose their ship is if after a trial—actually, a hearing—there is a fine and they don't pay it. Then the ship could theoretically be sold at auction to pay the fine. According to Doherty, that doesn't often happen—almost never happens—because the fines are never more than a hundred thousand, or two hundred thousand, never anything approaching the value of the ship—"

"And according to Doherty," Yung interrupted, "the only ships that tend to get sold to pay the fine are old battered small coastal freighters, the like of which aren't worth the cost of the fine. The drug people just let them go as a cost of doing business."

"So we was had, Ace," Delchamps said. "Not only was I led down the primrose path, but I held your hand as you skipped innocently along beside me."

"What's their angle?" Castillo asked, almost as if to himself.

"After my admission, I'm surprised you're asking me," Delchamps said.

"Come on, Ed. You made a mistake, that's all."

"I was conned by a guy I knew was a con artist."

"So what's his angle?"

"I have a theory, which of course I can't prove . . ."

"Let's have it."

"Weiss and Crawford are almost as old as I am. They're close to retirement, and I really don't think they've salted much away for their golden years. Can your imagination soar from that point, Charley?"

"They sold out," Castillo said.

"And justifying their actions—which wouldn't be hard, I admit—by telling themselves the company never appreciated all they'd done for it for all their long years of faithful service, the proof of that being Weiss riding a desk in Langley and Crawford being station chief in godforsaken Asunción, Paraguay. So why not take a few bucks for slipping the drug guys a little information from time to time? Everybody knows the damn drugs are going to go through anyway."

"I'll be a sonofabitch," Castillo said, softly. "That explains why nobody in Langley knew about their seize-the-cruise-ships operation; there was no seize-the-cruise-ships operation."

"It also explains why they were going to try—probably still are trying—to whack you. You were liable to stumble across something they didn't want you to hear or pass to Langley. So you get whacked, and they, of course, would have no idea who did you . . ."

"Isn't whacking me a little extreme?"

"So was Weiss coming to me at Langley, and then to you, with that bullshit story. Desperate people do desperate things, Ace. These guys are not only liable to lose their pensions, they're liable to get sent to the slam."

"Okay. Point taken. But doesn't that suggest they'll try to whack you, too? And Two-Gun?"

"And anybody else they consider a threat," Delchamps agreed. "And we must bear in mind they probably have access to the Ninjas."

"And anybody else would include Ambassador Lorimer and his wife. Shit!"

"Yeah," Delchamps agreed. "Including Ambassador Lorimer and his wife. Who will arrive in Montevideo shortly after we do."

Castillo exhaled audibly.

"And with us whacked and pushing up daisies," Delchamps went on, "nobody even hears about the bullshit seize-the-cruise-ships scenario they handed us, because we're the only ones they handed that line to."

"Except Dick Miller," Castillo said. "He eavesdropped on that conversation. And now he's coming down here . . . where they can whack him, too."

"They don't know he heard it," Delchamps said.

"He's close to me, so they whack him just to be sure. And blame that on the drug guys, too."

"Yeah," Delchamps agreed after a moment.

"So what do we do?" Castillo asked.

"Well, we can go to Langley and tell the DCI or Lammelle. *You* can go to the DCI or Lammelle without going through Montvale. And an investigation will be started—"

"Which they will hear of," Castillo interrupted, "and so long, Special Agent Timmons."

"Or we can get Timmons back and then go to the DCI . . ."

"Who may or may not believe us," Castillo said. "More egg on their face."

"Or," Yung put in, "we can try to find out where their money is. I don't think they'd have it in a Stateside bank. Or in Paraguay or Argentina. The Caymans, maybe. Or maybe in Montevideo. I ran across a number of accounts with interesting amounts in them that I couldn't tie to anybody."

"That possible, Two-Gun? That you could tie them to these bastards?" Castillo asked.

"Yeah. With some help. From Doherty, for example. It would take some time, but yeah, Charley. Now that we know what we're looking for."

"Say something nice about the FBI, Ace," Delchamps said.

"Hallelujah, brother!" Castillo said, waving both hands above his head. "I have seen the light! I am now second to no one in my admiration of that splendid law enforcement organization. Just hearing the acronym 'FBI' sends shivers of admiration up and down my spine."

"Actually, it's full of assholes," Yung said. "Inspector Doherty and myself being the exceptions that prove the rule. There may be one or two more."

There were chuckles.

"Sir, me too," Bradley said.

"You too, what, Lester?" Castillo asked.

"I heard what Mr. Weiss told you and Mr. Delchamps about the seize-the-ships op."

"How did you manage that, Corporal Bradley? You were not supposed to be listening."

"I was listening to hear what you were going to say about me going back to the Corps."

"Well, the DCI and Lammelle might have trouble believing you and me, Ace, but all they would have to do is look at the pride of the Marine Corps' honest face and know he is incapable of not telling the truth," Delchamps said.

"I can probably lie as well as any of you," Bradley said, indignantly.

"And probably a lot better than me, Lester," Castillo said. "I say that in all modesty."

"So what do we do now?" Yung asked.

"May I suggest we think that over carefully before charging off in all directions?" Delchamps said. "Wind up the rubber bands, Ace, and get this show on the road."

[TWO]

Forty-five minutes later, as the altimeter slowly unwound past 5,000 feet, what had been the dull glow of the lights of Montevideo suddenly became the defined lights of the apartment houses along the Rambla and the headlights of cars driving along it.

"There it is, Lester!" Castillo cried in mock excitement. "Montevideo! Just where it's supposed to be. Will miracles never cease?"

"So the data on the GPS indicates, sir," Bradley said, very seriously, pointing to the screen of the laptop.

Castillo looked. The representation of an automobile was now moving over the River Plate parallel to the Rambla.

What the hell am I going to do with you, Lester?

I can't send you back to the Marine Corps.

Not only do you know too much, but after everything you've been through, you're not going to be happy as a corporal pushing keys on a computer.

"And now if you will excuse me, Lester, I will talk to the nice man in the tower, after which I will see if I can get this aged bird on the ground in one piece."

"Yes, sir."

Castillo reached for the microphone.

"Carrasco approach control, Aero Commander Four Three . . ."

Five minutes later, as they turned off the Carrasco runway, Bradley said, "There's Chief Inspector Ordóñez, sir," and pointed.

Castillo looked.

Ordóñez was leaning against the nose of a helicopter sitting on the tarmac before the civil aviation terminal.

I wonder what he wants?

That's one of the old and battered police Hueys I am about to replace for him.

But that's an Aerospatiale Dauphin parked next to it.

I thought he said there was only one of those, and that it belonged to the president.

What the hell is going on?

And how the hell did he know we were going to be here?

Ordóñez was standing outside the Aero Commander when Castillo opened the cabin door.

"There has been a development, Colonel," he said without any preliminaries.

"And how are you, Chief Inspector Ordóñez?" Castillo said.

Ordóñez ignored the greeting.

"Would you be surprised to hear that your secretary of State has evinced an interest in the welfare of Ambassador Lorimer and his wife?"

"No. I wouldn't."

"I thought so."

" 'I thought so' what?"

"That you were behind what has happened. What's it all about? I don't like being pressured."

"Would you be surprised to hear I have no idea what you're talking about?"

Max exited the airplane and made for the nose gear. Delchamps, Yung, and Bradley got out and looked at Ordóñez.

"I'd heard you'd left the estancia," Ordóñez said to Yung. "By car, in the middle of the night, and had gone to Argentina."

Which means he has people watching Shangri-La.

Why not?

Is that what's got him pissed off?

"I wasn't aware he needed your permission to do anything," Castillo said.

"It was not in connection with your secretary of State? Is that what you're saying?"

"No, it was not."

"Then what?"

"In my experience, Ordóñez," Castillo said, "when someone in your frame of mind—to use the *Norteamericano* phrase, 'highly pissed off'—asks a question, he usually thinks he has the answer and is not interested in yours, even if yours happens to be the truth. Would I be wasting my breath, in other words?"

"I suggest you try answering and we'll find out," Ordóñez said.

Okay, bluff called.

When in doubt, tell the truth.

"Okay," Castillo said. "We have reason to believe—Yung found out—that the CIA station chief in Asunción is dirty. Ninety percent certainty. He went to Argentina to tell Delchamps and me, if he could find me."

Ordóñez looked at him very closely.

Somehow, I don't think that's what you expected to hear, is it, José?

"Wrong answer, José?" Castillo said, smiling at him.

"Not what I expected," Ordóñez said. "Is that true, David?"

Yung nodded.

"Then I apologize," Ordóñez said. "I had decided that you were entirely capable of doing something like that, and probably had. But I couldn't figure out why."

"Done something like what?"

"At eleven o'clock this morning, I was summoned—together with the minister of the interior—to the Foreign Ministry. The President was there. They had just been on a conference call with our ambassador to Washington. He reported that your secretary of State had requested a, quote, personal service, unquote, from him, and requested that he receive her at his earliest convenience. Half an hour later, she was at our embassy. She told him that she was very deeply concerned about the welfare of Ambassador Lorimer and his wife, who—against her advice and wishes—were already on their way to Estancia Shangri-La. She said the ambassador has a serious heart condition, which had been almost certainly exacerbated by the loss first of his son and then of his home in New Orleans during Hurricane Katrina.

"She asked, as a personal request, not as the secretary of State, that we do whatever we could for Ambassador Lorimer and his wife." He paused. "The President thought that was amusing."

"Amusing?"

"He said the lady may have gone to see the ambassador as a private citizen, but that inasmuch as she is the secretary of State, your American eagle was sitting on her shoulder."

"I'll tell you what I know, José," Castillo said. "She likes Ambassador Lorimer. I don't even know how she knows him, but she likes him. She doesn't want him down here, she told him that personally, and she sent me to Mississippi—where he and his wife were staying with Masterson's widow and her father—to talk him out of coming. I couldn't. My only connection with this was to send my airplane, the Gulfstream, to bring them here. That would at least spare them the hassle of going through airports.

"So, what I'm saying is that your ambassador got what he saw, a very nice lady worried about a nice old man. She had no other agenda."

"And what are you going to tell this nice old man about your plans for Estancia Shangri-La? Have you considered that?"

"He knows," Castillo said.

"He *knows?*" Ordóñez asked, incredulously.

"That was my hole card in trying to talk him out of coming. I played it. And it didn't work."

"Well, let me tell you how this very nice lady's concern for a nice old man is going to complicate things for you, Castillo. The President—not my chief, the interior minister, and not the foreign minister, but *my president*—pointed a finger at me and told me I was now responsible for the comfort and safety of Ambassador Lorimer and his wife as long as they are in Uruguay. If I don't believe I can adequately protect them with any of our police agencies, it can be arranged for a company of our infantry to conduct routine maneuvers near Estancia Shangri-La for as long as necessary.

"To spare the ambassador and his wife the long ride by car from here to the estancia—and to preclude any chance of a mishap on the road—I am to suggest to them that they accept the President's offer of his personal helicopter"—he pointed at the Aerospatiale Dauphin—"to transport them to the estancia.

"By the time the helicopter would have reached Shangri-La—this was the interior minister's 'suggestion'—I would have ensured that the estancia had been visited by appropriate police officials under my command to make sure there were no security problems."

He paused.

Castillo thought, *He's actually out of breath!*

"You sound as if there's some reason you can't do that," Castillo said.

"Can't do what?"

"Take the Lorimers to the estancia in the President's helicopter."

"How are you going to take them there in the dark?" Ordóñez said, gesturing.

"Speaking hypothetically, of course, I think that would pose no problem. What you do is fly there, and when people on the estancia, who are expecting you, hear you overhead, they turn on the headlights of their cars, which have been positioned to light the field near the house. And then you land."

"How are you going to find Shangri-La?"

"GPS."

"The Aerospatiale doesn't have it. I asked."

"I do," Castillo said. "Lester, show the chief inspector the laptop."

"You would trust this to get you there?" Ordóñez asked several minutes later, when Bradley had finished his demonstration. "Is it safe?"

"Absolutely and absolutely," Castillo said, "and what small risk it might involve is far less, I submit, than the alternatives, which are either to drive the Lorimers and everybody else all the way up there, or—even worse—to put them in a hotel overnight, which carries with it the risk that the secretary of state, not having heard from me that the Lorimers are safely at the estancia, might telephone Ambassador McGrory and enlist him in her cause, whereupon he can be counted upon to start making a lot of noise we don't need."

"I was worried about that," Ordóñez said. "If perhaps she hasn't already called the ambassador. If she had, I think we'd know."

"I think so. Let's keep him out of this, if possible."

Ordóñez nodded, then said, "We'd have to make two trips, right? We can't get everybody in the Aerospatiale."

"Is the pilot of the Aerospatiale any good?"

"Of course *they're* good. *They're* the presidential pilots."

"Okay. Then I go in the Huey and *they* follow me in *their* Aerospatiale."

"You mean with my pilots, of course."

"It would be better if I went as copilot."

"Can you fly a Huey?"

"No, but I'm a quick learner." When that got the dubious look that Castillo anticipated, he added, his tone bordering on annoyance, "Yeah, I can fly one, José."

Fifteen minutes later, as Castillo was talking to the Uruguayan pilots beside the Aerospatiale, he heard Miller's voice on the Aerospatiale's radio.

"Carrasco approach control, Gulfstream Three Seven Nine."

Castillo walked toward the runway to watch the Gulfstream land. Bradley walked up to him.

"I'm sure that's our airplane, sir," Bradley said, pointing.

Castillo looked at Bradley, then at the Gulfstream touching down.

"Our airplane," huh, Lester?

Another reason I can't send you back to the Marine Corps.

You not only consider yourself a member of this ragtag outfit of ours, but you have earned the right to think just that.

Three minutes later, the Gulfstream rolled to a stop on the tarmac in front of the civil aviation terminal and next to the helicopters.

Miller was the first to come down the stair door. When he saw Castillo, he tried—and failed—to make it appear he was able to reach the tarmac without difficulty.

Castillo walked to meet Miller.

"Who told you that you could fly that down here?" Castillo greeted him.

"I got tired of riding a desk, Charley," Miller replied, unrepentant.

"And if the Air Force couldn't operate the rudder pedals—for any number of reasons that come quickly to mind—then what?"

"If I had had to push on the pedals, I would have pushed on the pedals, and you know it."

Next off the airplane was a burly man whose loose raincoat only partially concealed the Uzi he held against his leg.

Christ, if Ordóñez sees the Uzi, will he make waves?

The burly man recognized Castillo—who did not recognize him—and saluted. Sort of. He touched two fingers of his left hand to his left temple. Castillo returned the salute with the same subtle gesture. Then the burly man, satisfied there was no threat on the tarmac, turned to the stair door. When Ambassador Lorimer started down the stairs, the burly man started to help him.

Lorimer curtly waved him away.

"Ah," Lorimer said. "Colonel Castillo. How nice of you to meet me. Entirely unnecessary, of course."

"How was the flight, Mr. Ambassador?"

"It made me feel like a rock-and-roll star," Lorimer said. "Where's your dog?" He looked around and finally located Max. Edgar Delchamps had him at the end of a tightly held leash.

"Ah, there you are, Max!" the ambassador said, put his fingers to his lips, and whistled shrilly.

Max towed Delchamps to the ambassador without apparent effort. The ambassador squatted and scratched Max's ears.

"Mr. Ambassador, there's a couple of small problems," Castillo said. "Would you and Mrs. Lorimer feel up to a helicopter flight of about an hour and a half, perhaps a little less?"

"To the estancia, you mean?"

"Yes, sir. Sir, the President of Uruguay welcomes you—this is Mr. José Ordóñez of the Interior Department . . ."

"On behalf of the President of the republic, Mr. Ambassador, welcome to Uruguay. The President hopes you will be willing to use his helicopter for the final leg of your journey."

"That's very kind of him," Lorimer said. "May I ask a personal question?"

"Yes, sir, of course."

"Do all officials of your interior department go about with a Glock on their hips?"

Castillo laughed. Ordóñez glowered at him.

"Try not to let my wife see it, please," Lorimer said. "And—partially because I think Colonel Castillo thinks this is necessary—I accept the kind offer of the President. There will be time when we get to the estancia for you to explain the nature of the 'small problems' Colonel Castillo has mentioned."

"Right this way, Mr. Ambassador," Ordóñez said, "if you please."

"Before we do that, I'm sure my wife will wish to powder her nose, as the expression goes, and I will need a little sustenance."

"You're hungry, Mr. Ambassador?" Ordóñez asked.

"Thirsty, actually," Lorimer said. "I've been told, Señor Ordóñez, that Uruguay's male population consumes more scotch whiskey per capita than any other such population. Is that true?"

"I believe it is, Mr. Ambassador," Ordóñez said.

"Then it wouldn't be too much trouble for you, would it, to come up with a little taste"—he held his thumb and index fingers about as widely separated as the joints would allow—"of, say, some of Macallan's finest? While my wife is powdering her nose, of course."

"I think that can be arranged, Mr. Ambassador," Ordóñez said, smiling appreciatively.

"You know, Señor Ordóñez, that according to Saint Timothy, our Lord said, 'Take a little wine for thy stomach's sake and thine other infirmities.' "

"I've heard that, Mr. Ambassador," Ordóñez said.

"If they had had Macallan in those days—even the eighteen-year-old, never mind the thirty—I'm sure He would have said, 'Take a little Macallan.' Wouldn't you agree?"

"I think you're right, Mr. Ambassador," Ordóñez said, nodding and smiling even more broadly.

Lorimer turned to Castillo.

"And while Señor Ordóñez is arranging a little out-of-the-sight-of-mine-wife sustenance for me, Colonel, why don't you get on that marvelous radio of yours and inform my daughter that her mother and I have not only survived this perilous journey but are now in your capable protective hands?"

"Yes, sir."

[THREE]
Estancia Shangri-La
Tacuarembó Province
República Oriental del Uruguay
2115 12 September 2005

After a quick—but, Castillo noticed, quite thorough—inspection of the big house of Estancia Shangri-La, Ambassador Lorimer said that he thought it would be a good idea if everyone "had a little taste—perhaps a Sazerac—to wet down our new home."

"*One*, Philippe," Mrs. Lorimer said. "One small one." She looked at Colin-the-butler. "You understand, Colin?"

"Yes, ma'am."

Mrs. Lorimer then said, "If you will excuse me, gentlemen, I'm going to have another look around the kitchen."

"And may I suggest the sitting room, gentlemen?" Colin said, gesturing grandly in that direction.

Everyone filed into the sitting room and watched as Colin prepared the drinks. When he was finished, he gave the first one to the ambassador and then passed the others.

"What is this?" Ordóñez asked, suspiciously.

"If we tell you, you probably won't drink it," Castillo said.

"This is a Sazerac, el Señor Ordóñez," Ambassador Lorimer said, holding up his glass. "A near-sacred New Orleans tradition, and certainly the appropriate libation with which to wet down my new home, but, frankly, I'm reluctant to have Colin offer you one."

"Why is that, Mr. Ambassador?" Ordóñez asked, politely and more than a little uncomfortably.

"Now that I am a retired diplomat, I don't have to drink with people I know are lying to me."

Ordóñez flushed.

"Who are you, really?" Lorimer asked.

Ordóñez was silent a long moment.

"I'll make a deal with you, Mr. Ambassador," Ordóñez then said. "You tell me who *he* really is"—he pointed at Colin—"and I will . . . *clarify* . . . my identity."

The butler looked at Castillo, who was smiling and shaking his head. Castillo nodded.

The butler said, "Chief Warrant Officer Five Colin Leverette, el Señor Ordóñez."

"You're a soldier?" Ordóñez asked.

Leverette nodded.

"And you are?" Ambassador Lorimer pursued.

"I'm Chief Inspector Ordóñez of the Interior Police Division of the Uruguayan Policía Nacional, Mr. Ambassador."

"Thank you," Lorimer said. "You may give him the Sazerac, please, Colin . . . or should I address you as 'Chief'?"

" 'Colin' is fine, sir," Castillo answered for him.

Leverette delivered the drink to Ordóñez, then said, "To *clarify* my identity, Chief Inspector: I am what is known in the profession as a shooter from the stockade. And now that I've told you that, I'll have to kill you."

Ordóñez shook his head in disbelief.

"To the ambassador's new home," Castillo said, raising his glass.

There was a chorus of "Hear, hear" and the drinks were sipped.

After a moment, the ambassador held out his empty glass to Colin Leverette.

"If you'll be so kind as to freshen that up, Colin, before my wife returns from her inspection of the culinary facilities, we can turn to the discussion of the few little problems Colonel Castillo mentioned."

Ten minutes later, Castillo looked around the room.

"Did I leave anything out?"

"That pretty well covered it, Ace," Edgar Delchamps said. "And actually, now that I've had a chance to think it over, it's not all gloom and despair, despite what the secretary of State has done to us with her decision to become Mother Teresa in addition to her other duties." He looked at the ambassador. "No offense, sir."

"None taken."

"Please tell me how that's not all gloom and despair, Ed," Castillo said. "My definition of total gloom and despair is when I have to admit I don't have a fucking clue how the hell I can stage a helicopter assault without helicopters. And the floodlight Secretary Cohen's shined on the estancia is so brilliant that there's no way that I can bring them in here black . . ."

"Doing it without them comes to mind," Delchamps said.

Is he saying that because he's stupid?

Or trying to bring me back from the depths of despair and gloom?
There's absolutely no fucking way I can do this without the choppers!
Without the choppers I won't even have any weapons!

"May I offer an observation?" Ambassador Lorimer said. "I hesitate to . . ."

That's all I fucking need. A diplomatic solution.

"Certainly, Mr. Ambassador," Castillo said.

"Perhaps I don't understand," Lorimer said. "The problem, as you see it, is that because of the secretary of State's concern for my welfare, and the kind response of the government of Uruguay, is that there will be so much activity here at the estancia that it would be impossible to bring the helicopters secretly here from the *Ronald Reagan*. Is that it?"

I thought I just said that . . .

"Yes, sir, Mr. Ambassador. That sums it up succinctly," Castillo said.

"Well, as I am speaking from a position of total ignorance, and you are the recognized experts in this sort of thing, I rather suppose you will think this question reflects my ignorance."

"Mr. Ambassador, I would love to hear whatever you have to say," Castillo said.

"What I was thinking when you first outlined the plan, Colonel Castillo, was that Mother Teresa had—certainly unintentionally, but I would submit, inarguably . . ."

He called the secretary of State "Mother Teresa"?

I really like the old guy.

I don't give a damn what he suggests, I'm going to let him down as gently as I can.

". . . provided you an opportunity to hide your helicopter-refueling operation in plain sight."

"Excuse me?"

"Listening to your original plan, I thought the one weakness was your belief that flying four helicopters in here at night would go unnoticed."

"Is that so?"

"They are not silent, and the noise they make is alien to the rural areas. Am I right so far? Please stop me . . ."

"Please go on," Ordóñez said. "That was one of my concerns, sir. But it was a risk I decided had to be taken."

"But now the first helicopters to come here . . ."

The first helicopter to come here was the one I flew during my failed attempt to repatriate his worthless son.

Doesn't he know that?

Of course he does.

What he's doing is being diplomatic and not bringing it up.

". . . attracting, I am sure, a great deal of curiosity, are government helicopters. Questions will be asked, I submit, and these will be answered by announcing that the government is doing something on the estancia. Thus, setting the precedent that helicopters here are legitimate."

"And what you want to do, Mr. Ambassador," Delchamps said, softly, "is pass Charley's choppers off as just more government helicopters."

"Taking care of that nice, sick old man and his wife," Ambassador Lorimer said, smiling, then finishing his Sazarac. "Nothing to be concerned about by the indigenous personnel or the local police. The more activity here, I would suggest, Chief Inspector Ordóñez, the better. All Colonel Castillo would have to do is make sure that none of his helicopters are here when yours are. A matter of scheduling, it would seem. . . ."

"And we could move all the fuel we're going to need onto the estancia in the open," Castillo thought aloud.

"The fuel to service the police helicopters will be brought to Shangri-La on Policía Nacional trucks," Ordóñez offered.

"May I infer that this suggestion has been helpful?" Ambassador Lorimer asked.

"You have just saved our ass, Mr. Ambassador," Castillo said, and then, suddenly serious, added: "And very possibly the lives of Special Agent Timmons and the two Argentine gendarmes those bastards are holding."

Ambassador Lorimer locked eyes with Castillo a moment.

"If that's true, Colonel . . ."

"It's true, Mr. Ambassador."

"I was about to say that would please me very much. I'm familiar with the philosophy that vengeance is the Lord's. But I am a sinner, and I would very much like to think I did some harm to the people who took my son's life."

Castillo didn't reply.

"And that being the case," Lorimer went on, "don't you think a small celebratory taste would be in order?"

"Yes, sir, I would indeed."

[FOUR]
Estancia Shangri-La
Tacuarembó Province
República Oriental del Uruguay
0355 19 September 2005

When the radio went off— *"Little Bo-Peep, Red Riding Hood One"*—Lieutenant Colonel C. G. Castillo, USA, wearing a dyed-black flight suit and puffing on a long, thin, nearly black cigar, was sitting at a somewhat unstable table. It was set up in a field about five hundred meters from the big house of Estancia Shangri-La and held a glowing Coleman lantern, two large thermos bottles of coffee, two insulated food containers, and the control console of an AFC communications system. Sipping coffee at the table were Chief Inspector José Ordóñez of the Uruguayan Policía Nacional, U.S. Ambassador (Ret.) Philippe Lorimer, U.S. Army Chief Warrant Officer Five Colin Leverette, and Corporal Lester Bradley, USMC.

"Answer them, Lester," Castillo ordered as he glanced at the Huey—once glossy white but now looking tired and battered—fifty meters away that belonged to the Policía Nacional.

"Go, Red Riding Hood," Corporal Bradley said into his microphone.

"We're due east of you, on the deck. Estimate five minutes," the voice said over the console speaker.

Bradley looked at Castillo for instructions.

"Acknowledged. No wind. Look for automotive headlights," Castillo said.

"Acknowledged. No wind. Look for automotive headlights," Bradley repeated into the microphone.

Chief Inspector Ordóñez stood up.

"I suppose I had best get back to Montevideo," Ordóñez said.

Castillo stood up, too.

"That's probably a good idea," Castillo said.

He put out his hand.

"Thank you, José."

"I realized just now why I really dislike you, Carlos," Ordóñez said.

Castillo raised an eyebrow. "Why is that, José?"

"You are a corrupting influence, like Satan. When I heard that"—he gestured toward the sky, meaning he meant the radio exchange—"instead of being consumed by shame and remorse for having done what I know I should not have done, I realized I was smiling nearly as broadly as you were."

"Not to worry," Castillo said. "That'll pass."

Ordóñez nodded and started walking toward the Policía Nacional helicopter. Halfway there, just as the pilot started the engine—and the lights of half a dozen cars and pickup trucks came on—he turned and walked back to Castillo.

"Tell your people to be very careful with my helicopters," he said.

"I'll do that," Castillo said.

Sixty seconds later, the Policía Nacional Huey broke ground. The sound of its rotor blades faded into the night.

Then the distinct sound of Huey rotors grew louder.

"I believe that is our bird coming in, sir," Corporal Bradley said.

"You're probably right, Lester," Castillo agreed.

Sixty seconds later, a Huey appeared out of the pitch dark, surprising everybody even though it had been expected.

The helicopter displayed no navigation lights; even the Grimes light on top of the fuselage had not been illuminated. The Huey quickly settled to the ground, and the moment it did, the headlights of the vehicles illuminating the field went dark.

And sixty seconds after that, Colonel Jacob Torine, USAF, and U.S. Army Major Robert Ward, 160th Special Operations Aviation Regiment—both wearing dyed-black insignia-less flight suits like Castillo's—walked up to the table.

Ward came to attention and saluted.

"Good evening, sir," he said. "I hope that is a cattle-free field. I would really hate to get bullshit all over my rudder pedals."

"And I hope you have not been letting that bluesuit fly one of my choppers."

"Screw you, Colonel," Torine said. "I say that with affection *and* sincerity."

"How'd it go?" Castillo asked.

"Getting off the *Gipper* was a bit of a problem," Torine said. "The Navy has a rule that they want to know where aircraft leaving their ships are going, and we of course did not wish to share that information with them."

"What did you do?"

"I told them the admiral would tell him after we were gone."

"Does he know?"

"No."

"Everybody got off all right?"

"At thirty-minute intervals."

"Which means we have to get you fueled and out of here right now," Castillo said. "Mr. Leverette—you know each other, right, Bob?"

"Hey, Colin," Ward said. "How are you?"

"My father just went to jail, and my mother just broke both of her legs. How about you?"

"And this," Castillo went on, "excuse me, sir, is Ambassador Lorimer."

"I have been waiting for the opportunity to say this," the ambassador said. "Welcome to Shangri-La, gentlemen. There's coffee and sandwiches. Please help yourself."

"As I was saying," Castillo went on, "Mr. Leverette has been checked out on the fuel truck."

"Charley, did you steal a police fuel truck?" Ward asked.

"I borrowed it."

"You do have that reputation for borrowing things," Ward said.

"I'll try for the third time to finish this sentence," Castillo said. "Mr. Leverette has been checked out on the fuel truck and has volunteered—"

"My crew chief would rather do that himself, Colonel, thank you very much just the same."

"Drive it over to the chopper, will you, please, Colin?" Castillo said.

"Carefully, please, Colin," Ward said. "Keeping in mind my crew chief test-fired his Gatling gun on the way here, burning six hundred rounds a minute."

"I thought it was *three thousand* RPM," Castillo said.

"The six-barrel M134D," Corporal Lester Bradley automatically recited, "is capable of firing per-minute fixed rates of three thousand *or* four thousand rounds of 7.65mm NATO ammunition." He paused. "At three thousand RPM, that's an extreme shot density of fifty rounds each second, the dense grouping designed to quickly suppress multiple targets simultaneously."

"Well," Castillo said after a moment, "we've heard from the Marine Corps . . ."

"Lester, you're right," Ward said. "And our weapons are tweaked for six-hundred-RPM test firings. Conserves ammo."

"Charley," Torine said, "why were you talking in tongues on the radio?"

"I didn't know if your pal the admiral might be listening," Castillo said. "Turns out we have a problem in Asunción. Yung found out the CIA station chief is on the bad guy's payroll. I couldn't take the chance the admiral—who I'm convinced is talking back-channel to at least one Pentagon admiral—would pass on anything that might wind up in Langley where another rotten apple would pass it on to Asunción."

"Jesus Christ, Charley!" Torine said, shocked. "That's one hell of an accusation. You sure?"

"Unfortunately. A long story. Delchamps will bring you up to speed when you're at Nuestra Pequeña Casa."

" 'Our Little House'? What's that?" Major Ward asked.

"A safe house, outside Buenos Aires. Your next stop. We're going to hide the birds there during the day and finish the ferry operation as soon as it gets dark tonight. And we'll give you the basic plan during the day. We have some really interesting satellite stuff."

"Finish the ferry operation how? And where to?" Ward asked.

Castillo looked at his watch. He didn't want to get into this now, but on the other hand, Ward had a right to know, and if he told him "later," Ward would be annoyed.

"The next leg is to Pilar. It's a little bit out of the way, but we're working with an Argentine cop on this, specifically a gendarmerie comandante named Duffy, and that's where he is. He's arranged fuel to be at a couple of the Argentine Polo Association's polo fields, ones sort of closed down for the day.

"Either Duffy's people—or ours—will take the crews to the safe house, where we can make the first operation briefing and get them something to eat and some rest.

"As soon as it's dark, the choppers—each having taken aboard a couple of gendarmes; in case you have to land someplace you hadn't planned, they'll make you legitimate—will fly separate routes to fields in the boonies for refueling. You'll get the coordinates at the briefing. There are redundant fields in case anything goes wrong.

"You'll wind up at a field in Argentina several miles from the Paraguay River and about ten miles from the target. This place has got a couple of big barns where we can conceal the Hueys and the shooters. The shooters are already moving there in private cars and trucks—mostly trucks—and again with a gendarme or two aboard in case they get stopped.

"As soon as everybody's assembled, and the choppers checked and fueled, we'll make the assault."

"No dry run?"

"No. That would attract too much attention, and you know as well as I do, Bob, that things happen—like dumping birds—during dry runs. You guys have done this sort of thing before; I'm not worried about that."

Ward nodded.

"What we're going to do," Castillo went on, "is make a simultaneous approach to the target. Three birds will take out the two generators, what we think is the main generator and its spare, and their radio. Duffy's gendarmes will cut the telephone and power lines at the same time.

"Three of the birds will use suppressing fire and get ready to put their shooters on the ground if necessary, while the fourth bird with a couple of shooters will land and grab the DEA guy and two gendarmes who these nice people have chained to a pole and, we believe, are keeping them doped up with some drug."

"You've located them?"

"Master Sergeant Ludwicz . . . you know him?"

"Skinhead."

Castillo nodded. "Skinhead penetrated this place and got a positive visual."

"So you know where they are?"

Castillo nodded again, then said, "Unless they're moved, which will probably happen. The fourth bird will put two shooters, plus an ex–Green Beret and a cop who both know the DEA guy—his name is Timmons—on the ground, grab them, put them on the chopper, whereupon the chopper will haul ass. The quicker we're in and out, the better."

"An ex–Green Beret and a cop? Where did they come from?"

"The ex–Green Beret is called Pegleg because one of them is titanium."

"Lorimer?"

"You know him?"

"Of him."

"Good man. And the cop, he's a detective sergeant, is the DEA guy's brother-in-law."

"You brought a cop in on this?"

"It was not my idea. But I don't know what shape the DEA guy is going to be in, and I don't want to have to fight with him to get him into the chopper, so maybe he'll be useful as a friendly face.

Major Ward did not look convinced.

"I know, I know," Castillo said. "Best scenario, we get them aboard the chopper and haul ass without having to put the shooters on the ground."

"Back to the field across the river?"

"The bird evacing the DEA guy will go to the airport at Formosa—a hundred clicks from the target—where the Gulfstream will be waiting. And there'll be medics, to let Torine know if it's safe for the DEA guy to fly, first to Uruguay and then home."

"Why Uruguay?"

"Because the Uruguayan cops get the choppers when we're done with them. The Gulfstream will also take all the pilots home."

"Where are you going to be while all this is going on?"

"I'll be flying the bird that lands to get the DEA guy."

Ward did not respond to that.

"Not to worry, Bob," Colin Leverette said, coming into the light of the Coleman lamp. "I'll be with him to make sure he doesn't do something stupid."

"Where did that idea come from?" Castillo asked. "For that matter, where the hell did you come from? I thought you were pumping fuel."

"My offer to be of assistance was declined," Leverette said. "Somewhat rudely, I thought."

"Your offer to be of assistance to me is herewith *politely* declined, Colin. I need you to stay with the ambassador."

"Anticipating what you were planning for me, I had Vic D'Alessando send the best available shooters from the stockade down here with the ambassador."

"I'll be fine, Colonel," Ambassador Lorimer said. "There are all sorts of local police, as well." He paused and added, "What is that phrase from Tactics 101? I think you've been *outflanked* by Colin, Colonel."

"Colonel," Leverette added, "you didn't really expect me to wave a tearful bye-bye while you and Jack Davidson flew off to do battle with the forces of evil, did you?"

Castillo was silent. Then he shook his head in an exaggerated fashion.

"I give up," he said.

"Colonel, what's the worst scenario?" Ward asked.

Castillo inhaled deeply, exhaled audibly, and said, "These people took out two of Comandante Duffy's gendarmes. He wants to leave bodies all over to make the point they shouldn't have done this. I can't stop him—frankly, I'm not sure I blame him—but I can't afford to get us involved in anything like that.

"So, worst scenario is that we get in a firefight on the ground. That would take time. I think Duffy's men are going to be in the compound where Timmons is within five minutes of the time we get there. I want to be gone by then, long before there's any chance of us taking fire—or casualties."

There came the sound of the Huey's engine starting.

"Well, Bob, I think you'd better take this old Air Force type to the house," Castillo said. "He's had enough excitement for one day."

"What I think we need, Colin, is a kinder, gentler commander," Colonel Torine said.

Almost exactly two hours later, at 0620, Castillo and Leverette looked out the side door of Red Riding Hood Four—around the Gatling gun—as the aircraft lifted off. They waved good-bye to Ambassador Lorimer, who was standing by the table in the field with the two next best available shooters from the stockade at his side.

XV

Castillo had an uneasy feeling that things were going too well, too smoothly.

Even the damn TVs came through.

All four of them. And in working order.

They were the sixty-four-inch flat-screen LCD television monitors from the quincho at Nuestra Pequeña Casa. He had mentioned idly to Comandante Duffy that it was a pity they wouldn't have one of them at what Edgar Delchamps had dubbed the Cathedral—"as in Saint Patrick's Cathedral"—meaning the huge warehouse buildings at Estancia San Patricio.

"They'd sure make the final briefing a lot easier," Castillo had said.

"Not a problem," Duffy said. "I'll have one of them there in the morning. Maybe we should send two, to be sure."

"Hell, take all of them. They're not going to do us any good here in the quincho."

And if we're really lucky, he'd thought, *maybe more than one will survive getting trucked over a thousand clicks of bumpy provincial roads.*

Thirty minutes later, one of the seized trucks from Duffy's combination headquarters-garage-warehouse had arrived at Nuestra Pequeña Casa. The cargo area of the truck was half filled with mattresses.

And the next day—yesterday, at lunchtime—when Castillo arrived at the Cathedral with Delchamps, Lester, Leverette, and Max in a confiscated Mercedes SUV, Sergeant Major Jack Davidson had all four of the screens up and running, displaying the latest satellite updates.

"This is great, Jack, but now everybody knows more than they should," Castillo said.

"Well, surprising me not a little, Duffy didn't argue with me when I told him that we were in the lockdown stage of the operation and that nobody leaves the Cathedral once they come in."

"You're a good man, Jack. Don't pay any attention to what people are always saying about you."

Comandante Liam Duffy, now wearing what was apparently the Gendarmería Nacional uniform for going to war—camouflage shirt and trousers, sort of jump boots, and web equipment that seemed designed primarily to support many ammunition magazines—walked up to Castillo, pointed at his wristwatch, and raised his eyebrows in question.

"Yeah, Liam," Castillo said. "It's about time."

Duffy bellowed a name.

An enormous gendarme with a sleeve full of chevrons appeared, came to attention before Duffy, and announced that he was at his orders.

"Form the men!" Duffy ordered, loudly.

The gendarme bellowed something not quite intelligible but what apparently was the gendarme command to come to attention.

All the gendarmes popped to their feet, stamped their feet in the British manner, and stood rigidly at attention.

Comandante Duffy grandly gestured for Castillo to precede him to the speaker's platform: the cargo bay of yet another confiscated vehicle pressed into service.

More than a few of the Americans in the room—two dozen Delta Force shooters and the crews of the Hueys—obviously found this military precision amusing. Perhaps even ludicrous.

Shit, the last thing I need is for the gendarmes to think the gringos are laughing at them.

But it's too late now for the speech about respecting the customs of your brothers-in-arms.

Castillo started to walk toward the pickup truck.

Chief Warrant Officer Five Colin Leverette put his hand on Lieutenant Colonel C. G. Castillo's arm, stopping him.

Leverette then screamed or shouted or bellowed, "On your feet, you candy-asses!"

This caught the attention of the Americans.

But no one moved.

Leverette then announced, at equal volume: "I will personally castrate any one of you candy-asses not standing tall by the time I get to the truck!"

Then, politely, he said to Castillo, "With your permission, sir?" and marched erectly toward the pickup truck, loudly and rapidly repeating "Up! Up! Up!" until he got there.

By then the Americans understood what was going on and had gotten to their feet.

Leverette jumped nimbly into the bed of the pickup, popped to rigid attention, and bellowed, "Assault force, atten-hut!"

The shooters and the fliers stood at rigid attention.

"Sir!" Leverette bellowed as he saluted. "Your assault force is formed!"

By then even the assault force commander understood what was going on.

Lieutenant Colonel Castillo marched across the Cathedral to the truck, jumped nimbly into the cargo area, put his hands on his hips, and examined his force as if he didn't like what he saw.

He turned to Leverette, who was still holding his salute.

"Very well," he said, quite loudly. "Carry on, Mr. Leverette."

"Yes, sir!" Leverette bellowed, then ordered the men, "At-ease!"

Leverette turned back to face Castillo. Neither the assault force nor the gendarmes could see his face. And they could not hear him as he softly said, "And to think you didn't want me to come . . ."

"I've never thought pep talks did much good," Castillo said loudly to the assault force and gendarmes. "So I'm not going to give one. And if there's anybody out there who doesn't know what he's supposed to do and when he's supposed to do it, he's out of luck. There's no time for that now.

"The only things I am going to say, and I'm sure Comandante Duffy agrees with me, is that the priority of this mission—above all else—is to get our people back from these hijos de puta. And to do that, we have to follow the schedule.

"This is one of those situations where one man, acting a minute too soon or a minute too late, can screw up the whole operation. Don't jump the gun! That'll get people—almost certainly the people we're going after, but members of the assault team as well—killed.

"And when your time comes to take action, don't hesitate. Hesitation will get people killed, too!

"And that's all I have."

Castillo looked down at Duffy, who stood beside the truck.

"Comandante?"

Comandante Duffy put his hands on the waist of a slight man in a gendarme uniform and hoisted him into the back of the pickup.

What the hell?

The gendarmes bowed their heads, and the slight man then invoked a lengthy, somewhat flowery blessing of the Deity upon the noble mission they were about to undertake.

It was only after everyone raised their heads that Castillo saw the clerical collar under the slight man's camouflage shirt.

Max sensed that something was going on that he was not going to be part of, but didn't protest when Castillo put him in the back of the Mercedes SUV and firmly lashed his leash to a metal loop in the floor. Delchamps would drive the truck, and Max, to the airfield at Formosa, where Torine and Miller had taken the Gulfstream.

Castillo had planned to send Lester Bradley with Torine and Max, but the piteous look in Bradley's eyes when he was told of this was even more piteous than the look in Max's eyes, and Castillo's resolve melted.

"Cover my back, Lester, and that's all," Castillo ordered.

"Aye, aye, sir."

Leverette intercepted Castillo and Bradley as they walked toward Big Bad Wolf, its rotor blades already turning. Lorimer, Mullroney, and two shooters were getting situated inside.

"Go get aboard, Lester," Leverette ordered. "I need a word with the colonel. And don't shoot anything until I tell you."

When Bradley was out of earshot, Castillo said, "Now what, Colin?"

"Would the colonel accept some friendly advice?"

"Not right now, thank you just the same, Mr. Leverette. I have a lot on my mind."

"Thank you, sir. How long has it been since the colonel has been referred to as Hotshot Charley, the Boy Wonder?"

"Meaning what?"

"May I remind the colonel that he is now a colonel? And that colonels—even light colonels, sir—are supposed to keep their minds free to make command decisions? Not drive helicopters."

Castillo stared at Leverette.

"Let the kid drive, Charley. He's good. I've been around the block with him, and the other kid, before."

Castillo glanced at the Huey, then looked back at Leverette.

"If the old man's memory serves, you've been around the block with me once or twice, too, Colin. Some people thought I was pretty good at this sort of thing."

"You were. That was then, this is now." He paused. "Let the kids drive, Charley."

"Fuck you, Colin," Castillo said, and walked quickly toward Big Bad Wolf. The pilot, a young captain, was holding open the pilot's door.

"Where would like me to ride, sir?"

"Probably there would be a good idea," Colonel Castillo said, pointing to the pilot seat. "That's where they keep the handles and levers and all that aircraft crap."

"Yes, sir."

"Big Bad Wolf light on the skids."

"Big Bad Wolf off."

"Big Bad Wolf. Commo check."

"One."

"Two."

"Three."

"Big Bad Wolf. M-Minute in ten. Engage computer on my bong."

"Bong."

This was far from the first time Castillo had flown an assault mission using the technique known informally as "flying the needles." But it would be the first when he would not actually be flying from the pilot's seat of one—usually the lead—helicopter.

I'm not flying. The "kids" are.

Colin was right about that. I haven't flown a Huey for a long time.

I am no longer Hotshot Charley, the Boy Wonder.

This is no time for me to fuck it up by thinking I am.

Castillo knew that the destination coordinates and the desired time of arrival—in this case, six hundred seconds from his bong setting order—had been all fed into computers aboard the Hueys. The computers would make the necessary computations and convert them to signals that activated indicator pointers—the "needles"—on the compass, the radar altimeter, and the ground speed indicator.

By keeping each helicopter's compass and its altitude and ground speed indicator's pointers lined up precisely with the computer-generated data—continuously making adjustments en route—as many as ten helicopters can arrive simultaneously (within two to three seconds) on target from several directions.

In our case—Big Bad Wolf and Red Riding Hood One, Two, and Three—from three different directions.

Making this damned difficult and complicated, and requiring pilots of extraordinary skill and great experience to carry it off.

And these "kids"—these Army aviators of the 160th—are the world's best damn chopper jockeys.

At M-Minute less three seconds, Red Riding Hood One popped up from its nap of the earth altitude east of the target and rose to one hundred feet above the ground.

There were faint lights visible within the compound beneath Red Riding Hood One.

At M-Minute, what looked like an orange ribbon flashed down to the ground from the opened side door of the helicopter. It lasted about ten seconds, and then Red Riding Hood One made a steep turn and left the area.

The orange ribbon had come from a Dillon Aero M134D 7.62mm "weapon system" mounted on a pintle in the helicopter. This weapon is patterned after the Gatling gun, a multiple-barrel weapon that was developed just in time for Private Tiffany of the jewelry firm Tiffany & Company and of the First United States Volunteer Cavalry, to buy several from the Colt people with his own money and in 1899 take them to Cuba, where he put them to use assisting Lieutenant Colonel Theodore Roosevelt in chasing the Spaniards off San Juan Hill.

The M134D—with six rotating barrels like the original Gatling, but ones electrically powered rather than hand-cranked—on Red Riding Hood One was fed by a 4,400-round magazine that could empty in just over sixty seconds.

In the ten seconds the weapon did fire, it sent from Red Riding Hood One almost seven hundred 168-grain bullets into a corrugated steel shed that contained a nearly new Cummins diesel-powered one-hundred-fifty-kilowatt generator. This caused the generator to malfunction—and the lights in the compound to go black.

A moment later, the diesel fuel in the tank behind the shed burst into flame.

Several moments after that, the electric lights of the compound flickered back on as an automatic system fired up the backup generator, an identical Cummins.

This coincided with the arrival of Red Riding Hood Two from the north at M-Minute plus five seconds.

And again there was an orange ribbon coming from the sky.

And again somewhere around seven hundred bullets flowed down, these striking the shed housing the backup generator—and causing the generator to malfunction, its fuel supply to ignite, and the lights in the compound to go out again.

As Red Riding Hood Two left the immediate area, Red Riding Hood Three and Big Bad Wolf appeared from the south.

Red Riding Hood was going to go in as low as possible to the ground and train its M134D on the corrugated steel building that the satellite imagery interpreters believed to be the compound headquarters—lots of people and a rather powerful shortwave radio station had been detected—and a motor pool behind that building.

Big Bad Wolf was going to land in the compound as soon as Red Riding Hood Three fired at the headquarters building, then off-load three shooters. The shooters would rush to the pole where DEA Special Agent Timmons and the two gendarmes had been chained, free them, and load them onto Big Bad Wolf, which would then immediately take off, under cover of Red Riding Hood One and Two, which by then would have returned to lay down covering fire.

Red Riding Hood Three by then would be seeing what it could do to facilitate the passage of the gendarmes from the highway to the compound, conducting what is known as "reconnaissance by fire."

Everything went as planned until Red Riding Hood Three picked up a little altitude to give it a better shot at the motor pool.

The pilot of Big Bad Wolf, the copilot, and Castillo—who was kneeling on the deck just behind them—almost simultaneously said, "Oh, shit!"

"Fuck, he hit a wire," the copilot said. "It cut the fucking blade!"

Red Riding Hood Three, which was tilted to the left, straightened out for a moment, looked as if it was trying to turn, then tilted back left, and was almost upside down when it crashed into the motor pool.

The pilot looked at Castillo for orders.

Castillo gestured impatiently at the ground.

"As soon as you're down, turn it around so we can take off the way we came in," Castillo ordered.

"Big Bad Wolf. Three is down. Repeat, Three is down. Two, go cover the gate. One, give us some covering fire."

"One on you, Big Bad Wolf."

"See what you can do for the guys on Three, Colin," Castillo ordered. "I'm going to get Timmons. Give me your chain-cutters."

Leverette gave him a thumbs-up and jumped off the helicopter.

Castillo turned to the two shooters.

"You go with Mr. Leverette," Castillo said to one, then to the other said, "And you come with me."

There was also a former Green Beret and a Chicago police officer on the helicopter, the latter grasping a snub-nosed .38 Smith & Wesson revolver.

"You stay on the chopper," Castillo ordered them.

"He's my brother-in-law," Mullroney protested.

Shit. That's why we brought him along in the first place.

Castillo looked at Lorimer and shouted, "I don't want him hurt, Pegleg. Got it?"

Lorimer nodded.

Castillo turned to Bradley.

"Lester, cover my back."

"Aye, aye, sir."

Special Agent Timmons was sitting with his back resting against the pole to which he had been chained. He was looking with confused eyes at what was going on. The two gendarmes were asleep.

"Hey, Charley," he said with slurred speech, dimly recognizing his brother-in-law and smiling. "What's up?"

Mullroney and Lorimer worked as a team to hold and cut through the chain. Castillo then hoisted the freed Timmons over his shoulder in a fireman's carry. He started trotting toward Big Bad Wolf. Mullroney and Lorimer quickly snipped the chains on the gendarmes, then followed Castillo back toward the helo.

Halfway there, Castillo suddenly felt as if somebody had hit him with a baseball bat in the leg, and then, a moment later, in the buttocks.

He felt himself falling.

"Oh, shit!"

He heard a burst from a CAR-4, then his lights went out.

"It's okay, kid, we've got him."

"Don't you call me kid, you oversized sonofabitch!"

"Goddamn, Charley, didn't you hear me when I said to remember to duck?"

"Where's Timmons?"

"You took a couple of hits—one in the ass, one in the leg—from what I'd say was that short Russian round, the 5.45×39. Not too much tissue damage, but you lost a lot of blood."

"Where's Timmons?"

"You want a shot? Or the happy pill?"

"I don't want either. Where the fuck is Timmons?"

"Not your choice, Charley, the one you took in the leg broke it. It's going to start hurting bad right about now."

"I don't want to go out, goddamn you!"

He didn't remember a needle prick, or any sense of being drugged, or even of feeling dizzy.

One moment, he was fighting with Colin Leverette.

The next moment, nothing.

[TWO]
Room 142
Hospital Británico
Avenida Italia 2420
Montevideo, Uruguay
1035 24 September 2005

"I shudder to think how you're going to answer the calls of nature in that apparatus, Colonel," Chief Warrant Officer Five Colin Leverette said to Lieutenant Colonel C. G. Castillo from the door of the room.

Castillo was suspended over—not in—his hospital bed. His left leg was encased in plaster from above the knee. Stainless steel cables attached to small D-rings in the plaster held the leg six inches over the mattress. This was necessary to keep the leg straight, this in turn being necessary to accommodate a cradle under Colonel Castillo's buttocks, which allowed his left buttock to hang free, which was also suspended from stainless steel cables attached to a frame above the bed.

Colonel Castillo gave Mr. Leverette the finger with his right hand. His left hand held a long black cigar.

"I don't think you're supposed to be smoking," Leverette said.

Castillo gave him the finger again.

"Where am I, and what am doing here?"

"You're in the British Hospital in Montevideo, Uruguay. I think the term is 'recuperating.' You apparently were involved in a firearms accident while hunting feral swine in the north."

"And Timmons?"

"Special Agent Timmons is undergoing drug detoxification in Saint Albans Hospital in Washington, D.C. Sergeant Mullroney is also in Saint Albans, recovering from minor injuries he suffered while shooting feral hogs with you."

"Anybody else get hit?"

Leverette shook his head.

"Amazing. They were waiting for us, Charley. A lot of them."

"What I remember is Three hitting an antenna cable and going in—"

"What it hit was a fucking cable, one of a bunch of fucking cables, strung across every area in that compound large enough to land a chopper. I don't see why everybody didn't hit one."

"But just Three did?"

Leverette nodded.

"And?"

"Bruises and contusions, one broken arm. We brought him here, too. They set the arm and put him on an American Airlines flight last night for Miami."

"Why here?"

"You lost a lot of blood, Charley, and your leg was a mess. Delchamps took one look at you in Formosa and decided you were in no shape for a ten-hour flight to the States. So he flew you here."

"And where is he?"

"He went on the Gulfstream with Timmons, Mullroney, and the guys from the 160th."

"Lester?"

"He took out the guy who shot you, and then started dragging you to the chopper. I was right."

He went into his pocket and came out with a small clear plastic zip-top disposable bag. He handed it to Castillo. It held three bullets, one fairly intact, the other two distorted.

"That's 9×39mm, PAB-9. I suppose the beat-up ones are the ones that did the damage to your leg."

"I didn't even hear any firing, and I thought I took two hits, not three."

"These are the rounds the FSB uses in their—suppressed—AS VAL Special

Purpose Assault Rifle. Odd that a bunch of drug dealers would have weapons like that, isn't it?"

"We were up against Russians?"

"Maybe. Maybe Cubans. Dead men tell no tales, and after Duffy got there and found his two guys full of holes from these things, that's all that was left."

"He took out everybody?"

Leverette nodded. "And then blew everything up," he said. "Spectacular! It looked like something from a Rambo movie. All kinds of secondary detonations. I was surprised nobody got hurt. Or the choppers."

"Our guys get involved?"

Leverette shook his head. "There was a moment—the first word was that you'd bought the farm—when I thought they would. But Jack Davidson stopped it."

"And you," Castillo said. It was a statement, not a question.

"What the hell, I'm a W-Five and Jack's just a lousy sergeant major."

"Where is he?"

"He and Lester are trying to sneak Max in here."

"He's still here? Why?"

"The Almighty has spoken."

"McNab?"

Leverette nodded.

"The verbal orders of our leader were 'You don't let that sonofabitch out of your sight until you can get him up here so I can ream him . . . a new rectal orifice.' Or words to that effect."

Castillo shook his head.

"You know the general, Charley. Any shooter gets shot, it's his fault for not shooting first."

The door opened, and was held open by a nurse.

A slight young man wearing dark glasses and tapping his way carefully with a white cane then entered, holding a very large dog on a leash.

Castillo grinned.

Lester, if those at Quantico could only see the Pride of the Marines now . . .

The dog, whining, very carefully put his feet on the bed and then licked first Colonel Castillo's left hand, then his face.

"It's all right, nurse," Sergeant Major Jack Davidson said. He was wearing a white nylon surgeon's smock and had a stethoscope hanging around his neck. "I cleared it with the chief of staff. And actually, canine saliva has a certain germicidal quality."

The nurse shook her head but left, letting the door slowly close by itself.

[THREE]
Room 142
Hospital Británico
Avenida Italia 2420
Montevideo, Uruguay
1650 24 September 2005

The very tall, well-dressed, somewhat ascetic-looking man entered the room without knocking and found himself facing a nice-looking teenage boy in a gray suit—who was holding a .45 ACP pistol aimed at his crotch. Beside the boy was the largest dog the man had ever seen, showing an impressive array of teeth and growling deeply.

The man quickly put up his hands.

"You must be Corporal Bradley," the man said.

"Who the hell are you?" Castillo demanded.

"My name is Frank Lammelle, Colonel. I'm the DDCI. Ambassador Montvale suggested I come to see you."

"You have any identification, sir?" Bradley demanded.

"It's okay, Lester," Castillo said. "I don't think he's making that up."

"May I put my hands down?"

Castillo nodded.

"And would you give the colonel and me a few minutes alone, please, Corporal?"

"Go get a Coke or something, Lester," Castillo ordered.

When the door had closed after Bradley, Lammelle said, "That looks very uncomfortable, Colonel."

"Until ten o'clock this morning, they had me literally twisting in the wind. That was worse."

"And now?"

"Now I have to lie on my side."

They looked at each other curiously.

"How did you know who Bradley was?" Castillo asked.

"Edgar Delchamps described him to me as a choirboy with a .45 who is seldom far from your side."

Castillo smiled but didn't say anything.

"Delchamps came to see me, and the DCI, immediately after he came from Saint Albans Hospital," Lammelle said.

Castillo said nothing.

"You didn't know he planned to do that?"

"No. But now that I think about it, I'm not surprised."

"He told us an incredible, unsupportable, unbelievable tale about several members of the CIA having, so to speak, sold out."

"Well, you don't have to believe Delchamps if you don't want to, Mr. Lammelle," Castillo said, coldly and softly, "but I'm going to tell the President about those two bastards just as soon as I can get to Washington. I suspect he'll believe me." His voice changed tenor. "Jesus Christ, did Montvale send you down here to talk me into going along with a whitewash of those two traitorous sonsofbitches?"

"My mother always taught me it was bad form to speak ill of the dead," Lammelle said.

"Excuse me?"

"We are both referring to Mr. Milton Weiss and Mr. Jonathon Crawford, are we not, Colonel?"

"I think of them as miserable CIA sonofabitch one and miserable CIA sonofabitch two."

"I'm afraid that I'm the bearer of bad news, Colonel. Mr. Crawford and Mr. Weiss are no longer with us."

"What did they do, catch a plane to the former Soviet Union?"

"They are deceased," Lammelle said. "Mr. Crawford was found three days ago in his apartment in Asunción. He had apparently been strangled to death during a robbery. With a garrote, actually. A blue steel garrote."

"And Weiss?"

"Mr. Weiss was found in his car in the parking lot at Langley yesterday morning. He died of a drug overdose. The needle was still in his arm—no, actually, it was in his neck—when his body was discovered."

"How interesting."

"Well, naturally, since Mr. Delchamps had raised these awful allegations against Mr. Weiss, our investigators had some questions for him."

"And?"

"Apparently, Mr. Delchamps had been involved in a marathon poker game at the house he shares with you in Alexandria during the time the coroner tells us Mr. Weiss got his fatal injection. With some other CIA veterans, now mostly retired. They have a small informal organization; they call themselves The Dinosaurs."

"So I've heard."

"Well, the CIA certainly is willing to take the word of such a group regarding who was where and when."

"That's probably a good idea."

"Some of those Cold War warriors, The Dinosaurs, tell fascinating stories—they can't be believed, of course—about what happened to traitors in their day."

"Such as?"

"I really don't like to get into this sort of thing, so let me just say it's rumored they acted as judge, jury, and executioner when they were sure one of their number had sold out. Just a legend, I'm sure."

"Yeah."

"Well, aside from saying that I don't think you could get arrested in Chicago for anything—Sergeant Mullroney has told both the mayor and the President of your courageous dash through fierce small-arms fire carrying Special Agent Timmons on your back . . ."

"Oh, Jesus!"

". . . that's about all I have. I have to get to Buenos Aires."

"Why?"

"Well, I probably shouldn't tell you this, as it's classified. Nevertheless, we've decided to beef up our operation in Asunción in light of what's happened there. Mr. Darby is going there to help Mr. and Mrs. Sieno get things straightened out. I want to see them before they go."

He put out his hand.

"It's been a pleasure meeting you, Colonel, and I wish you a speedy recovery."

[FOUR]
1040 Red Cloud Road
Fort Rucker, Alabama
1740 22 December 2005

Major General Harry Wilson, USA (Ret.), elected to park his Buick sedan on Red Cloud Road although he was fully aware that this was prohibited. There were several reasons he chose to do so, not the least of which was sitting next to him in the person of just-promoted Major General Crenshaw, the newly appointed post commander. Military Police only rarely ticketed post commanders for any nonfelonious breach of the law. Other reasons included that he and General Crenshaw had had several drinks on the flight from Texas, and he really could not handle more than one ounce of alcohol per hour.

Master Randolph Richardson IV was out of the Buick and up the lawn before either General Wilson or General Crenshaw could brief him on the best approach to the problems that were about to develop. Young Randy was holding something black and about the size of a shoe in his hand.

"Oh, shit!" General Wilson said.

"My thoughts exactly," General Crenshaw said. "But I'll deal with him."

"He's my son-in-law," General Wilson said.

"But I write the officer's efficiency report on the officer who writes his," General Crenshaw said.

"Point taken," General Wilson said. "You bring your animal and I'll bring the dead birds."

General Crenshaw opened the rear door and picked up a small animal more or less identical to the one Randolph Richardson IV had rushed to the door holding.

Generals Wilson and Crenshaw got to the door just as Lieutenant Colonel Randolph Richardson III opened it. His wife stood behind him.

"I made twenty takeoffs and landings," young Randy announced, then held up the soft black object in his hands for inspection. "And look at this!"

"You did what?" Mrs. Richardson asked.

"What is that?" Lieutenant Colonel Richardson asked.

"His name is Goliath," Randy answered. "General Crenshaw's got his brother, David."

"You did what?" Mrs. Richardson asked again.

"I made twenty takeoffs and landings in a Ryan PT-22," her son answered.

"That isn't one of those huge dogs Colonel Castillo had, is it?" Lieutenant Colonel Richardson asked.

"Not yet, Richardson," General Crenshaw said. "Right now Goliath and David are what they call puppies."

"Max had eight," Randy said. "Or his . . . the girl dog did. Colonel Castillo gave General Crenshaw one and he gave me one."

"How nice of him," Lieutenant Colonel Richardson said, carefully choosing his words. "But I'm not sure we'll be able to keep it, moving around the way we do."

"Nonsense," Generals Crenshaw and Wilson said, almost in unison.

"Every boy should have a dog," General Crenshaw added.

"Teaches him character," General Wilson agreed.

"A dog that size?" Lieutenant Colonel Richardson said.

"And Colonel Castillo gave one to a girl he knows in Argentina," Randy said, "a girl my age he says he wants me to meet some time."

"I would like to know what he means by twenty takeoffs and landings," Mrs. Richardson said. "Not by himself, certainly."

"What kind of an airplane?" Lieutenant Colonel Richardson said.

"A Ryan PT-22, open-cockpit tail dragger," Randy announced with a pilot's élan. "Hundred-and-sixty-horse Kinner five-cylinder radial. Cruises at about one thirty-five."

"Colonel Castillo has such an airplane?" Lieutenant Colonel Richardson inquired. "I don't think I've ever seen one."

"Uncle Fernando does," Randy said, softly stroking Goliath.

"You remember Fernando, Beth?" her father said. "Charley's cousin?"

She smiled somewhat wanly.

"You're calling this man 'Uncle Fernando'?" she said to her son.

"If he lets me fly his airplane," Randy replied matter-of-factly, "I'll call him anything he wants me to call him!"

"And what do you call Colonel Castillo?" his mother asked.

"He said that he's not my uncle so I could call him either 'sir' or 'Charley.' "

Beth exchanged a long look with her father.

"So this 'Uncle Fernando' took you for a ride in his airplane, did he?" Lieutenant Colonel Richardson inquired.

"No," Randy explained somewhat impatiently. "*Colonel Castillo* taught me how to fly *Uncle Fernando*'s PT-22. I made twenty takeoffs and landings. I *told* you."

"And you found nothing wrong with this, Dad?" Mrs. Richardson asked.

"Not a thing," he said. "I've always thought of the Castillos as family. Haven't you?"